BY SHARON SOLWITZ

Once, in Lourdes

Bloody Mary

Blood and Milk

Once, in Lourdes

Once, in Lourdes

A NOVEL

Sharon Solwitz

SPIEGEL & GRAU
NEW YORK

Copyright © 2017 by Sharon Solwitz

Published in the United States by Spiegel & Grau, an imprint of Random House, a division of Penguin Random House LLC, New York.

SPIEGEL & GRAU and Design is a registered trademark of Penguin Random House LLC.

Chapters 1 and 2 were originally published in different form in *Crazyhorse*.

Grateful acknowledgment is made to Special Rider Music for permission to reprint excerpts from "Mr. Tambourine Man" by Bob Dylan, copyright © 1964, 1965 by Warner Bros. Inc. and copyright renewed 1992, 1993 by Special Rider Music. All rights reserved. International copyright secured. Reprinted by permission of Special Rider Music.

LIBRARY OF CONGRESS CATALOGING-IN-PUBLICATION DATA
Names: Solwitz, Sharon, author.
Title: Once, in Lourdes : a novel / by Sharon Solwitz.
Description: First Edition. | New York : Spiegel & Grau, [2017]
Identifiers: LCCN 2016036717 | ISBN 9780812989236 |
ISBN 9780812989243 (ebook)
Classification: LCC PS3569.O6514 O53 2017 | DDC 813/.54—dc23
LC record available at https://lccn.loc.gov/2016036717

Printed in the United States of America on acid-free paper

randomhousebooks.com
spiegelandgrau.com

2 4 6 8 9 7 5 3 1

FIRST EDITION

FRONTISPIECE IMAGE: iStock/Sherry Talbot
Interior illustrations are by the author.

Book design by Simon M. Sullivan

For my friends, then and now

Then take me disappearin' through the smoke rings of my mind
Down the foggy ruins of time, far past the frozen leaves
The haunted, frightened trees, out to the windy beach
Far from the twisted reach of crazy sorrow
Yes, to dance beneath the diamond sky with one hand waving free
Silhouetted by the sea, circled by the circus sands
With all memory and fate driven deep beneath the waves
Let me forget about today until tomorrow

—BOB DYLAN, "Mr. Tambourine Man"

In grade school certain abstract nouns gave me goosebumps: Courage. Nobility. Sacrifice.

Ask not what your country can do for you.

In high school I needed friends, it seemed, to stay alive. There were four of us, a group, tender and loyal, more beautiful than I deserved. I'd walk the school's halls in the pretty armor of their image of me. And all around us, the shivery, breathless hum of erotic love.

Then came what, bad luck? A band of evil angels? What started as love uncoiled and bared its fangs like a serpent, a sea monster, like nothing I understood. And now I'm stuck with a question I can't purge from my brain. If I had been a stronger person, could I have saved us?

Part I

1

"The Haight"

I wasn't strong, I was shy and accommodating and—as nice people put it—on the heavy side. But my ambitious, ruthless stepmother had hopes for me. She had signed me up for Teen Slimnastics, sit-ups and jumping jacks in a group of kids all thinner than I was. The hour before that was summer school physics (likewise her arrangement), five mornings a week with the ripple tank and those strange nodal lines, where troughs met crests and canceled each other out. I was unsettled by nodal lines, by physics in general, concepts with no footing in my daily life, that couldn't even be diagrammed. But ever dutiful, I was battling through it all.

But every once in a while, for no reason you understand, you do something your known, familiar self could not have imagined. One August morning, the air thick as usual with damp summer heat, instead of taking my usual aggrieved, bewildered physics notes, I cartooned the chinless teacher as he tried to convince us that hot water could freeze faster than cold. Not in general, not most of the time, but it could happen, he said. Huh?

To my left, asswipe Gary Landry said, "That's counterintuitive." To my right, Andrea Holden rolled her mean-girl eyeballs. "*Could?* Do you mean in an alternate universe?" People laughed, though they probably didn't know what they were laughing at, and Mr. Carstairs turned red, and I felt his pain but of course said nothing. Then in my exercise class, after some rounds of torturous knee bends, I got stuck in my squat. The one good thing: We were aligned according to weight and I was on the end. Before shyness or reason could stop me, I had rolled out of line, grabbed my book bag, and was out the gym door.

In the parking lot a wave of terror flowed through me, though no one had followed me. I lay low, crouched between two cars, while my heart slowed down. It was a cusp moment, as we were starting to say. It was 1968, good people had been assassinated, enraged people were burning down their own neighborhoods, craziness was spreading, and in Lourdes, Michigan, population ≤11,000, nervously, inadvertently, I had joined in. I pulled on my skirt, stuffed my sweaty gym tights into my bag, and set off on foot to the park we called the Haight or, with humility, the Haight, Midwest. Even now I can see myself: clumping along in my ankle-length flowered skirt and extra-large leotard, like an immigrant dazed by the strangeness of it all.

Our Haight was Lourdes Metropolitan Park, named for Georges and Catherine Bellechasse de Lourdes, the first European settlers in our part of the state. When nothing else was required of us, it was where we hung out, we being my three best (in fact my only) friends. At the entrance was a large stone fountain fed by a spring that had saved the town from a drought in the 1830s; its water, some folks continued to believe, was curative. Every once in a while a crutch or an old wheelchair appeared at the base of the fountain, as if a cripple had drunk and been miraculously healed, though the items probably came from kids playing their idea of a hilarious prank. There was also a wooden sign we called "fascist"—PICNIC ONLY IN DESIGNATED AREA. NO ALCOHOL. NO LOITERING. HOURS 6 A.M.–11 P.M.—and beyond it a parking lot of shoebox-shaped cars where moms un-packed coolers to be hauled toward the picnic area ("Everyone helps, Doreen—did you hear me?"). By the restrooms that day, a mom was saying into the pay phone, "Haven't we had this conversa-tion before?"

I passed the baseball diamond, empty that hot noon, and the ten-nis courts with a couple of college boys hitting back and forth. I crossed a wide, grassy, weedy field where kids flew kites or caught bugs. And there, sprawled in the shade of our spreading maple by the bluff, their heads together, their backs to me, were two of my blessed three. Their transistor radio was on, they didn't hear me ap-proach, they were talking intently—and all of a sudden I was afraid to insert myself. I stood in the sun outside their oasis, wobbly with the heat and the pleasure of seeing them, waiting for something in their conversation to reach out a hand of welcome.

"If you *were* a homo," said Saint, "you might have an inkling, don't you think? It wouldn't just pop up out of the blue. What's so funny, jackass?"

CJ was squeaking with hilarity. He'd try to stop, then look at Saint and burst out again. "Man oh man, are you naïve!"

It was one of their games, insulting each other, their training pro-gram for the world's hard knocks. Saint as usual was on the defen-sive, but he was putting up a fight. "Let's say you're thirty years old with a wife and kids. And one day you wake up and go, 'Oops, sorry, honey, I have some bad news'?"

CJ shrugged elaborately. "I don't know this thirty-year-old guy of yours, but according to Freud—remember Freud?—we have drives we aren't conscious of."

Saint threw him a fake punch. Saint was tall and unusually strong; he could have picked CJ up like a suitcase and tossed him off the bluff. But he was a gentle, Ferdinand-the-bull sort of boy. He had strength he didn't use, that he protected us from. Verbally, though, he was no match for CJ, who had scored so high on the PSAT that he was invited to a genius camp in Telluride, Colorado. CJ had business cards that read HAVE BRAIN, WILL TRAVEL. "Seriously," said CJ to Saint, "we're not one hundred percent rational beings. We do things and we don't have a clue. We're driven by our unconscious."

"And how would you know?" Saint replied. "Are *you*?" CJ shrugged. The radio news praised a kid from the next town who'd been badly wounded in Vietnam, then played "God Bless America." Saint laughed, pleased with himself. "Is there something you're trying to tell me?"

"By definition," said CJ, "we don't recognize our unconscious drives. None of us! By *definition*!"

"All right, you win. Fuck you."

The radio was playing "Blowin' in the Wind," my favorite Dylan song. In the blowing wind, they lit cigarettes. They looked out toward the lake in different directions, in a cloud of smoke and annoyance with each other.

And, ta-da! Now I was needed, to clear the air. "Hello-o! Surprise!" I called out as if I'd just arrived. I stepped forward. Then my book bag slipped off my shoulder. I tried to catch it and tripped and fell—into them, onto them, sweaty arms and damp shirts. *Freudian slip?* The handsome pun came whole to my mind, and I'd already gauged it worthy of being said, but I couldn't say it while I was apologizing, and then Saint was helping to rearrange me, while CJ said, "You ditched physics, babe. Shame, shame."

I knew he was kidding, but I couldn't help it. Tears of genuine shame welled in my eyes. "Trust me, all I missed was fat camp," I said, feigning lightness. I feigned often in those days before Prozac, and I had another refuge as well. In my book bag were my stepmother's outdoor bridge cards, a metallic deck with a magnetic board that kept them from blowing away. Once a week she played contract bridge with her lady friends, and that summer the four of us were playing almost every day.

My life then, even with my friends, was High Anxiety, eased from time to time by gusts of Mild Anxiety. But bridge I found completely absorbing, more than movies or television. We started playing our junior year, reading bridge books, teaching ourselves with help from CJ, whose parents played. At school we were all on the same academic track (Accel) and got a hand in whenever possible, sometimes on top of one of our desks in the five minutes between classes. In the park now, in the shade of our wide-limbed maple tree, I dealt the cards onto the magnetic board, where they magically stuck. With three we could play Bid for the Dummy. But where was our fourth?

We didn't name her—it seemed disrespectful to talk about one of us who wasn't there—but I was a little anxious on her behalf. I'd called her the previous night, and her father hung up on me. Later I got Garth, her brother, who didn't know where she was, but his voice shook, which wasn't his style. Garth was a year younger than us, a quiet kid, but with gravitas. He played in a band and had friends in every group and clique in the school, freshmen, seniors; he transcended barriers. At the beginning of the summer he and his guitar had disappeared from Lourdes; not even Vera knew where he was; their father said good riddance. Then suddenly he was back home. A mystery.

I liked Garth, but their parents were straight out of Dickens: dad a bullying cop, mom a drunk—we knew though we didn't discuss it. Abuse, dysfunction, we didn't use those words. Nor did we discuss our fascination with Vera, though we all felt it. She had thick pale blond hair and blue eyes that darkened to gray at the rims of her irises, and narrow hips and high fragile cheekbones, and she moved lightly over the ground as if her personal force of gravity pulled less harshly than ours—and why not? She'd had dance lessons through grammar school, with no concern at all for her physical flaw, a malformed right hand: Her three middle fingers were barely emergent, with tiny fingernails, and the palm was undersized. It was a birth defect. Many people would have kept such a thing in their pockets or under long sleeves, but Vera wore tube tops and sleeveless blouses, and painted her tiny nails red, and when she raised a hand to answer a question in class it was always the bad hand. She'd wiggle her red nubs, daring anyone to react. My polyps, she'd say, my little anemones.

Even then, more than her physical beauty I linked the bad hand with her magnetism, the unmistakable power she exerted over us and others as well. She was utterly fearless. It was as if she had decided at a very young age that she had nothing to lose. She'd tell the truth as she saw it, regardless of social consequences; she'd say anything to anyone, harsh or sweet, cruel or kind, and sometimes your feelings were hurt but you trusted her. When she praised you or declared love for you, you knew she meant it. When she looked you in the eye, interested in what you said, agreeing, supporting you, you felt knighted, your shoulder tapped with her sword.

Waiting for her, I smoked a cigarette, though it hurt my throat. CJ and I played honeymoon bridge, Saint read the Tao Te Ching. The radio deejay was playing *Highway 61 Revisited,* all the songs in order, and we discussed whether Bob Dylan was as great as Shakespeare, whether God was malevolent or merely indifferent, where the *h* belonged in the word "rhapsodic," and whether the kids who burned their draft cards were heroes or chickenshit. Saint's draft card had come in the mail. He'd have to work like a dog this year if he wanted a scholarship to college.

The sun was right overhead when Vera appeared, a tiny figure across the field. So far away, hair to her shoulders, she seemed half-dissolved in light, like a fairy or an angel. I waited for her to come to us, but when I looked again she had vanished in the scattering of picnic tables.

I was the only one who'd seen her. Backs to the picnic area, the boys were discussing human consciousness, the phenomenon of it: that a mélange of molecules, made of the exact same stuff as the stars, had somehow organized itself to produce individual people with their own personal thoughts and desires. "And don't bring up God," CJ went on. "That's such a cop-out."

Saint and CJ usually took opposite sides on an issue, but not now. Saint sat up straight and almost clapped his hands. "The killer for me is how different we are. I grew up looking at grimy bricks out the window and you had plants and trees. I should hate you."

CJ laughed, agreeing. "You were poor; we were filthy rich."

"And you still are," said Saint.

CJ often sounded mocking even when he was sincere, but he wasn't mocking now. "So why *aren't* we walking around locked in our separate consciousnesses? Formed by how we were treated since birth and all the accidents that happened to us . . ."

"The accident of how we look," I said, joining in.

"The accident of brains," said Saint.

"But we aren't locked in," CJ continued. "*That's* the mystery. How, if we're so different, did we get to be so close? That's the central question!"

It was an opera now, our separate voices combining to create the whole. How had we managed to find one another? How did people ever learn to present themselves to one another and be understood? Even if only partially understood? Was that outrageous or what?

"Let us pray," I said, a joke, as we were all doubters in our different ways. But nothing weakened the excitement of our push toward insight. What we worshipped were words, precise and truthful words, bridging the terrible gaps between people. I wanted to cry from the beauty of it. "To language," we said. "Pass the joint," we said, another joke, since we had no joint.

The union of our minds seemed so important, Vera shouldn't be missing it. I went looking and found her seated on the bench of the most remote picnic table. The waistband of her cutoffs gaped at the back; her dancer's spine was straight as a rod; she looked fiercely alone. I sat down with her. "Come be with us."

She shook her pack of cigarettes, then turned it over. Empty.

"Are you pissed at something?" I said. "At one of us?"

"If I were, would I keep it to myself?"

"Right. Yes. I know."

"Do you have any smokes?" she said.

I nodded toward where the boys were sitting. "CJ does."

"Bully for him."

I winced on CJ's behalf. This was not where I wanted us to go. "So, how's your brother?" I asked her. "I mean, is he talking yet about his adventures?"

She climbed onto the table and stretched out on her back in the bright sun. It was a hot day and she was shivering. *Where were you last night, were you sick or something*? I wanted to ask chidingly. "You look cold," I said. She shook her head, eyes closing.

A failure, I walked back toward the shade of the tree. Beyond was the bluff over Lake Michigan, its entire open length fenced off by six feet of chain-link, on which hung a memorial plaque. I felt bad for Vera, laid out on the table like a dead person. I felt bad for the boy for whom the fence had been raised, Randolph Leonard Burke 1923–1929. I imagined six-year-old Randolph running for a baseball, backing up and up toward the perilous edge, and me, like the catcher in the rye, tackling him before he went over. I wanted something grand to do, an act of courage or self-sacrifice for the world or for my friends.

Half an hour later she stood over us, hands on her narrow hips. "So what's on the program?" She passed assessing eyes over our cards, laid out for Bid for the Dummy. "Wowie zowie," she said. "What a surprise."

Be nice! I wanted to say, but I was so glad to have her back, I didn't care if she wasn't nice. "Is this what they call fashionably late?" CJ said, but didn't press for details. We knew not to press.

Now, with us four seated in the four cardinal directions, bridge cards in hand, my world was complete. I could lose myself in the game's red and black geometry, the universe sketched out by the bids and confirmed by each ensuing trick under laws complex but knowable, from which arose a four-way intimacy that didn't endanger anyone. At school I had to study to earn B's, but I was gifted at contract bridge, shrewd and intuitive, the all-around most desired partner. CJ bid by the book and got confused with a less mathematical partner. Vera's bidding was good, but she'd hog the contract sometimes. As for Ferdinand-the-bull Saint, he'd make one bid and give up, as if saying to his opponents, "*Take* the contract if you want it so bad!"

That day Vera and I were partners, and I was glad; we usually did well together. She held her cards with her good hand and played them out with the other, using her thumb and first nub daintily. I wished myself a physical defect, not quite as bad as hers, something pretty and touching like a slight limp.

We were in sync at first, Vera and I. I was as happy as I'd ever felt, beyond self-appraisal in our oasis of shade, in the infinitude of summer, with friends of my heart. Saint made a tough contract; CJ gave him the V sign. CJ laid down the wrong card; we let him take it back. CJ's radio had run out of battery juice, but we didn't need music. We had the sweet growl of bees, the crickets' *chee*—pause—*chee*, a few faraway cries from the playground and tennis courts, and beating time to the song of our happiness, the steady crash of waves on the rocks a hundred feet below. Then Vera started overbidding, and it seemed on purpose. She bid a slam when we didn't have the points for game. She lost easy tricks. When the deal came around to her again she squeezed the deck between her palms. "I just can't anymore."

We looked at her. Someone said, "Uh-oh." Maybe it was all of us, a joint outbreath.

"I know," she said. "But could we pep things up? Expand our horizons?"

She smiled mischievously, which made me more uncomfortable; she wasn't a smiler. I wondered if she'd planned the move while lying alone on the picnic table. Or maybe she was just feeling her way with us, amassing courage, daring herself to tell us what she wouldn't be able to tell—her first caginess with us, the first lapse in her invincible candor—until the roller coaster of our calamity was clanking up the last hill. But that comes later. Right now she sat before us with her golden skin and golden hair, her eyes violet in our tree's shade, and asked us, challenged us, to reveal the darkest, ugliest part of ourselves, something we had never told anyone. Something so sick, she said, that thinking about it, we could barely live with ourselves. She laid four cards face-down on the game board. High card went first.

It was a conundrum. Being honest with one another was more than a point of pride with us; it defined our group. With tears sometimes, we confessed things that hurt us or that we were ashamed of. But to present for inspection what we considered perversions, things in ourselves we were trying to blot out or overcome—how was this a good thing? Saint's face was blank, but his hands were squeezed into fists; CJ's eyelid was twitching; my heart was thudding. No one wanted this, but there seemed to be no way out. In some ways we were still children. A game had rules, the first of which deemed noncompliance a mark of dishonor.

I drew the high card, a jack, and I tittered hideously. No one moved or spoke. Then, having no recourse, I opened my Lorna Doones, which I had snuck during physics, bringing my calorie count way past the prescribed 1,800, and presented a half-empty cellophane sleeve. "I've eaten seven today already. As an act of further self-debasement I will consume number eight in front of you. Show-and-tell. Happy, Your Highness?" I stuffed a cookie into my mouth and proffered the bag. "Next?"

Vera yawned theatrically. "We're looking for a story, missy. Lurid details, you know."

It was like standing on a high diving board looking down on the tiny, faraway pool.

"Take a risk, Kay. Blow our minds."

"You'll hate me," I said with a giggle, as if I didn't mean it. "Please?"

There was a low rumble of thunder. For a second I believed in a God who answered prayers, but the sky was clear overhead. Having no recourse, acceding to a will stronger than my own, I smiled around my thick tongue and described a summer night the previous year when I woke up in bed, went down to the refrigerator, and discovered an entire beef brisket, newly cooked and wrapped in foil. I hated describing what I did then, the compulsion and shame, but I forced myself, pressing each sickening word up and out of my throat. "It was sitting in juice, not even sliced yet—do I have to finish this?" They all nodded as if enrapt, Saint too. I talked fast. "I cut a sliver. The meat was pink, the fat was white and hard, but I ate it, fat and all, another sliver and another, till it was gone. All gone. Tomorrow's dinner."

"Well past the adult daily requirement," said CJ, "but at least it was protein."

I gazed at my lap, feeling slightly faint.

"Did you barf it up?" Vera said.

"Please shut up!"

It was late afternoon now. Shadows were lengthening, rooting things to the earth. But I felt stripped of crucial mass. The stage set of my life—tree, fence, my handsome, intelligent friends—stayed on the ground while I rose into the air and hung there on nothing. Soon my friends would cease their forbearance of me, eject me from the club of our four-way friendship. I took another cookie, pinched off a crumbly corner, and, immersed in the buttery sweetness, finished the story: Thus I had lost the right to learn to drive. I couldn't even take the written test. Consequences!

Saint hummed under his breath, a nervous tic, then gave me a naked-eyed look that divided the world's pain between us. Dear Saint.

I had always liked Saint's face, his reddish-brown curly hair, growing long in the back, and his high freckled forehead—so familiar to me in the two years of our friendship that I could have drawn him from memory. But now his forehead wasn't just high and broad, it looked noble, like a lion's. Saint looked like a sad, noble lion, like Aslan from *The Lion, the Witch and the Wardrobe,* while I felt so ugly inside and out it was who I was, even if I lost forty pounds. I took out my drawing pad and hunched over it, doodling, trying not to think too hard or long about any one thing.

CJ was next, with a story he said he was dying to tell. It was about his ten-year-old brother, Danny, a nice kid, and athletically gifted. To improve Danny's character, CJ had invented a club called the Vampeers, in which the boy held a membership as long as he earned sufficient Vampeer Points. And, CJ said with a show of pride, Danny was into it! There were numerous tasks for him to accomplish, and the boy was performing well. This week he stole a pen from Beck's Department Store, drew a swastika on the gray leather seat of their father's Buick, and took the blame. Grounded, Danny was bearing it nobly. His imaginary fellow Vampeers applauded him. "Nice," said Vera, "your little sadistic streak." CJ put his palms together and bowed like a Buddhist.

I looked at Saint but couldn't read his reaction. I felt sicker than before. We all knew CJ hated his father and envied his brother. But his father had survived Auschwitz. "That's—I'm sorry—it's *too* sick," I said. I wasn't used to speaking up, but it was a strange day, and more was coming out of me. "It's beyond sick, don't say you think it's fine!" I went on till his ears were red. He gave a helpless, apologetic shrug. But I had to ask, "Does Danny know what a swastika means?"

"He does now. Could we move on?"

His eyes were bright, and something like shame was coming off his skin, a sad sourness. I tried to breathe it in, my friend and this new information. I finished my cookie, took another, swallowed saliva. Their dad was a cold man, maybe even cruel. He was hard on both boys, but CJ especially.

Then it was Saint's turn. His face was blank, his voice uninflected. "I could tell you about the time Mike and Rick Gittles pulled off my pants."

"Oh dear," Vera replied, not very nicely.

"Mickey and Ricky, they lived on the first floor of my building, the last place we lived in Detroit, and for some reason they hated me. They called me queer and I didn't even know what it meant. They threw my pants in a dumpster and I had to climb in to get them back. What?" he said to Vera, who had taken a smoke from CJ's pack.

"Saint Sebastian. Saint the victim. How do you always arrange that?"

Saint's pause stretched out. His skin looked pale under his freckles. He said at last, "Does anyone know what she's talking about?"

His voice hurt my heart. Vera gave a brief shriek. "You're full of shit, St. John. You've never done a bad thing in your life? It's always done *to* you?"

I was used to admiring Vera's candor, but now I didn't know, with Saint, what she was getting at. He would ask for a glass of water as if he wasn't sure he deserved it. He read *In Search of the Miraculous* and *The Way of Zen*, he quoted the Tao Te Ching, he was genuinely nonviolent, and if someone tried to pick a fight with him he'd turn the other cheek, like Gandhi and Christ. *They know not what they do.* "Feel free to tell me off," Vera said, in the smoky, deep voice of a forty-year-old woman. "Stop me before I kill again."

I wanted to stop her, to stop this ugly game, but with CJ I'd blown my wad. Beside me, CJ was pulling up grass, sifting it over the knees of his jeans. Saint's face was still blank, but he was humming under his breath, trying to sit like a rock while the illusion of pain crossed the empty mirror of his mind. *Let's not fight,* I said to myself, eating cookie after cookie till I was drowning in sugar butter and there was nothing in my mouth but the hum of grinding and a little ache from chewing. "So, um, how about some more bridge?" I said. "Come on, guys."

"Aren't you forgetting someone?" Vera said. "You haven't heard my evil."

The sun was angled west now, and to stay in the shade we had moved bit by bit around the tree and away from the bluff. In a couple of hours my family would be having dinner, and some of me wanted to be home already, with people who had nothing to say to me that I hadn't already heard. On the other hand, I sought transformation—an enlargement not of the body (which I'd already accomplished) but of the spirit or soul. I was timid, ordinary, undefined, and if I died that day (I had fully imagined this) I would leave no mark, like a stone dropped in a lake. I had been raised to be "good," whatever that meant, and I was terrified of evil, cruelty, perversity, the dark side of human nature. At the same time I felt obliged to know it, as if somewhere in that frothy black murk was the embryo of my natural charisma, my latent, essential personal force. I put the cookies back in my book bag and awaited whatever was coming.

"I dropped acid yesterday," Vera said. "With my brother."

CJ hooted. "And now you're *schizo*. I'd call that a cliché!"

He was breezy about her news, though I was pretty sure he was putting it on. We sometimes smoked the grass Saint got from someone he worked with at Hamburger Heaven, but no one had braved the chancier labyrinth of LSD till Vera now. It separated her from us. Even her "dropped" instead of "took."

"I must say," said CJ, "I expected more from you, Vee."

"Let her finish," said Saint, who hated teasing of any kind, even of someone as quick-tongued as Vera.

Without looking at any of us she began to describe the experience: first a period of euphoria in which you think you're seeing the world almost like God. "Laws and rules—you remember them, but they just seem funny, ha-ha funny. 'Abnormal' makes no sense. And ugly? Beautiful? You can't figure out why one is supposed to be better than the other. Rust is beautiful. And wrinkles and scabs. You can see into your pores where the little hairs start." Her bright glance swept her malformed hand, which was shaking. There might have been tears in her eyes, though it seemed unlikely. None of us had ever seen her cry.

We were transfixed, but she remained silent. I couldn't tell if she'd finished or had lost track of her story. CJ folded his hands in his lap like a good little kindergarten boy. "That's all cool," he said encouragingly. "So did you go anywhere? See anyone?"

Saint: "Where did you get the stuff? Did your brother bring it back with him?"

CJ, before Vera could answer: "Hey, what happened to him down there, wherever it was? Does he talk about it?"

Then the Garth saga took us over, though we had only snippets. We knew he'd left after his dad said, *You're gonna get yourself a job this summer or you can find another place to live.* We had laughed: How literally Garth took the old man.

We got into analyzing Garth, though in an admiring way. Told, once, to pick up his toys, he threw them out the window onto the garage roof. He really did that. But he wasn't an asshole. If you didn't order him, he'd do what had to be done. He was his own person. Imagine him working in an office. Or in prison, say! No one wanted to go to prison, but it would make Garth crazy. Locked up, he'd kill himself—we agreed on that. "He'd make a crappy Vampeer," Saint offered. CJ cast him a loving look.

We went on awhile, imagining life for Vera's brother with his and Vera's dictator dad, none of us noticing that Vera hadn't joined the conversation. Till out of nowhere she said, "You don't do anything on acid you wouldn't do without it. Not that it lets me off the hook."

There was a little silence while this seeming bit of randomness circled our brains looking for a place to land. "What do you mean?" I said.

CJ cackled. "You're kind of rambling, girl."

Me: "No, go on. I'm so sorry. We're listening."

She took off her sandals, stepped out into the sun, and started dancing in the grass, barefoot, something she would do at times to calm herself down. It wasn't a performance. She moved as if we weren't there, without a slip or hesitation. But it was painful to watch. Her legs pushed at the ground as if to keep her body in the air where it belonged, while her arms, which seemed to have no bones under the skin, swayed helplessly, the dancer straining against something too strong for her but that she couldn't escape. I was scalded with awe, envy, pity, and love for my friend, a set of feelings so at odds with one another that instead of taking a cookie, I took up my pen and sketch pad and tried to draw her.

She ended the dance folded in on herself like a dead bird. "I am so, so, so, so sick."

What could we say?

She glanced at my picture. "You gave me huge, perfect hands. Are you blind, Kay?"

I was afraid to speak.

"Sometimes, Kay-kay, I wish I could crawl into your head. It would be such a vacation." Then to all of us: "Do you know what dance that was?"

But who would have known? In the deadness of our silence, slowly, dully, she resumed her "trip" story: The exaltation didn't last. You came down sad and hopeless, hating yourself. Gaps lengthened between Vera's statements, until she slapped her face with both of her hands. "That's it. I'm sorry." She looked up over our heads, as if for listeners with minds subtler than ours. "So, guys, it's bye-bye birdie. Adios. Sayonara."

What?

Saint's eyes, his whole body, strained toward Vera, who was—I saw now—trembling. Even CJ looked confused. She sat a moment more, dead cigarette on the grass beside her. Then she threw back her head and shoulders, swung her legs up and over her head, and landed on her feet.

It was a pretty set of movements, but unlike her dance it seemed show-offy. She stood in the golden light of late afternoon, face, hair, bare shoulders ablaze, but her voice was flirty and sly in a private joke with herself. "See that cyclone fence?" She nodded westward toward the bluff, the lake, the declining sun. "When the park empties out, I'm going to climb it. Then I'll spread my wings. My make-believe wings. My illusory wings."

She paused, her head balanced precisely on top of her neck, while we took it in, text and subtext. There was a breach then in the day's logic. A thread broke in the warp of the universe.

Anger—my own—has always confused me. I feel bad in a diffuse, all-over-my-body way and want to cry. Vera knew what my mother had done. I wanted her to take it back, to cut the last minute from all of our lives. For a moment no one said anything.

Then, thank God, the boys found their voices.

CJ: "LSD leads to suicide. Now, isn't that a cliché?"

"It's a threat," said Saint. "Why are you threatening us?"

CJ: "She's telling us so we can stop her."

"If you say so," she said.

She smiled coldly, in her own kind of rage. She bounced on her toes, as if about to waft away. I managed, at last, to get to my feet. I don't remember what I said—it's confused with what I wanted to say and what afterward I wished I'd said—but it was more or less this: "I want to believe you don't mean it. But if you do and you're our friend, I think you owe us." When it was clear guilt wasn't working, I tried logic. "Or maybe you don't owe us anything, but you could at least explain why you want to do something so . . . so final?" And then I was pissed. "It's just cowardly!"

"If you say so."

"Would you quit saying that?"

She arched backward till her hair and then the flats of her hands met the ground, and her body made a bridge. The slender bones of her rib cage stood out under her tube top. Prima donna is what my mother would have called me if I had made that move (my real mother, not the steplady). Not that I could have.

"What do you want us to do, stay and watch? Take pictures?" I said, though it was already dawning on me that we were irrelevant. Rising from her backbend, she looked at me from what seemed a sorrowful distance, as if she were already gone, in some heaven or fifth dimension. I was crying then, but I threatened to call her priest (it was all I could think of; Saint had the same priest). I tried to shame her into telling the rest of her story, as she had shamed me. "We told *you*," I said like a ten-year-old.

"If you try it, I may have to kill you," said Saint.

"To be or not to be. It's the central human question. At least according to Camus?" said CJ wonderingly.

We were all goofy in our different ways, and we stood before her—a goofy barricade—all determined to save her from herself, physically if need be. "You can't," I said. "We won't let you. We need you."

"It's true," Saint murmured, humming low in his throat.

Then her mood changed, or seemed to. She sat down again and crossed her legs like a kid in a kindergarten circle. As if we had no will of our own, utterly bound to her movements, we sat as well. She giggled eerily. "How *much* do you need me? Could you bear living without me?"

For the past three years I'd known her better than I knew anyone. And she knew me. At the mere thought of life without her, I felt myself growing dim to myself. Actions pointless. Gray days everlasting. I saw myself walking the earth like a zombie, cut off from the source of light and life. It was how the priests described limbo, hell for pagan babies, the soul cut off from God. "I couldn't stand it," I said. "I would die, truly." Which sounded false to my ears, overstated but lame, but the guys were nodding, and it seemed to touch something in her. Her body started to vibrate, not quite trembling, as if mild electricity were coursing through her. "I can't believe you mean it. But if you do, if it's true what you say, then maybe"—her teeth were chattering now—"maybe you would all like to . . ." The words "join me" hung before us in the air.

This was not my idea. It was not anyone's. Saint's hands were extended, either to hold her here in the world with us or to plead for our lives.

"All of us?" CJ giggled nervously. "Ooh, messy. Spilled on the beach. Picture it," he said, and I did: the plummet, the crash, our broken bodies.

I was shaking my head, no, no, but made no sound. As if it were still possible that her words didn't mean what they seemed to mean.

We were pleading now for our lives along with hers. "Do you want people talking about us behind our backs?" said CJ. "I mean, I'm sure they already do, but like we belong in the loony bin?" He put on a female voice: "That sweet Kay Campion, if only she'd asked for help! Like mother, like daughter? But I for one never trusted that witchy DeVito. And poor St. John, he might have had a chance if he hadn't gotten involved with what's-his-face, you know, the weirdo kike?"

Saint and I nodded concurrence.

"Seriously," said CJ, "think of the headline. 'Tragedy at LJHS. Teens Die in Deadly Pact.'"

I thought of my stepmother and stepsister; they might feel bad but not that bad. I thought of my father, who had managed to replace my mother. Wind hit the leaves of the tree overhead, and the rustle softened the sounds of the words in my mind. Far below us, waves clawed at the beach, hsssh hsssssh, like my mother, whom I remembered clearly, perfectly, humming me to sleep.

"You know that dance I did in the grass?" Vera said. "It's famous. It's called 'The Dying Swan.' It looks nifty, but it isn't that hard."

Then with a light hop she was up and running. We chased her, but she was fast. She was at the jagged top of the chain-link when Saint caught her ankle. He pulled, she slipped, he reached up, she fell. CJ and I stood on the outskirts as if paralyzed while they rearranged themselves at the base of the fence. Then she was a little bundle in his arms, held as I had always wanted to be held, and it got worse. He kissed her forehead. It got still worse. "I'll join you, if that's what you really want," he said, his cheek tender against her cheek, his wild red hair and her pale gold, so beautiful I could hardly breathe. "Don't leave me out!" cried CJ. He fell to his knees and curled beside them like a dog.

If I could have done exactly what I wanted right then, I'd have tipped my head back and howled, for as long and as loud as I had breath. Till glass cracked across town, in windowpanes and storefronts, and someone came to stop this terrible thing. Far too self-conscious to join their embrace, I just stood in front of them, looking for somewhere to rest my gaze. "This is so crazy. Guys, don't be crazy." I addressed Vera: "We *can't* live without you, that's the point, don't you see? We'll do anything for you. Isn't that something to live for?"

Now I knew what it meant to be beside oneself. This could not be happening. It was happening. CJ the rational, the ironic, kissed the back of Saint's hand. All three seemed swept out of themselves, in a genuine rapture. They were transported together, and I was alone. I was a bucket with a hole in it, never to be filled.

What happened next had a milky, shimmery haze around it—so much terror and giddy, exhilarated longing, and even a mystical kind of love, that afterward replaying it I didn't trust my memory. The three were entwined, breathing one another's breath. Every once in a while CJ laughed nervously. I watched from outside, from the borderlands. The air stirred, pooled, went quiet. Then Saint reached his large warm hand out to me. "Come on, girlie. Join the huddle."

"I love you," Vera said to me. "You're my sister. My twin."

"Let's not overdo it," said CJ. Then he too reached out.

I will never forget that moment, the sun in the late afternoon turning everything golden—the chain-link fence, the dry grass, our skin. The warm wind blew, waves beat on the rocks, and the weave of my mind began to loosen. Here was an answer to a question I didn't know I'd been asking. Words spilled out of me, things about myself that I'd never voiced and maybe only half knew, that I came to know as I spoke: I needed love but I didn't deserve it. I wanted to be better than I was, to submerge my weakness in something strong, to transform everything ugly in me into what was pure and beautiful.

I paused to swallow, and they waited respectfully. When my mother died, I'd willed my soul to leave my body like hers and rise up to heaven. I had asked God to help. Of course nothing had happened, but now again it seemed to be what I wanted and needed. There would be no pain, just the wafting upward of something not quite bodiless. Human life was a sea in which bodies floated like bubbles. Death was the bubble breaking.

I described my vision and they seemed to understand. Saint called me an old soul. Sitting cross-legged, erect in meditation position, he recounted the story of Siddhartha, which was also the story of the Buddha, a prince who gave up power, wealth, and human love to seek truth. I straightened my back, crossed one leg over the other. Vera blew a smoke ring, which swelled, rose, began to dissolve in the cosmos like our human souls. Life and death were illusions, yes? A ripple of peace washed over me.

"So," Vera said, "we have a pact."

Did we? How to be sure? The sky was so blue. I wanted, actually, to be both alive and dead. To know death while being alive in the knowing. I covered my face with my hands. I said, "Let's not rush this. We need time to think."

"About what?" she said.

"Everything. How to be happy."

"Thinking is pain," she said. "Right, Siddhartha?"

"Vera, shut up."

It was the second time that day I'd stood my ground with them, but there was nothing that day that I could have predicted. I'd wanted transformation, and here I was, on the brink. "Aren't there things you want to do in life? Go onstage and dance? You're so talented. . . ."

She curved her arms over her head like a ballerina, then flapped her bad hand at us.

"*That*? It doesn't have to stop you!" I turned to our friends. "What about you guys? If you had a year to live, or even a month, what would you do?"

"I'd go down to Chicago and see a Cubs game," Saint said. CJ smirked. "Asshole," said Saint. "What would *you* do?"

CJ made a fist and poked in a sly finger. We hissed, but he was unfazed. "With each of you! Or maybe all together?"

"I'd lose weight," I said. "I know it's vain and pathetic and means nothing in the face of really terrible things, but I'd buy a two-piece bathing suit and go to the beach. I'd walk along the sand in front of people. I'd sit down on my towel and put on suntan lotion. I would so love that." Tears were rolling down my cheeks but I didn't care. "Could we wait six months?"

No one answered. We sat in our patch of shade, the sun bright all around us. Backlit, my friends looked like gods. Vera was Hera, the queen; CJ was Hermes, the lightning-quick messenger; and Saint of the lion's mane—he was Prometheus, who gave fire to mankind and suffered for it.

Then Saint looked at me. Our eyes locked and a beam of light seemed to pass between us. And I felt beyond doubt: There was no beauty in the world without him in it.

"How about a month? Or two weeks?" I said. "I have to read *Siddhartha* and lose weight, and I have no willpower!" I was trying to be funny. But Vera's face was wet. Vera, who never cried.

"What's the matter, Vee?"

She shook her head from side to side. "I can't believe. You'd entertain the thought. Even for a second."

"It's just love." As I spoke, I knew it was true. "I would die for you. For all of you. Like those monks who burned themselves in Vietnam."

Vera held out her hand and I was pulled into the group. I felt as if I were ten years old again and a girl I'd liked from afar had just invited me to sleep over. Saint took my other hand. Tears poured out of me but without choking or sobbing, without pain or shame, sweet on my face and in my throat. I wrapped my arms around Saint's thick arm, I entangled my legs with everyone's. It was like a four-way marriage had been sealed, a pact like the covenant between God and Noah that kept the world alive. I loved these people. They loved me. God ran through them and through me, a circulatory system of friendship feeding all of us. "It's like we've already died and this is heaven."

We laughed ferociously. A compromise had been reached beyond our individual wills. For the next two weeks—exactly, only—we would make it our project to do everything we had ever dreamed of. Then, five days before the start of our last year of high school, on what was also, fortuitously, Vera's seventeenth birthday, we would climb the cyclone fence by the bluff, hold hands on the tippy-toe edge, scream, "Fuck you!" at the sad, silly, illusory world, and jump.

A pledge, it had to be inscribed. Vera dictated; CJ honed the word choice; I made a copy for each of us, on my college-ruled loose-leaf notepaper.

We, the undersigned, parts of a nearly perfect union, do hereby swear upon the Sacred Bond of Friendship that on August 29, 1968, before light from the rising sun hits the lake, we will leap together from the bluff at Lourdes Metropolitan Park, consigning our futures to such forces as may wish to govern them. The decision is ours alone and not the misdirection of any third party. We celebrate our will, our love for one another, and our sacred honor.

Katherine "Kay" Campion
Vera DeVito
St. John Scully
Christopher Joseph Walker

We had fourteen days.

2

Vera

———

It was dinnertime, but Vera stayed in the park. Pledge or no Pledge, the rest of us had to go, Saint to work, CJ and I to what Vera called our swank pads. We had pre- and post-dinner chores and, in between, the family dinner table. We would meet later at Hamburger Heaven when Saint's shift was over.

CJ drove me home, and in the car beside him I pictured Vera alone under our tree, maybe leaning against the trunk. The park had been emptying, moms assembling their children. When you know people the way I knew my friends then, you know what they're doing when you aren't with them, or you think you do. Words they uttered last year or an hour ago, their jokes and opinions, and sometimes their thoughts about things, including you, flit around your head like little demon butterflies, counterpointing your own thoughts, shaping the muddle of your day. Even years later I can see Vera in the park that evening just before sunset. She's feeling pretty good after all that solidarity, everyone's arms around her.

Then her good feeling starts to fade. Maybe it's confabulation, maybe I'm putting my own neurotic self into her, but it's getting dark and she's thinking of me in my air-conditioned house, with my family that, for better or worse, eats dinner together. She pats the back pocket of her cutoffs for the slight bulk of her copy of the folded Pledge. *As if,* she thinks, *Kay would actually honor the Pledge when it came due. As if anyone would.*

Vera was so utterly sure of herself—of the rightness of what she said and did—that it was hard for other people to sense her self-doubt. But it's so clear now. Swathed in fear and rage, she is moving toward the fence, glaring through it at the lake, at the flecks of light on the water. Fuck this, she thinks. She could climb and jump now, with the low sun shining on the waves and kids whining for ten more minutes on the swings. She can choose, her untold secret a knife to cut through any pledge.

This is what, at the time, we knew about her:

1. That her father was scum.

2. That her mother would be scum if she had enough substance to be wiped off of something.

When the mood struck she told us bits of sleaze:

3. Her father had had numerous girlfriends, currently a young lady in payroll, ten years older than Vera and great in the sack. (He told her such things.)

4. A possible cause of the man's faithlessness was his crazy wife (his term), who would clean the house from the cellar to the back of the closet in the master bedroom, then get in bed with a library book and a glass of vodka. Who could stand such a woman?

5. It was Vera herself at the root of every bad thing—her birth defect, to be specific, her essential governing symbol. It's what people saw, or worse, tried not to see. The rare times her mother spoke to her, it was to her forehead or where the wall of a room met the ceiling, far above the region of her hand. When her father enfolded her in his duplicitous, burly embrace or when he paddled her behind (still, in high school), his body would graze, as if accidentally, certain parts of her body but never her defective hand.

6. She had fucked seventeen guys if you counted the twins from New Jersey who were spending a week at their grandma's cabin. Who both shot off before they got anywhere.

7. At night in her darkened bedroom, wallpapered ten years ago in a repeating pattern of ballerina bunnies when her mother still had some life in her, she put a chair under the doorknob and had sex with appropriately shaped items—the handle of a hand mirror, a

bottle of roll-on deodorant, root vegetables. And reached climax—she even told us this—under the imaginary weight of the high school principal, a puffy elderly man with kind eyes. At least it wasn't her father, never her father. Nor (honestly) her brother, Garth, who ran away from home on the last day of school and had just returned, suddenly half a head taller than she was. Who still looked so much like her, hair and eyes, that people remarked upon it. They could be twins except for—what a shame!—that poor little hand of hers.

The thing she didn't say and had no plans to—what she wanted to tell and still held back from us, her friends, who did not hold back: that in the heart of her heart, where the deepest truth lay, she didn't really love us. Not the way we loved her.

That with Garth yesterday she felt something she had wished for her entire life without having words for it. Garth knew her, body and soul, and he could take her in whole—as if she were whole—without a qualm or the hint of a shudder.

That last night, too revved to sleep, with the dregs of the drug clogging her brain, she tiptoed down two flights of stairs to Garth's basement room to hear his *Sgt. Pepper*. And in her nightshirt, shivering in the belowground chill, she got under his summer quilt, just to warm herself up. And—I shouldn't know this, I never wanted to know—she screwed him, her flesh and blood, a hundred percent brother, sixteen months younger than she, with whom she'd watched Sunday cartoons, Elmer Fudd and Woody Woodpecker, and whom she used to mock and console, her brother who looked up to her. With whom, under whom—she can't stop thinking about it—her body hairs stood out from her pores when she came.

Now Vera is hungry but she doesn't want to go home. It's a problem that wouldn't exist if she hadn't signed the fucking Pledge. She takes the document out of her pocket to crumple it, but first she rereads it and mulls over the two weeks she conceded to her friends. She could violate it with no punishment. She'd be doing them a favor. Beyond the chain-link the lake is darkening. A feathery, weightless rain is coming down.

In the shelter of the tree she opens the green canvas Army-Navy Store satchel she calls her purse. Inside is a tiny film canister that Garth gave her yesterday, and inside that a square of translucent paper, which, against the sky, reveals a pale, dime-sized interior circle. You can't change the world but you can change how you think about the world: Saint said that once, or was it Timothy Leary? Shielding the scrap from the air's moisture, she puts it on her tongue, a sensation so slight, she can't tell whether the paper has dissolved or slipped down her throat. Or how in fact she has come to be walking away from the Haight, not home but toward the town center. She rejects hunger. She doesn't want to go home ever. Two weeks is a long, long time.

Two weeks ago Garth came back from Florida, where he'd lived in a van, he said, with a twenty-year-old woman and her pet tarantula. In the Everglades. He returned suddenly old and wise, older than her in some ways, knowing, among other things, a great deal about recreational drugs. Garth, her baby brother. He came back for her, he said. To be with her.

Weak in the back of her knees, still she moves townward, impelled by the left-right-left of her hands and feet, wet wind at her back. Near the lake are multistoried houses with screened back porches, cupolas with views of water, railinged widow's walks. Inland, the houses grow smaller and closer together. They become cabins or trailer hookups housing summer people, who rent for a week or a month and leave sunglasses behind, and damp paperbacks. Dogs yap. A girl in a bathing suit spins on a tiny lawn, arms out, head back. A man calls from a doorway, Kim? Lynn? The girl keeps spinning.

On the next, apparently untenanted block, Vera stops and puts her feet in ballet first position. She bends her knees, straightens, and rises onto her toes, plié. Relevé, feeling again the strength and pliancy of her spine, *la sagesse du corps*, as Madame Jarkov said of her body, which, for seven years in a row knew all the movements of ballet even as they were demonstrated, as if she weren't being taught but simply reminded. Madame Jarkov had singled her out for praise: *Elle flotte, n'est-ce pas?* And now she is floating again, over to the Red Owl for a pack of Camels, maybe a carton.

On Main Street, the two blocks of shops that constitute downtown Lourdes, the pierced lobe of one ear calls attention to itself. It's not pain; she rarely feels physical pain. Out of curiosity, primarily, she stops in front of the Coast-to-Coast and looks at the reflection of her ear and its heavy earring, a present from Kay. Oh, Kay. Behind the glass a fly settles on the chrome handle of a riding lawnmower. Then the fly is gone, only to reappear on the machine's grass-green seat, and Vera is off again to the beat of her earlobe, stepping high over the neatly tarred cracks in the rain-wet sidewalk. Someone overtakes her, a youngish woman, walking fast with lots of butt swoosh in white-stitched Kmart jeans that show the hip-hugger line of her underpants. Vera pities the woman, at the sad, inevitable point where looks don't matter anymore.

The acid is coming on now. To steady herself, Vera stops at a pet shop featuring a large aquarium. Fish dart through greenish water in which her face glimmers. Pretty? Ugly? She pushes her hair back from her ear; the lobe seems to breathe. A fish with brilliant blue stripes flits into and past the reflection of her neck, leaving a bright blue afterimage. Her earlobe swells, subsides, like an aquatic plant.

By the time she reaches the Red Owl the rain has stopped. Two men pass toting six-packs, bellies bobbing. A woman pushes an empty stroller, followed by a child of three or four, who every once in a while throws a stone at her leg. Tragically patient, the woman plods on. The child is lumpy, tuberous. It may be bad, this trip. Why don't people stand up straight? Her earlobe feels hot. A repeating sound issues from it, like a tapping foot. It's not especially annoying, but suddenly her hand has risen to her earring. Good hand steadying her bad one, she pinches off the metal back. And they are gone, the earring and what secured it.

She's on her knees but has already forgotten what she is seeking. Everything, lost in the soft green moss in the cracks of the sidewalk.

There are jewel-like iridescent chips in the pebbled cement. An ancient penny throbs green and dark gold. But she is happy. Beyond happy. The sun has struck the angle where it turns the world golden, the hour of kindness and peace and ego-rest before it goes down. On the damp, cool sidewalk outside the Red Owl her body and mind open like a baby's, like yesterday. Between beauty and ugliness, holiness and sin, there is only language, word-sounds turned into music in the incredible golden light. She could write a book, *Joy and Madness*, describing the miraculous truth that if you just stand still and look, everything in the world, good and evil, will flicker by like television. *The End of Ugliness*? She smiles at her shadow on the pavement, neither pretty nor ugly, eternally beyond comment.

"Hey, blondie, what'd you lose? A diamond or something?"

A boy maybe a little older than her, in mirrored sunglasses and an armless sweatshirt that reads BUD KING OF BEERS, has just exited the Red Owl. A cigarette sticks out of his fat Mick Jagger lips. He stops dead in front of where she's kneeling, a full shopping bag in the casual bend of his arm as if he's used to carrying much heavier things. Tall, with an oblong face, he is juicily arm-muscled, the kind of guy imitated by younger, weaker guys. The hand at the end of his muscled arm pats the top of her head. "Say, Marilyn. Is that hair for real?"

She stands up, trying to reknit the frayed ends of her social self. "*Va-t'en,*" she says crisply, French for "Get the fuck out of here." From his sunglasses to his loose lips over his long chin, this is not someone she wants to know. He has probably driven up from Hammond or South Chicago with a bunch of loser friends to play loud music at the campground and eat potato chips and leave cans of beer inside the fire ring. She is attracted, though, to his Red Owl shopping bag, over the top of which, behind some hot dog buns, she has glimpsed the corner of a carton of Camels. She'd walk a mile for a Camel. She has walked a mile.

"Hey, sexy lady! What did you lose, honey, one a them contact lenses?"

The question intrigues her, in particular the word "lose." "Lose face" comes to mind, though without an accompanying image. More important are the cigarettes, though she can't think about them without thinking of the camel-hair coat she used to wear to church. In her closet there's a camel blazer for college interviews, a birthday gift from her Texas grandmother, though she herself has no college plans. That's what she has lost, her college plans. She giggles, puts her hand to her mouth.

"Hey, beauty. Let me in on the joke."

She avoids his sunglasses, which present two distinct, warped pictures of her face. Below his shirt the narrow bands of his golden-brown abdomen taper into his unbelted jeans. Her hips jerk involuntarily. With her good hand she reaches out and touches his skin. It's softer than she expected.

"Do that again, baby," he says. His torso is washboard-hard. He holds her life in his hands. "You're really out of it, aren't you?"

His face is suddenly, obtusely sure of itself. She's at the point in her voyage when images assault. Oh, for the sweet rush of a cigarette. Her good hand presses her weak one to her stomach. *Give me please one of your smokes. Would you kiss my chest right here in the middle between my breasts? Would you hold me hard and not let go no matter what?*

She's trapped between the camel-bronze of his skin and the camel-colored camel on his carton of Camels when a second young man arrives. He has thick-lashed blue eyes, but he's short, with the stiff, self-conscious walk of the sidekick, the pale, diluted version. He pulls a stick of beef jerky out of his friend's bag and bites off the top. "Nice, amigo. She got a little girlfriend?"

Mick Jagger Lips looks her over again, his regard for her restored, perhaps, by that of his friend. "Sweetheart, you want to party tonight?"

His top lip rises to let the words out. In the twin lenses of his sunglasses is her forehead times two, swollen in the curve of glass. Her face deformed. In French, she knows, "face" is *"le visage."* Or *"la figure."* Once her mother said—a real live compliment!—*You have a nice figure.* But it's a lie; she is disfigured. *May I have a cigarette?* The words resound in her mind. Or did she say them aloud? His gaze is cool and warm at the same time down her face, neck, shoulders, chest. Her belly squeezes with nausea and excitement. *Would you like to fuck me?* She reaches for the cigarette carton.

"What's that?" His eyes lock on her bad hand on the carton it has made the mistake of touching. Fearful, ashamed of itself, the hand tries to hide inside its fist, then retreats to her midriff, which offers no protection. The boy speaks through closed lips. "What's with the hand, babe? Are you one of them mutant—" He turns to his friend. "What's the thing those prego chicks took? Thalo something?"

Coolly, unreflectingly, as if it has performed the feat many times, her good hand reaches up, grabs the front of his shirt, and turns him to the storefront window. Her voice too has refound its strength. "Look, moron! Someone should punch your chin back into your head! Do you think there's a girl in the state of Michigan who'd pull down her pants for you? Why don't you and Brother Dickhead hippety-hop over to your little Ford pickup and head back to the trailer park?" She flees, ballet-graceful, though her shoulder bag thumps against her side.

She's at the curb waiting for the light, about to cross the highway toward Fast Food Row, when she is grabbed by the hair. The flat of a hand slaps her face. Whap, whap, gonna teach you a lesson. In her head there's an annoyingly bright light, but her body is oddly tranquil. "Go right ahead," she says to the hand hitting at her. "Do you think I feel anything?" She thinks she is speaking. There's a buzz in her larynx.

Now she's sprawled across the curb with a woman striding toward her. "Are you okay?" The woman kneels, trying to see her face. "Beasts!"

"Thugs. Punks," says a man. "Let them beat on each other, but a girl? You didn't see that ten years ago."

"Her nose is bleeding. Pinch it, honey. In the middle, like this.

Mannie, do you have a hankie? My God, that eye. Should we call an ambulance? Or the police, maybe?"

They argue about whether to help her stand or make her lie down flat. Vera enjoys their ministering, their concerned, middle-aged expressions. They're her aunt and uncle, they're the grandparents she used to dream about, her mother's parents from Finland, who died before she was born. Then the word "police" accosts her ears. She's out of their helpful arms, running as fast as she can, across Lake Street to where Main becomes U.S. 12, heading north to Canada and south around Lake Michigan to Chicago.

Hamburger Heaven is the first restaurant in the chain of franchises on U.S. 12. Vera gets in the longest line with the hope of postponing a decision. Soon, though, she's at the white-tiled counter, face-to-face with a woman her mother's age, who is smiling with routine, weary friendliness. "If you're still deciding, young lady, would you mind stepping aside? Maybe you want to use the washroom?"

Vera steps back, bumps a little girl holding a woman's hand. The woman has a small upturned nose with gaping nostrils. Vera must elude their beckoning darkness. The woman pulls the child closer, but the child eyes Vera with solemn interest. It's hard to bear even the child's scrutiny. Sweat runs down her sides in individual drops.

Then the tray arrives, mother and child move off. The counter-woman says, "So, young lady, have you got it figured out?"

Vera looks around frantically. Faces are opaque, bodies block the door. Overhead is a picture of an enormous hamburger, striations of cheese, patty, onion, bacon, lettuce, tomato, and creamy sauce.

THE ARCHANGEL $1.95

No words come to mind to reaffirm her right to take up space on earth and in this restaurant.

"Miss?"

All she can do is point, but it's enough. "She wants an Archie," the woman calls, happy with her. A nice woman. "And to drink?"

Now it's easier. "Coke?" says Vera.

"Pepsi okay?"

"Yes."

"For here or to go?"

"Here?"

"Deluxe?"

"Yes."

"There's a wait on the fries, I hope you don't mind?"

"Yes! I mean no!"

The woman smiles forgiveness. "Now you better take care of that eye."

The transaction concluded, Vera is free to look around. By the door is a cigarette machine, in front of which stands a college-age couple. The girl buys a pack of Kools. When she pulls one out, her boyfriend strikes a match, cupping his hand over the flame with a tenderness that moves through Vera's chest.

She wafts toward them and toward the white and green pack in the girl's hand. Vera doesn't like Kools, they're too minty-sweet, but nearing the girl she inhales from the bottom of her belly and takes in what's supposed to be bad for her. At age five she loved so-called bad smells: gasoline, her father's sweat; they aroused a bodily shiver. Bad smells and touches. At three, in the back of the family car next to Garth in his kiddie seat, she stuck one of her polyp fingers into his sweet open mouth, and he sucked, and she shivered from her knees to the small of her back, a feeling so bad and so good she wanted to have it always and at the same time wipe it off the plate of her mind right into the garbage.

Now, cresting on acid, she breathes harsh, exhilarating hand-me-down smoke. And she's three years old again, beside little Garth in the back of the car. But now, age three, looking into his gray toddler eyes the same color as hers, she sees his thinking, so much like her thinking. She sees in his rapidly organizing brain that some bit of this experience will remain, accruing mass and odor like a rind under the fridge. And this time she puts a pacifier in his mouth, a rubber and plastic nipple shape that she can easily let go of, and not her nub of a finger, which goes into not his mouth but a little hole in the plastic seat of her mother's car. And she feels no nausea, sweet or otherwise. And for the next ten or twelve years, nothing burns in either of their guts. Yesterday didn't happen, could not have happened—amazing, this acid vision that contains truth. Time is malleable like modeling clay. Why, she can back up more than her sixteen-plus years, crawl up the birth canal, and fix the gene in the chromosome that screwed up her hand. So that here at the white-tiled counter, when her hands emerge at last from her pockets, either one can reach into her shoulder bag, unzip the wallet, and pull out a bill for the counterwoman, and it will make no difference which hand does what, since both are, at last, identically graceful and strong.

"Order up."

"*Un moment, s'il vous plaît.*" She pats her shoulder for the strap of her bag. She pats her hip.

"Miss?" The woman sets the drink on the tray beside the Archangel and the steaming fries. Hanging from Vera's shoulder is exactly nothing. Vera looks at her hands and finds them empty. Where else?

"Young lady? Yoo-hoo!"

Vera calls back, high, thin, adrift, "I know. Sorry. I can't find my . . ." watching the tail end of her explanation blossom into the word "hand," which is not what she meant to say. And she's out the door.

At first she knows where she's going; she can see the spot on the sidewalk where she dropped her bag. After ten steps, however, the mental image is gone. She circles the building that is Hamburger Heaven, white-painted brick shining under the parking lot lamps. Around back, past the trash cans, is a line of cars, head to tail, their windows open. Involuntarily she peers into one.

"Hello?" someone says.

"Who's that, Todd?"

"Beats me."

She moves up the line from car to car, eyeing faces, though for what purpose she doesn't know. At the front of the line is a car with an Illinois license plate, a convertible with two girls inside. Out of the drive-through window comes a large, freckled hand, closed competently upon the rolled top of a white paper bag. The bag changes hands, paper money changes hands, the car moves on. She steps up to the window and peers in, following the white-sleeved arm to a face she knows. Saint. St. John.

The car behind her blinks its lights; she pays no attention. A few days after Garth disappeared, Saint came to her house by himself, supposedly to talk, to calm her down about Garth, but he had nothing to say. It was almost a relief when her father came home and ordered him gone. Saint can be maximally annoying, especially his habit of blanking out for whatever reason. But now his presence soothes and almost pleases her, his hair netted back, his forehead high and shining like a priest's. She opens her mouth, hoping that what comes out will make sense.

The car honks; she gives it the finger and turns back to Saint. "I lost my bag, but it's cool. I lost my brother, but I don't know. I thought I found my hand, but I can't even find my handbag. Do I sound crazy?" Words pour like water. Her body is water lapping around his familiar form, just beyond the parallelogram of light from the window. "I was lost but now I'm found, apparently?"

"Are you stoned, Vee?"

She giggles, then reaches in to touch him. Behind her the car flashes its brights again and again.

"Could you come back at ten-thirty, Vera? With the rest of the pack? It's a zoo now, right?"

Ten-thirty was when they were meeting. The cohort, as usual. But it's more than she can handle right now. "I want just you."

He looks consternated, even annoyed with her.

"Call them," she says. "Please," says Vera, who never says please. "Tell them we'll see them tomorrow." Heat and light are radiating from the skin of his arms and face, and she imagines his tongue in her mouth, and now she is trembling. "And then buy me some cigarettes? Please, thank you, I love you."

3

Casa Campion

———

Through most of high school I did my best to avoid members of my immediate family. When they were home I'd don my cloak of invisibility at the door and waft up to my room, where I had supplies in the form of cookies and chips. My aim was a life apart, which I achieved—and was permitted—except for our so-called family dinners, from which I could neither excuse myself nor emerge from without a sense of my unworthiness to breathe the air of the nicely decorated room.

But that August evening, with the Pledge folded inside my bra, I was free of my usual dread. I washed my hands, took up four plates and four sets of silverware, and went straight to the dining room, where Dad was already seated and my stepmother, Arlyn (AKA Annoying Arlyn), was opening a bottle of wine—both of them tanned, attractive, even I could see it, compared to most people their age. I set the table. I kissed Dad, gave Arlyn a dutiful nod. One trial lay ahead, a test of my new aplomb. Across from my place at the table was the empty chair that would soon bear the athletic body of my stepsister. Generally I glowered abjectly. But now, while shower water was flushing from Elise any trace of perspiration roused by her tutoring job or tennis lesson, I had merely to touch the spot over my bra where the Pledge resided and I was inured. The chandelier beamed its fairy lights off the beveled glass tabletop, classical violin sang through the wall speakers, I felt largehearted if not rhapsodic. As if the four-way Pledge were all I needed for perfect self-love.

"Kay, what are you smiling at?"

Arlyn had spoken. I tried to loosen my jaw.

"Don't be shy," she said. "We like you perky like this. Do you have a secret?"

My father grinned. "I'll bet she's in love."

As usual the kidding felt like an assault, but I remained blissfully detached. Rays of light shot through the overhead circle of prisms and *refracted* (homage to Carstairs!) onto the bright white walls. Light seemed to bounce from the sprayed-on sheen of Arlyn's hair (set in what was called a bubble) to the white of her blouse to the glitter of her rings to the white platter of low-calorie chicken she was setting upon the table (to get cold in Elise's absence, but so what?) to my father's white golf shirt. *I am going to die,* I said to myself, suppressing laughter. *My friends and I are going to die.*

Then Elise swept in, in her white terry cloth robe: skin as white as snow, hair as black as ebony and smelling of apricot shampoo. There was something nauseating in the mix of food smells and shampoo that smelled like food, but I let it go. "I made you wait," she cried. "I'm sorry. Never again, I swear!"

"Want to make a bet?" my father said (*my* father, not hers), but he was smiling. She smiled back ruefully and kissed his cheek, then Arlyn's. The violin music swelled, as if just for her.

"What are you all listening to?" said Elise. "Wait, let me guess." She paused, her face bright with cogitation. "Mendelssohn's 'Violin Concerto.' But who's that playing—Heifetz?" She sat, finally, pulling her robe over the sculpted bones of her knees.

"Isaac Stern." Arlyn tossed her head, but her hair didn't move. "It's exquisite. But Heifetz sounds *thicker* somehow. Tom, honey, we have to get the Heifetz."

I had no opinion about either violinist. All I'd eaten today were cookies and I was starved, even for skinned chicken breasts broiled with lemon. But Elise had more to say. "Itzhak Perlman's my true love. He was on TV the other day. He played sitting down, and I had tears in my eyes! You know, he'll be in Chicago next month. I want to go down to see him. They have student rates." My father beamed approval, although before Arlyn and Co. he'd never turned on the stereo.

When we finally got to the food part of the dinner, it was cold as well as dry, but I ate, chewing slowly, counting to fifty, tasting with every part of my tongue the way the diet book advised. I forked some rice and chewed it to a sweet paste, imagining the people before me receiving the news of our tragic deaths: *Jumped! My God!* Turning shocked faces to one another, startled out of complacency. *How terrible. I don't understand.* Seeking in vain for words of genuine feeling. It occurred to me that the four-way Pledge might convey to some extent the beauty of our act, and I looked around the dining room for a good place to leave the document, where it would be found but not too soon. I decided to stow it in my desk drawer, findable after our bodies came to light. I could picture it: the gathering afterward at this very table, Arlyn pretending to be sad, Elise maybe actually (she had her authentic moments) a little sad, but she'd turn on some classical music or go march to end the war. An image of my father came to mind, crying real tears as he had when my mother died, for months after the funeral. But he sat now at his end of the table with his jokes and his looks at Arlyn, who had saved his life, he said. I forked a green bean and ground it to threads and beyond, counting till my teeth and tongue were chewing on nothing. I asked and was granted permission to go out this evening, pro forma if I gave details: CJ was picking me up. Our destination was Hamburger Heaven. I'd consume nothing but Tab.

"You know," Arlyn said, "you can take your driving test as soon as you lose . . ."

"You've mentioned that."

"Mom," said Elise, "don't you think thirty pounds is a bit much? Twenty's enough incentive." She beamed, like she was doing me a favor.

Here was another humiliation, one more rotten spot in the fruit of my family. I set my fork down on the edge of my plate. Elise took small, untormented helpings, competent with the serving spoon, wrists slim inside her loose terry sleeves.

For a while, to my relief, the subject wasn't me. My father described a chip shot he sank today from the sand. Retired at fifty, he played golf three or four times a week; this town was his paradise. "It was luck," he said modestly. Early tomorrow he and Arlyn were going to play a challenging course at a club they might join. Conversation ran like a pretty stream. Elise's boyfriend had just gotten into Stanford, where he had been wait-listed. The vice principal of the junior high school had crashed his car, probably DUI; no one was hurt, thank God. Luck: bad and good. With that mess in Vietnam, thank God they had girls, said my dad, and Arlyn raised her pretty hands in despair. She hated Nixon, but he had the best chance of working it out. "Mom," Elise said, "I can't believe you said that!" Tomorrow she and friends were driving down to Chicago to campaign for Eugene McCarthy. Clean for Gene. I glanced at my father, who had fought in Korea and feared Communism more than death. An avoider of emotional conflict, he was busy eating. I murmured under my breath, "I am really going to do it."

"Kay, you're in dreamland."

That came from Dad. At times I'd forgive his need to be loved by everyone in the world; then I'd hear him apologizing to Arlyn for me, which made me hate him more than I hated Arlyn. I eyeballed him till he looked away.

"How's the exercise program?" Arlyn said. "You haven't talked about that lately. Are they working you hard?"

"You do look thinner," Elise said.

"Do I? I mean, thank you."

Arlyn touched my arm. "And I want to know how you did on that physics test! You know, the one on, on . . ."

"On light," Elise said. "Waves, diffraction, refraction."

I didn't remember a recent physics test. I'd failed one on motion. Had there been one on light? I pictured myself walking down a hall, looking for a room in which a test was to be given. Corridors darkened. I couldn't see room numbers. Dream-panicky I tried to re-member the morning. Carstairs's glasses were smudged. "I hate that stuff," I said quickly. "I mean, it's not like I'll ever need it." A dead moment went by. I tried not to sag under the weight of Arlyn's opinion of me, and Dad's, their throats squeezing against my every swallow. "I got a B minus!" I said, as if embarrassed by the mediocre grade. My face felt hot. I hated to lie.

"That's solid," said Arlyn.

"Aren't you at least glad you're getting it over with?" said Elise. "Your load'll be that much lighter in the fall."

You have no idea how light my load is going to be, I said in my mind to Elise, who never doubted her own motives or powers or right to exist and was smart too. In the same month she was voted Lourdes Peach Queen and got into the National Honor Society, and she was going to Smith in the fall—to which I had been advised not to apply (why court disappointment?). Not that I wanted to go to Smith. Or anywhere. Campus, courses, professors. *Sorority. Dorm. Frat.* Who cared? *We who are about to die salute you.*

All three members of my pseudo family were staring at me now. I forked the last chicken slab from off the platter, cut it into pieces, and arranged them on my plate in the form of a cross.

"Kay," my father said, "maybe I shouldn't bring this up at the din-ner table, but these days it's the only place we get to see you." He looked at Arlyn, who nodded permission, then turned back to me. "You know, we've been a little worried about you lately."

His voice was cotton-candy soft and sweet. I filled my mouth with rice and started counting to fifty again. *One, two, three . . .*

"When one of us tries to talk to you," he went on, "you ignore us or try to get away as fast as you can. At least that's what it looks like."

Arlyn smiled. "It hurts our feelings, honey."

Their voices were faint, their outlines blurry. *Eleven. Twelve.* Through the thick beveled glass of the table my knees looked far away, my feet tiny as doll feet.

"Kay," said Dad, "you know we're on your side. But we expect a level of courtesy." He spread his large, clean hands on the table and leaned my way, radiating generic benevolence.

"I know that. I'm sorry." The two adults exchanged a look of relief and pleasure. I gripped the seat of my chair. All I wanted, now and forever, was to be gone from here. *Twenty. Twenty-one. Twenty-two.*

"I'm really glad," Arlyn said, "to see you taking your schoolwork seriously. You're on the right track."

In two hours CJ would come by. There was nothing in my mouth but I kept on chewing. *Thirty. What's after thirty? Trust no one after thirty?*

"You don't have to be a world-class anything," Dad said. "There's no need to be number one. Just do your work, that's all."

Time for the subject to change. I swallowed saliva. He said, "But don't pretend it doesn't matter to you. The door slams shut on kids who act like they don't care."

Shut up, shut up.

"Just do your best," Arlyn said. "Then we'll all be happy."

"That's what's important," I murmured.

"Kay," Arlyn said mildly, "there's no need to be sarcastic."

For maybe the first time in my five years of living with Arlyn, I looked her square in the face. "Of course I'll do my best. No matter how pathetic it is!"

"Kay," said Elise, "don't put yourself down."

"There's no *putting*," I said. "Down is down!"

"That's a lousy attitude." Dad's contribution.

"Please," Arlyn said more emphatically. "You've got to stop this."

I wanted to stop. But my mouth was moving, words were coming out, doing for me what words seemed to do for other people, raising up walls behind which I was safe. "It's not 'attitude,' it's *al*titude. I'm high as the sky!"

"You are excused from the table."

My stepmother's dagger voice pinned me to the cross on my dinner plate. But I was clever, powerful, thrilled with myself. "What did I say, Dad?"

"You heard your mother."

"My *who*?"

Arlyn sucked her cheeks in. Dad looked sad, or maybe embarrassed. *I am a good person,* I told myself. But something gray and sticky that had been gathering in my throat for the past few minutes swelled into a sob. I closed my mouth, swallowed it down.

"You're on thin ice," he said.

"As you well know," Arlyn said.

"You need to work on self-control."

"You can start by being more respectful to your father and me."

"Or you can spend the rest of the night in your room."

This last came from my father, who'd never talked like this, so cold and tight, until he met Arlyn. I looked at my watch. I decided to go to my room and give CJ a call. Maybe he could come early. "I'll see you guys later."

Elise looked like she was trying not to laugh, but Arlyn's lips were white. "Your plans have changed," she said.

Dad nodded agreement.

"You can telephone your regrets," Arlyn said. "With a little time alone in your room, you can work on your manners. You'll be grateful one day, and so will your friends."

"You don't know my friends," I almost screamed. "Or me or anything!" My voice was a balloon I was holding on to, pulling me up and out of here. "You're all just *crucifying* me."

"Kay," said Arlyn, "you are out of control."

"Mom, please. Let up," said Elise, then to me in a whisper: "But give her a break?"

They looked at each other. No one spoke. The music had ended and no one moved to put on anything new. The silence throbbed.

But there was no stopping it, what used to happen at the drop of a hat—what, despite the Pledge, my friends, my attempt at faith in a

God who loved fat girls, was happening right now. Sobs heaved out of me one after the other, scattering forever, it seemed, the shards of my self-respect. I ran for the stairs. Elise followed. "Kay, I know. She can overdo it sometimes."

She was trying to be nice, a part of me knew. But I couldn't bear her pity or the view of myself as pitiful. Then the phone rang and I picked up the extension in my room, but not before Arlyn had answered it downstairs. It was Saint, with Hamburger Heaven background noise. "Could you tell Kay we have to cancel tonight? Thank you," he said, and hung up before I could say anything.

4

Vera

———

While I lay on my bed wondering what I'd done to alienate Saint and maybe all of my friends, Vera sits outside Hamburger Heaven smoking Saint's cigarettes and watching a line of ants move across her table. By now dinner-eating families have given way to groups of local teens and lone sleazy men, but her table and its bench are reassuringly cemented to the ground and the little black ant bodies seem to be composed of tiny jeweled bits of color that may be their constituent molecules. A trucker sits down at her table, buys her a Pepsi, and tells her about a hot girl he picked up. Hot for *him*, he says. You ever hitchhike? She almost asks where his truck is. She has never fucked in a truck. But she isn't sure she wants to fuck this man, who is missing a bottom tooth. She looks at his hands, decides not. She smokes one cigarette after another, trying not to look at the ants, the tiny hairs growing out of their backs. She never noticed this before. Her eyesight has become painfully sharp. Overhead, the waxing moon is pale and irrelevant in the light from the restaurant window.

Then at last here's Saint through the heavy front door and walking toward her. By now the trucker is gone, and all the inside customers; the parking lot is nearly empty. She rises to her feet and hugs his arm. She lays her head on his shoulder and breathes his smell of soap, sweat, and slightly charred oil. He stands like a log, like he has no desires or needs inside of him, but she is ready for it. "Let's not play games," she says, "with the end so near."

He stares for a minute, as he does sometimes before he blanks. Then he's shaking his head. "Like this isn't a game? You're stoned out of your mind, Vee."

He walks to his scooter. His voice is ice-cold, which she didn't expect. The machine roars, then dies. He says, his back to her, "If I'm so feeble, what do you want with me now?"

"Who called you feeble?"

"Always the victim," he says. "I guess there's a hair of difference."

She remembers having said that, or something like it. But his reaction, so long after the fact, is one of the things she hates about him. "Don't take it like that." She looks at his face, sees an expression to be read, and does her best. "I didn't even know you were pissed, Saint. You were so . . . so nice and kind today."

He grabs her by the shoulder and holds on a moment, then pushes himself away from her. He jump-starts the scooter. "Get on. I'll take you home."

He is acting as if he dislikes her. Blood pounds in the shoulder he squeezed; she feels a sharp thrill. He flicks on the headlight, swings around. Blinded, she can only wait for what will happen next.

To her surprise, the motor goes off again. He's looking at her. "Jesus," he says.

She lowers her eyes under his perusal, wanting oddly to giggle.

He dismounts; with a gentle hand he touches her face. She holds still so as not to scare him off. "What happened to you?" She shrugs. So much has happened. "You have a black eye," he says, "didn't you know?" She may have known. It makes sense of some kind.

"Is it bad?" she murmurs, though it doesn't matter. She hopes it is bad. She's glad for a black eye, since it has softened him. She strokes the top of his arm. "There's no danger in touch, remember from chemistry? There's no actual contact, just molecules reacting to too much closeness by pushing one another away." She looks out at the world beyond the parking lot, the spreading fields silver in the moonlight. "I know I got on your case this afternoon, Saintly. It doesn't mean anything."

"You said what you thought. That's what you do. Brutal, that's you." But he leads her to the bright restaurant window, concerned like a doctor. "I think your nose was bleeding. It's dried on your chin."

"It doesn't hurt. Honestly." She tries to imagine what she looks like.

"Vera, there's nobody like you."

He shakes his head. His hand is still on her cheek; she presses it to her face. What she wants now is to lie down with him and feel his arms around her. His chest against hers. *I want to be naked with you.* Can she say that? There are dangers in words said, or said at the wrong time, though on acid she has lost all sense of protocol. "Smell is sexy, you know. Molecules of you are already inside me."

He doesn't pull away; he may have forgiven her. In the asphalt parking lot of Hamburger Heaven she floats on the prospect of pleasure. So often these days her body feels like a dead thing. Only during certain peak experiences like sex can she feel it, inside and out, scent and texture.

Abruptly he tilts her face up. "Well, are you going to tell me who pounded on you? Was it your father?"

"No!" she says. None of this has to do with her father. The thought disgusts her. She presses closer to Saint. "Let's find a place to sit down, okay?"

He glowers. "I also want to know what fucked you up this afternoon. Something happened."

She puts her hands over her eyes. Feels pain somewhere. Too much light? "Do me a favor," she says. "Go in and get me some ice. Please?"

While he's gone she walks to the edge of the pavement. There's a wood fence and beyond it a field of soybeans, softly swaying against the dark. She puts her forehead to the top of a post. He returns with the ice, and they sit on the warm asphalt, backs to the fence. He takes off his T-shirt and wraps up some of the ice chips, holds the bundle to her eye. "Thanks, Doc," she says.

He doesn't smile, though. He's pressing with his questions. He has a right to know! She takes a piece of ice in her mouth, presses her cold lips to the back of his hand. "Saint, be nice to me."

"All you think about is you."

"That's all anyone thinks about," she replies, and mulls for a moment the problem of selfishness. She wouldn't have to think about herself so much if someone else were thinking about her. This is a notion she has had before, more than once, but she wonders now if it's true. She asks him if he called their friends, he nods yes, and she doesn't know if her concern shows her to be selfish or not completely selfish. When all the ice is gone they climb the fence and sit on the top rail looking out over the field, side by side but not touching. "I think about *you*," she says. "More than I want to." If it wasn't true before, it seems now to have become true.

They scarcely breathe for a moment while her words enter and spread through him. Then he takes her hand. Holding on to each other, they slide down onto the field, into a trough between two raised rows. Ordinarily it would be uncomfortable in the dirt, if not disgusting. Mulch pokes into her back. Her hair is filthy. But there's no cell of her skin that doesn't want to be right up against his skin. They nuzzle. "It's crazy," he breathes, in the same cadence as "I love you." She pulls him on top of her, wraps her legs around him. "If I had sex all the time," she says, "I could make it through life."

"That's kind of scary, Vera."

She beats her joyful heels on the ground, unsnaps her pants and his.

"Shit. Vera, what does this mean to you?"

She licks his neck. "No talking during sex. It's a rule."

He pushes a little away. "I know you've been with a lot of people."

"So have you."

"Name one."

It's ridiculous and irritating. He had girls in Detroit. And when he moved to Lourdes, for a few months there was Cathy Kirk, who starred in school plays and was a Future Teacher of America. Vera will not think about Cathy Kirk. "Saint, dear. I have a huge amount of respect for you."

He shrugs, but it doesn't matter; she is pressed against him. Little tickling waves in her body become bigger, slower. She wriggles out of her cutoffs and top and flattens them under his head. "You too," she says. "Give me *my* pillow."

He sighs. "Vera, I feel . . . *used*."

"So let's use each other." She passes her good hand over his fly. His torso bucks. "I can see you hate this."

He seems to give up then, or give in. He kisses her all over her face, then on her forehead, like a blessing. His eyes are closed. For some reason she wants to weep, but her vagina pulses with the prospect of pleasure. Some guys can hold her on this brink indefinitely, especially older ones, and afterward, light and airy, she feels like dancing. His jeans are off and she moves slowly with him, trying not to mess things up. He wants to put on a condom, but what's the point, right? Given the Pledge? Then he is inside her and there is no trying or thinking.

Afterward, she lies beside him looking up at the sky, which has fogged over. Night is a smoky cave around them. Her hand strokes his hip, unreflectingly grateful. There is no need to move.

"You're so confusing," he says. "I still want to know. . . ."

"No, you don't." She strokes his leg, stroking him silent.

"Listen," he says. "Do you ever get these black holes in your mind? I don't mean in a dream. Sometimes I'm walking along or, just, I'm talking to someone, and all of a sudden I don't know anything. It's like my electricity shuts off. It's pitch-black in my brain. Like, if I take a step I'll fall into a pit."

This is new information. She isn't sure what to do with it.

"It might have started when my dad walked out, but I was so young I hardly remember. Maybe I've always had it."

She has been holding her breath. She thinks of Poe's "The Pit and the Pendulum," the prisoner feeling his way around the torture chamber, in whose center, unbeknownst to him, lies the thicker, deeper blackness of the beckoning pit. What a terrible image. She wants to erase it from both of their minds. Up in the sky a bright patch of cloud is hiding the moon. She slides down his chest, takes him in her mouth.

"Wait."

She doesn't believe in waiting, doesn't believe he wants her to wait, how can he?

"Oh God, Vera! It's like you're sucking my brains out."

"I'm a nympho," she murmurs. "Take advantage."

"Vee, I don't know if I'm—"

"You can think about Cathy if you want. Go ahead, if it turns you on. I don't care."

"What?"

"Never mind."

"I don't give a shit about that stupid cunt."

"Okay. Forget it."

She believes him about Cathy. She's pissed at herself for even bringing it up. She licks the crease between his leg and groin. She kisses up and down his stomach, trying to shoo away his bad feeling.

"Slow down a little, could you? I'm not, you know, completely . . ."

She tries to slow down. When her mouth and her good hand prove insufficient, she adds whatever erotic impetus her weak hand will provide. It does its assigned job, cupping his balls while her good hand caresses. Her jaw starts to ache. But his dick, incredibly, has shrunk away from her. Her shame is toppled by fury so fast that she feels no shame, and why should she? She wants to squeeze harder, hear him shriek. She lets go, jerks herself to sitting. "Fuck it, St. John. Are you some kind of homo?"

He doesn't speak, of course. In a moment her clothes are back on. She's over the fence, across the parking lot, racing across the highway away from him—his deadening silences, his body's disgust with her.

She walks quickly toward town while everything liquid in her dries rough and hard like slag. She has what's left of Saint's pack of cigarettes and she smokes one after another, blotting out the erratic swing of her arms, the shape of her hands, whose asymmetry offends anyone with eyes. In the light of the streetlamp at Lake and Main she sees clear as day: her fetal hand, finger nubs white and boneless.

With her good hand she slaps the bad one as hard as she can. There's a small, sharp sound but very little sensation. Swiveling for momentum, she swings her bad hand out from her body like a tetherball. Whap. The back of her hand strikes the pole of a streetlamp. Tears spring to her eyes, a burnt-orange flash. This is her quest—for pain focused enough to draw the ugliness from every part of her mind and body.

Then she's home, on her front porch, inhaling the damp cool of the summer night while her hand throbs, unrelenting. She leans against the railing. That was crazy. That was the acid. She will do no more acid. In a minute or so, she'll unlock the door, tiptoe into the kitchen for ice. There are pills in her mother's drawer. More tiptoeing, but her mother won't mind. Already seeing herself in her bedroom, her bed, hand wrapped, burrowing into the thicket of sleep, she nearly falls asleep standing. It's only when her mouth opens in the tight-jawed yawn of the end-of-LSD that she remembers that along with her purse she has lost her key.

5

My One True Mother

When I was eleven, my mother killed herself. Elizabeth Campion—Betty—my first and only mother, who tended the garden but not the sprawling house we lived in, whose blackened pots and frayed furniture our cleaning women shook their heads over. Like everyone, she had her problems. She yelled when she was frustrated (she was easily frustrated), and until the last year of her life she was substantially overweight. But she sang in the church choir with a voice that rose up to the angels, and she had a way of looking at me, her only child, that made me feel embraced.

We lived in Evanston then, on the northern edge of Chicago, with the beach a walkable distance away and the luminous city spreading south from the Evanston Express, a train I would be allowed to take downtown by myself when I turned thirteen. But at thirteen I moved with my father and stepfamily to the other side of the lake, to Lourdes, Michigan, where we had a cleaner but less accessible beach and a new house in a woodsy development three miles inland—white paint, blond wood, tall sheets of glass. This Lourdes promised no miracle healings. No one believed in the spring-fed fountain. But away from reminders of our catastrophe, my father thought we'd learn to look forward instead of back. I had a new mother and sister. I would be happy again.

In Evanston at age ten and before, I was reasonably happy. We were Episcopalian but I went to a Catholic grammar school, where I was an above-average student, shy with rare, reckless bouts of extroversion, chubby, maybe, but not fat (that would come later). My presence incited no special mockery. I had a best friend, a Chinese girl named Cynthia, who had a large wardrobe of clothes for her Ginny doll. I had a mother with a pretty singing voice who loved me more than anything on earth (she said once, on the way home from a doctor's appointment) and who cooked wonderful dinners for me and my father. My father worked long hours and paid us fairly superficial attention, but he was exuberant about the things he enjoyed—golf and making money—and he laughed at people's jokes: a man who made good company. I myself did not make particularly good company. I was thin-skinned; so Dad had announced at my Uncle Ted's Christmas party to excuse my tears at something my cousin said, and I examined the skin of my arms, which seemed, in fact, fragile as tissue paper. Desperately inarticulate, I would cry when angry. But until my mother killed herself, I walked through my days in a fuzzy, warm cloak of dream and routine.

For a few days after her death, my dreamy chrysalis remained intact. During the wake and the funeral, amid the tears and pat-patting of my parents' friends and the relatives who'd flown in to shudder and mourn, I was commended for my maturity and self-control. In fact, though, while I accepted embraces, I focused on my science project due the following week, the two bean plants on my windowsill, one growing in sand, the other in potting soil, and about playing jacks during recess with Cynthia. I was good at jacks. Eventually the consolers dispersed and I went back to school. Cynthia was glad to see me. But there was a hush, a dead space between me and the other kids. "I'm sorry about your mother," they'd say, as if they'd practiced it in my absence. As if there was something about me that scared them. As if they knew what my mother had done, though my father had said not to talk about it, it was nobody's business. As if someone had poked his head between the shrubs behind our house and peered through our basement window.

My so-called self-control persisted until my counseling session at the end of the week. Sister Mary Pat reached across the neat piles of paper on her desk and took my hand. "No matter what she did, you must remember she loved you," she said, and I forgot the dictum I was trying to live by, not to embarrass myself. I snatched my hand back and covered my mouth, but a crazy laugh pushed up through my throat. "I'm sorry," I said, but I couldn't stop the freakish sounds—at the words "no matter what she did" and at the image I had been trying to quash, to expel from memory, because a girl can't live with that in her head.

The day my mother died, I'd brought my pajamas and tooth-brush to school in a little bag because afterward I was taking Cynthia's bus to her house for a sleepover. But I'd forgotten my oil pastels and I went home to retrieve them, thinking my mother could drive me to Cynthia's; she was always there when I came home from school. And I was even glad to be seeing her, because something had happened that afternoon. A girl in my class, Therese Agostino, had started to "menstruate." She'd announced it to all of us girls in the gym line using that exact word, a word I could never have released into the air of a room: Was it brave of her or shameless, and what was wrong with me? But already in our front hall I felt my balance returning, because, in the midst of cooking or TV-watching or resting in bed (which, on her new strict diet, she'd been doing more of lately), Mom would make fun of Therese Agostino, and I would laugh. In fact, walking through the house in search of my mother, I was smiling at the prospect of her familiar face in a familiar room. I checked the kitchen, bedrooms, bathrooms, enclosed porch, pan-eled basement, and garage out back. And after a number of passes, in which I perused the same rooms stupidly two and three times (had she dieted herself down to nothing, as Dad was predicting?), I found her by the workbench in the unfinished part of the basement. That is (there is no good way to say this), I found her alongside my father's seldom-used woodworking bench, hanging from a pipe by a length of yellow clothesline.

Later, revisiting the image, I understood that I wasn't meant to see it. What she had done was for my father, her response to something that he had done or said, the last word, so to speak, in their marital dialogue. Later still, I understood something about the point that my mother had only one way to make to her backslapping, exuberant, unreflecting husband, who let dust collect on his workbench and took phone calls in the middle of dinner. Who wept at his wife's funeral but fourteen months later married his accountant, a thin, pretty, energetic, divorced Jewish woman with whom he may have been having an affair. *You can bet your life on it!* said Aunt Natalie. *But is that any reason to kill yourself?* said Aunt Shirley. Not to me directly. But this sort of commentary filled the air around Evanston, which may have been what prompted my father to sell his three sporting goods stores and move us away from everything that had to do with the craziness, as he called it, to devote himself to his new family, his golf game, and buying and selling Michigan real estate. What had my mother wanted to tell him? *Do you see me? Take a look now!* Or: *Why did you buy yourself all those fancy carpenter tools if you weren't planning to use them?*

But at eleven, in the walled garden of my shyness, I had no context for what lay before me. Emotionally unclothed, thin of skin, as my father said, I registered the outside world like a burn victim; even the lightest touch could cause pain. And what I saw at that moment cut so deeply into my awareness that five years later I'd wake up in the night with my knuckles pressed into my eye sockets— against the image of Mom's bare feet dangling, thin-ankled, below the hem of her light rayon dress, recently purchased at Marshall Field's downtown for the pretty new self she was shrinking into. I was there when she bought it—navy blue with little white flowers, belted waist, flared skirt. For dancing, she said to the lady who rang her up. She wore it out of the store, patting her flattening stomach: *Like a model, right?*

If she and Dad went out dancing in the two or three weeks between the purchase and her death, I have no memory of it. As far as I know, the dress hung in the closet till that final day. But it still afflicts me, the first thought that came to me in the cinder-block room in our Evanston basement where I found her. There is a disturbed kinship for me between being thin, being pretty, and being dead. She had been dieting strenuously and was unquestionably thin, the dark flowered rayon even looser on her hips and stomach than it had been at Field's. And she was wearing makeup. She had lipsticked lips, blush-rosy cheeks, silvery-blue-shadowed eyes. Under the blush her skin was the color of skim milk, which I used to call *skin* milk. I stared up at her dead face while the thought hardened into words: *She is so beautiful.*

At the funeral people hugged me, murmuring to one another, "It seems so unfair," and with an intake of breath, "Poor thing. She was the one who *found* her!" Wiping their eyes, shaking their heads at what they imagined I'd seen—while my eyes were dry. For Sister Mary Pat's sake I tried to give my grieving heart over to Jesus, though there was nothing in me, it seemed, to be given over. Counseling concluded at the end of the year. We moved. But afterward, nearly every day for years, I cried over something—a news broadcast about a fire in which a child was lost or saved, an insult to my pride or someone else's, the death of a celebrity I'd never heard of before.

My eyes were dry, though, the night of the day my friends and I pledged our lives to one another. Confined to my quarters, I called CJ, then Vera, to see what was going on with Saint; no one answered at either house. I sat at my desk drawing cartoons of my family: Dad's peace-at-any-price grin, Arlyn's big, capped horse teeth, Elise years later on her psychiatrist's couch: *It was hard for me being smart and pretty!* But even then I knew that Elise meant more or less well and that whatever evil I attributed to Arlyn and my father wasn't that dark. I took the Pledge out of my pocket and tried to recall the afternoon's grand euphoria, but nada. I started sketching out a logo for the group, number and letters tight against each other—

4EVER

—and then the bedside phone rang. It was CJ, with an explanation for the change of plan: Vera was big-time messed up and needed to talk to Saint. He sounded amused in a brittle, irritated way. "What if *we* need to talk to Saint? And what's the matter with *our* advice?"

It was the kind of social upset that adults often encounter and learn to overlook, but it hit my sixteen-year-old heart like a fist. We four were different from other high school cliques in that we had no secrets from one another. What you told one, you told everyone. And now Saint and Vera seemed to have paired off, made their own pact from which we were excluded. My head clogged with every social shaming I had ever received. *Do you realize you walk with your arms bent up? Instead of a straight skirt maybe you could wear an A-line? You're always smiling; it seems kind of phony.* This was four years ago when I was new at Lourdes Junior-Senior High School, and now I was back there, too diminished even to say how I felt. "It doesn't matter, since I'm grounded," I said to CJ, and recapped my sorry brawl with Arlyn. He commended my courage.

A knock sounded on the door then: It was Arlyn with my book bag. In silence she extracted my physics book and held it out with both hands like an offering. Something in her face felt like warmth, and I was blinking back tears. Thank you, I thought but didn't say. In a kind of trance, then, since with the Pledge in operation physics was moot, I opened the book. We were on electricity, defined as the flow of electrons. A set of problems was due in the morning. I could picture electrons coursing through an electrical cord like blood cells through a vein; I only needed to learn the formulas. I took out my notebook.

But there was no formula to stop the electrons flowing from Saint to Vera to Saint, or to change their course. I drew his face from memory, firm chin, noble brow, electric hair, and in his eyes the confused pain I wanted to help him bear. I called his house and left a message with his sister. *Call when you come in, I don't care how late.* For a reason I didn't ponder at the time, I didn't call Vera.

I was asleep in my clothes, but at the first sound of a ring I had the phone in my hand. Usually Saint's voice had an intermittent bass note under the tenor, but he was all tenor now, strung tight. I turned onto my stomach, phone to my ear under the pillow, just his voice and mine. "Did you just get home?" I whispered. "What time is it?" He laughed, but not at anything I understood. I sat up and turned on my nightlight, as if it would clarify. "What? What's the matter?"

"That bitch," he said.

"Don't say that."

I listened to him breathe while my heart alternately shrank and sped up. "So you guys didn't resolve it? The problem? Whatever it was? Please don't hang up."

My hand was wet on the receiver. This was new territory for Saint and me. Till now with him, I was the friend in need—with my wicked stepmother, my mediocre grades, my pervasively low self-esteem. I'd complain and he'd make me feel better. But here was an occasion for me to rise to. "If there's something I can do, Saint, you just have to ask. Anything." He remained silent. I had to pull words out of my mouth. "You've always helped me," I said. "You'd find me in my dark corner and lead me out."

"Glad to serve."

"Stop it." I forced speech past the lump in my throat. "Isn't that kind of a weird thing to say? I mean, whatever happened tonight with you and Vee, please don't take it out on me—"

"Get out of my head, will you?"

I should have been angry then, but I'd started shaking. "Saint, I'm grateful to you, or I was until you—" I was whining; I cut it off. "I know it's ridiculous but I was trying to make you feel better."

"Sorry."

"Are you?"

He was silent so long I was afraid he'd walked away from the phone. Then he said, with pauses between words, "I can't stand it."

The remark was spoken as if to himself, but it circled my brain. What couldn't he stand? Something to do with Vera or my daft attempts at comfort? Or was it the Pledge this afternoon? Further back in time there was the girl who broke his heart who still went to our school. "Listen, please, Saint—you're such a good person. People love you, Vera and CJ and I, and even that B-I-T-C-H Cathy Kirk—"

A loud crash sounded on his end of the line, like he had put his fist through a window. I dropped the receiver. I'd have picked it up, but it was spewing swearwords. It occurred to me how similar we were, Saint and I, our thin skins, the one difference being that when he couldn't transcend his hurt he could turn it into rage, while I was stuck with my ineffectual tears. In the dresser mirror I gazed at my face, round like a cabbage. I was ugly, inept. Then I heard my name. "Kay, I am so fucked."

Eventually I returned the phone to my ear. I liked the way he said "Kay," in two syllables, Ka-ay. "I don't know, you were just—"

"A jackass."

I smiled, though he couldn't see it.

"Will you tell me the truth?" he said. "Will you be completely honest with me?"

I knew he knew he'd made me feel bad and that he was sorry. Later that night I would realize that was when I started to love him. But at the time I was busy trying to meet what I wasn't even sure were his expectations. I felt a test coming on, and the possibility of transformation if I passed, and my words tripped over each other in their rush to serve him. "I always tell the truth, to my friends at least—"

He broke in: "Do I seem . . . ? Shit. Do you think I'm . . . shit! I can't even say it."

"You can. Say it."

He swallowed so hard I heard it over the phone. "Do you think of me, well, as . . . Kay, do you think I'm *manly?*"

"Manly?" Stupidly I repeated the word. Did I hear it right? I murmured apologetically, "What do you mean?"

"Get it out, just get it out!" he said, but he was yelling at himself. "Do you think I'm a . . . ? Fuck, do I have to spell it out for you?" His voice rose and cracked, and when the words finally came, they sounded strangled. "Kay, babe, do I act like a homo?"

"Are you kidding?" I started to laugh, then cut it off. Knowing he wasn't angry with me, I could think more clearly. "You aren't, of course you aren't!" I avoided the terrible word. "I don't even know where you got the idea! How you could think that!"

He took a breath, but his voice was still ragged. He wanted relief, and I wanted to relieve him. But I was laughing hysterically. It had begun halfway through his question and was now unstoppable. Every time I managed to calm down, the notion took hold of me as if for the first time. "You are so . . ." I began. But my stomach was killing me. My eyes were streaming, my chest heaving with blissful pain. "Saint, are you making fun of me?"

"Why won't you answer my question?"

My lips were sore from my biting them, my stomach hurt from

my hysteria. Homosexuality then was nearly unspeakable, the word "queer" synonymous with all things disgusting. *You queer. You are so queer.* I felt certain that Saint was not, if only because he attracted me. When I smelled his sweat and deodorant, even his faintly sour breath, my insides went loose. But my mind had filled with the ugly, arousing jargon of sex—screw, fuck, ball—and stomach-hurting laughter was squeaking out of me, at these words that I'd never have said aloud and at my giddy terror at waking my family.

At some point I gathered myself and managed to say what I thought, nodding like an idiot to underscore my words. Then afterward I lay in bed, trembling. In the middle of my chest something had softened and warmed. That he'd asked me for help? It pleased me more than I would have admitted. My heart thudded, and between my legs what felt like another heart was beating too. I wrapped my arms around my pillow, put my lips to the cotton pillowcase. "I love you," I said, then added self-consciously, "as a friend."

Because it was our code of conduct, albeit tacit, that affection must flow among the four of us equally. Verboten was the preference of any of us for any particular one of the other three. The group was the ideal family, where differences were not only respected but cherished and no one felt the sear of envy.

6

Saint

————

Saint arrived in Lourdes halfway through our sophomore year, and after the Cathy mess he gravitated our way. He wasn't a talker, especially about himself, and maybe for that reason he became for each of us what we thought we needed. Some quietness is thin and weak, as if it comes from fear or because the person has nothing to say. But Saint's silences seemed to contain depths of pain felt and transmuted. His steady gaze, the bass notes in his warm voice, made you think of good kings, wise rulers of nations—of people with power they didn't abuse. He had pale eyebrows, a large, straight nose, and a wide, openhearted face, like a Greek statue except for his freckles. And he was physically strong enough to pick me up and twirl me as if I were made of air. Until he asked me if I thought he was queer, I didn't think he was afraid of anything.

He came from Detroit, and gave us enough of it to convey the family's downward trajectory. To us he was exotic, not because of Detroit but because they had been poor. Genuinely, rats-in-the-basement, trouble-paying-the-rent poor, which got worse after his father left. In Lourdes they were better off; his mom cleaned and cooked for the wealthy Kirk family, and they lived in the pretty carriage house behind the main house. But Saint was the only one of us who worked because he had to. I wondered sometimes if the disparity bothered him, though he showed no resentment.

Once, we were disparaging our families as we often did, and he told us his first full-blown memory. He was three or four years old, too young for school, and he came down to the kitchen to find the world gone crazy. Plates, cups, saucers, once stacked in cabinets he could reach only by standing on a chair, lay broken on the floor. He was barefoot, in summer pajamas. It was early morning.

He'd done something wrong: That was his first thought. Gloria, who watched them when his mom went to work (there was a younger sister and baby twins), was going to wallop him, or his mom would when she got home, or Dad, later, harder. And if not him, then his mother would get it. On nights after sunny days when no one wanted his father's cab, Saint would pull the covers over his head or curl up on the rug by his sister's crib, praying to find in the morning a bouquet of flowers on the table. It happened sometimes: his father weeping and kissy-hugging his mother, then picking him up, squeezing his breath, saying he was the best boy in this godfor-saken world. And they'd all go to Mass, then to Honest John's for pancakes.

That morning, however, he knew pancakes to reside in a world far, far away, and he tried to fathom the part he had played. He re-membered the previous day, he and his sister up in their bedroom, and parent-voices like out of a dream: *John, Megan, I want you down here at the table right now.* His father's voice came from the foot of the stairs: *If I have to come up there's going to be trouble.* Megan went, thumping down backward with pleasure in her new skill. But Saint was deep in the conflict between the dinosaurs and his army men, Stegosaurus against General Eisenhower. *Please! Just a minute!* he said, or said in his mind, while slow, heavy shoes made the stairs squeak. He could picture now the strong, weary legs of his father, and he said, aloud and not in his mind: *Just one minute. Okay?* But instead of lifting him with a laugh and a hug, his father knocked him onto the battlefield of his plastic and metal figures. His created world was gone, an eradication so abrupt and complete it under-mined his sense of a stable earth and of himself as a person on it, and he threw himself at his father's legs. And even though once, at Mrs. Gloria's, he'd had to sit in the coat closet for biting someone, he bit the hard, hairy flesh under his father's trousers. It was wrong to bite—he knew that even before the coat closet—but how to stop with your ears abuzz, your mouth full of saliva, teeth ringing to close upon something? He was prepared for a time-out. Instead, his father kicked him.

It had hurt no more than other blows from his father, but the pain held on. Megan was crying, his mother screaming, the room full of noise and people.

"Will, he's a child!"

"He's a vicious dog!"

"Someone has got to control themself!"

"You better control that kid or one of these days he'll get himself killed."

His mother bent over him. "You mustn't bite, Johnny. It's animals that bite!" Megan toddled over and touched his face. He tried to stand but couldn't move without jiggling what felt like a knife in his back. He lay on the floor taking shallow breaths.

The rest of the evening was blurred by motion and bright light. There was a backseat ride to the emergency room, a ride on a cart to a small curtained place where shoes tapped by down a hallway. A baby was screaming for longer than he thought anyone could scream. There was an X-ray, which didn't hurt, and wide white strips of tape connecting his back to his front, which hurt a lot. In the car home his father cried, and he started to cry too, and his mother held him. The smell of soap and his mother.

That night in bed, as he lay under his sheet breathing lightly against the binding tape, it had started to rain. Rain came in through the open window, then it seemed to him that his father came with the rain. His father shut the window, kissed his forehead. This had never happened before—his father had no gentle, kissing love for him, only bear-hugging, jerk-your-neck, scrape-your-cheek love, and Saint (named St. John and sometimes called Johnny) took the kiss back with him into his dream, forgetting the whole thing till the following morning when, barefoot in pajamas, he stood in the kitchen doorway. All over the blue kitchen linoleum, piles of white broken things shone in the sunlight coming through the window.

Meggie, who'd crawled downstairs behind him, padded into the rubble in her footie pajamas. She picked up two pieces of something and tried to join them, then sent them clacking across the room. "Tee ha!" The twins were still upstairs in their crib, probably talking to each other as they always did: "A ba ba ba ba ba ba bah!" Soon they would be crying. His mother, who usually skated from one project to another, taking care of everything, was nowhere to be seen. He found her sitting on her bed smoking a cigarette, and he stood at the door, willing her to get up and make coffee and bring it to his father at the kitchen table in his work jacket and Tigers cap. Though downstairs and up, there was no trace of his father.

Eventually her wide white feet marched down to the kitchen, and he followed, waiting for the explanation. She picked Megan up, deposited her on the living room couch. "Stay put, the both of you. Out of the War Zone." He didn't move for a while, just sat next to Megan outside the hurricane kitchen with no coffee smell or newspaper and his father's chair pushed flat to the table.

Later that day, after his mother had swept the shards into a grocery bag and vacuumed, she told him and Meggie that their father was dead. Unfortunately, he'd got sick and died, she said. It was very sad. And they'd have to work extra hard to get along without him. St. John made a fist and punched her arm, and when she didn't punish him or even yell, he started crying.

"He's gone and that's it," she said. "If someone asks, it was galloping pneumonia." She made him repeat the two interesting words. Then a week later Alicia Porter Smith across the street said his father had gone away to live without them in the state of Texas, and he hit Alicia as hard as he could—a girl, yes, but older. To his relief, she hit him back.

His grandmother from Boston came to stay with them now that the jackass was gone, her word for his father. "Their wedding china, from my mother in Ireland!" She shook her angry head. "That man is an animal!"

"*You're* an animal," he said.

She pulled him toward her. "What did you just say?"

He looked at her blankly. He had said it wrong; *he* was the animal. But he couldn't explain, and she shook him till his teeth clattered. "No man goes off and leaves his children to starve—no one who calls himself a man!" she cried, and sent him to bed without supper. Where he lay in the dark with his hand over his mouth of dangerous biting teeth, thinking crazily: *I turned him into china and smashed him to pieces.*

That happened in Detroit, in the only house they would ever own, which they would vacate for a rental in a loud, decrepit neighborhood. Even in Lourdes, where the house was quiet and safe, it still wasn't theirs. And in Lourdes now—August 1968—having recently smashed an innocent drinking glass in the kitchen sink, Saint is confounded by repetition. He picks splinters out of the sink, first with his fingertips, then with a damp paper towel, glad only that Kay didn't actually see him smash it. He doesn't want to think what she must be thinking of him. Not to mention what Vera is thinking.

He gets down on his hands and knees and towels up invisible fragments (his mother has enough on her hands without his craziness). Is he a destroyer? Better a destroyer than a homo, he thinks, feeling for the last splinters with the flat of his hand.

After the breakage is safely stowed at the bottom of the trash bag, he takes off his work jeans and carries them to the laundry hamper on the porch, checking the pockets as he was trained to do. There are five quarters (keep the change, kid), half a dead joint, and his copy of the Pledge signed with everyone's name, including his own. His heart jumps at the thought of his mother finding it. He goes outside and locks the paper in the only receptacle to which he alone has the key, the box on the back of his scooter. There's one thing he knows for sure: Pledge or no Pledge, he will not jump. He will not be a jackass like his father.

He was in fourth grade when his father returned. Six years had passed, his grandma was dead, his mother no longer smoked or drank and felt sorry for people who did. Their flat, the first floor of a three-story house, was small but clean, and every Sunday they went to church, although Megan fell asleep and the twins whined or giggled. His mother begged God to help Sean and Percy to learn respect, to help Meg with her reading, to free St. John from the vice of anger that had afflicted his father.

With God's grace St. John seemed to be managing this. One shimmering dawn with no one else up, he had looked into his future and decided to be a priest, and God helped him build a wall in his mind between what he thought and what he did. In his new school he rarely spoke in class, but his teacher liked his calm, handsome face and praised his thoughtful answers to test questions. He had neat handwriting and he never left his seat without permission. Then one night, in the quiet of after dinner, with his mother at the sink washing the dishes and St. John at the kitchen table cutting out of brown construction paper his careful rendition of the state of Michigan, the doorbell rang and there was his father, smiling like he'd been gone a week. He walked into the kitchen and fell to his knees before his wife, on the floor that St. John had just finished sweeping.

Sean and Percy were in their mother's bedroom watching television, Megan with a friend next door. St. John sat back down with his project, not glad at all to see their father miraculously alive, and especially not on his knees like a slave or a baby. St. John shot him a covert glance, since it wasn't polite to stare, wondering irrationally (sacrilegiously) if the man had returned to life because St. John had prayed regularly for his soul. Perhaps his father's return was his reward for working so well at self-control, but it didn't feel like a reward. St. John worked his school scissors around the bottom of Lake Michigan while his father tugged at the hem of his wife's waitress skirt. "Forgive me," he said.

She looked down at him, her braid of red hair coiled around her head like a helmet.

"Mary, I can handle it now. I'm ready, I swear to God. Let me come back."

He touched her leg. She stepped away. "Never in a million years," she said, brisk and light as she might have said, "I hope you enjoyed your meal." She wiped her hand on her apron and pointed toward the living room, the door beyond.

"This is my family," his father said, rising to his feet. "These are my children. Do you have someone else?"

Her face was stone.

His father, so strong, was weak now. St. John's hands felt weak. He thought he should say, "Give him another chance, Mom." A truly good boy, one destined to govern the spiritual lives of other people, would know the words to reconcile his parents; his holiness would bless their lives. "Get out," his mother said, "or I'll call the police. I mean it, Will." St. John opened and closed the blades of his scissors while his father went out the way he'd come and his mother locked the door behind him.

Moments later there was a knock on the back door. "Leave it," his mother called from the sink. There was pounding. "Ignore it." St. John ran to the door, but she pushed past him. She chained the door, then opened it a crack and yelled, "Go back to Dallas! None of us want you here! Do we?" she said to St. John, and put her arm around him. She smelled of hairspray and sour rags.

A little later the doorbell rang again, angry, impotent, and heartsore. "That man," she said, "has a problem." Back at the sink she Ajaxed the porcelain, shined the spigots and faucet, wrung out the rag, and set it to dry over the back of a chair. "He was stinking drunk, could you tell, John-John?" She was humming to herself. "We need him like a hole in the head." She pulled the band off the end of her braid and shook out her hair. "Weak men make monsters out of women. Where did I read that?"

Now St. John is almost seventeen, soon to be, if not for the Pledge, a high school senior like all his friends, and he believes he has shamed himself beyond recovery, but it's time for sleep. He rinses his face, brushes his teeth. Stripped to his jockey shorts, he lies down on his bed across from the twins' bunk, hears their sweet sleep-breathing. Shame or not, tomorrow is an early shift. He doesn't look at the clock. When a bad thought comes he shunts it away with the mantra he found in a book he ordered through the mail: *A Glimpse of the Clear Light: The Path to Buddhahood*. He pulls his sheet to his neck, burrows into his pillow, and chants, *"Nam myoho renge kyo."* He hopes he's pronouncing it right.

But he can't sleep. He gets out of bed, feels his way over to the screened porch. He squats, grasping the shaft of the set of barbells his mother bought for his fifteenth birthday. He rises with the weights, meeting their heaviness, drawing the shaft to his belly, chest, neck, and then, with an extra push that ripples his back, raises them over his head. The sequence is effortless and thus useless. He performs it ten times; his back and arms heat up. Another ten and he's sweating like crazy, but his mind won't blank. The nearly full moon is shining through the window screen onto the slats of the floor when he sets down the barbells. He's thinking about Vera and what she called him, thinking he ought to hate her. He throws himself down on his stomach, lifts up on his hands and toes, straightens his back and arms. Then he's moving fast, down, forehead to the wood, then up again, not counting this time, waiting for the ache of arms and back to slow his mind. *"Nam myoho renge kyo."* He's Siddhartha by the river, ever moving and ever the same. But there are faces in the shimmery water, and they look like Vera's.

Before Vera, there was Cathy Kirk, whose mother is his mother's employer. Cathy, who still, not that it matters, lives in the large house in front of theirs. Cathy has large breasts, which he was permitted to touch under her shirt but not under her bra; who made those rules? It seems almost funny to him now that Cathy's breasts no longer interest him. For weeks after Cathy he didn't speak to anyone at school, and barely to his family. And now on hot summer days, Cathy can sunbathe in her yard a hundred feet from "the servants' quarters," and it's nothing to him. Cathy barely exists in the light of Vera.

Continuing his push-ups, though more slowly, effortfully, Saint pictures a woman of twenty-five or thirty, tall and fleshy, with a kind face, someone he has never met. Patient in the ways of love, she knows when to move and when to lie still, so that on the verge of orgasm they both pull back and there is only their breath, hot in each other's faces. *"Nam myoho renge kyo."* Saint breathes the words out as if they're dirty talk. Pushing off the mat one more time, he's at the brink without touching himself, about to come, crazy for it and for the woman in his mind, and then he does—accomplishes this feat ascribed to serious yogis!—sweat running down his sides. Vera's insult still makes him wince, but he can now reject it, since obviously he is not that. She said it in anger and at this very moment might be wishing she could take it back. He too has said things in anger that he would like to take back, many things.

Saint was in junior high the last time he saw his father. It was his mother's thirtieth birthday, and she'd stayed home from work to make herself a cake. In the late afternoon Sean and Percy were licking the beaters, Megan was talking on the phone, and he, still the good helper, was washing the mixing bowl when the buzzer rang. They lived in an apartment building; you buzzed people up. "Happy, happy," said a male voice through the intercom. "Hey, Queen Mary! I have a present for you!"

"Shit!" said their mother. "I mean shoot."

She didn't seem frightened, but John followed her to where the dining room met the living room. Her hair was still red and long down her back. She held it in one hand like a rope while she opened the door. "Hello, Willy," she said, sniffing the air theatrically. "What, liquid courage? Our little midday pick-me-up?"

By this time St. John knew they were divorced. He was pretty sure his father sent money, though his mother didn't open the letters and sent them right back. There were phone calls, his mother calm, sometimes triumphant, always resolute, after which she'd eye him and shrug, tall and strong, a wall between the children and their bad father. That's how she stood that birthday afternoon, her big pale freckled hands on her hips, blocking their father in the doorway like a reared-up mother bear.

Sean and Percy, who didn't remember their father, peered with interest from the kitchen. Megan continued talking on the phone but kept an eye out. St. John, who had fully embraced his mother's view of this man as a shame to them, an embarrassment, didn't even try to see past her wide back. Then a muffled squeak came from her mouth. She bent over, then fell to her knees. Sean started crying. Megan dropped the phone.

Their father stood at the door with a puzzled expression on his face, as if he didn't know what he had just done, as if it had honestly surprised him. But to St. John it was as if no time had passed; all barricades were down between thought and action. He was punching his father, right to the jaw, left to the gut, where the man had punched his mother.

They were the same height, though St. John weighed less. He doesn't remember whether his father hit him back. He knows he got in at least two punches before he fell, and that when he clambered to his feet his father was gone. "No, we're okay," Megan said into the phone. St. John locked the door and helped their mother over to the sofa.

Saint considers a shower, which might relax him enough for sleep, but the water creaking up the pipes will wake his mother, who gets up early to brew the Kirks' coffee. He puts on jeans, goes out, and lopes around the house, alert as a gunslinger. The moon is down or behind clouds, and the darkness soothes him, but his jeans feel heavy on his legs; he goes back inside and replaces them with an old pair of cotton shorts. His bare chest expands, the ache of anxiety turning to energy. Strong, alive, awake as in daytime, he jogs barefoot over the soft grass through the scattered trees on the Kirk property and out to the empty, silent road.

His bare soles hit gravel on the road's shoulder, but he doesn't slow down. It's as if his feet and the black stony earth are made of the same thing. After a hundred yards or so, he becomes aware of the bob of his dick. He could use a jockstrap but doesn't want to go back. He tries to take it in stride, so to speak, but the jiggle annoys him and the shorts are tight. Wanting to keep up his pace, he tries holding his dick through the cloth of his shorts, like meat wrapped in paper, like the stalk of a plant. Yes. Jack with his beanstalk, he's high-stepping through the wooded subdivision, over the newly tarred road, smooth and warm under his bare feet, and his dick is hard in the grip of his hand, and he laughs out loud as he considers where he seems to be heading. He could jack off under her window, he thinks, and laughs again. He'll throw a stone at her window and hide in the bushes and tackle her when she comes out. It's what she wants, right?

He's imagining sexual pleasures given and received, appreciated, and even words of love exchanged, when something comes crashing out of the woods. It's right in front of him, a deer, a big one, antlers and all, gone almost before he can blink. But not before, in his leap away, he has ripped his shorts, right down the middle and almost to the waistband. He stands in the warm wind looking down at his jockeys, ghostly through the parted curtain of his shorts. With the flourish of someone with nothing to lose, he steps out of his torn shorts and his stinking old underpants and tosses them into the weeds.

Body and mind are one right now. Overhead, stars gleam. It's good to run without the constriction of clothing. All around, swaddling him, is the hum of insects. The air is warm and wet as if he's moving inside a cloud. When every once in a while a car approaches, he leaps into the roadside weeds, impelled by an arrow of fear that translates so wholly into action that it passes out of him with no anxious residue. He'll make love to Vera under the peach tree in her backyard and afterward speak of their lives together, lives that—fuck the Pledge—will last a lot longer than two weeks. His callused soles beat the soft asphalt. He bounds down the invisible road.

Crossing Route 12 into the commercial district, he feels the skin on his back tighten. There are pools of streetlamp light. Is he nuts? To be running through town without clothes on? He ought to go home. Surely he has burned off all his excess energy.

Then awareness of his absurd and flagrant nakedness falls away as quickly as it came. What is the meaning and function of clothing that isn't served as well, or better, by the humid night air in which his skin vibrates with strength and joy? If there's danger, it's not from some dry old Puritan who hates the human form divine. Danger is cosmic and inevitable, like the H-bomb; danger is worlds away, like Vietnam. There is nothing to be done, nothing to fear but fear. On the crest of his rising exaltation he runs toward Vera through the warm dark.

He has leaped the curb onto Lake Street in downtown Lourdes with a joyful, powerful rhythm that won't flag, when a car passes. It brakes with a squeal, then backs up. It's a police car. A window rolls down. An amused, badgering voice: "What the fuck is this?"

Trying to protect his exhilaration, Saint continues running. But his skin has begun to cool. His legs are white in the glow of the headlights. "Get your psycho ass over here. Jesus Christ. What are you high on?" The door swings open.

Completely unmanned by the tone of this voice, Saint comes, at last, to a stop. Standing alongside his car, the cop regards him with the snide jollity of low-level authority, like every cop that has ever taunted him with curfew or sent him moving along a city street. Saint's hands ball into fists but loosen immediately. Without clothing, he is without power. He dons a cloak of humility, though it wraps his naked body in sticky, shamed outrage, and says in a voice that rings sickeningly high in his ears, "I don't do drugs, Officer. I have no interest in drugs."

The man glances into his eyes, suspecting mockery, and the glance stays there. "Is this a bet? Or some weird initiation? You're fixing to join one of them high school fraternities?" He laughs like he knows something. The corners of Saint's mouth curl, dim-witted and slavish, a response Saint despises in other people but most of all in himself. *Nam myoho renge kyo.* He follows his breath in a long slow stream, in one nostril and out the other.

"It takes balls," says the cop, and directs his gaze pointedly downward. "To coin a phrase." He laughs again, a man whose jokes don't need an audience.

In a sudden shift of perspective, Saint sees himself through the cop's eyes, fucked up, a real weirdo, and who's to say he's wrong? Not Saint, hopeless at verbal sparring. Saint wants to mow the man down. He could. He could duck his head and ram him like a bull, break his windpipe. But—*nam myoho renge kyo*—he still has options. With the bound of a deer, Saint is streaking around the corner toward the darkness of a side street.

"Stop, you son of a bitch! Does your mother know how you run around?"

The words pepper his bare back, and he imagines the nose of a gun leveling, the cop sighting down the barrel. In a dodging run, he leaps a curb, races up a driveway toward the chain of small backyards of the houses that flank the commercial district. A car passes and he keeps on running, impelling his legs over the tiny lawns that alternate with cement driveways. There's an occasional low hedge. These he jumps, maintaining his speed although his side hurts and his breath rasps up through his throat. Crazy barking starts up; yards away, a dog pulls at his short chain. Saint loops sideways, running even faster through the adjoining yards onto a street empty and silent except for the ever present wind.

By the time he rounds the corner of Vera's block, his sweat has dried and his muscles feel tight and stringy. He tries to imagine holding her—her narrow back, the unexpected, unimaginable softness of her skin. He looks up her street toward the house he knows is hers but feels the return of his shame. His abject, naked body is unworthy of her.

He would like to be home now, in bed trying to sleep even if sleep won't come, but the town is too well patrolled for return passage. Avoiding lights, he moves west and north as quickly as he can, through the woods north of the park to the wooded lake path, which he follows until he comes to a low stone wall that borders a long rolling lawn, closer-cropped, thicker, and more darkly blue in the starlight than the Kirks'. He steps over the wall. At the end of the lawn, immense and ancient-looking, is the house where CJ lives, its gabled roof rising into the night sky.

Compared to this place, the Kirks live in a trailer. CJ's dad has bucks up the wazoo, money that needs only the slightest attention to keep reproducing itself. The Walkers have other homes in other climates. They have servants who call them and you Mr. and Miss, not playfully or even ironically, servants who have waited on rich people all their lives without resentment, as if it's a privilege, not like his overworked, outraged mother.

He looks back once through the fringe of trees that holds off the bluff's erosion. Here the bluff is less sheer; wooden railroad ties dug into the earth form a stairway that angles down to the beach. On the slope below him are dark patches of the Walkers' lawn, every year more of it slipping down the dune from forces even the Walkers can't stop. In this is something vaguely comforting.

He scampers across the soft back lawn, so kind to the soles of his feet, and along a paved walk between bushes, and arrives at a spot below CJ's second-story window. The window is dark, but he cups his hands around his mouth and emits the one animal sound he can mimic, the yodel of a cat in heat, a talent he has not yet shown the folks in Lourdes. Is the window open? He doubts it; these folks like their air-conditioning.

The first pebble he aims at CJ's window hits the ledge; he tries the yowl again. Already the sky seems a shade less dark. Company could come at any minute—the gardener, or Mr. Walker himself out for a predawn stroll. He feels like Adam after eating the apple, appalled by his nakedness. He needs a place to hide till CJ finds him, between a bush and the side of the house, although CJ could wake up and leave without ever visiting his backyard.

What a moronic idea, this naked run. He imagines himself caught, handcuffed, paraded nude through the streets of Lourdes while the good citizens hoot from their doorways. Then he sits down in lotus position on the smoothly paved walk. *Om namah shivaya.*

7

Vera

_____

Alone in the dark in the dying glitter of LSD, Vera remains fucked up. From the small bones of her neck down her spine to her aching hip bones rolls a wearying energy, fatigue speckled with kernels of anxiety, as if she were lying on electric gravel, though in fact she lies on the smooth stone of her own front porch. At her feet, concrete steps descend to a narrow walk between two neat patches of lawn. Behind her head rises the dark brick of her house—not the largest on the block but surely the sturdiest. Ropes of caulk insulate the window frames, fresh mortar seals any spaces between the bricks of the abode of the third, smart little pig. No one can blow this house down. Nor can anyone enter. In the past hour or two or three (she has no sense of time; even her heartbeat seems random), she has jiggled the knobs of the front and back doors, tried to raise the kitchen window, tried the car in the garage (four doors all locked), smoked all but one of Saint's cigarettes. Right now all she wants is to sleep, no matter where. She lies prone facing the street, her head on the thin rubber comfort of the welcome mat.

She remains, though, oppressively alert. The damp elastic of her tube top constricts her chest. Sweat beads on her eyelids, under her bottom lip, in the shallow cleft between her breasts. Each drop of perspiration is separate and distinct on her face like a bead of mercury, and the sensation makes her dizzy, like she's underwater with no sense of up or down. Which way means air? She'll lie here till her father comes out for the morning paper and she'll accept his punishment; he is not imaginative. She squeezes her hands together, squeezes her crotch till it hurts, hating the chemical she swallowed that raised her up high and splendid but won't drop her completely back down.

She'll fall asleep, she tells herself, if she stops trying to sleep, so she tries not to try. Something bites the back of her neck. A bad-tasting juice rises in her throat and she swallows, hating her mother, useless in her sedated sleep. She could maybe pound on the door loud enough to wake her father, who sleeps downstairs in the den. Who'll be less angry now than tomorrow morning when he sees her empty room.

Then comes the shade of Garth, a seeming murmur in her ear: *Try me. I'll let you in, sister.* Her teeth start to chatter. She could knock on the basement window, which is right over his bed. Why not? Hell is absurd, hell is nothing to her, a nasty fable to scare the children. But the thought of her brother fills her with shame and self-disgust. *Please, Mom,* she says in her mind, *do something for once!* Although the only evidence of her mother's strength of character was her refusal to abort her, a decision she made against the wishes of the good-looking asshole who was scared enough of his own fa-ther and the pain of hellfire to marry her. She was a sophomore in high school. Vera closes her eyes as if to shut out the image of her mother young and hopeful, and the concrete seems to shift beneath her. She can't countenance hell, but limbo makes sense, a floaty place between lost and found, evil and good. She wants to throw up, though there's nothing in her stomach. Oh, to lie under covers, under the weight of something.

On the next block a dog starts to bark, then two more, a chorus of need and desire: *Chain's too short, collar's too tight. Get me out of here. Pet me.* She's dizzily awash in the harsh, lonely sounds, and then, with no sense of having arisen, she's descending the steps. On flat ground she puts her heels together. Fingers curved softly, she raises her hands over her head and sways in the wind, in the damp starry night. She's a feather in the acid aftermath, a husk, so wasted that a harder gust might waft her away. And then she's wafting, around the house to where a rhomboid of electric light shines on the side lawn. Through the low, narrow window comes the muted wail of an electric guitar: "Purple Haze," and Garth trying to kiss the sky. Garth, the white Jimi Hendrix. Garth bemoans his singing voice, which is too sweet for the music of rage and pain, but Vera has always loved it.

She stands above the window but doesn't rap on the glass. What passed between them fills her even in memory with a searing terror, as if her brain is being tweezed from her skull through her eyeballs. Making love with him seemed simple and pure, beyond pleasure, an expression of their deepest selves. She felt whole—at one with him, the world, and herself, as if there was nothing more to strive for, a state of mind she seemed to have wanted all her life without ever believing it possible. But afterward, almost immediately, she was mired in shame. As high as she had been, she was struck low, obliterated, mind and soul, banished from the world of goodness and ordinariness like Lucifer after his rebellion, banned from the sight of God. Not that she believes in God. She drops to her knees, expels a thin, bitter liquid.

Back on the porch she sits on a middle step, leaning against a riser, eyes wide in the dizzy heights above sleep. A mosquito whines in her ear. She lights her last cigarette. She tends not to mind bug bites; normally her skin resists sensation, as if it weren't skin at all but an elastic, flesh-colored sheath. She runs her fingers along her arm, the small, hard swellings. Inside her elbow a latent itch flares, then one on her anklebone, and more: on the small of her back, the back of her neck, the soft skin over her eye. She turns quiet inside with the desire to scratch, resisting at first, then submitting as she sometimes submits to sex, voracious and jubilant. Her fingers are clawed, she is about to scratch, when the porch light snaps on. The screen door swings open. "Get yourself in the goddamned house."

She's inside before the sentence concludes, standing at attention on the hall rug while her father inspects her. "You got yourself beat up." He sounds concerned, but that's how it starts. "Well, what's the story?"

"I ran into a door?" The smart-assery comes out too fast to be checked; she lets it flow. "It could have been a tree?" What will be will be. A laugh tickles the back of her throat. "Sorry."

"That bastard Mick," he says. "That slimebag."

All residue of the drug is gone. She's in a play in which she knows all the lines. "It wasn't Saint, Daddy." She exaggerates the girlish breathiness of the underling, the powerless one. He touches her cheek softly.

"I'm going to kill him."

Tears spring to her eyes, although they don't seem to have come from anywhere inside her. She stands motionless under her father's oddly gentle touch, gazing at the wooden crucifix on the wall behind him. Tucked behind it is the dried, frayed stalk of a palm. *Hail Mary full of grace the Lord is with thee*. Her voice almost breaks: "You don't know him, Dad. He's a nice guy. Really. I'm the crazy one." Then, embarrassed by her unwilled earnestness, she tilts her head up, displaying her eye in all its damaged glory. Her father's mouth tightens, but he makes no other move. He's controlling himself. "It was some tourist creep. A piece of male shit." She smiles wickedly. "I may have provoked him."

He takes her by her bare shoulders and she feels what he's feeling: her tiny bones in his hands like chicken bones. But he is in command of himself. This too she can sense. He took a course in impulse control at the police academy.

"Are you," she says, "disappointed in me?" He takes a breath, looks into her eyes as if he's trying to understand something. "Let me have it, Dad. Show me who's boss."

"Why should I waste energy on a girl without a smack of decency or sense?"

"A girl who opens her legs to every dick in the neighborhood?" This is *his* line. She smiles demurely.

"Look at yourself!" he says. "Where's your self-respect?" His eyes traverse her breasts under her tube top, the span of naked flesh above her cutoffs. He wants to slap her; it's coming. "Don't think this is over."

She shrugs, then sticks her hands into her pockets like someone who hasn't a care in the world, and encounters the folded Pledge. A shiver of triumph courses through her. In her ferocious, sustained battle with her father, victory is almost certain. "Let's hope not," she murmurs, almost loud enough for him to hear on the way to his bed in the den.

As a little girl, Vera loved her father the way a religious person was supposed to love God. On his nights off, after dinner, they'd sit on the TV room couch watching gangster movies. She liked Edward G. Robinson's pebbled skin, his barrel chest like her father's, his gritty snarl of a voice: "Ya want me ta mess up that pretty face a yours for good?" She'd mimic it to her father, who would reply, "You're going to be trouble, angel!" as if he admired her burgeoning willfulness. To her malformed hand he gave no special attention, and neither did she. His opinions were her opinions. She felt safe with her father, who was stronger than other kids' fathers, armed with all the paraphernalia of protection—the belt that held his nightstick and gun, the sweeping light on top of his car, the righteous rage of his siren. Her mother, who was back then strong enough to get an idea and carry it out, had enrolled her in ballet class on Saturday mornings, and sometimes her father would pick her up in a police car. Once, waiting in that car in a parking lot while he was inside a store, she slid into the deeper warmth of the driver's part of the front seat, pushed a button on the steering wheel, and the siren went off, like a wild animal raging around the car. When her father leaned in and turned it off, she was sobbing with panic. He said, then had to repeat, "Which hand was responsible?"

Of course he was going to punish her. It was so right and certain that she had already extended to him the hand that had pushed the button—her small hand, which was also her dominant hand, the first volunteer for any manual task. Her head was raised bravely, her shoulders hunched for the blow. He had hit her before, and she never thought to protest; if he'd chopped off the offending part, she'd have borne it bravely. But this time he only tapped her hand. "Never again, right?" he said, then kissed it, her runt of a hand that didn't know its place, and in her heart there was no doubt: She was in love with her father, who could punish or forgive at will like God.

Throughout grade school, as her mother relinquished her maternal duties one by one, her father assumed them. On Sunday mornings he took her and Garth to Mass and sat between them, sometimes holding her hand. He would pick her up from school and take her to a friend's house or to Woolworth's for a Coke. She was the most important person in his life, it was clear to her, and he in hers.

Then, in sixth grade, a new girl started at Immaculata, a girl with shiny dark hair who couldn't stop talking about Vera's hand. Having seen it all their lives, Vera's classmates were used to her defect. It was a fact; why mention it? But this girl, whose name—Bonnie Thibodot—even now stirs Vera's rage (though Bonnie Thibodot left Lourdes for a school in Hong Kong the following year and was lost to history), took a look at the hand at the end of Vera's right arm and cried, "Ee-ew, like a fetus!" for everyone to hear, and Vera understood then that one single person can change everything. Although no one in her class knew what a fetus looked like, they were suddenly sickened, these girls Vera had played with on the playground, who had come to her house after school. They tried not to look at her hand, and the effort made them squeal with laughter. They looked through their fingers, gasping with hilarity. *This is how it will be,* she thought, *for the rest of my life.*

She didn't take it meekly. She pulled Bonnie's shiny dark hair, she scratched her face. So it was Vera who was restrained, lectured, threatened with suspension. Not the sort to ask adults for help, Vera bore their disapproval in proud silence. But silently she was engorged with rage, a lens through which she now saw the world and herself. In ballet she had been a star, the soloist at recitals, but after that she couldn't raise her small hand over her head without thinking of Bonnie. In ballet class several months later, she landed on the side of her foot and broke her ankle, and quit lessons for good, although the ankle healed. "I never wanted to dance," she told her mother. "Why did you make me?"

She wanted to quit Immaculata too. But, required to finish out the year before she could start at the public junior high school, she reworked her personality to meet the new circumstances. Formerly courteous and diligent, she started mouthing off to the nuns. She spurned her former friends, even the ones who made small overtures of apology, pointing out their errors and physical flaws, which were suddenly crystal clear to Vera's eyes—a broad nose, gaping nostrils, creased neck, pocked cheek. A lisp. A stupid answer in class. At home she refused to do chores. "I must protect my beauty-hands," she'd say in an exaggerated Southern accent. She'd make Garth cry, especially when her father was in the house, just to see what he'd do. Sometimes she still felt love for her father, profound love, but she was compelled to taunt him. Once he grabbed her in frustration and she stuck out her tongue at him. He slapped her then, and it seemed to her that this was what she was waiting for, the bright flicker of pain in her cheek. Soon punishments became regular—after which she'd dissolve into abject tears and throw her arms around her father, obliterate herself before his greater strength and knowledge. But still, the next time and the next, her will pranced out to meet his, David smart-assing Goliath, a half-grown dog teasing a bear.

Left alone in the hallway, Vera doesn't know what to do next. She drags herself to the foot of the stairway, which is solidly built and will make no sound under her weight. She stands with her hand on the banister. The stairs to her room are steep and there are so many of them. Who is Vera, she thinks, this wisp of a body, these thoughts that pass so fast she can't remember any of them?

Then with no movement of hers that she can remember, utterly without volition, she is standing at the door that leads down to the basement, two painted cinder-block rooms and the laundry, the space Garth made his private headquarters after returning from Florida. She touches the door lightly with the flat of her hand, a symbolic "good night" to her brother. But the thick wood actually throbs under her hand. She turns the knob. The lights are off, but a roll, from drums and a bass guitar, comes at her like a wall of water. Trumpets. Garth is listening to *Revolver*, turned up so high the darkness is thrumming.

When her eyes adjust, she tiptoes down and makes her way past the room with the ping-pong table to the second room, which doesn't have a door. The bed is empty; at first the room seems empty. Then, on the far side of Garth's bed, she sees a candle burning low and her brother asleep on his little rug. His T-shirt has ridden up, his ribs are fish-bone long and fragile; she sees the shadows between them. She loves the base of his spine where his jeans bag out. His back, as lean as her own. *Hail Mary full of grace the Lord is with thee. Blessed art thou among women and blessed is the fruit of thy womb Jesus.* Perhaps there is a hell, she thinks, hell and heaven, downstairs and up. She chooses heaven, though she doesn't believe in it, walking quickly up the linoleum stairs, glad for the torrent of sound that hides her footfalls.

In the bathroom across from her bedroom she showers with the hottest water she can stand, rubbing herself hard with a stiff washcloth; she brushes her teeth till her gums sting and puts on a pair of her old flannel pajamas. But ready for bed, she isn't ready to sleep yet, and it's as if she never will be. She finds her old toe shoes and pas de bourrées over the carpet in her room, her long hair dripping. The house is so sturdy the floor doesn't shake. She does *changements* till her heart is racing, cushioning her landings with softly bent knees. Then the door swings open. "Dad, get out of here!" But it's not her father. "Oh shit. Shit!"

Garth leans against her doorframe, straight, tall, and leggy-thin, like a plant seeking light. His shoulders are just starting to broaden. His jeans hang on his hips. Her heart swings wildly under her breastbone. "Go away. Please, Garth."

"I just got here!" He clucks. "Come on, give me a break. Hey, what's with the eye?"

Pat-patting the floor in her toe shoes, she walks to the window, turns the fan on, then off. She presses her hands to the fabric of her pajamas, the bones of her chest. She sits down on her bed, stands up, sits. "Jesus! Do you have to burst in on me?"

"I learned it from you." He looks hard at her face. "Did Dad do that?" He gazes gravely, absorbing all her displeasure with him. He has wonderful posture. Even as a child he had the straight back of a soldier. He says, "I'll report him. I will. He can't do that to you."

"Who will you report him to?" When he says nothing, she shrugs. "It wasn't Dad, it was some hillbilly type. You should see what *he* looks like."

His brow knits as he absorbs the new information. "Why do you always get in trouble like that?"

She scowls and he turns away. For a moment she wonders if he'll start to cry. As a little kid he sometimes cried for no reason she could fathom, but he hasn't cried in years. Mr. Cool now, he struts to her nightstand, turns on the radio.

"Hssh, Garth, you'll wake Mom."

"Want to bet?"

His face, though, isn't angry or mocking. He sits down on the floor at the foot of her bed, maintaining his perfect posture. He has eerily white-blond hair like hers but his teeth don't need braces. Hers could have used them, though she refused. She clicks off the radio, sits, and takes off her pink shoes. He picks one of them up, puts it to his cheek. He runs the satin along his lower lip. "I remember you dancing."

She keeps her face neutral, remembering him in grade school, how quiet he was. *Garth is very bright but he should contribute more to class discussion,* teachers would say, but even then he had presence. Friends would call him all the time and invite him over, boys and girls both. She stands up, motioning for him to stand as well. "Goodbye, Garth." She cocks her head toward the door. "*Adieu, mon frère. Dors bien.* I'm getting into bed."

"That's what I've been waiting for."

She shakes her head firmly. "It happened once. It will never happen again. Don't give me any shit about free love."

"I'm not sure you know, Vera, that you are a very beautiful woman."

"Quit that!" Stationed at the head of her bed, longing to lie down, she regards him sternly but he won't look away. Eyes on her face, he crawls to her and takes hold of her ankles. Runs a hand up her calf to the back of her knee. The tiny hairs of her legs stand on end. She whispers, "Don't you feel the least bit weird about this?"

He smiles up at her like an intelligent, happy baby. "You know those super-tall swings behind the school? With the chains, that it took forever to pump? If you could get yourself high enough the seat would start jerking, and it was like if you went any farther it would dump you or take you over the top. I'd always chicken out." He puts a finger in his mouth and bites the corner of a fingernail. He tears it off contemplatively, from one side to the other. "And now it's like I've done it."

"Good for you."

"I've done it and it's okay," he says. "It's better than okay. It's what I always wanted."

A wave of fright washes over her. She turns off the light, gets into bed, pulls the light bedspread to her chin. To the air she says, "You're so strange, Garth. Like you were behind the door when they handed out guilt."

"Isn't that a good thing?"

"Stop it."

He sighs. "There's so much stupid pain in the world, think about that. There are so many ways to feel bad. You have to balance it out. Does that eye feel as bad as it looks?"

She doesn't reply. She lies under her covers with her eyes closed, but she sees his face in her mind more clearly than her own. Does she want him? She wants something so much she has forgotten to breathe. She rolls away from him toward the wall, shielding herself with the bones of her back.

The move was a mistake, though. There is now room in her bed, and he crawls in behind her, takes hold of her bad hand. He kisses the small palm, then each nub of finger, as if the monstrosity is precious, like a starfish or the hand of a new baby. He puts her thumb in his mouth and sucks gently. She moans involuntarily. "Vera, is it okay? We don't have to do anything. I'm sad and you're sad. We'll hold each other."

She doesn't speak or move, but it's as if she has acquiesced. He nestles against her back as if he belongs there. He smells like dirt and salt. "For a minute," she says, yawning self-consciously.

"I can relax you," he says.

"Where did you get that line?"

He giggles, and she loves the sound. His hands move up and down the cloth over her back. She takes a shallow breath. He pulls up the back of her pajama top and touches her skin. "Lots of zits here."

"Mosquito bites. Stop, you're making me itch."

"You have a ton, man," he says almost reverently. "Do you want some lotion?"

"No. Why don't you go back to bed now?"

"I'll get you something. For your eye too."

He leaves and returns with Caladryl. Gentle as a parent he turns her on her stomach, squirts the lotion into his hand, and coats her shoulder blades. "I've thought it all through, Vera. After we graduate college we'll get an apartment together. We'll get along great since we know each other so well and we're so much alike."

"The weird DeVito kids."

"We'll go to New York. You can dance in the New York City Ballet."

"How about the New York City zoo?" she murmurs. "Or the circus?"

"Or San Francisco, where nobody knows us," he goes on. "It's a new world there. No rules about love. I'll get a job. We could have a family."

"Kids with two heads."

"Two heads are better than one."

"That gives me the creeps!"

"One day you'll see," he says. "The world is changing."

His voice trembles uttering his last statement, but she doesn't know whether it's from uncertainty or its opposite, an apprehension of the enormity that he is contemplating. They look at each other, inches apart, her nose at the level of his mouth. She inhales his breath, which tastes sweet whether or not he brushes his teeth. How she loves Garth, no one but Garth. Then with an urge so ambivalent, so weakened with doubt and resistance that the gesture makes her arms and chest ache, she pushes him away from her. "Garth, you disgust me."

He lies where she moved him, hard and still. He's hurt, she knows. And when she's gone, he'll hurt more. Tears spring to her eyes. How long has it been since her eyes were moist? She has always disdained notions the nuns would throw at her. *Listen to the voice of God in you. Be quiet inside and you will hear. Blessed be the Father, the Son, and the Holy Ghost.* While, in fact, she has no idea what combo of God, Satan, and her own twisted psyche, rotten as her hand, wants her to be with Garth and no one but Garth. *Thy kingdom come, Thy will be done, on earth as it is in heaven.* She puts her feet against the small of his back and pushes him out of the bed, propels him out of the room, shuts the door, and hooks a chair under the knob. She pushes her desk in front of the chair.

On the desk are her cutoffs, which smell rank. She takes them to the closet, starts to scrunch them down into her laundry bag, and feels the Pledge from a million years ago, which she is glad she signed. She and her friends, her trusted, trustworthy, cherished friends. She folds the paper into a tinier square and transfers it to the deep side pocket of her good winter coat, which, having already been cleaned, will escape her mother's compulsion until next spring, when it will all long have been over.

8

CJ

It's three-thirty A.M. by his nightstand clock, but he's into his book and reading fast, with only thirteen days to finish this and all the other books on his shelf. This one, *The Last of the Just,* is about a Jewish boy in Nazi Germany. CJ craves Holocaust stories. His father, who was interned and survived, will tell him nothing, not even the name of his camp, though CJ was able to prize this fact from his mother. In bed now, propped against pillows, CJ imagines himself in Auschwitz, starved and terrorized down to his essential savagery or heroism. With skeletal legs and arms, will he share his bowl of scummy soup? Will he suck up to the Kommandant? He imagines himself as the Kommandant—obese, charismatic Hermann Goering, or perverse, pitiless Dr. Mengele, his nod directing a line of trembling humanity toward life, toward death.

After some minutes, though, he closes the book. He shuts off the light. He closes his eyes and presses twin spots in their inner corners, lost suddenly in the wilderness of wanting. Wanting? It's a feeble word for what he feels. Lust? Love? No single word can contain it. It's "want" to the hundredth power. CJ pictures the face of his beloved but won't say the name even under his breath. Wanting and unable to speak, he feels as if he's about to die, though his heart beats stoically.

Back on goes the light. CJ returns to his book and reads about the German schoolteacher who, in class, kicks the Jewish boy in the stomach for not being able to sing properly. No one protests. Tormented and outcast, the boy wonders if he might be one of the Lamed Vav Tzadikim, thirty-six righteous men who aren't known to one another or even necessarily to themselves but whose business is to suffer so the world can go on. What a job, CJ says to Mick Jagger, who looks down on the room from a wall poster. CJ gets out of bed, retapes a loose corner of the poster, aligns the spines of the college catalogues that have been arriving all summer, though he didn't send for them. He shivers, which isn't strange—the air-conditioned room is freezing—and opens a window, inhales some of the damp, warm night. Among the thirty-six, the worst off are the ones who don't recognize their earthly purpose. They ascend to heaven so cold that God has to warm them between His fingers for a thousand years. CJ puts on a sweatshirt, not that he thinks he's a Lamed Vavnik. He's not even sure he is a Jew. Does Jewishness disappear from one's blood when it isn't practiced? Named Christopher Joseph Walker, he sounds pure Aryan. Of course, Hitler would think otherwise.

A bit disoriented in the endless middle of this night, he puts the book down and plucks a college catalogue from the shelf. On the cover handsome young men and women walk curving paths before an old stone building, in which agreeable discussions no doubt occur, ideas batted back and forth with the fervent courtesy of tennis players: Cornell University. In the foreground a slim girl holds the hand of a broad-shouldered boy the right number of inches taller than she. There's a catalogue from Harvard too, where his father wants him to go, though he won't admit it. Inside is an application form, questions to be answered seriously. "Describe yourself and what you see as your place in the universe." CJ rolls his eyes up at Jagger, who seems to share his derision, his wide pink lips like some internal organ.

CJ gets up, sits at his desk, and turns on his electric typewriter. He writes, *I exist in opposition to the word "no." I challenge the 613 Judaic commandments and a few more. Thou shalt not deposit the pickings of thy nose upon the underside of thy desk, even if thou art seated in the back row. Thou shalt not enter thy brother's bedroom with the purpose of pressing a pillow upon his seraphic face. Thou shalt not cut off thy dick and leave it to bleed on thy father's desk no matter what he does to emasculate you. Thou shalt not call S____ (my love) in the middle of the night no matter how much you want to talk to him. Thou shalt not call S____ (my love) at any hour of the day or night.*

He rather likes what he's written. At least it doesn't kiss ass.

Now it's four-fifteen; in an hour the sky will lighten, but his horsefly brain is buzzing. Almost of itself, his body rises from the chair. On quiet feet he walks darkened hallways till he arrives at the door behind which his parents sleep. Almost involuntarily he turns the knob. He steps onto carpet thick and soundless. There's his mother's light breathing, and from his father the occasional rattle of a snore. The sleep of the just? The sleep of a former Auschwitz inmate, an honest-to-God survivor who married a shiksa, named their firstborn Christopher, and joined the Unitarian Church, his demons buried deep or maybe too stupid to locate him—crafty old Judah Wachsberger, hiding out as Dr. Jack Walker, orthopedic surgeon, in this row of gentile mansions-on-the-lake. Not even his German accent gives him away. You think scientist or even Nazi before you think Jew.

Across from the king-sized bed, silently CJ slides open the top drawer of his father's bureau. There's a giant economy-size pack of condoms, squares aligned like thin mints. He has checked these out before, surprised by the rapidity with which the contents diminish. They won't be needed for a bit, as tomorrow Mrs. Walker is flying to New York to spend time with her sister, who recently lost her husband.

CJ gazes down at his sleeping mother, who loves her sister and seems to like most of the people in the world. There's a nugget of goodness in everyone, she says, you just have to find it. But she had no response when he said, *Even Hitler?* She prefers his brother, he's sure, though she denied it the one time he confronted her. Her dominant feeling for him seems to be worry, which makes him worry about himself. *You have such high standards for yourself,* she said. To which he said, *Isn't that a good thing?* To which she replied with a little sigh, *Just give yourself a break sometimes.* He still wonders what sort of break. He used to adore his mother. She was the one he sat by on airplanes, at restaurants, or even at home on the couch watching TV; he would cry if he couldn't have her beside him. For a moment he regards her in her tranquil, good-sister sleep, rocked by dreams as blithe as Broadway musicals, and he considers her reaction to the news of his death—which might occur while she and Aunt Lottie are out shopping, or at a play, or visiting Uncle Jed at the cemetery. She will not know, then she will know. The image disturbs him. With a forcible tug from his will, CJ exits the room, along with two of the items that exist to save him from acquiring a second younger brother.

Danny's room is next to their parents', and the door is open as usual. A nightlight reveals disorder of an athletic strain—gym shoes, tennis and golf balls, a deluxe hockey game with players that swivel and charge. The boy himself looks frighteningly vulnerable lying on his back in his cotton pajamas. Ten years old and tall for his age, he still sleeps with his cheek against an ancient stuffed dog. For a fraction of a second CJ's eyes start to water. It will be strange never to see Danny again, if only for his look of wondering pleasure when CJ tells him something he doesn't know. Where does that dauntless openness come from? CJ stands with his hand on the doorknob till the question subsides into the broth of other unanswerable, irrelevant questions, and he is once more intact.

CJ's final destination is the large Victorian-style bathroom that adjoins his bedroom. Dropping his boxers, he balances on the curved side of the old claw-foot tub and regards himself in the framed mirror over the sink. He is no Greek god for many reasons, chief among them a disproportion remediable only through butchery, his lean frame made ridiculous by a cock so pornographically large that, after the misery of overnight camp, he faked asthma in order to get permanent leave from gym. Faked it well enough to fool both his doctor-father and his allergist. On a shelf in the medi-cine chest is his bronchodilator, which he discharges every so often. He's good at acting—at anything that heightens the ecstatic shame of what is about to happen.

Perched on the side of the tub, eyes fixed on the mirror, he touches himself, imagining popular, brainless boys from his school standing just outside his door, nauseated but transfixed. There is pleasure in being disgusting, he has discovered, a refined pleasure akin to what nineteenth-century lords probably felt when they vis-ited a brothel. Contemplating any new lewdness, a man of courage has no choice but to act on it. He puts the condom on, lubricated and nearly translucent, watching his hands in the mirror as if they belonged to someone else. To S, perhaps (but who, pray, is S)? He runs a hand along the shaft of his cock, thinking, *The compadres like me, but they don't know this part of me, not even Vera, who applauds perversion.* If they saw his soul, their warmth would turn to revul-sion; no question. But it's his destiny to seek revulsion. His excessive dick points at the ceiling. In the mirror he sees its seamed and riv-ered underside. He is not happy, he will never be happy, but he feels strong and right, like Christ on the cross apprehending his place in the scheme of things. Like a martyr of the Talmudic persuasion, a concentration camp internee, one of the thirty-six just, whose an-guish sustains the world. Balancing, cresting on his fantasy of sacri-fice, he doesn't ejaculate.

Back in his room now, the finale exceeds grand. Lying in bed he imagines himself to be former Reichsmarschall Goering in his cell at Nuremberg. It's October 15, 1946, eighteen months after V-E Day—the sad finish to the German stab at glory as Goering conceived it—and fifteen days after the tribunal's verdict came down: death by hanging, despite the Nazi leader's passionate nine-day defense of himself. Hermann Goering, just a poor old Nazi bastard now, lies on his back in his bunk, reviewing the events of the trial, if you could call it that. He spoke well, he believes, with the same humor, sincer-ity, and intelligence that raised him to National Socialist power, buddy of Hitler and designated successor. That the trial was a sham doesn't bother him; how, after a war like that, could the Allies let him live? But as an officer he has the right to a firing squad—to be executed as the enemy soldier he was. He claimed this right with his head high, but *die Schweine* wanted the last full measure, his Aryan blood not even spilled on German soil but left to rot in the veins of the carcass of a hanged man.

In the confines of his father's condom, CJ pulses with Goering's shame and fear. He can see the man on his last earthly night, prone on the wooden slab in his cell. Physically—ironically!—he's feeling good, fifty pounds lighter on the prison diet. Gone, the old yen for morphine. Then his buddy, an American lieutenant—hunter, lover of woodland like himself, the one friend he has cultivated from among the conqueror dogs and pigs—gives him the news: *It will be tomorrow.* CJ can hear Goering's sincere thank-you, his German accent with its slight British inflection like CJ's father's. At which, following instructions, the kind and able American locates the stored suitcase and extracts from under the quilted lining the poison capsule Goering has hidden there for just this occasion.

No, Goering already has the capsule—he has always had it, his final escape—wrapped in foil in the bottom of a jar of pomade on the table in his cell. Under the eyes of the guard posted to prevent exactly this, he rises as if on an afterthought and locates his comb along with the jar. Immaculate to the end. He almost smiles, probing the creamy bottom of the jar. Shortly afterward, hair oiled and combed, he returns to his cot, feeling in the waistband of his boxers the sticky, foil-wrapped capsule. Then, even as the guard's eyes are turned upon him—a Brit this one, slow-witted and incorruptible, ensuring the world that no "German criminal" will cheat the gallows—he reaches into his clothing as if to scratch. The movement is almost absentminded, and afterward he lies still, listening to his heartbeat, picturing his two handsome wives (he was a lucky man), his dear, disappointed Hitler, and the Fatherland in a thousand years, freed at last but by someone else. (Still, they'd fought a good fight.) Then, casually covering his yawning mouth, he inserts the cyanide cap that will end his days with the only sovereignty that remains to him. But sovereignty it is. Gazing upon the guard's young, stupid face, he suppresses the urge to wink at him, and bites down. CJ lies in his own bed, breathing in gasps, thinking first of Goering in his death throes, his hand maybe in the hand of the kind American, who is trying not to weep, and then it's he and Saint hand in hand on the edge of the bluff.

He comes ferociously.

He is trying to move from that pleasure straight into sleep when he hears the shrill rising yowl of a cat. They don't have a cat. Cocking his head he hears it again. He raises the window screen, sticks his head out, and sees in the paling dark before dawn's early light a vision from a dream. He whispers the name, "Saint." He clears his throat, holding on to the windowsill, hating the expression he must have on his face. But it is Saint, his wild hair, wide shoulders, and—my God!—his large, pale body sitting on the walk below his window, naked as the day he was born.

9

Our Story

———

Before we of 4EVER caught the first glimpse of one another, when the idea of a cherishing group was just a yearning in our disparate minds, while my mother was still pretending to be a happy Evanston housewife and Saint was finding safe routes to and from his various apartments in Detroit, CJ was out East at boarding school. He was ten, eleven, twelve, almost thirteen, trying to find a place in the world of competitive, confident boys—unlike himself, he thought, but he could fake it. He was not only brainy in a school that lauded brains, he could bat a dime across the room with the side of his pencil. In seventh grade he was first in singles on the Grosvenor School tennis team, and he played shortstop on the Grosvenor baseball team. Then one afternoon, with a lousy batter at the plate, he saw in the bleachers a blond, square-jawed eighth-grade boy who had played the sax in a school assembly—played it tenderly, swaying from side to side—and his dick swelled. An easy grounder rolled through his legs. Before the game was over, he had made three more errors.

Though his team still won, and though the coach only told him to get more sleep, and though his teammates' gibes were friendly, he labored to understand his lapse, which was involuntary and seemed uncontrollable. He read Aristotle on causality, sought an efficient cause, and came up with something that made sense: There were only boys in his life. He spent all his time with boys.

With only a month until summer, CJ was able to keep his eyes and mind on the tasks in front of him. Back in Michigan, he told his parents that he no longer saw the need for them to spend their hard-earned cash on a private school for him. When they proclaimed their eagerness to continue doing so—what else was money for, a good education unlocked doors, etc.—he mentioned his desire (which was true!) for a more mainstream cultural experience; as it was, the only kids he knew how to talk to were snotty rich kids. He didn't need a third argument, populism being something both parents felt obliged to encourage, though it made them nervous.

So his place was canceled at Grosvenor, and he felt on the verge of hopeful. His brother was glad to see him. There was a girl a few houses down who didn't seem to mind talking to someone younger. But starting eighth grade at the local junior-senior high school, he found that the kids he used to play with had knotted into groups with their own jokes and vocabularies. They didn't purposely exclude him, but he felt excluded, like a foreign exchange student, and he spent time trying to figure out if he was superior or inferior. Lonely, bored, and angry, with five years of the same yawning before him, along with homework on subjects he had already mastered, he sassed a teacher who should have retired years ago and received a detention.

It was that afternoon in the cafeteria when the potential for kinship opened to him. In the shuffling silence of the twenty or so detainees trying to amuse themselves without attracting the monitoring teacher's attention, a high, musical voice rang out: "Man, oh man, I broke a fingernail! Does someone have an emery board?" Heads turned, including CJ's. There was something interestingly theatrical in the delivery. His eyes came to rest on a small blond girl two tables away with a savagely comic expression and long red fingernails. She was waving her manicured hand. "That's okay," she said, "I'll take care of it." She stuck a long-nailed finger in her mouth and bit down, bit it off, her finger, the whole thing past the knuckle. There was a room-wide gasp. The teacher approached; some kids snickered. Then the girl spat out a red and white glob, which turned out to be the masticated wax remains of a red-nailed vampire finger. In the maelstrom of laughter CJ picked up his books, moved to her table, and met Vera DeVito, who was whip-crack smart and didn't give a shit about that or anything.

It was a match. Adolescent misfits, their alliance gave them pleasure and safety. They hung out after school, honing their acerbity. Kids who messed with either of them dared double ridicule; soon there was no messing. But in certain ways they were too similar. Some weekends they spent alone because they were both too proud to make a phone call. They were wary of each other. Their affection was anxious, tentative.

Then (ta-da?) I entered the picture. It seems weird to applaud myself, but CJ and Vera both told me that the seed for what we would call 4EVER only began to sprout when I joined the group. It wasn't love at first sight. I had arrived at LJHS the same fall as CJ, and we three had some classes together. But they were kids I avoided, clever and sharp-tongued, and what would interest them in me? I spoke in class only when called on and ate lunch with other quiet, solitary girls.

The second semester I was further perfecting my isolation. I had art right before lunch, and the teacher allowed me to eat my sandwich in the room and keep working, a privacy undisturbed till the day CJ walked in. I remember my drawing, a pen-and-ink of a nude woman with bigger-than-regulation hands and feet. I had just finished it and signed my name, Kay Campion. CJ eyed it awhile, then he said with a kind of drawl, as if he were acting the part of someone impressed, "So *this* is a *Kay Campion*?" But inside the joke, I felt real admiration. I looked at what I'd done, and it seemed good to me too, and suddenly I had a voice. "Yes, it is!" I said. "Are you familiar with, uh, Campion's work?"

We riffed on our similar tastes in art and our good luck in finding this rare piece, the artist being such a recluse. That sort of verbal play wasn't anything I could keep up. And even now I sometimes wonder why they liked me so much. I was a novelty, a big cuddly doll that eventually they would set aside. But they kept calling, they didn't want to do anything without me, and slowly, slowly, I started to trust them and like them. Once again I had friends. By tenth grade the three of us had earned if not high regard from the other students, at least the secure status of a rebel group. Vera and I stopped setting our hair, and CJ let his grow, dark curls springing out from his head like Bob Dylan's. Girls still had to wear skirts to school, so I asked for a sewing machine for my birthday and made myself and Vera some long flowered skirts. Hippies, people called us, and we reveled in the gibe as it fell upon us, light and glittery like fairy dust.

Three was a triumvirate, a trinity, enough legs to hold up a stool. Except to play contract bridge, which CJ and I were teaching Vera, we didn't need a fourth. Then halfway through the year, a boy from Detroit walked into CJ's homeroom, tall, good-looking, probably bound for popularity despite his late arrival on the scene. At lunch in the cafeteria we checked him out brazenly. A face man, said CJ. Dumb jock, said Vera. I said, *Please don't talk so loud!* I had no caption for him. I liked his face, and it made me nervous.

As we predicted, the new guy was embraced by the kids who thought most flamboyantly well of themselves. St. John Scully, with the broad, handsome face, big chest and arms, played football and basketball, liked the Doors, spoke mildly but with assurance, and started dating Cathy Kirk. Then out of nowhere, it seemed, a rumor started. St. John Scully didn't try hard enough on the basketball court. He held back; didn't care; didn't play with heart. Facts about him were scrutinized, first by the boys who called themselves Trojans, and then by the general populace of LJHS, that (1) his mother was Cathy Kirk's cleaning woman, (2) he wore the same three shirts to school on alternating days, and worst, (3) nothing you said to him would piss him off. One afternoon Cathy got on the school bus, and instead of taking her usual seat she said something that was reported as *You give me the creeps* and passed him by. It must have been hell for him. The hallway taunts crescendoed, kids competed in the invention of pejorative nicknames—Squirrely, because of his clothes, Gandhi because he wouldn't fight back, St. John of the Cross because it sounded good. Someone would bump him accidentally-on-purpose just to see what he'd do, and kids would stop to watch what they had come to expect: Saint eyeing his attacker with mournful gravity, then walking on, swinging his long arms as if nothing had happened.

It was so sad and terrible that one day, in a burst of fellow feeling, I sat down at his lunch table. I didn't know what to say. I almost got up in confusion, but CJ and Vera were on their way, if only to get a closer look at his fatal flaw. "You're un*real*, man," Vera said as she put her tray on his table. "Do you realize that?"

He shrugged, swallowed the food in his mouth. "How do you know what's real?"

Vera and CJ were merely curious at first, but there were no questions of theirs that this kid wouldn't answer, no part of his life that he held back from us, and soon we were telling him and one another things that we had kept secret before. If my advent helped our group to like one another without reservation, it was Saint's that turned the feeling into love. For Vera too, even when she gave him a hard time. "You're a fucking *saint*," she said, and that's what we called him. And he was, an angel, agent and object of our yearning for beauty and goodness.

10

CJ

―――――

With the darkness thinning toward dawn, with his father's rubber hanging from his dick, CJ leans out his bedroom window toward the beam of Saint's upward gaze. An organ in his body that seems to reside between his stomach and his heart hurts so badly he could weep, but he knows only how to be amusing. *"But soft,"* he stage-whispers. *"What light through yonder window breaks?"*

"Fuck you!" Saint's voice rises to his ears. "You've got to help me."

His friend's problem is obvious. But CJ is lost in his cleverness and *Romeo and Juliet,* despite the fact that his lines belong to the figure standing below. It's what he wants Saint to be saying to him: *"Deny thy father and refuse thy name . . . and I'll no longer be a Capulet!"*

"Shit, man. I'm freezing my ass off!"

"But you look so fine! You look so—how you say in America? Cool?"

"CJ. Please?"

There's pain in his friend's voice. He hears it, and it strengthens him. "Don't go away," he cries absurdly, and pulls off his sweatshirt, his stupid rubber. "Hey, man, just keep your *pants* on!" Naked, he dances around the room in anticipation of something he hasn't dared to imagine, free of everything that used to weight him to earth. Still naked, he descends the stairs, bursts out onto the dewy lawn. "You Looney Tunes! You fucking mental patient!"

Saint stares a second, then he puts a hand over his eyes. "I didn't mean to set a trend. All I want is a pair of jeans. Shorts. Something?"

His friend's request is a disappointment. Under other circumstances, CJ would have deflated and started in with the gibes. But in the predawn light there's a weird radiance around them both, though CJ can't tell if it's coming from Saint or his own brain. In the middle of Saint's chest is a patch of curly red hair; CJ wants to touch it. Saint stands with his weight on one foot, in the fluid S-curve of the statue of David. "At least," Saint implores, "get me a bathing suit!"

There are times in a person's life when, even as an event is occurring, you know you might not ever understand it. CJ has often conjured scenes of sex, love, pain, and death, but in the realm of the actual, he is at sea. In the breaking dawn, his friend's large, pale body obliterates everything that CJ has ever conceived. Like a young child—the only persona he can inhabit now—he reaches out and tags Saint. "Touched you last!" he cries, and gallops off across the lawn, arms outspread in a dream of flying.

He falls but doesn't hurt himself. The grass is soft in Eden. He starts rolling over the damp, cool lawn, dizzying himself till there's no top or bottom, no ground or sky, just this moist, sweet-smelling semi-dark all around him. He remembers a family car trip to Canada, the moment when, after a night of wakeful car sleep, he opened his eyes to pale green foggy hills in a fragrant newborn world. Saint is standing nearby, arms awkwardly folded. CJ leaps up and dances just out of reach. "You're it. Loosen up, boy."

Saint runs clumsily, only half into the game, like an adult entertaining a child. Fine with CJ. He runs a circle around Saint, then dances back. "You can't catch me."

Saint's long arm whips out and tags him. Saint takes off.

CJ must now reassemble. Saint, the clumsy hippo, is suddenly swerving, dodging. He takes cover behind a tree, pops his head out. "Evil creature!" cries CJ. "Foul fiend!"

It's all around the mulberry bush, the monkey chased the weasel.

It's Sambo's tigers running round and round the African tree, chasing the boys till they all melt to butter in the heat and speed. Saint stumbles. Close behind, CJ trips. They fall, skin on skin. There's the taste of salt, CJ laughing or maybe weeping.

Sprawled, the boys don't look at each other. It's not the first time they've touched. The group exchanges hippie hugs as a matter of course. They pat, they stroke T-shirted shoulders. But their hands on each other's sweaty backs this morning feel dangerous. Personal. Intentional. They move apart, gazes sliding by each other. CJ is suddenly afraid of what Saint is thinking. "You came all the way here in your birthday suit. That's so bizarre," he says.

But it's not what he means. It's not bizarre as in freakish, it's bizarre as in marvelous, miraculous; a wish granted, idea made flesh. He chances a look in Saint's eyes, conveying these thoughts telepathically. Saint's freckled skin looks fragile, easily scratched. His smile is frightened or generic.

CJ is very close to panic now. Saint keeps smiling his stupid smile, his gaze every which where, and CJ knows what Saint isn't looking at. CJ himself doesn't even have to look to know. A final attempt at coolness, he sits up and crosses his legs, allowing his dick to do whatever it wants. He pushes it down into the grass, and it pops back up, pop goes the weasel! Trying to be funny. Is he funny? He wants to laugh, to duck himself back into the silliness of a few minutes ago—he's rarely silly and longs to be (if only Saint's cock were as unruly). But Saint looks uninvolved, his smile seems to hide pity, and what did CJ expect?

More than ever now, CJ needs to be cool. Which means make a joke. *Is that a banana in my pocket or am I in love with you?* Or he could say, *Do you think I want to fuck you, huh?* in a tone that renders the notion absurd. But the feeling of more-than-disappointment, of bereavement, of being booted out of Eden, obliterates irony. He wants to tell his friend that he dreams about him, that he loves him, not just sexually, but that too. When the time comes he will happily die with him, or for him. But his jaws are locked, his mind stalled out. If he were standing at that moment on the bluff, he'd jump without anybody's hand in his, he'd jump and that would be that, dust to dust, like Goering in final, uncontestable control of his life.

Then, like the man in the Zen story who hangs by his fingers from a cliff while the hungry tiger prowls below, CJ gives himself over to the moment. His hand, as if accidentally, grazes Saint's thigh. Saint's dick stirs. He strokes again, as if he's in a trance, he doesn't know what he's doing. And in the silence of the spreading yard, he hears the sudden intake of his friend's breath. CJ's eyes are closed—if he looked at Saint he would surely die—but his hand has closed over Saint's dick and he can feel Saint feeling pleasure. It's like touching himself, but so much better. He thinks of soldiers dying for their comrades, and of Moses closing his eyes before the face of God, and then Saint's arms are around his back, they are touching each other at the same goddamned time, and there is nothing else to think about.

Afterward, breath slowing, CJ is ready to die. It should happen exactly now, at this peak, after which everything that is not this is half-assed and ordinary. But he is alive, the sun is rising, and questions ring in his mind: *Did you like it? Do you hate me now? Or, oh God, do you love me?* Saint's wide-open eyes convey no information.

"Hey, man. Where are you?" CJ says at last, but Saint doesn't seem to understand the question. "So, uh, er, do you still want them there blue jeans?" He laughs like a cretin. "Or do you want to flash back up Main Street and scare the tourists?"

Saint's mouth curves into a frightened smile. CJ wants to embrace him, but Saint's blank face walls him off. "I'll take you up on those jeans," Saint says at last, casually. "And a shirt, if you have one that's big enough."

"You can have one of Dad's."

Their words are painfully offhand. Saint has to work today. CJ, who would do anything for Saint, does the few things he is asked to do. He gives him clothing and drops him off at his restaurant.

Part II

11

Chicago Run

————

And then? With the Pledge, we might have seemed to be courting death, but it was also joy we were after. We wanted to feel our birthright, what we thought other, happier people felt—the sense of endless possibility, the world shimmering around us. To dance beneath the diamond sky.

And I think we did, at times, at first. But we were also at war within ourselves, and the next day, or even that night, we felt for the first time uncomfortable with one another. I didn't know what had happened between Saint and CJ but it was easy to see that Saint kept himself on the far side of wherever CJ happened to place himself, while CJ's jokiness became more frantic. To my shame, though, I wasn't thinking much about CJ; my secret eye was on Saint and Vera. I had promised Jesus to die with His name on my lips if he kept them apart and, to my surprise and relief, that particular prayer seemed to have been answered. All of a sudden, of the four of us, I was the one Saint wanted to be with, which left CJ with Vera, and all of us shrill and nervous as we tried to re-create our mutual affection as if from relics and old parchments.

The weather remained hot and densely humid. The wind off the lake peppered our arms with sand and tried to blow our magnetic cards off the board. But playing bridge imposed on us a sort of formal harmony, and we spent almost all of our waking time near the bluff that would witness our Grand Finale. Vera would come early to the park and stay late in order to avoid her father and brother. When

Arlyn dropped me at school, I'd enter the right-hand door, count to fifty, and exit the left. Saint maintained his work schedule, but otherwise he was with us. As for CJ, with his mother gone and his father at work, his time was his own. Even with Saint acting like he didn't exist, where else could he spend his last days?

Then toward the end of those stultified days something loosened up in us, or at least in CJ, since it was his idea. On Tuesday, Saint's day off, with eight or nine days till the Pledge came due, we would go down to Chicago to see a Cubs game. We'd arrive in time for the opening pitch and return—after a postgame beer (courtesy of our fake IDs)—in time for Vera's and my curfews. CJ was floating, almost giddy at the prospect of something new. And the following morning, dressed in bright blue, Cubs cap and Cubs T-shirt, he was parked outside the school with Vera and Saint in the car. He had a blue plastic Cubs change purse with four fat joints. "Root, root, root!" he cried. "I crave Cracker Jack!"

Still more impossibly wonderful, he had secured his mother's convertible; we smoked the first joint with the top up on the way out of town. Then alongside a spreading cornfield we pulled over and rolled back the top. The smells were green and brown, the corn as high as an elephant's eye, sun pouring down like honey on this land that was our land. Things were going to be good now. CJ took his shirt off; Vera, beside him, pulled her tube top down to her waist, casually exposing her small, pretty breasts. Less daring, I pulled my granny skirt up over my knees. As usual those days, I was in back with Saint, and on left turns the car rocked me against him. When CJ hit the gas, hot wind whipped my hair; it was hard to take a breath, but God! To feel so wind-rushingly alive! We passed a car pulling a boat, we passed a line of trucks. Vera turned up the radio. Mick Jagger couldn't get satisfaction, but he didn't seem to feel that bad about it, and neither did we. We sang at the top of our lungs, screaming at truckers and cute kids in the backs of station wagons until the empty road hummed under our tires, a shiny band dissolving at the horizon into sky. No traffic. No thought, no pain, no relief from pain, no longing or relief from longing. Just the four of us breathing the hot wind and one another's skin as we raced toward the future, of which we had full control.

Outside Gary, the air turned thick, sour, and oily, but we breathed it in, still exulting. Flowers and shit, all one. Traffic was sparse across the Skyway and up Stony Island, but Lake Shore Drive was crawling, as if the whole world were going to our baseball game. Across from Buckingham Fountain we stopped for so long that CJ put the car in park, stood up on the seat, and sang "Take Me Out to the Ball Game." He had a nice voice; other people joined in, among them a family of five in the next lane. In Grant Park people were erecting a platform for the Yippies, who were coming to the Democratic convention to speak against the war. Kids carried signs, one of which read ELECT PIGASUS. This was Chicago, the teeming, frothing heart of it all.

The congestion got even worse at Belmont, supposed gateway to Wrigley Field. Exiting took fifteen minutes. After circling for another half hour, CJ paid a boy twenty dollars to park on a slab of concrete behind his family's apartment building. Out of the car I started to feel a little paranoid. The locals wore shorts, sandals, psychedelic T-shirts. CJ had on expensive cowboy boots. "I fear we are overdressed," he cried, hip-butting Saint toward a husky young man in a Che Guevara shirt. "Watch it," CJ said to Saint, "you want to pick another fight?" Saint apologized to Che for his asshole friend, and Che flashed a V for victory. He was cool. No problem. "See?" cried CJ.

CJ was getting crazier by the minute as he herded us through the crowd toward the stadium. He kissed my cheek, he kissed Saint's. "Up north we're trouble, here we're straight as a string. Us boys, at least." He stopped in his tracks. "Oh my God! Soul mates!"

In the general sweep of bare legs and primary colors were two men in boots and the same long jeans CJ and Saint were wearing. One wore a cowboy hat. CJ opened his arms. "I love you. Be our friends?" They turned. Buttons on their shirts said NIXON'S THE

ONE! and DEFEAT = DISHONOR. CJ held up a hand. "We'll wait for the next incarnation." Tipping his Cubs cap to them, CJ turned to Vera in her trademark cutoffs and tube top. "Hey, dollface, does your daddy know how you walk around?"

Vera ignored him; he said it louder. I tried to shush him, but it only gave him energy. "What's the worst they could be thinking?" he said. "What are those hicks doing in the big city?"

"Please," I said. "I feel like an escaped mental patient."

"But you look like an Earth Mother." He pulled me into the shelter of his arm. "I'm a loudmouth, please ignore me. We're good-guy aliens. We come in peace."

Our group seemed fragile now, out of place. CJ trying to fit us in, acting as if we already belonged, just made it worse. My granny skirt and embroidered peasant blouse that were a statement in Lourdes seemed phony in Chicago. *That farm girl thinks she's a hippie,* I felt people thinking. I dropped back beside Vera and kept my eyes on the ground, trying not to step on anyone's heels while CJ guided us toward the stadium.

We hadn't bought tickets ahead of time, and at the Today's Game window we learned there were no decent seats left, no four together anywhere but upper deck reserve, where you couldn't see the pitches. CJ, though, was in his glory. "Since when," he said to the ticket seller, broadening his Midwest accent, "does a fourth-place team sell out, tell me that."

"Stay home," the woman replied without heat. Middle-aged, with a rose-colored blemish on her cheek the shape of the state of Indiana, she was in no hurry to serve the next fan. "That's what I tell you diehards. Go on strike. Keep your money. Make SOB Mr. Wrigley spend some of his."

CJ nodded sagaciously. "You've got a point, ma'am. My pa was a union man. Until he died, but that's another story. Here's our immediate problem. My friends and I woke at dawn to get here. We've been in the car for four hours. Are you sure, in one of those drawers back there, there aren't a few really good seats? For hotshots that probably won't show?" His voice mimicked the woman's cadences. I was impressed, and even more so when she handed him two pairs of prime seats, upper deck over home plate and field boxes by the Cubs dugout. She waved away the twenty-dollar bill that CJ offered. "You are a magnificent human being," he said to her.

"You're a funny young man."

"I've been called worse. But I treat nice people nicely."

I grinned, liking him.

"They're all talkers down here," he explained. "At home, you start a conversation with someone you don't know, and it's *Hunhh?*" He was especially happy about the seating, which separated us into twosomes, girl with girl, boy with boy. He handed Saint one of the field box tickets, gave the two upper deck boxes to Vera and me. He was scanning for an entry gate when Vera asked to see my ticket. Without a pause, as if she'd planned it out beforehand, she handed mine to Saint and Saint's to me.

I didn't mind the transfer, but CJ was unhappy. "Girls get the view, boys get to catch foul balls. That's the American way," he said. "Come on, be nice!" He held out his hand for the ticket she'd snatched. She put it in her pocket.

"Kay will help you catch your foul balls."

Saint's face was blank, as if any seat was fine with him. CJ evil-eyed Vera. "You're a little Napoleon, aren't you?"

"And you're a male chauvinist pig."

I too wanted to sit with Saint and considered offering that arrangement as a compromise, but Vera crossed her arms, small and dense as a meteorite: This was how it would be. And it was a nice day. Agreeable hours stretched before us. "Okay," I said to CJ, "let's catch us some balls."

12

Vera

———

Alone with Saint, Vera doesn't feel like Napoleon. She's not even sure why she maneuvered the seat switch. What does she want from a guy who declined the pleasures she offered? The image assails her, his dick proclaiming what he couldn't or wouldn't put into words. He should be the one appeasing her, trying to accommodate her, while all week he has avoided her, and she's not a girl who chases guys who reject her. Or is she? Her actions suggest otherwise. And it's hard even to walk beside him, let alone probe his inscrutable brain. She keeps her bad hand in her pocket, wishing she'd worn a loose shirt. She feels underdressed. Under-somethinged. If someone remarks on her hand or even looks her way, she thinks she might scream.

On the long ramp, as she climbs ahead of Saint, rage supplants her insecurity. That it was she who had to implement the reconciliation, that Saint couldn't take charge once in a while—it's what she hates about him. Rounding a bend, she looks back. There he is, gazing up at her, for reasons known only to his Zen mind. She walks faster, elbows out, past clusters of loud-talking fans; no one impedes her. When the ramp ends she selects the entrance with the number corresponding to that on her ticket, sidestepping down the row as if she's done it a thousand times.

Then she is seated, with the sky overhead and the field spread out below, and her mood shifts again. She has never been here before; the novelty is both soothing and stimulating, the green-painted slats of the seats, the metal chair arms, the smell of beer and old cement. All around her, along with the steady wind, is the relaxed urgency of human voices en masse, thousands of them, a constellation of sound that rises and falls like breathing.

When Saint arrives, to punish his weeklong coldness she focuses harder on her surroundings. They are in the third row on a steep incline. Down below, the green of the playing field is heightened by the white patches of the bases, the soft brown collar around the infield. Over the stands, over the jagged crests of the high-rises, the sky is a tender blue. Between two buildings there's a hazy bit of lake, a tiny white sail. "These are good seats," she murmurs, an unwilled appeasement (what's wrong with her!), but he doesn't respond. He doesn't comprehend small talk. Her fingers slide down into her pockets. This is her first visit to a major league ballpark. She tells him so, but nada. Why does he make it so hard? Her gaze crosses the field, travels up the bleachers, the red and blue dabs of fan T-shirts, the enormous scoreboard. It's definitely nice up here. Her thoughts lighten and drift, as if in response to the wind or weakened gravity. "We don't have to talk," she says sarcastically. "Let's just sit here like we don't know each other." From Saint, nothing.

She's irritated, but with only part of her mind. Another part seems involuntarily to be seeking something. She wiggles her stubbed fingers. Among these strangers, without thinking about it, she has been hiding her bad hand away in her pocket. Now she liberates it; she uses it to scratch her ear. Why not? She has nothing to lose. Daring herself, as she does in school when she feels challenged or simply when the impulse assails her, she raises it over her head and holds it there for the viewing public, all these yo-yos come to watch men swing a stick, who are no more dangerous or important to her than her Lourdes schoolmates: *Look! Mock me! I dare you!*

Then, while her hand is aloft, before she can return it to the shelter of her lap, there's a wild cheer. Applause, whistles. Her heart jumps, her hand descends, and she looks at it as if she has never seen it before. Behind her, two boys scream, "Santo! Santo!" Down below, men are running out onto the field. "Number ten, Ron Santo" comes through the loudspeaker and the cheering mounts. Her cheeks burn at the thought of her egotism. She is not central to all the world's thoughts, for better or worse. Shouldn't she know that by now?

She raps the back of her hand, not hard, a check to any renewed notions of its self-importance. On her other side, a man her father's age is telling the woman beside him about his costly divorce. Rows of strangers stretch before and behind her, none of whom are looking at her. They have no opinions about her whatsoever. Is that bad? It doesn't feel bad. They order beer and hot dogs from the vendors; she passes food down the row and money the other way, unimportant, unobserved. Nothing seems that important. "Be honest with me," she says to Saint. "Are you wishing I didn't finagle this?"

After a beat he says, "I'm kind of wishing I knew why you did."

She gives a short scream. "He talks! That's amazing."

He looks at her.

"Don't quit now."

"What do you want me to say?"

She wants to scream again; he's maddening. "Sometimes I haven't the faintest idea how your mind works." He doesn't help her out. "Come on. Would you rather be sitting with CJ? If so, you should have said so."

"Why would I want to be sitting with CJ?"

She is exhausted. Why is talking so hard? She wants a cigarette but doesn't want to ask Saint, who fills the whole span of his seat, his leg angled into her space. Inadvertently, slightly, her bare knee touches the fabric of his jeans.

On the field below someone hits a high ball. A cheer starts to swell, then the ball is caught near the wall; the cheer crumples. She closes her eyes and tries to guess what's happening on the field by the sounds. *What the fuck do you want?* she says to Saint in her mind, over and over, but she has extended herself enough. She's a rubber band stretched as far as it can go. More and someone will get hurt.

On the field below, the game is a slow, unfathomable modern dance.

By the time the crowd sings "Take Me Out to the Ball Game," Vera is wishing for the simplicity of the company of Kay and CJ. She wonders if she could find the car, or a bus station—every city has a bus station—not that she has money for a ticket home. Then under cover of the communal noise, Saint puts his head next to hers. "Vera, tell me please, what do you want from me?"

She regards his freckled arm on their shared armrest. "What makes you think I want anything?" she says coolly.

"Why did you bring me up here? To give me shit about that night?"

"What night?" she says.

"You're still PO'd, aren't you?"

"'Pee-Ohed'? Is that how they talk in Detroit?"

He starts his zombie hum. She gives the man on her other side a look of scorn that he no doubt deserves for something and leans toward Saint. "I'm sorry. But with you I just feel so fucking . . . I don't even know the word." He's like a door she's pounding on that doesn't sound under her fists. She's worse than powerless. "Tongue-tied?"

"Is that my fault?" he says. "I don't think it's my fault."

She closes her eyes. "Look. You're so, I don't know—heavy on me? I can't move, around you. Or even think."

"I don't know why that should be."

She shrugs.

"Tell me what to do."

"There's nothing to do."

He watches the game, and she sits breathing the ether over the green of the ballpark. She lets herself float on the rise and fall of crowd pleasure and pain. *Boo. Go Cubs.* Then, after it seems that the game has gone on for as long as a distant and pointless ritual could possibly go on, the crowd stands and screams as a body, Saint along with them. She stands too, though she can't see through the wall of people. She leans against Saint. When they sit down she murmurs, "Just be nice to me. That's all."

"Vera, you could drive someone crazy."

"So could you." She smiles at him with her mouth only.

"I just want things to be more—"

"Fluid?" she says.

"Equal."

"That is such crap." She's shaking, though sweaty and hot. "It *is*!"

"Some of the things you say," he says, "are really hurtful."

"That's not my intention."

His gaze remains blank and clear, but his color has changed, less like stone than hard-baked clay. "I don't think you know your effect on people."

"That isn't fair! What people? You don't know *your* effect either. You treat me like I'm made of shit."

He shakes his head, but whether he means no, he doesn't and never did think she was shit, or oh dear, it's all so confusing, she doesn't know and doesn't feel like asking.

13

Wells Street

———

Our seats, mine and CJ's, were low and close to the field. From there the game looked two-dimensional until a ball arced up. Baseball is slow and easy to follow. I could see the pitcher arching back and raising his leg before the throw. CJ had binoculars, and through them I could even see the batter's hands on the bat. I liked the way the man crouched, waiting, then the ball snapping through the air right into the catcher's glove like a message understood. It was hot, the sun beat down on my hair and arms, but the players were sweating a lot more. Their shirts got wetter and wetter each time they trotted out of the dugout and back to the field.

My only problem with the game was that one team was winning too easily. The Cubs scored four runs in the first inning, and I liked cheering with the rest of the crowd, but I felt bad for the Atlanta Braves, who were brave, I thought, to keep on playing when they were so far behind. Then a Brave scored a run, and I clapped, but people were looking at me. Oops!

"Cubs are blue and white, Braves are gray," CJ said. "Good guys, bad guys. Don't you know your colors by now?"

"Oh shut up!" It was my usual clever retort.

Still, Saint and Vera were out of my mind, for once; I was enjoying the day. The Braves caught up; the power balance became more just. And I understood the game. I'd played softball in Evanston, and although I couldn't throw well, I could catch when the ball came at me, and I could bat. I liked hitting the heavy, thick-skinned ball over everyone's heads and trotting around the bases.

"CJ," I said, "this was a good idea."

I didn't know the whole story yet, but I wanted to make up for Vera's little coup. "She doesn't know what to do if she isn't in charge of things. It isn't fair, but it doesn't hurt to let her rule us sometimes. I hope you don't feel bad?"

"You're a wise woman," he said, as if he didn't entirely like me for it.

"Is that good or bad?"

He laughed, and the tension that could have buzzed me all afternoon, made me anxious and tired trying to understand it, dissolved in the bright green heat of the afternoon.

After the game, we met at the car as planned. A guy on the corner was playing the saxophone, the same song over and over. Saint threw a coin into the instrument case while Vera gazed hard in the opposite direction. They seemed more at odds than ever; they didn't even know the score of the game (6–5, Cubs) or that it had gone an extra inning and been won by a home run. I tried not to be glad.

Though so much was unresolved, no one wanted to go back yet. We left the car where it was and joined the crowd swirling out from the ballpark, moving with it wherever it had a mind. Down Clark Street, past bars that looked dark and cool in the hot white sunlight. Sweaty, thirsty, we saw a bar with the hospitable name Mother's and walked in with composed adult faces. But even before he saw our IDs, the door guy rolled his eyeballs. "Anyone here remember Ike Eisenhower? How about Sputnik?" Grooving on his own wittiness, he held CJ's driver's license up to the light. "Who you gonna vote for next fall? Hey, did you just get back from Nam?" People were laughing. We ducked out fast.

We bought Cokes at a corner grocery and lounged under the L tracks in the hot, sooty breeze. Soon the bottles were warm, the

Coke too sweet. I thought of Vera's curfew and how far we were drifting from our car. Vera didn't seem worried, though, and CJ was good on logistics. And the sun was high; the day still stretched before us. He hailed a cab and asked the driver where the real action was—Grant Park, Lincoln Park, the Amphitheatre? We sank into the air-conditioned backseat.

We were let off on a narrow street of row houses, whose first floors were little shops selling fudge and popcorn, hookahs and rolling papers, adult books. The street was jammed with people and things. Soap bubbles swelled out of a pipe in front of a store called Bizarre Bazaar. Peddlers wound up their tiny metal animals to dance on the sidewalk. Metal snakes hissed and writhed at our feet; an elephant raised and lowered its metal trunk. People's voices fought the occasional grinding roar of the L.

A tourist trap, CJ said. Middle-aged couples gaped at the booty in the shop windows; children hopped along the sidewalk holding round, flat rainbow-colored suckers the size of their faces. CJ started gabbing with a guy selling Mickey Mouse wristwatches; he bought one for me, and I put it on. "I'll wear it always," I said, then amended my statement. "Well, for the next week or so!" I loved the watch and the tiny pretty shops, the pervasive smell of popcorn. Little kids in sunsuits stared at teenagers in ragged tie-dye sprawled on stoops in large laughing groups, and I stared too. A boy in a doorway with hair to his shoulders asked me for a quarter, and I emptied my pockets for him. Beside him, a girl said, "Spare grass? Spare acid?" I apologized for not being provisioned, and she smiled forgiveness. I was thrilled at how readily people talked to us. In another doorway two guys were sharing a joint. One of them passed it to me and wouldn't take it back. "Blessings," he said. I gave it to CJ, who blew them a kiss. Saint and Vera, though, seemed not to feel the collective warmth, walking apart in their separate daydreams.

At one of the kiosks in Bizarre Bazaar, CJ bought a hash pipe and rolling papers. A few stores down was a tattoo parlor called Marc of Cane—Marcus and Jillian Cane, proprietors. Signs proclaimed a friendly environment, free consultation, sterile needles, walk-ins welcome. CJ entered and we followed our captain. There were posters in the waiting area of Albert Einstein, Jimi Hendrix, Day-Glo elves and devils. There were large Mylar-wrapped sheets of designs of varying complexity: a tiny rose, a heart, a swastika, a snake emerging from a skull. Five to five hundred dollars. "My treat," said CJ. "Price is no object."

He waltzed through as if he knew the place. In an interior room reclining chairs were aligned in front of a long mirror. There was no door or curtain; a man in plaid Bermuda shorts lay with his arm strapped to a board while a woman with stark-white hair down her back injected him with ink. From under the lids of his closed eyes, soundless tears ran down his cheeks. It looked like a demon's beauty parlor.

By this time I was ready to leave. In 1968, tattoos were for sailors and Hells Angels. Nor was there any part of my body I wanted to decorate or otherwise call attention to. Saint, though, was checking out the designs; Vera too, seriously. On the man's arm a lizard was emerging, black and green, elegant in an ugly way. I hoped consensus would turn against the idea for us, but it did not. The only conflict was over which tattoo we would get. We had to agree, since the image would represent our bond with one another. Vera argued for a bird, Saint a yin yang sign, CJ either Scrooge McDuck or a severed hand with the bone protruding. Think small, I said. Then someone brought up my logo, the symbol of our four-way unity. I redrew it, extending the foot of the R into a bird in flight. My vision of our immortality. I was on board.

Marcus said he could do it. A sign declared the minimum tattoo age to be twenty-one, but Marcus found no discrepancy between our faces and our fake IDs. It would take at least thirty minutes per client, a couple of hours in all, but less if no one else came in and the proprietors worked simultaneously.

Now it seemed we had refound our purpose. *The solution to the problem of life lies in the disappearance of the problem*—who had said that? Alan Watts? Wittgenstein? It didn't matter. Vera and I had curfews. Should we call for permission to come home late, permission that might not be granted? I called and Elise accepted the charges. When our parents came home she'd say I'd be back by one or so. Drive safely, she said, and the problem was gone. Vera chose not to call, knowing permission would never be granted, but her eyes were shining. She was flying under the radar; no one even knew where she was. She would either sneak in or bear whatever consequences ensued. I hugged her, and we embraced as well the prospect of pain, shared and for a greater good. And who could harm us? Our souls were eternal. And in nine days, freed of our souls, our bodies on the lakeshore would bear the same eternal image.

So in the brief, glowing present moment, on the island of Here and Now, the tattooing commenced. CJ and Saint had theirs etched on their biceps, where they could be concealed if necessary inside short sleeves. Mine was on the outside of my calf, hidden under my skirt. I didn't cry and was impressed with myself. "It doesn't hurt that much! Really." The last to go, Vera wanted hers on her breastbone. She pulled her tube top down a notch and pointed to the shallow dip between her breasts. Jillian tried to dissuade her. Over the bone it could be bad. "Do it where there's some flesh," she said, "not that you have a lot of flesh." A tattooed beanstalk ran up Jillian's arm to her fleshy shoulder. She suggested the top or back of the thigh, but Vera was adamant. She had a high pain threshold. "Don't worry about me," she said, and lay back on the chair, chest bared.

Her procedure took longer than any of ours, and Jillian spent as much time wiping off the blood as inserting the dye, but under the needle Vera lay still, dry-eyed.

It was getting dark when we left the tattoo parlor, but the street was rocking. The smell of popcorn was replaced by muskier odors, conjuring images of evil and pleasure hidden under the daytime tourist veneer. Authentic or not, we didn't care now. It was Halloween, Mardi Gras, an event, not a place. It was Brigadoon, a town that exists for a single day every hundred years. We bought fudge and lemonade, then, still hungry, went to a restaurant and ordered slabs of barbecued ribs. Saint and Vera began to talk, though not exactly to each other. CJ took the check, as he had been doing all day. He put an arm around me, the other around Vera. "Call me Sugar Daddy."

"You're not *my* sugar daddy," Saint said, more belligerent than seemed called for, but CJ rose to the occasion.

"I pay your tab, I own you."

"We'll see about that."

CJ plunked his elbow down on the table and dared Saint to arm-wrestle him. After an awkward pause, Saint agreed. Biceps swelling under their bandages, they clasped hands. CJ's arm, so much narrower and shorter than Saint's, was upright far beyond expectations; the table beside us cheered him on, the obvious underdog. Saint won, of course, but CJ looked radiant, as if something had been achieved. The constriction between them was easing now. There were no rules in this city, or different rules. Tattoos burning on our skin under sterile gauze, we breathed the beckoning, arousing, lawless air. It glowed inside us. "We're buddies," said CJ. "Brothers in arms."

"Oh yeah?"

I nodded encouragement. At least Saint was looking at CJ. It loosened a knot in my chest.

"Anything can happen," CJ said, and I seconded him. Anything could happen. It was that kind of world.

I felt almost sure then that we would all have lives beyond the Pledge. I could picture CJ at Harvard, then law school, and Saint in Asian studies somewhere planning a semester abroad in Japan. Vera, who had an ear for languages, would study French while she taught ballet to little kids, or performed—why not?—while I graduated from the School of the Art Institute of Chicago and had my first show. The idea pleased me, and I stashed it in an out-of-the-way place in my brain.

By now most of the suburbanites had gone home, but the street traffic remained dense. The narrow, adjoined buildings were black against the sky, which had a purple cast. Purple haze, violet sky. Hendrix, Dylan—they knew this place. Across the street two men walked together, not touching but as if their bodies were connected, the way couples walked. CJ watched them. Then Vera took my hand and we started skipping like little girls.

It was time for us to head home now, but CJ had copped some hash and he wanted to try out his new pipe. Then we'd get a cab.

We started arguing safety concerns. Vera pointed out a car in a no-parking zone with the telltale plates of a plainclothes cop. Pigs were everywhere. CJ was herding us toward an alley where we could get high, and I was worrying about getting Vera home even if she didn't care, not to mention the fact that any guy in jeans could be a policeman, when someone plowed between us and hurtled past, gasping, a young man obviously running at top speed. He had a bag or a package under his arm.

We followed in his direction and found him again, hunkered down between two parked cars. Some people glanced his way but without much interest. He had black hair to his shoulders and wore a loose white embroidered shirt like the kind sold in Mexican shops. His face was turned streetward but I saw his profile—jutting cheekbones, beak of a nose, beads around his neck like a hippie or maybe an Indian, someone America abused. I wanted to kneel beside him, offer him things, money, a place to stay, a ride out of here. His white shirt was spotless. Then a siren ripped through the night, blue lights swept a wide circle, a loudspeaker voice yelled, "Police action! Clear the area. Spectators, clear the area."

"Right," said CJ. "We do need to clear the air."

Saint muttered, "Unload that dope, will you?"

"Not on your mother's life!"

People were close, pressing us against the cars. CJ put the pipe in his teeth and extracted a lighter. "Toss it," said Saint.

"I don't know you," said Vera.

CJ grinned. "I won't name names. Trust me." He lit the pipe.

Traffic was stopped dead. The bullhorn kept warning pedestrians back and away, but they didn't hear or didn't care or couldn't move. Then the crouching man stepped into the pulsing blue pinwheel of light with his hands raised, either in surrender or to show he had no weapon. The bag had fallen to his feet; he kicked it away. A shot rang out and he fell.

There was silence at first, a mass intake of breath. Then murmurs and light, tentative screams. Panic rose like a tide. We had to escape, to get off this street, though to where, who knew?

Vera was beside me. We grabbed hands and slowly made our way to a quieter block, where a car of kids squeezed us in and drove us back to the ballpark. Eventually Saint and CJ arrived. Safe inside our car but still shaking, we tried to reconstruct what had happened. The guy could have stolen a purse. Or a car stereo. But even so, they didn't have to kill him. Not that we knew for sure the man was dead. I didn't remember seeing blood. Was he black, a light-skinned black? Man, he could have had a bomb in that bag, what did we know? But he was trying to surrender!

"I hope it was a bomb," I said. "If not, it's pure evil."

"Or stupidity," said CJ.

"Cops are evil," said Saint.

"Cops are motherfuckers," said Vera.

I kept wishing I'd done something. As he stepped down into the blue light I should have grabbed him, pulled him back onto the safety of the curb. I could have knelt by the guy when he was down, stroked his head, held his hand. Made sure, if he was breathing, that no one came and finished him off. I saw him in my mind's eye stretched out on the street in his shining white shirt. "We could pray," I said.

No one seconded me.

"Was he dead?"

Saint shrugged, but beside me I could feel him shaking. CJ shook his head no. Vera laid her head against the window and closed her eyes. All the way back home I kept picturing the purity of his white shirt in the light from the streetlamp, as if his mother had just washed and bleached it. If there had been blood, I'd have noticed. I sat straight up in the backseat, breathing in out, in out, as if it were his breath I was breathing, as if my breathing would keep his chest going up and down.

14

Vera

It's two-thirty A.M., the house is blessedly dark, and she has never turned a key so silently, thanking the craftsman in her father that oils locks and hinges. There's no sound downstairs; everyone is sleeping as they ought to be. *4EVER* burns reassuringly in the hollow of her chest.

In the upstairs bathroom she removes the bandage, cleans the tattoo with Ivory soap, as she was told, and pats it lightly dry. She applies baby oil. Keep it moist, Marcus said. Don't let it scab up. In the mirror the letters over the dip of her breastbone look clean and sharp, as do the wings and beak of Kay's artful bird. Done bleeding, she hopes. She fastens two wide Band-Aids over the area to protect it while she sleeps, then towels off her underarms, towels her front teeth, careful not to run water. No toilet flushing. Back in her room she drops her clothes in a silent heap and slips naked under her covers, a violation of two of her mother's edicts. In every way, it's delicious.

Under the light, cool, clean sheet, lying on the edge of sleep, she imagines Saint loving her the way Garth does, with every part of himself—hands, lips, dick, and heart. Before her friends drove away she'd leaned over the open car, grabbed hold of Saint by his Zen-zombie head, and kissed him hard on the mouth, daring him to remain *beyond desire* when the point in life was getting what you wanted, and whoever denied it was a coward or a hypocrite. The guy who was shot tonight—he too wanted something that made him run like crazy. She's sinking into sleep when her door swings open, admitting the smell of beer and sweat that means her father. She feigns a sleepy turn to the wall, winding herself inside a protective sheath of cotton sheet, but there's no avoiding him. His bulk magnified by the emanations from his pores and his mouth, he plunks himself down in the space she vacated. "So what's the story, girl? More midnight rambling?"

Master of herself, she grips the side of the mattress to keep a gap between them. She says, still sleepily, "Please get out of here." He squeezes her upper arm.

"How much more do you expect me to take?"

"More what?"

"Don't get smart, Vera. I know you like a book."

Since when did you start reading books? runs through her mind, but she sits up wearily, holding the sheet to her chest. "Just punish me, okay? Get it over with. Hit me. Whatever you want." She wants to kick him off her mattress. She'd try, if she had clothes on. "Or go back to bed."

He leans toward her, pressing upon her his smell of alcohol and rank adult maleness. He's not much taller than she is, with a belly of middle age, but his arms are strong and his chest is thick; sandy hairs press through his T-shirt. He played high school football, a little guy who'd break your collarbone if you messed with him, and sometimes when he just felt like it—he'd say that about himself. His hard, hairy thighs angle away from each other from out of his boxer shorts. "There's no point in lying, Vera. Your brother told me."

Her head jerks back and bangs the wall. Under the covers her toes grope for a hold on the mattress.

"He says you're screwing around. Are you?"

She straightens her back. Her voice hurts her throat. She doesn't believe Garth said anything like that. And to their mutual enemy. "Could you be more specific?"

He grabs her arm. "You have a mouth, little girl."

"The better to eat you. I mean, to have a good heart-to-heart talk with you?" What is she saying? Her teeth are chattering. She raises her head to look him in the eye, but his upper regions seem cloaked in fog. Some nights are like that. "I don't know what I mean," she says.

His grip tightens. "Your baby brother says you're a slut. He says you're fucking one of your so-called *buddies.*"

An involuntary squeak rises up through her throat. She stares at her father, trying to see through his coarse features to what Garth might really have said. Lying to the perp is probably standard interrogation procedure. Divide the team. Sow distrust. She feels distrust. The little fucker, she'll strangle him. Laughing airily, she tugs her arm away from her father. "Detective Garth? FBI Agent Garth? I can't believe you believe him!" Especially confounding to her is the fact that she feels innocent of these particular charges, as if an event could be canceled out by what happened afterward, if that changed your feelings about it. She rubs her arm, which hurts where he squeezed. "He's that *age,* Dad. Boys—that's all they think about. They think everyone's doing it but them!"

He nods like he has her number, like he's cool. But he's simmering down. He turns on her bedside lamp. Light shines on the wide sweep of his brow. He looks like a fierce but well-meaning soccer coach who just wants his team to win. "Why don't you come down to the kitchen with me, make me an egg sandwich," he says. Then cagily, proud of his shrewdness: "I knew you weren't sleeping."

She resists the temptation to roll her eyes. This is his benign, *Father Knows Best* mode. She doesn't trust it for a second, though at age ten and eleven she'd get out of bed and cook him something, points for her in the old competition with her mother. "I don't know, Dad."

"You don't know your *dad*? Listen, honey. Did you know I got a promotion? Got the news yesterday. Detective DeVito, in charge of District Nine. Somebody shoots someone's dog from Grand Rapids all the way to Traverse City and I get to pick through the blood and fur—what do you think, sweetheart darling? Are you proud of your old man?" He stands. "Put on a robe or something, come on, rise and shine."

When he's gone, she looks for nightclothes. Her baby doll summer pj's are flimsy, her winter flannels too hot. She puts on underpants and a long blue bathrobe that came from her aunt in L.A. She ties the sash tight around her waist on her way downstairs. Between the living room and the kitchen is the door that leads to the basement room where the traitor Garth abides. Certain things seem clear now. Toward Garth she feels only rage.

In the kitchen her father is at the table drinking orange juice. She glides around him like a capable housekeeper, clicking on the gas, melting butter in the frying pan—wanting to get this done, for the night to be over. The place is clean like her mother left it—her mother, owning less and less of herself, who can still muster enough to put dishes away and sweep the floor. It's almost a violation to rummage through the orderly drawers, to take eggs and butter out of the refrigerator, and Vera maintains her mother's system, washing and drying everything as soon as it's used, wiping down jars, lids included, even when they're not sticky. Her robe slips down her shoulder and she pulls it closed. One of her Band-Aids has lost its stick. Turning her back to her father she presses the end to her chest ferociously. *Stay put!*

He wanted his eggs over hard, and he waits for them at the table like an ordinary father, one who loses his temper from time to time, regrettably. "I was lying in bed," he says, "but the old brain won't let go. They're sending me down to Chicago for training. Things are changing, honey, and I'm changing with them. Do you know that, except for the army, I've lived in this town all my life? I didn't go away to college. That's an advantage you'll have." He laces his fingers in front of him, then cracks his knuckles one by one. "God," he says, "if I could talk to your mother like this."

His voice hums with sudden respect for her, for what, she can't tell. Within his beer smell is the faint chemical sweetness of maraschino cherries. An ache gathers at the base of her throat. She's repelled and soothed. She pierces a yolk, mashes it down. The hardening whites of the eggs slap against the pan. In this mood of his, she might not even be grounded. In the morning he'll have forgotten it. He shouldn't drink, she thinks; he's almost sweet when he's sober. She remembers mowing the lawn with him on bright summer Sundays, her small hands between his large ones on the handle of their old push mower. She flips the eggy slab, slides it onto his buttered toast: "Chow's on." He laughs. She turns away from his bright eyes.

"You're something, daughter," he says. "Not just pretty, but smart like your mother. And stubborn as a mule. You'll go somewhere, no doubt about it!"

He plants a kiss inside her wrist. She retrieves her hand, but gently. Was her mom once smart? She quit school when she got pregnant.

"She was a brain," he says, as if he knows what she's thinking. "I was lucky she looked at me. She could have married a college professor. She used to say, anyway."

Then how did she get to be the way she is now? Vera says to herself. Her robe has loosened again; the silk is slippery. She yanks it closed. There's egg on her father's lower lip. She hands him a napkin, washes her hands.

"Don't go. Please?"

The eager, plaintive note in his voice surprises her. But before she can take the seat across from him, he pulls her toward him and kisses the side of her mouth. Stifling a gasp, she jumps away. He booms a laugh. "I thought you liked romantic kisses. That's what you called them. You'd climb on my lap and say, 'Kiss me like the movies.' Those were your words. If I tried to put you down you'd have a fit."

She wraps the sash twice around her waist and knots it. She folds her arms across her chest. "How old was I, five?"

With a face of mild and courteous regret, as if for a memory lapse, he gets up, washes his plate, and sets it in the rack. He cleans the frying pan, dries it over a burner, and sponges the sink with the slow care of a drinking man who is respectful of his wife's wishes, all the while describing Vera's future as he sees it. Business or politics, she has a head for both, unlike Garth, who was behind the door when they handed out brains. The kid's out of control. Old enough to get a job, and bolts—skips town like a felon!—when he gets what he deserves for disrespecting his father. Yvette is no help. He's thinking of military school for Garth, though it will cost. "You have no idea," he says to Vera, "what it's like to be a parent."

You didn't have to use your belt, she thinks but doesn't say. She says quietly, "I don't think you should send him to military school."

Drying his hands, he sits back down at the table, his eye-beams like a net around her. He's worried about Garth. Is the kid doing drugs? What kind of friends is he hanging out with? He knows how close they are, so maybe she can help him. What the hell happened down in Florida? If only he could talk with Garth like he can with Vera.

Vera looks hard at her father, who, in her opinion, knows her no better than he knows Garth. But before anything smart-ass can come to her lips, he's on to Deedra, his newest honey. He's a family man, but her mother doesn't really love him—Vera knows that, doesn't she?—and Deedra doesn't have Yvette's brains, but she's crazy about him. He's on the verge of weeping now. He wants a divorce, but how can he ask, with her mother sick like that? Once before, he wept in front of Vera, for angry envy of his two hotshot older brothers, who work for their wives' fathers and make big bucks sitting on their tails. Now across the old kitchen table Vera resumes her seat. She puts her head down on the varnished hardwood, trying not to think about anything at all while he praises her understanding of the world and of him.

She must have nodded off during the barrage, because when awareness returns, the tribute is over. He's standing over her, angry again. "Do you think I don't know what time you walked in to-night?" She shuts her eyes, then reopens them; he's still there. "Let's have the truth for a change."

A laugh starts, very deep down in her. This is how it starts.

"Vera, I'm responsible for you, until you're eighteen I'm responsible. We both know your track record."

She wishes for a moment she could just tell him the truth. What was wrong with driving down to Chicago with her friends? He didn't punish Garth when he got back from Florida. But lying is what she does with him, her part in their unfurling drama. "I was at Kay's." She swallows, takes a breath, then hands him another crumb of information lackadaisically, as if it's beneath her interest and ought to be beneath his. "We watched a movie on TV, and in the middle of it"—she simulates a yawn—"we both fell asleep. I know I should have called, but it was late, I didn't want to wake Mom." She presses her lips together against the seepage of irony. "I could have slept at Kay's, but you know how you get when you wake up and I'm not home. I'm really sorry."

He scoots his chair to her around the table, hoists her leg onto his lap, and begins to massage the ball of her foot. This too has happened before. As always, bumps rise on the back of her tongue. "You shouldn't be smoking," he says.

"We shared *one*. One cigarette! It gets in your hair. But you're right, I know that."

He presses on her arch with both of his thumbs, prodding deeply this side of pain. It feels good and it feels worse than awful. The leg not attended to begins to tremble, and she folds it onto the seat of her chair, wraps it in the slippery cloth of her robe. What would a normal girl do right now?

"It's my last one, I swear," she says.

"Do you think I don't know when you've been smoking? Do you think I'm an idiot?"

"Do you really want me to answer that?" She smiles quickly, defusing her joke. "I know I shouldn't smoke. I know I should have called."

"One of these days, you're going to learn respect, Vera. If I have to take you over my knee." He has the ball of the foot of her extended leg in his hands. He pulls the shelf of her toes back, hard. She waits for the crack of the little bones. "You were with the Mick tonight, don't you dare lie to me." At that, she opens her mocking eyes wide upon him. He has iron-gray hair thick as a rug, a wide, sloped forehead, and the strong, dull, single-minded glare, she thinks, of a Viking. There are things she can say to him, snottinesses so subtle he won't even know to be pissed. His gaze lifts to the V of her robe. "What's that?"

She pulls it closed too late. A Band-Aid is sticking out.

"What the fuck," he says, "have you done to yourself?"

"Would you believe open-heart surgery?"

His ears redden.

She has no heart for this. She wants to get back into bed and think about Saint. But it's a game they've been playing for years. She'll tell him the story eventually—of the car trip, the baseball game, the tattoos, the shooting, with a final crack about trigger-happy cops. Then he'll ask who drove, who paid, who all went, who sat where. And eventually she will supply those answers as well, countering his incipient rage with her mildness successfully, until she admits that Saint was with them. Now she goes straight to the end of the story. "We got tattoos, all of us: Kay, CJ and I, and Saint."

"Saint? What kind of name is that?"

"Dad," she says softly, "why do you like to pretend you never heard of him? He's been our friend for two years. His name is St. John. Scully," she adds.

She's as sincere and respectful as she knows how to be, but it seems to come out snarky, or maybe it isn't, but it's tainted with the snark of times past.

"It makes me sick!" he shouts. "It breaks my heart! You're balling a piece of shit that calls himself Saint!" He stands over her chair and his head seems to brush the ceiling. Other things in the room look large as well: table, refrigerator. With the tips of his fingers he slaps her face, not hard, nearly a pat, the way you chastise a lapdog.

"Stop, please, Dad."

His face is so close she's bathed in his maraschino breath, a metallic sweetness. Does she want to be hurt? She's tired of pain. Bone-tired. Nerve- and brain-tired. Her good hand raises her weak one in front of his eyes, where it dangles limp as a hankie. He pauses, then slaps her hand down. "Really, Dad. You don't want to do this."

They eye each other like boxers circling in the ring; both are panting. Then he puts a hand to his head. "Do you know how important you are to me?" he says. "You're the most important thing in the world." He pats her arm. There are tears in his voice. "I don't want you to make mistakes. I couldn't stand it if anything happened to you."

She regards his massive hand on her arm, regards his shame and apology. When he lets go, her arm bobs a moment, testing its freedom. She stands on wobbly legs.

"I'm sorry. But Jesus, Vera, don't ever lie to me! It screws up everything." His voice trails off as he rises and walks away, back to his bed in the den. "You're a beautiful girl. You'll grow up and meet lots of men who'll appreciate you. Don't waste it on . . ."

She holds on to the back of a chair while his door clicks shut.

Then behind the closed door between kitchen and living room she hears the scramble of feet descending stairs; she flings the door open. It's dark but she feels his presence, the shithead who started this. She can't find the light switch, but she shuts the door behind her and makes her way down. There's no light from Garth's room either, but she strides in that direction; she shouts into the darkness, beyond caring, "You fucking spy!" Feeling her way along the side of the ping-pong table, she arrives at his doorway. "If you keep following me, Garth—if you say one more word to Dad about what doesn't concern you—"

"It all concerns me," he says.

They are face-to-face on his threshold, though they can barely see each other. Garth's voice trembles with emotion, but she's too angry to take it in; she hisses into the dark, "If you stick your nose in my business, if you fuck with me and my friends one more time, I will come to your room at night and put my hands around your neck and strangle you!"

"Feel free," he says. "Sweet death at your hands."

"Stop that! What do you know about anything? It's sickening, this idolizing love shit. It's *mental*!"

Perhaps cowed by her force, he has stepped back into his room, which seems alien to her without music playing. She steps forward—she has points to make, things he has to understand—and her foot hits something large and light. It scrapes the cement floor. "Turn on the goddamned light," she says, then finds the wall switch.

On the floor by the wall lies the guitar he bought last year with money he earned shoveling snow. Knobs and bits of plastic surround the body of the instrument, which is cracked down the middle, attached to its neck only by the strings. It's like a dead thing—or worse, and though she steels herself against the image of a murder committed, she can't escape the resultant horror and fear. Uncharacteristically, she wants to cry. "Oh, Garth, you *love* your guitar."

"I love lots of things."

"You moron. You'll get yourself locked up."

"In a cell with you, big sis."

She makes a fist with her strong hand and punches his shoulder. "Did you learn that from Dad?"

She snorts fiercely, helplessly. "Do you think that's clever?" She folds her hands across her chest. "Understand, Garth. You don't know *any*thing." Her brother, who seems to be losing his mind, stands loose and limp like a rag doll. She says, more gently, "What do you want from me?"

He looks straight into her eyes. "Do you think you can do . . . whatever you want with me, then act like nothing happened?"

"Please," she says.

"Why are things different now? Don't you love me?"

"Love you? Of course I love you. I'll always love you." She pats his shoulder where her fist was.

"More!" he says. "I like your silky robe thing. I'm feeling swoony.

I'm going to faint, Vera." He hangs in her arms. She settles him onto the floor. "You're just pretending," he says, "to be a hard-ass."

"I'm getting out of here."

"Don't. Please don't." He lies on the floor in a pile of himself. "Vera, we're perfect for each other. We fit together like yin and yang. Like Ian and Sylvia!" He smiles loosely, as if whatever she wants to do with him is A-okay. "I don't know what I'd do without you."

"You'd take care of your stuff. You'd go out and play basketball." She pats his cheek, feels his shudder of gratitude. She rises quickly. "Come on, let's restore, you know, normalcy?" With the side of her foot she begins pushing the breakage toward a central pile. "Get a shopping bag. We can finish before Mom gets up. Otherwise you'll have to pick someone to blame it on. One of your druggie friends came over and had a meltdown?" She picks up his guitar, neck and body, and sets the pieces on the shelf beside the record player. "What did you take, Garthy? More acid or something? Or is this your natural psychosis?"

He picks up one of his records and Frisbees it across the room. It hits the wall and breaks.

She feels a rush of what might be despair and wonders for a moment if this is what her mother feels when she opens a door onto mess. The floor of his room is awash in dirty clothes, books, crumpled pieces of paper, the detritus of his hopelessness. In frustration she kicks at a pile of rubbish and something spins across the floor. It's a pistol, smaller than their father's, like a well-made toy. She picks it up—hard, black, and heavy for its size. "Where did this come from?" She holds it by the butt, careful to point it at the floor. "Garth," she exhales, "what is this for?"

"Holding up banks."

"Oh shit. Oh shit."

He walks to her, breathing on her the warm, sweet, small animal breath of someone with outstanding teeth who never brushes them. "It's for protection. So I can walk the streets of Lourdes without being afraid." Is he telling the truth? He presses his lips to her cheek, then offers his cheek to her lips, at the same time grabbing for the gun. She turns and blocks him.

Guns are not unfamiliar to her. When she was seven or eight their father would empty his service revolver and let her open the chamber and look inside. She's not sure if Garth received the same training. Once, under her father's supervision, she loaded it, cocked it, and pulled the trigger, aiming out at the lake, and she laughed with the blast and muscle of it, though the recoil hurt her arm. But this one looks even deadlier—its very smallness, its anonymous density. Circling to keep her back to Garth, she clicks open the chamber. Her hands work together, the small and the large, master and servant comfortable with their roles. A single bullet falls onto her palm. "Where did this come from? Florida? Or do you have some new friends? Tell me, Garth. Are there more bullets?" He doesn't answer. Her voice thins and rises to a soft wail. "You know, you would've fallen asleep and forgotten about it! Mom would have found it when she came to clean!" What their mother might have done with it, she will not think about. With the gun in one hand and the bullet in the other, she makes for the door. He runs in front of her.

"Kill me. Come on. I dare you."

"Stupid talk."

"Vera, listen to me. We did it once and the gates of hell didn't open! This floor didn't split open and swallow us down."

The gun rises in her hand, points at her brother. Both know it's empty, but he stands with a little martyred smile on his face, arms out. When after several moments she lowers the gun, he remains before her, head high, eyes open wide, looking straight at her like a brave man facing a firing squad. "I don't want to talk about it," she says. "Ever again." Her knees are shaking. Sweat drips down her sides.

He gazes on her brightly, with his eyes that take in the world's sadness and turn it hard and clear as crystal. She touches his arm, his skin softer than a boy's is meant to be. She lets go. "Chill, brother. Don't act weirder than you absolutely have to." She walks to the door, then turns around. Her heart is beating neutrally now, rationally, the heart of a normal sister. Please, God, may it remain so. "Whatever you think you know about me or my friends, keep Dad out of it. Okay?"

"Wait."

"What?"

He walks over. Stands close. "I didn't tell Dad about you. I swear. But there's stuff I could say. That I could have said—"

Her cry rises to where only a dog could hear it. "Is this some weird blackmail? Don't be a psycho!" She takes his hand in both of hers, kisses it tenderly, then gives it a shake. His face looks so much older and wiser than anyone else's face. But he is crazy. Or what he is saying sounds crazy to her. She pushes away from him, shuts his door as quietly as she can. Back at last in her own room, she quickly stuffs the gun and its single bullet into a thick wool sock and stows it at the bottom of her backpack, which she puts in the closet between two quilts. Then she lies down and tries not to think about Garth or Saint or anyone.

15

Saint

———

The boy was seventeen, Saint hears on the radio. He was Saint's age, and he had a name, Dean Johnson, and he was a Sioux from South Dakota. Or maybe he wasn't a Sioux, he was just from Sioux Falls. The facts get murkier as they accrue. He was with a friend; he was alone. He'd come for the convention; he'd come for work. He was shot three times; Saint heard only one shot. But did he have a gun? That he pointed at a cop? All Saint saw was the kid raising his arms in surrender, although *"according to police, Johnson's gun misfired. . . ."*

Saint dislikes conflicting information. He is further unsettled by the one fact the reporters agree upon, that Dean Johnson is dead. The death seems indisputably wrong. The whole saga makes him feel muddled and stupid about himself. But at the same time he is happy this morning, intensely. So he is bopping along country roads in the dawn's early light, riding to the Haight before his friends will be there. After a week of trying in vain to expunge from his brain the "thing" with CJ (the lapse; craziness?)—after meditating long and hard to ban any trace of a naked male from his brain (even as he knows that banning an image is the best way to summon it), suddenly, blam! the worry is gone. Vera might have kissed him last night as a joke or a taunt, but it aroused him. He was aroused by a girl, and he still is; he wants a girl! He feels only compassion for CJ, whose feelings he has hurt, though unintentionally. He must find a way to make it up to him.

The Pledge will come due in eight days, but it's nothing he has to think about now, as he enters the park. After circling the empty field, he parks his bike by the pay phone near the restrooms and calls Vera, so happy at the prospect of the sound of her voice he doesn't even plan out what he'll say. Unfortunately he gets the old man, who recognizes his voice at the first stammer. "You go anywhere near my girl I'll have your balls, do you hear me? I'll cut them off and hang them from my rearview mirror—" The threat follows Saint back to his scooter.

He rides to Vera's street, chains his bike to a tree around the corner, sits and watches the sun rise. People pass—a boy on a bike, an old man with a carved wooden cane, a woman with three tiny dogs on one leash. The sky is brightening, with heat on the edges of things. He's about to head back to the park to wait when he feels a flicker at the base of his skull like an electrical charge. He doesn't even have to look to know it's her.

She turns in the opposite direction without seeing him. He calls her name, but too softly. He stumbles to his feet like a drunk and follows her, a block or so behind, reluctant now to make his presence known. Is this a weird thing to do? Well, he's doing it. At the Haight, instead of crossing toward their spot by the bluff she turns south into the woods, moving fast, and now he wishes he had his bike. Still he continues along the groomed path through the trees to the narrow sandy trail along the bluff. The trail moves downhill as it goes south, the drop to the beach lessening. He thought she was going to CJ's, but he passes the wall at the edge of the property without a glimpse of her. He follows the path, quickening his pace till he comes to the flight of railroad ties that descend to the beach.

He has lost her. The lake stretches below, almost white against the blue sky. Patches of fog lie on the water. The lake is still, except for its regular slow, foamless swells, a gentle rise and fall like the chest of someone sleeping. Perhaps she jumped CJ's wall and is back there hiding from him? It makes no sense, but then Vera doesn't always make sense. With a deep breath, slowing his heart like a yogi, he makes a choice and starts down to the beach.

Halfway down the slope, he sees a swimmer out in the lake, hair fanning behind like a trail of seaweed. Now he's hurtling down, almost falling. He lands on his knees and ignores the pain; he flies across pebbly sand and—no time to undress—flings himself into the water, clothes and all.

He's not a great swimmer; he didn't learn till he moved here. And it's slow going in sodden jeans. A few more brain cells and he'd have taken his shoes off. He pulls them off now, jeans too, and hurls them backward over his shoulder without turning to see what hits the shore. The water is cold and it gets colder the farther out he goes, but he can move now. Then the sandbar falls away and he's swimming forcefully toward where he thinks she is, though with his eyes full of water he can only guess, and he's splashing too hard to hear anything but himself.

At that thought he stops, treads water, and there she is, ahead but not far. Her crawl is steady, efficient, not frantic; he can't tell what's on her mind except that she's resolutely swimming away from the beach. With a dozen laboring strokes he's past her and circling, in the way of wherever she means to go. He has strength, if not skill. No harm will befall her on his watch, even if it makes her angry. He tries to keep his head above the swells, to keep her in sight. Then she ducks under a wave and suddenly vanishes. When he sees her again she is yards away, swimming toward shore.

He follows, not unhappily. His surge of energy is depleted, and he concentrates on moving one arm, then the other, lifting his head only to keep her in view. On the sandbar, where the water comes to his waist and her chest, she regards him without pleasure. A horsefly lands on her forehead; she swats it; it plunks between them. He feels her disgust with the insect body, its heft, its mere and purposeless (to her lights) existence. Her small breasts bob in the surf. She was smart enough to take off her clothes. The bandage over his tattoo has loosened; he pulls it out from under his shirtsleeve and watches it float away, then start to sink. There's a sting on his arm that he hasn't noticed till now. His gaze moves to the mark between her breasts, *4EVER;* he's glad for the link between them. She says, "What the fuck are you doing here?"

"Christ," he says, "I thought you were . . ."

"What?"

His eyebrows scrunch stupidly together. "I was afraid . . . Shit. I'm sorry."

"Sorry?" Quickly, as if her mere speaking is a favor to him, she says, "I know what you thought. You thought I was going to drown myself." Her face is so cold upon him, it makes him dizzy. "You don't know the faintest thing about me."

He finds his jeans rising and falling with the shoreline waves. Back on the sand, he wrings them out and pulls them, dripping, up his legs quickly, before she finishes dressing. He wants to feel her wet body against him, but it's not an option. He tries a joke. "I thought you were swimming back to Chicago." She doesn't laugh or even smile. "Knock knock?"

"I can't relate to you, Saint."

"But would you like to? Relate to me?"

Her look is pure ire.

"Yesterday we related, didn't we? You keep changing on me."

"What are you talking about?"

With her hair flattened to her head, her features are sharp and terrible in the light of morning: her brow, the high ridge of her nose. It hurts his eyes—her beautiful, skeletal face with the day swelling open. "Nothing happened yesterday," she says. "Nothing between us. Why is everyone following me?"

The thing he loves and hates most about her is how she changes on a dime, for nothing. Her flickering moods emit a kind of iridescence. He has gone blank; there are no words in his mind, nothing to hold on to. He's about to fall into the hole of his weakness and idiocy; then for no good reason she wraps her arms around his arm. He's afraid to move. She kisses his shoulder, touches his cheek, then smooths her hair behind her ears and looks around. It's blue toward the Haight, bright and hot. Southward is fog. "Thank you for try-

ing to save my life, Saint. For wanting to. Really." She picks up her
pack and sets off south along the sandy beach, leaving a buzzy spot
on his shoulder where her lips touched.

He stands still, inside his chest a cup of water that he mustn't spill.
He respects her need to be alone. He scans the beach for his
sneakers—there's no money in the house for a new pair—and finds
them so clogged with sand he has to rinse them off in the waves. No
time to put them on. By now Vera has shrunk with distance and almost vanished into the fog. Like an idiot he starts after her again,
barefoot, far enough away so as not to intrude.

When the big rocks start, she clambers up without slowing, leap-
ing from boulder to boulder like a goat, while he's a lumbering zoo
rhinoceros, a flapping seal. His wet jeans rub against his legs but he
pushes on, along the spill of boulders, shifting, slippery, sometimes
sharp under his feet—and soon he's farther down the beach than he
has ever been. Looking up to see how far away she is, he steps on
something; blood is seeping. The skin of his thighs is burning and
so is the tattoo on his arm. He shoves his feet into his dripping
shoes. When he checks for her again, she's gone.

Anger clogs his throat. *Saint the victim.* This is the story of his life,
it seems, though it's only two or three years that he's been chasing
girls who treat him like shit. But he pushes on over the boulders, *om
namah shivaya,* till he comes to a wide, flat rock that tilts so steeply
he has to make his way around it. On the lake side he finds an opening. A shallow bunker has been formed by the convergence of four
boulders, wider at the bottom than at the top, like a flask. And inside, sprawled on the sandy floor, Vera is looking up at him as if she
has been waiting way too long.

"Yes, I followed you, so what? So I'm a stalker." He lowers himself down. The temperature drops; the air feels wet. Dismissing a
shiver, he sits across from her. The place is almost entirely enclosed,
a hideaway out of a solitary child's dream. "Just talk to me. After we
dropped you off, was it okay? Did anyone hear you come in?"

She shrugs. Her eyes are closed. "I was quiet as a little mousie."

He moves closer. "Vera? You said your dad can be a real . . ." He trails off, picturing the mouse bones of her rib cage going in and out. He thinks of Lennie, the retarded guy in that novel they read last year who accidentally kills someone. *All he wants is to pet soft things.* The line is all he remembers, though it made him queasy then and still does. But on the damp sand in the murky grotto, she's a little fairy light, and he wants to keep it alive. He sits on his hands so that he won't accidentally damage anything and tells her what he has been thinking. Her quick, shallow breaths scrape his heart.

"I want to be with you," he says. "I'll even play by your rules. When we're not together you can screw whoever, just don't tell me about it."

"Is that what you think I want?"

His brain floods as if with a caustic liquid that burns away the delicate connections. "I thought you thought I was too possessive."

She rolls her eyes.

"Honestly, I don't want to control you or anything," he says, feeling his cheeks heat up. It's so hard, with her, to say what he means. Sometimes he doesn't even know what he means, he's like a worm or a mole, blindly pushing its way through dark earth. "Sometimes I think you want me to . . . I don't know, be more of a bruiser? More *forceful,* does that make any sense?" She regards him fiercely. "Vera? I mean, what *do* you want?"

Her skin is perfectly clear and white, without discolorations or freckles. How can skin look like that? He wants to lick her like a dog, her eyelids and down the side of her nose. He should leave before he gets even more pathetic. He clambers to his feet. "Okay. Well. See you later."

"Where are you going?" She's rooting through her backpack.

"I'm sorry. I don't want to bug you."

"What is wrong with you? Don't go—do you hear me!" He blinks. She's pointing a gun at him.

After the shock it's instinctive. He ducks, lunges at her, and in a moment he has the gun. But he's shaking. Sweat is pouring out of him. His palms, his underarms, are soaking wet. She's rolling her eyes again. "Saint, it was a joke!"

He stands, gulping deep, enraged breaths of air. *Saint the victim.* She is smoke, ungraspable; how come he never saw that before? "You have a problem, Vera. How could *anyone* be with you?"

She explains where the gun came from. Her brother's a mess. She doesn't know what to do about him. She's telling the truth, he imagines, but something doesn't jibe. "Don't change the subject," he says.

She apologizes for screwing around with the gun. It wasn't loaded. But it was stupid, a bad joke. Not funny. She shouldn't have done it. "I am truly sorry," she says.

She might still be mocking; how would he know? "You apologize so easily, Vera."

"It's *not* easy. I *hate* apologizing." They look at each other, trying to understand what underlies each other's words. "Here's another truth," she says. "I really don't want you to leave. Do you believe me?"

Now it's hard for them to pull their gazes apart. They seat themselves again, face-to-face, in the flask-shaped haven from which it's hard to depart with any panache. He isn't cold anymore. Talk is easier. She predicts that he won't keep the Pledge. He'll marry a good Catholic girl and take their kids to church on Sunday. He loves looking at her. "I like bad Catholic girls," he says, and takes her hand.

With a sour smile, she withdraws that hand and offers the other, the small one. Her eyes are glittery hard. But tenderly, as if gathering up the petals of a damaged flower, he draws the hand to his lip and kisses the back, then the palm, trembling. "Would you mind now—you don't have to, really, but would you mind," she whispers, "kissing my short fingers? Sucking would be acceptable too. If it's not too disgusting?" She looks frightened by her own request, b₁ he is humble and eager, the way he felt touching a girl for the f₁ time, thrilled and desperate with wanting. He uncurls the hand one by one, puts her nubs in his mouth and sucks hard like a calf. She's shaking from the small of her back, violent waves of what might be pleasure. When he lets go she withdraws the hand to the shelter of her tube top. She says, "Was that disgusting?"

"Nauseating. Revolting." He reaches for her hand again. Failing that, he touches her knee. "I'm kidding, Vera. I learned it from you. It's the opposite of disgusting."

Now, quickly, she pulls down her cutoffs. He's ready to oblige. More than. He folds his jeans into a pillow for her head, apologizes for their dampness. But something is wrong. In the field beside Hamburger Heaven she was fierce with wanting, her skin hot, her body pushing toward his hands. Now only her voice moves, and her skin is cool and dry. She starts dirty-talking, but beneath him her body is inert. He rolls onto the sand beside her. "Do you want me to do something special?" She covers her face with the side of her arm. "Vera?"

He puts his arms around her, not like John Steinbeck's Lennie but carefully, gently. Then, precise and flat, as if she's reading from a book, she tells him what happened with her father in the kitchen last night. The mind-fuck of it. He didn't hit her hard. Saint says, "He should be locked up."

She rolls her eyes. It was nothing new. In a way she was asking for it.

He feels simpleminded with her, as he often does, but he can't accept her self-critique. He berates her father, and anyone who abuses their power, and though she might not accept his reasoning, she seems to accept his fury on her behalf. He wants to do battle for her. Martial images ride through his brain.

When she starts to talk again, it's flat and murmurous, as if she's singing him to sleep, as if she wants him to fall asleep so he won't hear what she is compelled to say. But he's listening harder than he has ever listened to anything. It wasn't the slaps that fucked her up. They didn't hurt. And she doesn't mind pain; at times she craves it. "My brain is wired wrong," she says, squeezing her eyes shut. "I don't know how else to explain it. Sex and violence are mixed up in me. And even that's not it, exactly." She moves out of the haven of his arms. He shifts in order to accommodate her. "Last night at first I tried to avoid a fight. I tried to appease him. I played small and meek." She squeezes her hands between her legs. "I have no control over anything. Oh God. Even that's not it." With a gasp of weary sadness so deep it seems to come from down in the earth, she heaves out, "The thing is, I *wanted* him to hurt me. I know it's sick."

She sits on the sand like a featherless bird; he gathers words for her like worms. "All four of us are fucked up some way. And maybe everyone is?"

She takes hold of his hands. "I'm not that scared of him, Saint. I'm scared of myself." She swallows. "There are things I could do— that I've done. . . ."

He thinks he knows exactly what she means. "I love you," he says, and he feels it (he is not queer). He is smiling like an idiot.

A few minutes later they walk back, she to the Haight. He goes first to his scooter to lock up the gun, which she placed in his care along with the woolen sock and its single bullet. Then he rides to the Haight, awed by what he is coming to know about this girl, and exhilarated by her reliance on him.

But all that day at the park with their friends it's as if the events of the morning never occurred. She is sheathed in a giddy friendliness toward him that's worse than nastiness, and he understands his terrible mistake. He has violated love's rule number one. You have to stay on the brink. You must resist the State of the Heart Address, immediately after which (as your teeth come down on the *v* in "I love," even before the "you") you feel the bite of loss. While he—in the clutches of pity for her or his sublimated lust or just his usual pitiful self-abasement—threw himself on the mercy of a court he already knew was merciless.

16

Vera

The following morning, she arrives at the Haight in a pair of her mother's old Bermuda shorts and an extra-large T-shirt from a package her father hasn't opened yet. The shirt swallows her hips, the shorts hang past her knees; she's done with looking good. In seven days her thinking will stop once and for all, and the point now is for time to pass. She has brought the blanket from her bed for people to sit on. She will babble and riff with her friends and play contract bridge with them on the blanket. She plays well when she puts her mind to it. Partnerships rotate, and they are keeping personal scores; she is close behind Kay.

Today she is Kay's partner, and CJ and Saint have just bid an unmakeable slam. With four trumps headed by the queen/jack, and seated behind the declarer, Vera has resisted doubling for penalty, though she's not sure whether it's from care for Saint, who made the wild bid, or fear of alerting CJ, about to play the hand, to a situation he might be able to handle if he expected it. CJ eyes the dummy and openly glowers at Saint. "You talk about the Clear Light—what all you Buddhists are questing for!—but right now you're lost in the fog. Are you high by chance?"

Saint flushes easily; his freckled face is bright pink in the shade of the tree they are seated under. Kay is laughing, and even Saint joins in. Vera puts her hands under her big shirt and hugs her midriff. Who said truth will set you free? Even when her sins were venial— a creepier word than "mortal"—confession was a joke, since in pure and simple truth she hated the sin less than the sound of the priest's absolving voice, not to mention her own voice in false acquiescence. She remembers a hideous gap in the flow of Father Guston's words, in which he was no doubt picturing exactly what it meant when she said she had touched herself under the covers. After which she by-passed that particular sin, along with others so subtle or complicated they were hard to describe. She would tell him she had disobeyed her mother but not that she hated her mother for being someone she was supposed to love but in truth despised and, worse, was afraid she'd turn into, which felt like the real sin. All of this she has kept to herself until yesterday, when she made the mistake of telling Saint a few seamy truths. Oh God. She could have blabbed on till everything came gushing out.

She casts a glance out of the corner of her eye at Saint, handsome and awkward amid people's laughter, trying to be a good sport. Her heart squeezes. He loves her, or so he said, tempting her to confess what could never be told, as if he could grant absolution.

Is he looking at her? She's afraid to lift her head.

Yesterday was so . . . "uncomfortable" doesn't hit it. Freakish. His "I love you" offered absolution without penance. It could heal nothing. He may have meant it; he doesn't speak idly. But in her experience, and in her own heart, love can come and love can go.

Inside the casing of her big shirt, she tries to take in the love he declared without pushing it past its capacity to succor. But how to gauge the sturdiness of someone's love? She needs the heavy-duty kind that will surround her like padding, swathes and swathes of durable love, to hold her aloft like a bird or cushion her fall from a height. She's actually not sure it exists, but she has known its close cousin exactly twice in her life, with Garth on acid and once long ago at a performance of *The Nutcracker* when the tiny ballerina leaped into the air and her mother whispered in her ear, "You can do that too." She named it "white wonder," the closest description of the experience that she could find. For a moment she felt the world and herself as one entity, free of boundaries, a vision so intense and encompassing that she couldn't imagine anything outside it. She couldn't even imagine an end, though of course there was one. Protecting her fragile psyche with the one simple policy: *not to need*. She must float above the hard ground of need, for love or any other thing.

"Earth to Vera," says Kay. "Time to play a card?"

They play the hand, which Vera allows CJ to make by offering her jack to his king, her queen to his ace. Kay stares openmouthed at the lapse of mind, which cannot be accidental. "I mean, Vee! It's like you want them to win?" Vera begins to apologize. Then Saint is looking at her as he did in their cave, and it's like a light all around her.

Dazzled by irrational joy, she puts her arms around Kay's waist, pulls her up, and tries to swing her around. Kay shrieks, "So now you're Supergirl!" Kay is laughing, having forgotten the botched game, and Vera laughs too. Wind blows their hair. Wind blows through the pores of Vera's skin, in and around the striations of her muscles, between the slats of her ribs, over and under the tattoo between her breasts. She's beyond the sexual fray, the wheel (as Saint says) of desire and temporary, limited satisfaction, of birth and rebirth. She's high on chastity like a virgin priestess, and she loves Kay, dear Kay. "Kay," she cries, "it looks like you've lost a huge amount of weight. Do you know that?"

With a last surge of whatever has filled her, she lifts Kay a foot off the ground and sets her down softly, then flops back onto the blanket under the tree. Saint lies on the far side of the group, his eyes closed. She looks up at the dark underside of the maple leaves, the bits of sky between them. CJ turns up the radio. "Mr. Tambourine Man" pours across the field onto the playground, the tennis courts, the lake beyond.

It's one of Saint's favorite songs. Riding home after a night shift he'll sing it at the top of his lungs over the engine roar. Vera listens and tries to hear it as he does. But her radiant energy is gone now.

Feeling cut off and weary, she changes the station. "Do you mind? Let's hear something more upbeat?"

The others object. With uncharacteristic compliance she returns to the station. "The group rules," she says.

But she's a mess now. As soon as she gets a good feeling it collapses. Pleasure, pain, pleasure, pain. The wheel of dharma, of death and rebirth. She waits for the song to end, the ache to lift. *I love you,* she says to herself. Which Saint said to her—she reminds herself!— yesterday afternoon but hasn't repeated. Has she made him angry? Without wanting to, she sometimes makes people angry, she knows that. She shuffles the deck. Praise God for bridge, and hallelujah for Kay and CJ, four so much better than two. But the game has stalled in the magnetic field of the Dylan song, which seems to her excessively long. CJ's mouth moves with the lyrics. Saint says, "I've heard it a hundred times and it still gets to me."

Vera is careful not to look at Saint, but she looks in his direction. Even if he loves her as she wants to be loved, she's not sure she loves him. As a friend, yes, but not romantically. Sexual doesn't mean romantic. She considers whether to tell him that but hopes she won't need to say anything. No law says she has to feel what he feels. Someone's rich, someone else is poor; someone goes nuts, another sits in control and comfort—so it goes.

Without looking at Saint, however, she hears him in conversation with CJ, his voice steady and sure and unaware of her, and now she isn't at all certain of him. She is, in fact, a little frightened of him, because, even though she doesn't love him, she would feel bad if his mind changed about her. It isn't fair, of course, or reasonable. But if he decided that he loved someone else (unlikely as it seems) she wouldn't like it. At all. The others are sprawled on their backs. She moves closer to where Saint is lying.

Suddenly she thinks of a joke. Not a great joke—just something she heard somewhere. She rarely tells jokes. She's crappy at it, rushes the buildup, mistimes the punch line. But this one is just a question and answer. "Hey, compadres. Why do guys have bigger brains than dogs?" With an eye on Saint, she waits the appropriate beat. "So they won't hump your leg in the cafeteria!"

There's a general hoot, with Kay the loudest. Kay and CJ proffer jokes of their own, but Saint makes no comment, lying on his back with an arm over his eyes. Was he even listening? She nudges him with her knee. "Hey, asshole?"

He opens his eyes. They're blank, not even perplexed. He smiles as if he's forcing it. As if he feels sorry for her. A sprout of fear pushes up from her heart. She lifts her chin, presents him her profile to re-awaken his dignified, subdued longing for her, sorry now that she's dressed like a bag lady. Of course, she reminds herself, nothing has happened between them that she can't retreat from or cast into the void of insignificance. She wants to get up and walk away from them, to a picnic table or home; fuck them all. She thinks of the day seven days from now that they call P-Day, which went unmentioned today. As if it didn't matter to anyone but her. Not that she needs company.

As usual, at dinnertime CJ and Kay depart. But Saint remains, though his job starts at four, doesn't it? *He loves me,* she says to herself. Though what a person said yesterday doesn't guarantee *now* and maybe not even *then.* The connection between words and feelings shifts even as you speak, and again as the other person looks back at you, she reminds herself, while Saint lies still on the blanket with his eyes half-closed, his hands folded under his head like a surfer boy's.

She stands groggily, puts a steadying hand on the tree trunk. Across the field some middle school girls are playing softball. Beyond the chain-link fence the sun is sinking into the lake. Splats of red and gold dance on the blue water. There's a little rainstorm in her brain, then a narrow blade of light, a pain that flares and refuses to die away, and it occurs to her that she loves Saint. The insight isn't joyful or even agreeable. She walks to the fence, looks through it and down, considers jumping, and doesn't want to. Not now. She is in pain, but all of a sudden she doesn't want it to end.

On the edge of the blanket she finds a place as far as she can get from Saint and sits, hands in her lap, her brain pulsing like a small dying sun. She is burning out while Saint, at rest, is fully alive, his freckled skin and even the red hairs that grow from the top of his lip. Then, without volition, she has uncurled, she is snaking toward him, aligning herself with the length of him. His arm gathers her in. His lips are moist on her forehead. She feels the kiss, takes a cautious breath of him. In her mind she says, *Wait a little; wait till I want you more.* Overhead the darkening bones of the branches arc into a fili-greed dome. A bird calls out. The tree is full of birds twittering. The air is cooler, the sky a deep, luminous blue. She touches the tufts of his eyebrows, the soft skin of his eyelids and temples. She places her palms, large and small, on the flats of his cheeks.

His body is vibrating as if it were connected to what generates the turning of the earth, and he pulls her toward him. "Not yet," she whispers, though all of a sudden she wants him so much she could cry or die. On the tennis court a hundred yards away someone is riding a bicycle, around and around. "Time to go, Jamie. Okay, once more, but that's it!" The picnic area is empty, and so is the playground, and at last the baseball diamond: no one to see or care. She rubs a bare sole over the hairs of his leg, hides her face in his neck while her body simultaneously clings to him and pushes away.

Darkness gathers; a thumbnail moon rises over the lake. Mosqui-toes and sand fleas dart, attack, and Saint and Vera hold on to each other. They kiss each other's faces any which where. Sometimes as their intensity mounts, to slow their hearts and their breathing they talk. He tells her about the girls he loved before her. *Thought* he loved, in the wasteland before he met her. No one came close.

The wind is cool, and they talk to keep warm. She tells him about her prior—not *loves,* never loves—but amusing or crazy-wild or gross *fucks,* condensing for the sake of brevity. One she leaves out. It can't be said now, with her legs wrapped around his leg, her soles pressing his bare calves. It can be contained like Garth's gun, in a little storage box in her brain.

He might have felt the small lurch of her thought. At any rate, he moves back a little. "Now you know everything about me," he says.

"Do I?"

"Everything that's important."

"Is that a good thing?" She feels him seeing her, and herself being seen. The sensation is not entirely pleasant. But she is careful not to impede what is running between them. "Two people can't know everything about each other. And even if they could, who says it's good?"

He snorts. "You're doing that weasel thing."

"So?" With both hands together she touches his cheeks, his lips.

"You can be a bitch, Vera. You always have to have the upper hand."

"True."

"Vera." His voice trembles. He asks for the truth once again. Why she wanted to jump. It will bring them closer, which is a good thing.

"I'll tell you, but not today," she says.

"Do you still want to?"

"Don't you?" she says. Though she already knows what he'll say.

"I might have done it before," he says. "But now, Vee, I swear to God, if you get anywhere near the bluff, I'm going to tackle you. I'll bring you down."

Her lips reach for his mouth; he holds her off. "Now tell me your secret." She wants to kiss him but he won't let her. "Tell me," he says. "Be brave. Do it and see what happens. I dare you."

"Saint, you are such a goofball." He lets go of her; she refuses to feel bad. "Can't I be mysterious?"

"You're plenty mysterious," he says. Then: "Will you tell me tomorrow? Swear to it?"

Her long sigh fills the spot where she is supposed to swear. "I love your tongue."

"Love," he says, calling it into being and at the same time naming what's there, what maybe (they both consider the possibility) has always been there.

17

Tennis Game

———

By the tenth day of the Final Fortnight, my waistbands were loose and my skirts sagged around my hips, though I hadn't attended a single Slimnastics class. The physics final came and went without me. I found this funny, along with the fact that I'd dropped ten pounds. Ten in ten days. It sounded like a diet scam. Maybe without physics I'd turn into Einstein?

Lighter of foot, burning with the intensity of our four remaining days, four days to walk, breathe, smell, think, twenty-four hours times four, I arrived at the Haight just after dawn. I was alone, the ground wet and sweet-smelling. I walked to the chain-link fence and started to climb—not to jump prematurely, just to see if I could haul myself up and over. Last night the others had done it, as a preview or dress rehearsal. "No thanks!" I said lightly. "I don't want to collapse it!" Mocking myself so no one else would.

Of course no one did. A joint was rolled and passed to me through the chain-link. On the lake side they gave one another pretend shoves toward the brink, while I played Anxious Mom: "Stop, children, you'll give me a heart attack!" I leaned against the fence, my back to Saint's with only the mesh between us. I wasn't jealous; in our presence, at least, he gave Vera no special attention. He smelled of sweat, soap, and deodorant, and I breathed him in while Vera and CJ dangled their legs in oblivion, superior to other people who didn't live their lives poised above death.

Now alone in early daylight I tucked my skirt between my legs and into my waistband and climbed—without fear or superhuman effort—to the barbed top of the fence. Westward, pure and clear, was the tender junction of water and sky. The lake had separated into two colors, emerald at the horizon turning khaki toward the shadowed shore. An occasional curl of water frothed high enough to catch the light, though mostly the waves broke gray and hushed. Before fear could overtake me, with a sharp breath blanking out thought, I gripped the crown of a post with both hands, hoisted a leg over, and shifted my weight onto a toehold on the lake side. Then my skirt came loose, my sneaker slipped, a barb caught the back of my thigh. With all the strength in my underused arms I held on to the post long enough to free my leg and dropped.

For a second it was like enacting the Pledge four days early and all by myself (a terrible accident!). The ledge was flat and wider than it looked, with room to lie down and even walk a few steps to either side. But with nothing between me and it, the lake pulled at me. I clung to the chain-link and kept my gaze inland. The tennis courts were empty, the tops of the trees sunlit, the sky heartbreakingly blue, while behind me and down, down, down, waves broke on the shore, and my leg throbbed with their breaking. I couldn't look at the injured spot. Skin was an organ, we'd learned in biology. I asked the members of my imaginary jury, which was always in session, *Is it right or wrong to inflict on my body the mayhem that will result from my jump?* I'd signed the Pledge on the crest of something that was hard to recall now. Because excommunication had seemed worse than death. And because, I must have been hoping, in the two intervening weeks something would divert us.

There were still four days.

With my pulsing wound and the distinct sensation of blood running down the back of my leg, I was gathering strength for my return climb when two girls I knew arrived at the courts, Lynda Miller and Susie Epton, who had never talked to me and never would, for whom I was beneath even taunts. Their bright yellow balls skimmed the net and landed near the baseline. Then CJ was crossing the field.

I shook the fence, and he started running my way. "Bad girl," he said upon arrival. "You want to do the deed all by yourself? Do you always have to be first in everything?"

"I'm just a born leader?"

He laughed. I sat down on the lake side of the fence while he squatted on the park side, nonstop rapping to me about soap operas, which he considered brilliant satires of midcentury America. He could talk about anything without instigation. I had no views on the essential nature of soap operas, but I liked the sound of his nasal, insinuating voice and wondered what he'd be like to kiss (the first time the thought crossed my mind). I liked his face of a merry sprite, his thick-lashed dark eyes. Gone was the pain in my leg. Until he turned to look back across the field. "Have you been wondering," he said, "where our friends are?" Then I was wondering. It was ten o'clock by the Mickey Mouse watch he'd bought me. Four hours had passed with me in dreamland. "What do you think?" I said.

"Who knows, fucking their brains out?"

"What? Do you mean with—"

He shook his head unnecessarily hard. "Oh dear, oh dear. I mean they're attending Mass. Or reading Schopenhauer. Improving their minds. What was I thinking?" He lofted a parodic eyebrow. "Don't freak, Kay. It was a joke."

"Not a good joke."

CJ wrinkled his forehead; then he was off again. "Oh dear, oh dear, oh. CJ forgot to take his Librium! Should he up the dose? The doctors are so confused!"

"CJ, cut it out."

He turned and scanned the field as if playing the part of someone scanning a field. "Fear not. Saint has to milk his goats. The great Vee needs her beauty sleep."

I stood. This was a violation. We four did not pair off to discuss one another. Even nice things said behind someone's back could be disloyal, a ring of words locking a person in to be known and diminished. I unstuck my skirt from the back of my leg and resecured it to my waistband, about to try the fence again—the gash hurt, but it wasn't bleeding now—when we saw someone walking in our direction. It was a boy from our high school, from the shadowy, blurred masses beyond our group of four. With a bound, CJ had scaled the fence and was standing with me. "Save me!" he cried.

"From who?" said the boy. "I come in peace."

It was Gary Landry, the asswipe from my physics class. He was on student council, and as Vera had said he permanently acted like he was running for office. He wasn't hateful, though. He seemed to like the sound of his own voice overmuch, but he was friendly, he'd talk to anyone: an asswipe, not asshole. Not wanting to look weird to him, I tried to climb back over the fence and managed it without a mishap. He was carrying two tennis rackets and smiling. CJ stayed where he was, clutching the chain-link, peering through like a prisoner.

I was embarrassed for CJ, but Gary didn't seem to think anything was amiss. "Would one of you like to hit with me?" he said, gazing democratically from one of us to the other. "Kelly didn't show, the dweeb." CJ regarded him as if he didn't quite understand what had been said. "Or I can take you both on. Canadian doubles. I'm sick of working on my serve."

CJ pressed his face to the chain-link. One eye was half-closed, his lips squeezed into a slot in the mesh. "I'm not allowed out."

Gary looked confused, which only inspired CJ. He shook the fence, emitting a yodeling wolf howl. "Don't be a jerk!" I mouthed. Gary shrugged, smiling apologetically, and started to walk away. "CJ, what is *wrong* with you?"

"Hey, man," CJ called out, "don't let me freak you. I'm only moderately insane."

Gary turned around. His head sat square on his slightly stocky body, his face was placid and frank, and he looked at CJ the way a well-behaved child looks at a zoo animal. I'd never spoken to him before, and my face was hot, but I had to say something. "You're in physics with me." Thinking, Oh God, he *knows* we're in the same class, or if not it's because my presence is beneath consideration.

"Where were you last week?" he said. "You missed the final. Were you sick or something?"

I wanted to say something clever, but my mind was empty. CJ leaned into the fence, his arms outstretched like Christ on the cross. "Physics and I don't get along," I said. Gary smiled generously, but something more was required from me. "Uh, how did you do on the final?"

"I don't know yet. I got a C on the midterm."

I nodded enthusiastically. "Me too." It wasn't true. I had gotten a D. "I hate physics."

He laughed. "Who doesn't?"

I went on more forcefully, "Every time he called on me my mind went blank."

He laughed as if it was easy to laugh. He liked laughing. "At least you hid your ignorance. I talk even when I don't know anything."

"But you aren't afraid to ask questions. That's a good thing!"

" 'The question is,' said Humpty Dumpty, 'which is to be master?' "

The interjection came from CJ. But instead of attaching him to our fragilely constructed society, his remark broadcast his isolation. He'd dropped the Christ pose but remained behind the fence. "To be or not to be. Maybe *that's* the question?" he said. "Hey, I had Carstairs last year. He's not exactly inspirational." Gary set his bag down. CJ twitched his small, amused squirrel's nose. I prayed for words to charm the boys, merge the worlds across the chain-link. I leaned back on the fence and whispered fiercely to CJ, "Go play tennis with him!"

"Okay, Mom."

Quick and fluid as a squirrel, he scrambled up and over, jumped, then gave us a bow. "I can play a little tennis," he said. "I can also talk and chew gum at the same time." He sprang into a handstand, arched his back, and declaimed, in a British accent: " 'When in the course of human events it becomes necessary for one people to dissolve the political bands which have connected them . . .' What kind of bands did they have in those days? Help, youse guys!"

Gary couldn't look away from CJ, who shifted his weight from hand to hand, maintaining the arch of his back. CJ went on, with a German accent now: "Undt to assume amonk the powersss of the earth the separate and equal station to vich the Lawsss of Nature and Nature's Gott . . ." He flopped over onto the grass. *"Sieg Heil!"*

I couldn't smile like this was funny, nor could I roll my eyes and side with Gary against CJ. My stomach ached, not only for CJ, who barked at strangers like a jealous dog, but for Gary, who seemed honestly bewildered.

"Were you named, by chance, for Gary Cooper?" CJ asked. Gary said he was named for an uncle who died in the invasion of Normandy, but CJ wasn't listening. "Do not forget me, oh my darling," said CJ.

Every once in a while, as I said, you act against type; you can't help it. There were times in my life as a shy person when my shyness would suddenly vanish to the point where I would risk near-certain humiliation. On the bus once, on my way home from day camp, I responded to a call for volunteers by standing up in the aisle and trying to lead the other campers in a song I didn't know, and didn't know I didn't know till I tried to sing it. I sang a line or two, then stood like a dolt till someone else took over. That day in the park, feeling bad for Gary, I offered myself as a tennis partner, although my tennis history comprised two sets of lessons: an Evanston Park District summer course, in which I was the worst of six children my age, and two years ago at Arlyn's club, where I was more coordinated but more inclined to fatigue and had to sit down every twenty minutes. "This is my tennis dress," I said, pointing to my skirt configuration. "Do you still want to play?"

On the court Gary was skilled and patient. His balls came gently; he flooded the court with goodwill. But the grip of the borrowed racket made it feel like a club, and I swung as if at a marauder I was hopeless against. On the adjoining court Lynda and Susie's balls hopped rhythmically back and forth over the net. Their legs were slim and tan, their waists narrowing to meet their tennis skirts. To keep my skirt tucked I kept a hand on my waistband. "Sorry," said Gary each time I missed. Then a ball came that I thought I could hit. It lofted over the net and dropped like a shuttlecock. I drew my racket back and waited for the bounce as I had been taught, the rise and partial fall—there would be time this time. I stiffened my wrist, swung through, and watched the ball sail into the girls' court. Lynda sent it back. "Thanks, Lyn," Gary called out, and then to me, "Take a step back."

I followed his advice and that of my former tennis instructors, bringing the racket back before the ball bounced, swinging from the shoulder, but my goal had become to give Lynda and Susie no reason for further annoyance with me, and I either missed the ball or hit into the net. By now the sky had turned white. Wind blew. My hair came loose from my rubber band and caught in my mouth. The hem of my skirt fell out of its tuck. I'm *so bad*! I wanted to call across the court, as if the self-censure would console poor Gary, who was sending out patient ball after ball. But my breath burned my throat, and I didn't want my apologetic voice befouling the clean, sure sounds of good tennis.

The wind intensified, the girls waved goodbye. From overhead came the rumble of thunder. The sky was thickly clouded now, the air gray and damp. But the rain held off, and Gary gave no sign of impatience. I hated the heavy air in which I could barely move, I hated my skirt dragging on my legs, I hated Gary's superhuman patience with me and my failure to control the ball, not to mention everything else in my life, and I swung at the hard white whizzing thing as hard as I could. It flew over Gary's outstretched racket and the fence behind him. So what? Let him despise me. The next ball I hit hopelessly. It cleared the net and dropped down on the other side of the court inside all the lines.

On his bench outside the court CJ applauded theatrically. Gary was grinning as he hit the ball back to me. But that was enough. I staggered to the net, dripping sweat. "This is a good place to quit. Yes?"

He made me play a few more balls so I'd know it wasn't a fluke, and after a few tries I once again landed a ball in the right general area. "All right, Billie Jean! Seriously, isn't it kind of fun? Just the running?" He followed me off the court, bouncing a ball on his racket head. He loved everything about the game of tennis, he said. The smell and feel of a USLTA-approved ball, the bonk off tight strings.

My cut leg hurting again, I collapsed on CJ's bench. "Don't say a word," I said. CJ batted innocent eyes. But, as it turned out, he had a new agenda. He took my borrowed racket and sprang to his feet. "I haven't played in a while," he said to Gary. "Will you put up with me too?" His offer accepted, CJ bent to tighten his sandals. "I'll have to play like a country boy."

"We'll take it easy," Gary replied.

It was broiler-oven-hot now, the rain clouds pressing down on us without unloading. I sat on the bench with pain ticking in my leg. But I was moved by Gary's pleasure in being on the court, which reminded me of my feeling for bridge. Courteously, the boys offered each other the advantage of the first serve till Gary prevailed. Because rain was coming CJ declined practice serves. I watched lazily. He planted his sandaled feet behind the baseline, tossed the ball gracefully upward. His racket arm rose. Gary had time to turn, that was all, as the ball veered to a corner just inside the service court.

CJ served assorted slices that bounced erratically. Gary could reach them but couldn't return them with any power. It began to drizzle, but the game went on. Gary's first serve was strong but inaccurate, and the next one CJ pounded back. I wanted to yell, *Go easier on him!* but didn't want to call attention to the inequality.

The set was over in thirty minutes and CJ had won every game.

The boys shook hands over the net. "Ouch," said Gary, smiling with some effort. "You aren't bad. Why aren't you on the team?"

"Want to play one more? The rain's stopped."

"Thanks, I'll take a pass." Gary held out his hand for his spare racket, then said more genially, "Just wait till I take a few lessons."

Something in his voice gave me goosebumps. His courage, if that's what it was, or resilience. "I have to confess," I said to Gary, "I got a D on that test. Our physics midterm."

His face loosened. "Really?"

"I'm sorry, I don't know why I lied."

"Me too," he said.

"What?"

"I got a D too. God knows how I did on the final. I'll probably have to take the course in the fall."

"Oh, screw physics!"

We laughed at the same time. The joint laugh felt good in my throat and to my ears. I was liking Gary.

18

Busted

———

After Gary was gone, CJ couldn't stop talking. "Why aren't I on the team, since I am amazing? Darling, speak to me." We walked over to our tree. I sat down with my back to the trunk and looked around for something to look at. "Kay, love, what's the matter? I can beat anyone with a weak backhand. With all my lessons I should be at Wimbledon." He talked to the air. "Are you pissed? He's a dork. You aren't pissed, are you? You don't get pissed. Do you hear what I'm saying?"

I heard. I was pissed. I had nothing to say to him.

"Tell me. Or do you want me to guess? Okay, twenty questions. Does it start with a *G*? Is it our friend Gary Cooper? Should I have lost to him, is that what you wanted?"

"He's not a dork! He was *nice* to you, really nice! To me too." I couldn't speak without crying, but I was angry. "Asshole!"

"He didn't feel that bad. Didn't you hear him?"

"Yes! Yes, I did. I heard everything!"

I glared in CJ's direction, waiting to be swept over and demolished by one of his breezy, unanswerable remarks. I wanted to say mean things, knock him off the pedestal of his superiority over everyone. I stared hard into his eyes till he looked away.

Then I felt bad. "I'm sorry," I said. "I didn't mean to yell at you." He was my friend, and Gary obviously could take care of himself. "Isn't it amazing?" I said. "That he could lose like that and not be crushed?"

CJ was silent for an unusually long time. Then he agreed.

Soon afterward, our friends showed up. Vera and I went over to the spring-fed fountain and she helped me rinse my cut with the alleged healing water—which would work, she said, if I only believed. "Do *you* believe?" I said. We'd never talked about this before. She cut her eyes at me, then patted my leg dry with the hem of her shirt and blew on it lovingly, like a mother would. "It's working!" I cried. We checked out each other's tattoos and how well they were healing. Hers was perfect. Mine was getting there. Ceremonially, we dabbed the images with the miracle water and placed our Band-Aids in a nearby trash can.

Saint was in a great mood. He put an arm around CJ, then he picked me up and ran me around the field. I was teary with pleasure and relief. He had brought a joint, and we smoked and played cards, all of us In the Moment, beyond everything that might have oppressed or distracted us. Then, light and free in the bronze sunshine of late afternoon, I strolled off from the group, and everything I saw reinforced my joy: the perfect oblongs of the tennis court nets, the low orange sun hanging over the lake. The crowns of trees glowed green as if lit from within. I held an imaginary ball of string, with one end tied to the tree where my friends sat, and it played out as I walked. From time to time I looked back to make sure they were there. Then the lowering sun cast a net of gold over the lake. The shadow of the fence on the grass was crisp as lace, and so were the shadow-tendrils of my hair, blowing. Forgetting the Pledge and its time constraints, I thought of growing my hair down my back. My hair was wavy and kind of thick. Would it look good long?

I arrived home as the family desired, with plenty of time before dinner. Elise was setting the table. Feeling sisterly, I lifted my skirt and showed her my tattoo. "We all got them," I said. "The same one. It's almost healed."

She smiled, then shook her head at me. "You're in trouble," she said.

"Groovy," I said. The dregs of the joint were still with me and I was starving. I took a bowl of grapes out of the fridge. "Are these washed?" I bit down on a grape and my mouth took in the pleasure of the squirt. "So, um, how's the campaign? Did you change any capitalist pig minds?"

Her look of concern hardened. "Don't you want to know what's going on, Kay?"

"Not really," I said, then added, since something else seemed required, "Trouble is my middle name."

She stood in the middle of the kitchen with forks in her hand. "You're being incredibly casual."

I put another grape in my mouth, then spit it out into the Disposall. I didn't need this grape. "You're always happy," I said to Elise. "How do you do that?"

"I'm not always happy. Listen. Mom tends to get obsessive about things. Be cool and she'll mellow out. Seriously, do I really seem that happy to you?"

"Yes. Well, no. I don't know."

I made a pro forma contribution to the table setting, then went up to my room. Before I could shut the door, though, Arlyn was standing before me, in gold sandals and pants so crisply white she might just have put them on, though she had probably worn them all day.

"You look nice, Arlyn. The table's done. Is there anything else I can do?"

She gave me a brisk, disapproving nod, a far cry from her usual strained friendliness. "I'm glad you're home. Let's go outside. We need to talk." A tiny shiver ran down my spine.

"I'm not the least bit hungry," I said, which had become true. "I don't even need dinner."

She was halfway downstairs, though, and I followed, taking in less and less air with each breath. At the sliding glass doors I was panting. She was already out on the patio, waiting for me in one of a pair of lawn chairs set side by side. I tried to focus on the flower beds, the newly mowed lawn. I wanted peace tonight. Even counterfeit kinship. I wasn't ready for any kind of struggle. Beside the patio was a young tree she had planted, its slim trunk wrapped in wire mesh. At the end of the yard my dad was putting a golf ball toward a machine that shot it back. I sat down in my appointed chair. "That's a nice tree," I said. "Do you know what kind it is?"

"Jonathan apple. It'll bear next year. But that's not what we need to talk about."

I scanned for other objects of my stepmother's interest. Arlyn loved having a yard. In Chicago she and Elise had shared a one-bedroom apartment on the tenth floor, with a view of the lake if you craned your neck from the small balcony. I watched my father's golf ball roll smoothly into the machine. I watched the arc of its just-as-smooth return over the short grass. Elise came out with a book. She pulled a chaise lounge far enough from us not to intrude but close enough to hear us. "Tomorrow I'll come home earlier," I said to Arlyn. "I'll help cook."

"The problem is not," said Arlyn, "your household chores. We got a call today. That concerned you."

Any contrition of mine was instantly gone. "Great," I said. "My application to modeling school?"

Elise giggled, then put a hand over her mouth. I was suddenly glad for her presence. But Arlyn wasn't amused. "It was Jill. Your Slimnastics instructor, does that ring a bell? Kay, the class was for your benefit."

I could have guessed Jill would call. I nodded overvigorously. "But I wasn't getting much out of it, I didn't think I was *bound* to it." I sucked my stomach in, showed her my loose waistband. "I've been losing without it."

"Kay," Arlyn said, "do you have any idea how overweight you are?"

"I didn't ask for Slimnastics, did I? *Did* I?"

"Elise," said Arlyn, "how much weight would you say Kay should lose?"

"Keep me out of this, Mom."

"Thirty pounds," said Arlyn. "Maybe forty." I tried to shrug, but my shoulders just twitched. Her eyeballs sliced into me. "It's not just how you look, Kay, there are health concerns." She listed numerous problems that arose from extra poundage, as if a person living in 1968 could maybe not know this. Did she think I was retarded? "I don't think you realize how much you've gained this past year. What size do you wear now?"

"Mom," Elise murmured, "you're making too big a deal about this."

"Let me finish, honey. I don't think you have an accurate notion of your body, Kay. Those full skirts of yours—"

"I'm not blind. Do you think I'm an idiot?" I pulled up my skirt. My calves looked fine, especially the one with the tattoo. I sat with my tattooed leg crossed over the other, *4EVER* distinct and beautiful in the light of early evening. Arlyn, though, made no mention of it.

"You're not an idiot, Kay! Will you let me finish?" She spoke rapidly, a woodpecker drilling at my sense of things. "I have a girlfriend with the same problem. She'd look in the mirror, and I don't know what she saw, but it wasn't reality. It took her husband, friends, and a therapist to make her see. And after Weight Watchers, you wouldn't believe how great she looks! Please, Kay, this might lengthen your life, and it'll definitely make for a better last year of high school. Isn't that right, Elise? Larry, what do you think?"

Across the lawn, Dad was chipping now. I had never had golf lessons, though I'd have preferred them to tennis. I liked the look of chipping, the clipped, unhurried half swing, the way the ball hung in the air, then hit the grass and stayed put. He cocked his wrists and sent the ball in a pretty arc to the base of the poplars between our lawn and a neighbor's. I used to love his large, regular, handsome-man features, the aggressive congeniality that got him good tables at restaurants. "Excuse me," I said to Arlyn, and walked over to him.

I apologized for interrupting him, whispering, as if it were more polite. "But, Dad, I've been needing to talk to you. I have this problem with . . ." I said, cocking my head toward Arlyn. "Maybe I should say she and I have this problem." I almost took hold of his arm, I was so glad at last to be talking with him. But he looked at me as if he didn't understand what I'd just said. I labored not to whine. "She's on my case all the time about the weight thing."

"Kay, honey. Honey." He wiped a dazed hand across his forehead. "She might go overboard sometimes, but she means well. She has your best interests at heart." His voice was deep and sweet, like the voice of a TV newscaster. But this was not going well. "I have to be honest," he said. "We were both upset about this Slimnastics business."

Then Arlyn approached, alarmingly resolute. "Tell him what size dress you wear. Go on, Kay."

"Please. Stop her, Dad."

He patted my shoulder, addressing Arlyn. "Let's not put too much emphasis on her weight," he said. "It was a problem for her mother."

"And I'm trying to make sure it doesn't happen to Kay. I talked to her instructor. We had a long talk, Jill and I. She's concerned and she has some ideas. She works with the kids on diet too, a sane calorie-based diet that will get the weight off and keep it off." She was fervent. Her voice rose. "Kay may not think it matters, but one of these days she'll have to get a realistic notion of herself or I don't know what's going to happen to her."

"I know. You're right. I just don't want things to get out of balance."

"Out of balance? Look at her, Larry. Don't make me the bad guy!"

"Of course you're not the bad guy."

"All I asked was her dress size—"

I covered my ears. "Shut up. Shut up, both of you!"

He dropped his club and put his arm around Arlyn, who was

stiffly shaking. To me he held out a placating hand. "Please try to calm down. Why not answer her question, sweetie—what's the harm? Tell her your dress size."

It was a trap, I knew, for my good-girl self, taught by my mother to answer when spoken to. And for my idiot self, who never knew whether to tell the truth or roll my eyes or cry. My head filled with commonplace numbers—my age, sixteen; my Evanston house number, 1911; the first five digits of pi after the decimal point, 14159; the year American women were allowed to vote, 1920—which I'd never bothered to memorize and here they were! Of course I knew my dress size. "I wear a junior eleven. Sometimes a thirteen."

On her patio chair Elise closed her eyes. Arlyn looked faintly, infuriatingly sad.

"I do! Go look in my closet and see!"

"Kay," said my father, "I'm less concerned with your weight than this class-cutting." He shook his head. "You lied to us. That's not the sort of thing I expected from you."

My chin was quivering. Dad used to look young for his age, younger than other kids' fathers, much younger than my mother. But after Mom died his face started to get puffy, and right now it looked swollen, if not rotten inside. If I touched any part of him, I thought, my hand would sink in. "Obviously," I said sternly, "you're on their side."

"Don't talk like a nut, Kay. I'm on your side too! There are no sides!" Shining upon me his face of pseudo love and pity, he said, "I want life to be easier for you."

"Kay," said Arlyn, "in less than two weeks you'll start your senior year. Wouldn't you like to go out on dates? And to the prom? You have such a pretty face."

A sour rumbling had begun in the pit of my stomach. There was a name I wanted to call Arlyn that I'd never said aloud. It sat on my tongue like a piece of walnut shell. "I have no interest in the prom."

"You think so now," Arlyn said, "but what will happen when everyone's talking about it? High school could be such a great time for you."

"No one will talk about it. No one with brains!"

"Oh, Kay, I just don't want you to miss out on—"

"There's nothing to miss out on, nothing I want!"

"Keep your voice down."

Obviously, there was nothing to be gained here. I closed my long-suffering eyes.

"Look at us, Kay, when we're talking to you."

I didn't know what to do. Generally with these people I'd assert myself for a few volleys, then apologize, or choose not to apologize and suffer in a different way. But now I couldn't bear the sight of Arlyn's pretty forty-year-old face. I saw Arlyn as my father might have seen her when she interviewed for the accounting job—petite, outspoken, with the casual self-assurance of a woman who'd supported herself and her daughter for ten years, a woman with a college degree. My mom made beds, meals, small talk. She became weak and could barely drag herself up the stairs. Relentlessly energetic, Arlyn was the opposite of my mother. I could not look at her. I would not.

"Look," said my father. "You chose to quit your exercise class. From now on your weight is your own business—your problem to solve. But you lied to us, which I consider more serious. You are grounded tonight and tomorrow. Is that clear?" He and Arlyn exchanged a look of frustrated patience. "When your physics grade comes, we'll revisit this."

"Uh-oh," I murmured. "Just wait till you see my physics grade."

Now I had his full attention, though it gave me no pleasure. I had simply pushed open a door onto a new corridor. For better or worse we were strolling down it. "What makes you think I've been going to physics class?"

Elise had given up all pretense of reading. Arlyn's jaw was working. "Kay," said Arlyn, "did you fail physics?"

"Well, there's a chance I won't fail if the world comes to an end. Or if what's-his-face Carstairs loses his grade book. He's kind of spacey."

"Kay," Arlyn said, "you are so *hostile.*"

My father said, "Are you trying to get my goat?"

"Why would I bother?" I stood my ground. "You're such a dork! And she's a"—I spelled it out in a stage whisper—"B-I-T-C-H." I squeezed my mouth shut against the burgeoning tears.

"You're confined until further notice. Don't walk away, young lady."

I turned and ran into the house, out of range of them. But I heard it anyway: "Larry, she hates me. I've always felt that." Elise followed, trying to explain or give comfort, but I couldn't stop for her kindness. Up in my room I locked the door, spurred by the remembrance of something my mother had said to me the week she died. The words had frightened me so much I must have put them in storage, retaining only, at times, a feeling of mild dread. But now a murmur arose in a fold of my brain, threatening to ignite into consciousness. I rummaged frantically through my middle dresser drawer for the bag of chips I had hidden. Gone! Like a scared wild animal I turned around and around in this room that wasn't mine and never had been.

Voices clawed at the door. "Open up!"

"Please, Kay."

Pounding. My dad: "I'll let you know when this is over. When school starts, senior or not, you're coming right home after school! I'm not joking."

Arlyn: "Do you think you're the only person with feelings in the world?"

It was a flimsy lock. He opened it with a screwdriver, marched in, and removed the phone. "You can use this again when you receive our permission and not before, do you hear? You're not too old to learn respect."

When he left, I relocked the door, though it was obviously useless. A little later there was a knock of the quiet sort. Arlyn, softly: "I have news for you, not that you'll appreciate it. I talked to Mr. Carstairs. There's a chance he'll let you take the final. He'll let us know tomorrow. I'm leaving your book bag outside the door." Her footsteps walked away, then returned. "In the meantime, I hope you'll be thinking about important things. Like the kind of person you want to be."

I was still pacing. Something in Arlyn's voice conveyed genuine concern for me. She had obviously gone to a lot of trouble. But, as always, when my gratitude met Arlyn's composure it shriveled and died. When her husband died, she found my father, who was richer than her first husband and probably loved her more. This was a woman for whom things would always turn out right. Certain people were like that.

Fully clothed, I burrowed under my covers and fell asleep. In my dream my mother sat on the edge of a lawn chair, leaning forward with her mouth half-open, as if she was about to speak or throw up. I woke just before midnight with the back of my leg throbbing. It had just occurred to me that when P-Day came I'd be up in this room. I snuck downstairs to the kitchen phone and called Saint, then CJ, then Vera. No one answered. I found a Band-Aid and put it over my cut.

Back in my room, unable to sleep now, I sharpened a pencil and started a sketch of Saint on his motor scooter, but the handlebars looked wrong and so did his arm. I turned off the light and lay down again, feeling grossly heavy. I was a prehistoric mammal on the verge of extinction. A vegetarian dinosaur, weakened from foraging tundra that couldn't produce a leaf in the glacial cold, too tired to flail out of the tar I was sinking in. My mother's words came again, distinct, inevitable, not her last words but the ones I would call to mind from now on, on the brink of anything: *Your father doesn't love me anymore.*

19

The World Without Me

The last week of August 1968, five months after Martin Luther King, Jr., was killed, less than three months after Bobby Kennedy was killed, Democrats gathered at the International Amphitheatre in Chicago to nominate for president the lusterless, well-intentioned man who would lose to Richard Nixon. College students, hippies, and Yippies drove or hitchhiked to Chicago to back Gene McCarthy, protest the war, or just see the show. The Yippies backed Pigasus, a live pig that was led around Grant Park on a leash. To maintain order, Mayor Daley instructed the police to shoot to kill. Kill arsonists; cripple looters.

There were hot days, and nights almost as hot, in which protesters, journalists, and bystanders would suffer tear gas and bloody beatings captured live for TV. But up north in Lourdes, we, the renegades of 4EVER, weren't watching TV or reading the papers. It was P-Day minus three, and I was still in seclusion, phoneless, my friends banned from contact with me. Whoever called got my father or stepmother and the same facts—house arrest till further notice. Cruel and unusual, but what could my friends do? Explain to my jailors that my punishment interfered with our plans for suicide?

I longed to be rescued. I wanted a ladder propped against my window in the dark of night and to ride off behind Saint on his scooter like Guinevere with Lancelot. To that end, I left my window open. But they had even removed the phone from their room so I couldn't use it when they were downstairs. And there was always one of them in the house.

The best moment for me was when my friends drove up with signs they had made: FREE KAY CAMPION. KAY 4EVER! "I love you all!" I screamed from the window. They left and returned with more emphatic signs: END FASCIST PARENTHOOD. CAMPIONS CRUEL TO CHILDREN. They marched up and down the driveway—I could see from my room—till a cop pulled up and confiscated the signs.

Most frustrating, though, was not knowing what was going to happen on Pledge Day. Would they do it without me?

I cried as they drove away, imagining dawn in sixty hours, when they would jump and I wouldn't be there to join them—or (my secret wish) to stop them.

20

CJ

P-Day minus two. The early, desultory male dinner has concluded (lettuce with Wish-Bone Italian dressing and frozen pizza) and CJ doesn't know what to do with himself. Saint's mother wanted him home with the family tonight, and Vera declined without giving a reason. The three will get together tomorrow morning and discuss how to liberate Kay. Meanwhile, CJ lies down on his bed and tries to bring himself to climax with only mental images, a feat that Saint said he had achieved. CJ is not successful.

Already depressed, he becomes even more so. His mother is coming home early from her mission of mercy—coming tomorrow, in fact, with her sister, who needs to be, right now, with people who love her. Aunt Lottie is a talker. There will be long dinners where he and Danny sit with napkins on their laps while the sisters discuss people that only they know, alive and dead. There will be at least one private mother-son discussion of how he has spent this summer in which he neither worked nor went to summer school; is something bothering him? She won't call him lazy; her great fear is that he's unhappy and she's somehow responsible for it. And even if he swears that he's happy, it will end with her feeling bad. He used to see her as weak-willed, since she quit work to raise the children and never contradicts his father. But she has a variety of friends who are always calling to talk or make plans with her. With her gone, the phone hardly rings. She has a good heart, he is starting to think, not that it matters. He has stopped seeing his shrink, his MAOI inhibits nothing, and maybe he's just imagining it, but he's felt a current of something arcing between Saint and Vera that makes him contemplate his death with less aversion. Right now he is eager for P-Day, after which, unavoidably, the group will have refound their four-way equality.

With nothing else to do, CJ goes into his parents' room and checks his father's stash of condoms—untouched (good man) during his wife's absence. In the master bathroom he opens the drawer belonging to his mother. Among other tools that serve female beauty is a cache of lipsticks of multiple hues. He selects one called Gypsy Rose and brings the tube back to his room, where he tries it first on notepaper, then on the side of his hand. The red is darker than he expected. Then comes a tap on his door and his father's overenunciated English: Would CJ kindly join him downstairs in a game of pool?

There is but one right answer. CJ's father has an aura of unassailable correctness that CJ has never been able to undercut, and a pool game is the usual prelude to a shaming. To sustain himself CJ applies the lipstick to his lips, heavily, unambiguously, a transgression for his father to note and overlook. Try to overlook. It may be interesting.

The game that ensues in the dark-paneled, Oriental-carpeted game room is standard for them. CJ breaks, shoots till he misses. Better than usual tonight, his lips moist, he drops three balls before turning the table over to his father.

The man's hands on the cue stick are the precise and urgent hands of the surgeon he is, a man who snips unruly cartilage, who files down a renegade spur of bone. If the hands belonged to someone else, CJ might have loved them, loose on the stick but in absolute charge—stopping the cue ball dead as its mark hits the pocket. He marvels—at the hands, the stick, the sequence of balls, the locus of force transferred so deftly that the final drop is almost silent. Half a dozen similar nudges and the table is clear. After which the man sets the stick down and delivers the expected coup de grâce. "I need your assistance."

"Oh dear, you know how busy I am." CJ eyes his father in his pale gray summer-weight suit jacket. It's six-thirty P.M., and soon the man will drive off to rehearse with the Midland Quartet (he conducts), but now he wears what he wore this morning to the hospital. The word "dapper" comes to mind. "Natty." CJ says extra-casually, "What could anyone do for you that you couldn't do better yourself?"

The man coughs, which might or might not signal something, and spends the next game courteously—or perhaps evilly—disregarding the fact that his son pokes at the ball without taking aim and that, if he manages to sink a shot, drops the cue ball right behind it. CJ has done no wrong but feels that he has and hates his baseless, fathomless guilt, and his father for engendering it, and his own weak will for not casting it off. Meetings with his father are tests of a part of himself that his father wants to destroy, that CJ must use all his intelligence and cunning to preserve.

"That's two flawless victories for you," CJ says. "Want to go for three?"

His father's hand rises to his mouth, slow and terrible like a drunk faking sobriety. CJ's pulse speeds up. It's his personal goal to see his father at a loss. Even in Auschwitz, CJ believes, his father was in utter self-control—this slight, pale, balding, righteous man, tapping the floor with the end of his pool cue the way God wanted Moses to tap the rock. He sets the stick down, casts a glance at his watch, and says with the mildness of authentic sobriety, "At some point in our discourse as father and son, you could oblige me with respect. In the meantime, courtesy will do."

He sits down at a leather-topped table, opens a drawer, and takes out a stack of envelopes addressed to deans of admissions at various universities. Open, already stamped, each holds a signed check and a stapled sheaf of questions with the responses typed in. "Since you apparently haven't found the time yet, I've taken the liberty of organizing your college applications. I hope you don't mind."

"You've gone beyond organizing."

His father, of course, lets the remark pass. Back to his normal briskness, he arranges the envelopes in order of preference. On the bottom is Michigan State, where his father earned his B.A. and then his M.D. and where CJ is almost certain of admission. He hands him the first packet. "Please sign by the X?"

Suppressing a roll of the eyes, CJ scans the sheets that show Princeton University how desirable he is. He has—honest, really—nearly perfect scores on his Scholastic Aptitudes. His extracurricular interests do indeed include tennis, literature, and film. He speaks and reads German (*Entschuldigen Sie, wo kann man die Toilette finden?*). Under the entry *Describe an incident that changed your life* is a long, single-spaced paragraph, typed, no doubt, by his father's secretary, describing how he learned to "move on" after the death of his grandfather, who drove in from Lansing on Sundays to play chess with him. CJ loved his grandfather, and he still misses him, but he smiles coldly. "I was a sensitive lad."

His father nods, overlooking the irony. "The most selective schools give considerable weight to the personal essay. It provides an indication—"

"If I'm psycho or not."

"Not at all. But it will tell them something about your emotional range and how effectively you can express yourself. Your level of maturity . . ."

CJ shakes the page in his hand. "I didn't feel that bad when Grandpa died. It was worse when Adelman moved to Seattle. And I didn't even like Adelman."

"Do you think your confused anger at the departure of one of your shrinks will get you into a good college?"

CJ glances over the application. "To my knowledge, I do not and have never felt 'bereft.'" He fans himself with it. "What are 'mores'? Like those chocolate marshmallow things you eat around the campfire?"

His father coughs, a sound as precise and conscious as his gestures. "Feel free to change it as you see fit. We can retype." He holds out a pen. CJ waves it away.

"And why the fuck did you name me Christopher? You should have come right out and called me Jesus! Do you really think people don't know you're Jewish? Man, I'm surprised I was circumcised."

His father looks at him, but so briefly that the glance is lost in the quick-flowing words. "Please, Chris. Don't speak of things that you don't understand."

Now his angry energy is suddenly gone. He goes through the stack and signs everything *Christopher Joseph Walker*, although the name is so phony he sees directors of admissions laughing at it. CJ considers slipping the U of Michigan letter into the envelope addressed to Michigan State—it would be interesting to see what, if anything, ensues—but any pleasure in the prank sinks in the marsh of his father's determined serenity. The man is actually humming to himself.

"We want the best place, naturally, for your abilities, which we both know are considerable."

"Good thing they didn't ask for a photo." CJ presses his lipsticked lips together, extends his slim legs.

His father, who has never acknowledged in CJ anything either obnoxious or humorous, nods without looking at him. "You ought to be welcome anywhere you want to go, but it is competitive. Your recommendations will be mixed. Activities are nil, unfortunately. I'm trying to be realistic."

"Varsity tennis, ninth grade."

"You were good."

"Danny's better."

"What are you talking about? He can't beat you."

"In two years he will. Next year."

"You should have continued."

"I despise tennis."

A flash of something that CJ reads as contempt tightens his father's mouth. One by one, the man checks the envelopes, taping over their seals. CJ lounges in the brocade chair, kicking his feet on the wooden legs like a little kid. He wonders what Saint and Vera are doing. He can picture Saint watching TV with his younger siblings, their mom coming into the room and sinking into a chair, but he has no idea about Vera. Then he notices the absence of his father's favorite school from among the applications. In an exaggerated Boston accent he says, "Where's Harvard?" pronouncing it *Hah-vad*. "Aren't I Harvard material?"

His father's eyes shut, then open again. "Do you know how many senior class presidents will be applying to Harvard? Boys who play football and volunteer to help needy people and still earn their A's?"

"Isn't there a chance?"

"It is not impossible. Is it what you want?"

His father sounds suspicious but hopeful, but CJ is on a roll. "Harvard or nowhere. Harvard or the U.S. Navy. Join the Navy and see the world. Harvard or"—a brilliant idea strikes him—"a kibbutz in Yis-ra-el!" He grabs one of the envelopes, addressed to a school that isn't Harvard, and tears it in half. Deliberately. With dignity. His father sucks his cheeks in.

"If you wanted to go to Harvard you should have followed my advice at the beginning of high school." He looks off into a corner. His eyes, nose, and mouth are small and fine-looking and give the impression of letting one another discreetly alone. "Well, who knows? We'll send for an application. As people say, it's only money."

"Ha, fooled you!" cries CJ. "Fuck Harvard. Who wants to go to any crappy school?"

His father stands, pushes his chair against the table, stacks the rest of the envelopes, and sets off with them across the room. "Please control yourself."

"I have control! I have total control! It was a *waste* to fill out those stupid forms! Really, since in about thirty-six hours I'm going to kill myself. Thursday at dawn, to be precise. So, Dad, you can tear up those checks. I'm *dead* serious!"

CJ tosses the speech like a kick at his father's retreating back. But when the man turns, gazing full upon him with an open, sad, vulnerable face, CJ's arms reach out. Part of him labels the gesture stupid, pointless, humiliating, inane. Like he needs a hug? But for a moment in the middle of the game room, he sways back and forth, arms extended like the leaves of a plant on the verge of animal movement. Evolving.

"CJ, your mother would be upset if she heard you talking like this."

He could cry now. He is supposed to cry. The very thought helps him rein himself in. "She's given up on me." It comes out less wry than he intended, but he plunges on. "Danny's her one hope. Her last, best hope."

His father's mouth compresses, as if he'd just bitten down on something hard. Then his hand gives a slightly absentminded wave. "Keep this up and we'll have to call Dr. Lowe."

CJ closes his eyes until the tears go back to wherever they came from. He rocks for a moment in the wake of his father's leaving. Then he addresses himself to the game of pool with a hypothesis to test: Will he play better with his father gone?

He is racking the balls when Danny walks in, nodding his usual universal approval of everything. "Play *me*, brother?"

CJ squints along the cue, banks a stripe into a side pocket. "Are you dressed appropriately?"

"I want to play with my clothes *on*, okay? Mom could come back anytime."

"Mom's in New York. Do you know how far away that is?"

"There's Dad?"

"At rehearsal. Seven to ten. Strip, sonny. And chalk your cue."

CJ sinks two—clip, clip. In neutral, cleansed of feeling, incapable of error, he observes Danny forsake his reluctance. Danny is often unforgivably stupid, but sometimes the light of courage shines from his face. The boy wriggles out of his T-shirt, unsnaps his jeans. Goosebumps raise a patch of hair on top of CJ's head. "Hold up, boy. We'll both do it. Every miss we take something off, you and me both. That's fair. How's that, brother of mine?"

"Cool," says Danny, resnapping his pants without self-consciousness. "Or how about this? When you sink one, I take something off and vice versa?"

"You got it."

Danny rams his head back through the neck of his shirt. "Sometimes men take off their clothes and women watch. There are places."

"Who says?"

Danny's eyes shine, though his shirt is inside out. CJ feels slightly sick. It's frightening how easy it is to make his brother happy. A person shouldn't be so exposed and vulnerable—it puts the burden on everybody else. On the other hand, Danny loves the game of pool. He can play down here for hours, just angling balls off the table walls. And recently Danny beat him for the first time, sinking perfect ball after ball in his birthday suit, with the grace of a little baby Greek god.

Tonight Danny promises to be as good. His break sinks one and sets up a second. CJ removes his watch, a shoe. He feels the burn of adrenaline; he'll have to work now. When Danny misses shot number three, CJ takes command and manages to relieve his brother of both shoes and his Batman ring. The game proceeds with equivalent successes and failures until one ball remains on the table along with the cue and the eight. The boys, six years apart, are both barefoot in their jockey shorts. "Gerald and Rupert," says CJ, not that Danny will understand. The boy is giggling.

"This is fun, isn't it?" Danny says, and looks at him. "Hey, you're wearing lipstick."

"So it would seem," CJ replies, his voice ringing highbrow and phony in his ears like his father's.

Danny guffaws. "And you have a tattoo! When did you get a tattoo? It looks cool. I'm going to get one."

CJ wonders then what would happen if Dad left his music at

home and came back suddenly. What would their mother say if she saw them? *We're sick,* he says to himself, soothed by the "we," the league of him and brother Danny. *In league.* Complicit.

He is still in charge, although uneasily. Danny's last miss lined up the balls, but on the far side of the table, a setup if his arms were a foot longer. He calls the corner pocket, stands on tiptoe, reaching for the angle he can see as if traced out on the green baize. Then behind him comes the breath of a giggle. He turns his head: The chalky tip of Danny's cue stick points at his butt. CJ grabs the stick and flings it across the room. "Fetch!"

Danny is laughing like an idiot. He covers his mouth; giggles spill out between his fingers.

"See that stick?" CJ says. "Bring it back to me." Still laughing, Danny sets off. "Not like that. Like a dog. *Fetch,* Rover!"

Danny drops to his hands and knees, making his way around the table along the edge of the Oriental rug. The boy sometimes gets like this, so silly it destabilizes the kingdom and CJ has to find new and creative ways to restore order. Now Danny is crawling back with the long stick between his molars. The stick is about as long as he is tall; it's tough, maneuvering between the wall and the table legs. The stick falls and Danny labors to pick it up with his teeth, like a real dog. He doesn't cheat. Spit drips down his chin. "Good lad!" CJ cries.

CJ's heart is beating crazily. In the way, way back of his mind, eyes narrow on him with disapproval. But the game has power over him. It's not about to let him go. He reclaims the pool stick and pats his brother's doggie head.

Having reestablished his authority, CJ draws back the stick again. But when he tries to hit the ball, the stick won't move. He turns to find his brother's hand on the end of the shaft. Danny tries to squelch his laughter, but it keeps coming. He seems unable to let go of the cue stick. He squeaks with hilarity.

"You know, boy, the Vampeer committee has sanctions for such as you. Who dishonor the Great Chain of Being."

Danny drops to his knees as CJ has taught him. Laughter at last is vanquished. "I'm sorry, Majesty."

"Do you deserve forgiveness, earthworm?"

"I sincerely hope so, Lord of the Planet."

CJ checks for irony in his brother's sweet-voiced delivery. "You are without redeeming facet."

"I know that, Lord."

Rising to his feet Danny bows and steps back. CJ sinks the shot. Without a complaint Danny removes his jockey shorts. CJ watches the boy's lower body emerging from his clothing, the small globes of his butt white as marble below his sturdy brown back. On an impulse, CJ drops his own shorts, exposing his body, its lean, neat muscles. He and Danny are equal now—naked, proud young gladiators. "Beautiful," says CJ. "Gerald and Rupert!"

"Who?"

He tells Danny about the two main male characters in *Women in Love,* who love women and each other too. In his favorite scene they wrestle in the library in front of the fireplace. "On a polar bear rug in front of a fire," he says. "I might have made it up, the rug, but it's a scene to pay attention to. By a guy you're going to start reading on the Vampeer program. D. H. Lawrence."

"Was he a homo?"

"You schmuck! What's the matter with you? Just because you love men doesn't mean you're a homo!"

"Do they marry the women? What happens in the end?"

"One of them gets married."

"What about the other one?"

"Read it and find out."

CJ won the game. He could rest now in the fullness of Danny's trust in him. While they dress, though, preliminary to a second game, CJ gets an idea. "How about this? Same game, no stripping. Whoever makes a shot gets to make a command. Not just me. You too."

"You'll do what *I* say?"

"Yup. Even steven."

"What about a time limit? Not forever."

"Five minutes."

"And we can only command one thing. Not two things. One thing with each turn."

When Danny at last falls silent, CJ makes the break, but as usual the so-called random universe aligns against him and nothing falls. His brother drops the first shot. "Go, boy," says CJ. "I am yours to command." Danny looks delighted and a little frightened. "Go ahead. Do your dirtiest."

After a brief hesitation Danny orders CJ to get down on his hands and knees and bark three times. CJ complies, emitting three sharp barks and a fourth for good measure. "That's it?"

Danny nods, but when his next shot goes in, he directs CJ to skip around the room with his hands on his hips. After one circuit CJ is to curtsy before him and say, *I am a sugarplum fairy.*

"Is that *fairy* as in *fag*, Master?" says CJ. Danny screams with laughter.

"Come on, just do it!"

CJ does it fast, the small shame passing quickly up and out of him, like a burp. Danny applauds, eyes watering. His face is red. He's giggling hard, choking. Then he misses, and CJ sinks his shot; CJ is in charge again.

Now that the scepter of government is back where it belongs, CJ is aware of his brother without looking at him—sturdy and handsome, at ten nearly as tall as he is. He has a square chin, a good chest for his age. He looks like their mother, who is as tall as their father, prettier than their father is handsome. When they grow up—were they both to grow up—Dan would be taller by far. CJ discovers, then, a staggeringly miraculous idea. "Go up to Mom's closet and bring down a dress."

Danny looks at him, measuring with his eyes.

"Something kind of fancy. With a brassiere. The Kommandant commands you."

"She won't like that."

"Go, boy-o. You know how the Vampeers regard people who go back on their word. And bring down some of her makeup too. It's in the bathroom."

Danny returns with a lipstick, a brassiere, and a white sleeveless summer dress with a zipper in the back. "It's time to get dressed," says CJ. "You have a dinner date. The bra goes on first."

Danny holds the bra at arm's length, as if gauging the scope of the transgression. CJ thinks only of the power he has acquired, whose boundaries and limitations he has yet to investigate. The bra is huge even on the tightest pair of hooks. CJ discards it but helps his brother into the dress and zips it up. It's a little loose, but with the belt buckled it doesn't look bad. CJ's heart is knocking around in his chest. "You're looking good," CJ says, "but a woman can't go out without her makeup." He applies lipstick to his brother's lips and smears a little on his cheekbones. The brothers breathe shallowly, the only sound the conditioned air coming through the vents.

The transformation touches CJ. Dan's dark hair curls over the top of his ears. His face is smooth and hairless. In a hat and earrings he'd look like a beautiful young girl. A sound is coming out of CJ unlike any he has made before, like the screak of the rusting door to an ancient dungeon where prisoners were disemboweled. "Danielle," he says, "you're gorgeous! You should look in a mirror!"

Danny does not want to look at himself in any mirror. Feeling weak in the knees, CJ is ready at last for the game to end. He hops back into his jeans, then brings Dan's clothes over to the table, where the boy stands in his mother's dress, seemingly paralyzed except for the rapid chuff of his breathing. CJ unzips him. "You did good, son." CJ nods in support of his encouraging statement and pulls his own shirt back on. "You were willing, that's what counts. You passed with flying Vampeer colors." He tries to smile.

"Don't call me Danielle." Danny's teeth are chattering.

"I won't," CJ says gently, and hands him his shirt.

When they are both fully clothed, they stand beside the pool table, but Danny won't look at him. Something feels wrong to CJ, but he can't quite fathom it. He feels generous toward his brother. And loving, like an elder sibling ought to feel. He hands Danny one of his socks, so that he can remove his makeup. "I know what you're thinking," he says. "You forgot we were playacting."

Danny is trembling. CJ too now. His breath lurches up his lungs and out of his mouth. Before tonight he felt Dan's attachment to him, but not its depth. Something is wrong that he must make right. CJ pulls back his narrow shoulders, straightens his spine, pushes his chest out against the fabric of his T-shirt. "Pay attention, Danny. If something like this ever comes up again, with me or with anyone else, if you don't want it to happen you don't *let* it happen, do you hear me? If someone tries to fuck with you, you have my permission to cut off their balls. Do you know what I'm saying?"

Danny swallows. "Am I a homo now?"

CJ takes him by the shoulders. "No way. You're a red-blooded American man. A he-man. Superman. It doesn't matter what you wear."

Danny nods.

"Tell me. I don't know you know till you tell me. Tell me what you are."

Danny declares his manhood.

"Let's shake."

The boys shake hands, then Danny puts his arms around him, burying his head in CJ's chest. "Cut it out, Dan." The boy lets go immediately; CJ pats his back. "It's cold in here. Who's in charge of the air-conditioning?" He ruffles his brother's hair, thick and soft as fur. "Danny, don't love me so much."

Danny smiles like an angel. "Who said I loved you at all?"

"That's the idea!" They walk upstairs together. In front of Danny's room, CJ takes him by the shoulders and keeps hold, grinning to still the quiver of his lower lip. "That's what I like to hear. You stand on your own in this world. Say it, brother."

"Right. But there's a lot of stuff we're going to do together."

"Sure. For sure." CJ leans on the doorframe.

"Like what?" Danny says.

"I don't know. Like what? Fishing? Hunting?"

"Yes! And getting high together!"

"We'll get high and rob banks?"

"We'll be spies for the CIA. I'll be a spy and you'll be a counter-spy!"

On an impulse too strong to suppress, CJ kisses the top of his brother's head.

Back in his own room CJ is still shaking. For some reason he can't look in the dresser mirror, though it's something he often does to calm himself down. It's as if a train is speeding through his body. If he could get on it, he could find a seat and get some rest, but it won't stop for him. In his heart or gut is a very bad feeling, and he doesn't know its name.

The phone starts ringing, but CJ doesn't pick up. On the wall Mick Jagger is looking at him as if he has his number. *Who is this creep?* Jagger is thinking. But what has he, CJ, done? Nothing happened! The ringing continues, but he's not ready to talk, even to Saint. On his desk a copy of *Women in Love* is open to the chapter in which Gerald lies down in the snow and freezes to death. Under the weight of Jagger's condemning gaze, CJ lies down in his bed. He hasn't hurt anybody, so why does he feel bad? Jagger is no angel.

CJ is arguing with imaginary Mick Jagger on the place of evil in the universe when the phone starts up again. Someone is serious. He answers. It's Kay.

"You won't believe it, CJ. I'm out! I'm free!" She gives a short, exultant scream. "I went to Saint's, but he wasn't home. I walked miles and miles in the dark. I'm at the park now. God, it's so freaky!"

Her voice wobbles, as if she is crying or trying hard not to. CJ would like to beg her forgiveness. Which she would bestow, he knows, without asking what for. Kay the rock. Kay the good and true. "I'll be right there," he says. "As soon as I get some things together."

He takes a suitcase out of his closet and packs the book first. He has never belonged in this house. He's not sure, even, whether he belongs on the earth. He adds jeans and a T-shirt to the suitcase, underwear, a pair of sneakers, and five twenties that one of his grandmothers sent for his birthday. He walks down the hall.

It's almost ten o'clock this hot August night. Danny has gone right to sleep, his cheek to his ancient, hairless stuffed dog. In the master bedroom their mother's vacancy is marked by a biography of John Kennedy, who would have made the world right if he had lived, their mother said. CJ used to love her like crazy. Now he forgives her for preferring Danny. The world in general prefers Danny. And why not?

He puts her brassiere back into her drawer, hangs up her linen dress, and selects one—black, sequined, with shoulder straps, of a stretchy fabric he can maybe squeeze into. He finds clip-on earrings, a handbag, a pair of high heels. She's a large woman, his height, with feet as long as his and nearly as wide. Who knows where or how tonight will end? He finds a pair of long gloves that almost reach his tattoo.

Back in his bedroom he puts on the dress. It's loose on top and tight at the waist, but, hey: Black is forgiving. Now, where did he hear that? He clips on the earrings, stones too big to be real. He reapplies the lipstick, rubs some on his cheeks. He combs his hair, which has grown out this summer, curling past his ears, and at long last he looks in the mirror. On the expanse of his forehead there is no mark of excommunication, nothing to set him apart from the world of human beings. He stows the gloves and the tube of lipstick in the beaded bag. Then, suitcase in one hand and purse in the other, in his mother's dress and shoes—not too high to walk in and tastefully black, like the dress—he is on his way.

21

Quantum Leap

The third day of my captivity, I was sick of drawing and bored with Archie, Betty, and Veronica. I tried rereading *Gone with the Wind,* but Scarlett's mindless selfishness just annoyed me, and the fact of her eighteen-inch waist. On my desk sat my physics book—unopened, although Mr. Carstairs had caved to Arlyn's efforts on my behalf. My makeup exam was scheduled for sixth-period study hall on the first day of school, generous of Carstairs, who would miss a free period. I wondered absentmindedly what story she had told him, whether it was my physical or my mental illness that had waylaid me. Regardless, I was presumed to be creeping back to the fold. My house arrest would end that day, and if I passed the exam with a B or higher, I could go for my driver's test. There were hints of a secondhand car for me. Elise had no car. Big stick, yummy carrot.

The dilemma was false, of course. In light of the Pledge, what was summer school physics? I had already decided that if I didn't hear from my friends, when the sun rose on P-Day, while they were falling from the bluff I would be diving headfirst from my second-story bedroom window. In the meantime, all I wanted was for time to pass. With nothing else to do, I started rifling through *Modern Physical Science (PSSC)* till I arrived at the chapter on light—what, figuratively, we all were seeking.

To my surprise, then, some event or rearrangement seemed to have occurred in my brain, because the concepts were suddenly comprehensible. I could picture it: Waves. Particles. Electrons, with their fixed little bundles of energy (quanta) obediently circling their home atoms, hit by new quanta and jounced into wider orbit. Farther away but still joined, still circling. A quantum leap? I had questions. What kept them circling? Why didn't they float off? Did it depend, perhaps, on something measurable, on the quantity of energy in the quantum or the distance between them and the nucleus?

I ate dinner downstairs with my jailers without mentioning my seeming acquiescence to their wishes. Back in my room, I returned to my physics, reading the textbook like a novel, letting images pop into my head and vanish, not trying to retain anything in particular. Then on a page with no diagrams or pictures, I came upon a string of words that stopped all my thinking and feeling:

Neither the wave theory alone nor the particle theory alone can account for the behavior of matter in all forms and under all conditions.

I reread the sentence, startled to have found among the formulas, models, and laws of physics this one hesitation. The prose remained formal, and I proceeded cautiously, but the book drew me further in, a not-quite-friend teasing me with odd, dashing turns of mind. *On a large scale, the predictions of Newtonian physics are fully confirmed by experimental data, but on the molecular plane, in the atom's interior, no single system or model applies. In fact, when many quanta are present, the existence of discrete, separable units cannot be verified. It would seem, then, that quantum mechanics is an extension of classical statistical mechanics rather than Newton's deterministic laws. Most startling is the breakdown of the causality principle. . . .*

Ordinarily, by this time my thinking would have stalled out, but now comprehension filled me like food. This thing called matter was like my *self*, predictable and ordinary at a distance but indeterminate at close range, following unverifiable laws or no laws, words and actions only loosely related to intention. You could, for example, hate your two chins in the mirror and then gobble down a quart of ice cream. You could love a person, perform all manner of loving kindnesses for them, and they'd yell or ignore you. Someone could hold you in her arms crying how dear you were, you'd feel her cherishing you and your life together, and the next day she would be gone from your life and her own too. You might even love your life and, thrilling with tender hopefulness, perform an action that horrifies every cell of your body. Causality, what? This breakdown I had already felt below the level of language, and here it was in words on a page. Who or what had caused my mother's death? Not I. Not even my father and Arlyn. My disorientation, my inability to declare myself for or against anything, was not just a fault of character, it mirrored the wishy-washiness—the essential indeterminacy!—of the universe.

So without trying to be quiet, in my normal galumph I walked downstairs and out the front door, as if no one could stop me. And no one did.

I waited for CJ on top of the slide in the playground, while below in the parking lot three boys played bicycle chicken. It was ten P.M. by my watch. Then a pair of lights swung into the lot, a station wagon, with heavy bass pounding through the windows, and the kids rode off on their bikes. Over the lake sat the nearly full moon, larger than usual and pumpkin-colored. The air was damp and fragrant, but I was nervous, like something bad was going to happen. I had never been here alone at night.

A second car (still not CJ's), a gray Plymouth sedan with spray-painted rust spots, pulled into the lot and parked as far as possible from the first. It belonged to Tweedledum and Tweedledee, high school juniors who ate lunch together, held hands in study hall, finished each other's sentences, a pair who'd been born, it seemed, thirty years old and already married to each other.

Soon the wagon drove off, leaving behind the diminishing sweet wail of the Beach Boys. A cloud passed over the face of the moon. In the new silence and darkness, stars pricked the sky, nearly too vast to bear. I turned my face to the wind, to the lake, though I couldn't see it, imagining it as wide as the Pacific and me a teenager from the real California, from, say, Santa Monica, named, say, Monique—slim and tan, suffering an alienation so universal it was like community.

I floated on the soughing wind, the faraway hum of highway traffic. When the wind fell, I thought I heard a new sound. It would merge with the rhythmic slosh of the surf, then rise above it, whimsically, like a spate of hiccups or coughing or two dogs going at it. I held my breath and scanned the lot, the playground, the fields, the woods; it seemed to come from wherever I wasn't looking. It amplified, quickened, a shrill gasping like a runner straining to win a race. Then there was only wind in the trees, the faint, irregular beat of the surf.

The moon rose above its cloud, shrinking and whitening. The metal swing set, the fence around the playground, the Plymouth's bumper and aerial shone in the moonlight, along with the slats of the monkey bars, the weedy sprigs in the sea of grass flowing out to the bluff. Hard, cropped blades like a silvery sea. It was almost September. Twenty-nine years ago the Germans had marched into Poland. Down in Chicago the cops were bashing college students. They beat someone unconscious, Elise had heard. There were no rules out here, not ones that people obeyed.

For a moment I wanted to return home. I could sneak back without being seen. I knew how to live with people who both punished and approved of me. They would let me out to buy school supplies. They would drive me to Woolworth's, glad I was at least trying to pass physics.

But to live without my friends? To walk into school where they wouldn't be? To walk the earth without them? Those three days alone in my room I could barely eat. I lived for the messages sporadically relayed: "Your friend Vera is worried about you." "St. John—I think that's his name—says hang in there." I dreamed of us seated at a perfectly square restaurant table, then woke cut off from the world of 4EVER, while their friendship, without me, knotted into something I couldn't untangle.

. . .

Moments later CJ turned into the lot and parked at the far end from the old Plymouth. As I slid into the passenger seat, I saw in the car's overhead light a beautiful woman. Glittery dress and earrings, lipstick and blush, face framed in softly curling hair. "Yikes," I said. "I mean, hi?"

"Settle down, girlie."

His eyes looked wary. I felt a little bad for him. "You look dressed for the prom. You know, if I were a guy I'd ask you." I opened my window; the night wind cooled my neck. I smiled an apology. "As a girl, you look better than me. Seriously. I mean that."

He seemed on the verge of pleased. Crickets sang around us. In the distance, the surf gasped for breath. But there was still that weird moaning in the air, as from a ghost, though it might have been a cat. "Isn't that weird, CJ?" He listened a moment, then turned his lights back on. They shone on the field and the woods. Nothing moved. He backed the car up and reparked it. He opened his glove box, found a pair of binoculars, put them to his eyes. He shook his head and looked harder, lips pressed tight together. "Do you see something out there?"

He shook his head again, as if irritated; his earrings jangled. His eyes were wide-open, his dark eyelashes thicker than mine. His line of sight moved slowly from left to right.

"What? Talk, CJ."

He laughed scratchily. "Oh, I could speak. I could tell tales." He lay back against the seat and closed his eyes. I picked up the binoculars and tried to see what he'd seen.

"Do you really want to know? Think about it."

"Quit that! You're scaring me!"

He began in a murmur, with his eyes still closed. "At the edge of the woods, there's a motor scooter lying on its side. A red motor scooter. Do we know anyone who rides a red scooter?"

I didn't like where this was heading, but he went on, louder now, as if he was enjoying himself. "And there's more to the picture, my love. Just behind the scooter, there's a blanket on the ground and two people are lying on it. For sixty-four thousand dollars, Kay, who's on the blanket? It's a tough question, but think and you'll figure it out. Or we can play Twenty Questions. Name our two mystery fuckers." He smiled into the air.

"You are so obnoxious!"

"Obnoxious is as obnoxious does. Not to mention, look before you leap. Have I addressed the question of haste making waste? We all know ignorance is bliss. But on the other hand, three strikes and you're out, dear Kay, Kate, the sweetest Kate in Christendom. Tell me, who is that masked man? And that skinny little woe-man? Turn the little wheel and focus, my love."

I got out of the car, looked at the sky, and tried to merge with the indifferent stars, but names for the lovers leaped to my mind like toads from the mouth of the ugly sister in the fairy tale, who wouldn't clean the crone's cottage and abused the beautiful sister. When I was thinking right, I was what I wanted to be, largehearted enough to rejoice in another's happiness apart from my own. I could love Elise for being seeded fourth in junior tennis in the state of Michigan, I could forgive Arlyn for being more beautiful than my mother and a competent person in the world. I could forgive Arlyn for being alive instead of my mother. Sometimes I felt my heart truly expanding, my spirit transcending the world that gave beauty and cleverness its best rewards. Then CJ leaned toward me and whispered the names of the lovers on the blanket. "The plan was to meet tomorrow morning. To work out how to liberate you. They seem to have come early."

Half of me was in despair, but the other could still argue. "You know Saint is working tonight." Through the binoculars I saw what could have been a scooter, half-hidden at the edge of the woods. I couldn't see anything behind it. "He always works Tuesday nights," I said. "Other people have scooters."

"You block, you stone, you worse-than-senseless thing."

"You're crazy, CJ."

"Let's check it out, why don't we? Let's see for our naïve, unsuspecting selves."

"You're evil," I said.

"I'm Cassandra, cursed to be always right and always disbelieved."

It could have been comic. In gown and heels, he led me across the field, his skirt swishing, his high heels at times sticking in the ground. I followed, laughing in a way that hurt the diaphragm, but I was shaking too. Then he slowed down and we walked together, pushing through the thickening air till our long, thin moon shadows touched the scattering of trees where the woods began. I recognized the scooter.

But even so, there were explanations. Even if the bike was Saint's, who's to say he wasn't alone? And even if he was with Vera, who's to say what they were doing? Then, husky and dead sure, came a voice that broke my heart: "Oh God, I love you." I pressed my hands to my mouth, as if to stifle more of these words.

We turned and walked the other way quickly, stumbling. "I'm the serpent, Kay. Did you like my apple?" His voice was amused but quavering. I shook my head with no awareness of what I was disputing. I knew only one thing—there was nothing inside me. I was gutted, bled, stripped to bone. I was a husk, ash for a breeze to blow away. No, I was immensely heavy, sunk in the ground like a boulder. A block, a stone, worse than senseless, truly too stupid to be alive.

"So what's the plan?" he said. "Shall we join them? Shall we make—how you say in America—a foursome?"

"No!"

"We should at least stop by and say hello. It's rude to ignore people. Especially your closest friends."

"Stop that!"

"Come on." He stood, motioned back toward them. "Let's congratulate them on their engagement. We'll say mazel tov."

I wanted to break away from him, but there was nowhere to go.

And even crazy, he seemed stronger than I was. "Please," I said. "Let's not make it worse!"

"Could it be worse?"

The question repeated itself in my mind while he went on about how he *must* see them, starting to babble, though it was clear he had no intention of visiting Saint and Vera in the woods, of being a part of whatever they were doing there. Clumsy as drunks, we walked toward the parking lot. We halted on opposite sides of the car. Audible as birdsong was a clear, high laugh that had to have come from Vera, happy or stoned, followed by Saint's, lower, flatter. There was the moon overhead, almost full but small as a dime in the sky. CJ said, "It's you and me, babe."

Later, I would understand that his wound was as jagged as mine. But I still don't know if mutuality lessens pain or expands it to infinity, like two mirrors facing each other. His face was white in the moonlight as if his inner deadness was coming out. And this was how I felt as well—inwardly dead—since the love that was supposed to be divvied up four ways had been dealt out (unfairly) to two alone. I couldn't decide whether it was worse to be with him or alone. There was the whine of bugs, the rustle of leaves, the ka-loosh of waves, his slightly asthmatic breathing. Even sounds hurt, like the bites of insects. My hands were cold, my cheeks cold, as if I'd lost the strength to keep myself warm. "Let's get in the car?" I said.

"But where should we go?"

There was nothing snarky in his voice, just the unanswerable question. There was not just nowhere to go, there was nowhere to be. The two arenas between which I had swung like a pendulum those years had both disappeared. First, the door of the house in which I ate and slept had clanged behind me like an iron gate. Now the grassy acres between the parking lot and the lake looked not just alien but indifferent, although I'd been here so often I knew the bare spots in the grass under the tree, the rust of the scattered trash cans, the flaking paint on the tables, the old fascist sign: PICNIC ONLY IN DESIGNATED AREA . . .

"Let's go to San Francisco," I said doubtfully.

"That was good last year. Now they're all wasted. High on smack."

"I've never tried smack."

"It may not be too late."

Luckily he didn't wait for my response. We got into the car and set out for nowhere.

22

Vera

———

Just inside the fringe of woods, nearly invisible to anyone not looking for them, Saint and Vera occupy the plaid wool blanket from Vera's bed. Vera turns onto her side and runs a hand along Saint's back, which—interestingly—is soft and hard in different places. The knobby chain of his spine seems oddly fragile, while the two triangles of muscle from his neck to his shoulders are thick and hard. She would like to chomp down there, close her jaws, almost, but not quite, to the point of puncture. Then she is distracted by the valley alongside his right shoulder blade, which deepens when he moves his arm. On the inner slope of the valley sits a small, dark brown mole, slightly raised. She tests it with the tip of her tongue, then lays her cheek on his back and listens to him breathing. Over and around them is a tender blanket of small outdoor sounds, crickets, wind in the leaves, the purr of a distant highway. Above, gaps in the branches open onto the overarching night, an immensity toward which they seem to be moving, clicking upward as if in the back car of a roller coaster. There's no getting off. She takes a small, tentative breath. She can maybe accept that.

Saint raises his head. "I think they saw us."

"Ooooh," she says sleepily. "Get the gun." She doesn't look where he is looking. Then after a moment: "Who?"

He laughs. "Kay and CJ. He's wearing a dress, but it's definitely him. They were looking this way."

"She escaped! Good for her." Like a friendly dog she takes nibbling bites of his arm flesh, contemplating the vast and bewildering range of human behavior. "CJ in a dress? Seriously?"

Their voices are murmurous and silky. "Why do you think," she says, "he put a dress on?"

They kiss. He sighs. "This isn't good," he says.

"I'll bet he looks fine in a dress."

"No, I meant—"

"I know what you meant. I was being silly." Then she addresses what, of course, he meant. "They'd've had to know, before, that we . . ." She doesn't want to complete the thought.

"We'd've told them tomorrow."

"Should we go talk to them?"

"Probably. Or we can wait till tomorrow."

They kiss awhile, then Saint looks out across the field. "They're gone."

She laughs with relief. "Maybe you imagined them."

"I think I'm imagining *this*," he says.

Their lips are so close they almost brush as he speaks. She could drink his breath. "Say that again."

They want to keep murmuring together, fanning the embers of the agreeable tension. "They saw and walked away," he says.

"What should they do, join the party? They're being polite. Showing tact."

"Should we go find them? We ought to talk to them."

She sticks her foot over the edge of the blanket, feels pebbly ground then retracts the errant limb. Her one venture outside their little haven. "You first." She glances into the lighter dark beyond the trees. She thinks she sees headlights. "We'll both go," she says, trying to remember how she talked when she was more sure of things. "Just say the word. Well?"

"Well?"

"Or we could postpone it. What time is it?"

"Should I get my watch?"

She rolls back to him, puts his hand on her breast. "We're not being good friends."

"We'll be good friends later," he says, and kisses the base of her neck. She kisses his neck right under his ear. They lie on their sides face-to-face. Later is almost unimaginable. "It's definitely hard to get up right now."

"I'll second that."

"I like the smell of your mouth."

"Tooth rot and cigarettes."

He rolls her onto her back, bends over her, and licks her teeth under her lower lip. It tickles, not quite pleasantly. Something is poking her from under the blanket, but she doesn't mind. His lips move down her neck, over the top of her chest. She gasps for air, but she doesn't need air. She needs something she has no name for, but she can wait and it might be better to wait. He says, "I love you, Vera."

She shivers, reaching for the warmth he is offering. She can barely speak. "Me too," she says.

"You love yourself too? I could have figured."

She nods giddily. Joy is nearby, almost within reach. "There's some left over for you." She has already told him she loves him. A stingy part of her doesn't want to repeat it, as if the store of such utterances is limited. She can't remember now why she wanted to die. That is, she knows why but can't re-create the feeling. She pulls him onto her, wraps her legs around him, squeezes till he's pushing back. The poky thing is still there, and with all her strength she arches the two of them up, reaches under the blanket, and extracts Saint's Tao Te Ching. Earlier today he read some of it to her. "It was hurting me."

"I'm sure it didn't mean to."

She runs an edge of the book down his spine.

"That feels weird."

"Spine to spine. Laugh, Saint."

"I am, but just to make you feel good."

"I usually hate puns. What's wrong with me?" Into his ear she chants, "The Tao that can be named is not the Tao," then bites the side of his arm till he yelps.

"Stop that."

"It could save the world," she says, a remark he once made to her.

She opens the book but can't read in the dark. She remembers lilting, inscrutable lines. Did he really understand them? She licks the side of his neck. "Salt. With a sandy aftertaste."

"You're in a silly mood, Vera."

"I know," she says. "But I'm worried, a little. Are you?"

"Are you getting cold feet?"

She startles. "Not about *that*," she says sharply. "I meant our friends. I'm afraid they'll . . ." Actually, she's not sure what she's afraid of.

"Maybe they're falling in love with each other at this very moment?" Saint offers.

At the possibility, however unlikely, their serenity returns. Through the screen of trees the moonlit field is silver and silent. She kisses him till she loses her breath. "The bomb has dropped. We're the last people on earth."

"Kiss me with your eyes open."

She tries to keep her eyes open on his open eyes, but as his face comes toward her it's like an approaching train and she turns away. Then the cool, damp wind makes her skin want his skin again, a phenomenon she finds remarkable. She puts her lips to his fragile temple, imagining later riding behind him on his scooter, the thrum of the motor, her chest to his warm back. Imagines them stopping on the shoulder of the road to embrace. Maybe finding another place to lie down, on leaves, pine needles; let the bugs bite. It seems remarkable as well that they are here now and remarkable that tomorrow they will be here or somewhere, and after that? After that, time is a gaping hole, beautiful and terrible, if they don't do what the four of them have pledged to do. And for the first time since they signed the Pledge, she seriously wonders what would happen to her and to them if, for whatever reason, they all declined to jump. If the day after tomorrow came and went, and the next day, and more days after that, so much time, to be filled by her and Saint finding places to lie down together. They could tear up the Pledge, all four of them together, with the plan to live happily, at least until they're not happy anymore. The wind comes harder, blowing dust and grit; she is frightened now. So much thinking is required. She isn't sure how Saint would respond to a change of mind from her. She is not a girl who changes her mind. Would she become someone whose views could be overlooked—someone ordinary, weak, in need? Would that be terrible?

Then, for no reason, her body jerks.

"What's up, Vee? You fell asleep?"

She shakes her head fiercely no. But her mouth hurts; her teeth are clenched. For the past day or so she has forgotten Garth.

Saint has gone back to kissing her face; she smiles resolutely. Since he doesn't know and she doesn't have to tell, the thought may return to where it came from. Words have this nasty function of preserving things, of making them real for good or ill. And what could she say to Saint about her brother's slender body? His skin, soft everywhere unlike the body beside her, which is only soft in specific places, the temples, the inside of his elbows. She presses against Saint, kisses him back, quickening her breath in time with his.

Vera has had sex so early and often that the instances have blurred together. She remembers mostly the clash of pleasure and pain. There were usually three stages:

1. Breathless loss of self, like a dream of flying.

2. Burning tearing, in which the good feeling swells till it bursts.

3. Clear-eyed stillness. After which comes the driving urge to be somewhere else and alone.

But it was different with Garth. Besides the thrill and the pleasuring pain, there was a sense of inevitability—of the two of them at the center of events that converged at the single point of her joy and shame. She remembers part of a poem she memorized for ninth-grade English. *Out of the night that covers me, / Black as the Pit from pole to pole, / I thank whatever gods may be / For my unconquerable soul.* She and Garth—they have the same soul, made to fight to the death whatever tries to overpower them. With Garth there was no stage three, no stillness or urge to withdraw, just the sense of having started something that couldn't be stopped.

But maybe it could be stopped. Her ribs ache around the throb of her heart. *I am the master of my fate: I am the captain of my soul.* She takes in sharp, frantic gulps of air.

With Saint too the stillness eludes her. His part in the ballet of sexual intercourse is so groping and wondering that she forgets there's a direction and an end. Sometimes his lips stay closed like a little kid's, and her mouth (this has never happened before) swims with saliva, and she has to open his mouth with hers, which makes her want to die of tenderness. She comes and it's not enough; she must come again, and it isn't enough. There is no resting place, just the endless cliff-edge spin of wanting. Perhaps that will sustain her?

She looks over at Saint on his back beside her, hands clasped under his head. He has his T-shirt back on; she can't remember when he did that. Despondently she kisses the cotton over the swell of his shoulder. She is trying to be brave, though she doesn't know what there is to be brave about. She tongues the salty, sourish crease between his groin and his leg. She sticks out her tongue at him. He lies heavy and still. She puts a hand on his stomach under his shirt. Should she tell him about Garth? Would speaking her sin shrink it in her mind or make it larger and more disgusting? Would it weaken the spell of the taboo or whatever still holds her in thrall?

"Saintly?"

He's asleep. The affront adds to the affront of the newly donned T-shirt. *Fuck you, pal.* She curls into herself, gathering the strength to rise, to trot off home. But strength needs will to set it in motion. Saint lies encased in his shirt, the armor of his indifference to her, while from her own naked body, it seems, the protective epidermis has entirely dissolved. She has been flayed, filleted, laid open.

And then it returns—love, or something close to love. When she believes, body and soul, that unless he does something to restore her she will lie here forever, living but dead, he drapes a mammoth leg across her legs and kisses the back of her neck. His hand wanders the rise of her belly, a finger brushes the topmost curls of private hair. Warm, sweet honey milk laps the edges of her. When it reaches her heart, she turns around in his arms.

Now on the crest of pleasure, she is careless of pain. Her mouth opens; his too. Their tongues flick virginally. *If you don't mind. Please.* She kisses him harder, murmuring "I love you" for the sound alone, but it must be love that she is feeling. Her skin melts onto her bones, there are no separate stages, no plateaus, just the sensation of rising. Could it last 4EVER? "Saint," she whispers, "there's something . . . about me"—there are pauses between the clumps of words—"that I think you should know. . . ."

She's trying to swallow what is blocking her words when the roar of an engine, distant but amplifying, breaks the night's silence. Brakes squeal. It's annoying but no big deal. From time to time cars arrive in the parking lot. Now a beam of light sweeps the trees over their heads. They shut their eyes. The light swings by again, unusually bright, like the parabolic beam from a car lot. They can't see for a moment. Saint breathes against her neck, "Some crazy guy."

She lifts her head, blinking through the afterimage, and is blinded again. She sits up, feeling around for her clothing. "We should get out of here."

"I'll bet it's the compadres. Giving us a hard time."

"At least let's move farther into the woods."

"The bugs will eat us alive."

"Then let's pack up. We'll walk the scooter and leave by the north exit."

He sighs heavily, stretching his legs. The revolving beam catches the jungle gym in the play area, soars into the blackness over the lake, finds the jut of his nose and brow. He used to be chunkier, she thinks, a solid core cushioned with baby fat. His flesh has hardened lately, like the body of a guerrilla in the hills above Hanoi, honed to its necessities in the constant readiness for fighting.

For a moment she rests on her dream of him in the crazed sweep of dark and light. Then the engine cuts off, the light goes out. The weave of small noises rises up again—crickets and wind. But it's like a cobweb, almost instantly rent by the firm click-open of an oiled car door. She knows the sound. It afflicts her dreams. "Saint, we've *got* to get out of here!"

He turns, kisses the side of her leg.

"Saint, it's my father!"

"How do you know?"

"Please don't be stupid!"

In the dark she finds jeans, thrusts her legs into them. Too big. She rips them off, throws them at him, grabs her own. She can't find her shirt.

"Calm down, Vera." He sits up, blows her a kiss. "All right. But don't freak. The park's open till eleven." He yawns. "What time is it?"

Who cares! she'd have screamed if there were time. But sliding into her own jeans she hears—click-click—the open and shut of a glove box she knows is her father's. It's clearly audible to her although he closes it quietly, always quietly, because it's important to care for your things. Once at age five or six, after climbing down from his car, she slammed the door too hard, a shiny blue door that she pushed with both hands and all the strength of her small body to make sure it stayed closed (there was a distinct and satisfying ka-thunk), and he placed her bad hand on the clean, oiled inside of the door and pretended to slam it—"That's how the car feels!"—grand in the righteous anger of punishment. "Learn to value what belongs to you!" He didn't hurt her, but she couldn't stop crying. Her father believes in punishment, its sacred necessity. She pulls at Saint's arm. "You must have a death wish."

"I thought we wanted to die."

"Not like this."

"I'm not afraid of your father."

"You dick!" She turns his jeans right side out, pushes a leg hole at his foot. "This is a *cop* we're talking about. He has a fucking *gun*. He's licensed to kill in the state of Michigan and he isn't crazy about you." Saint doesn't seem to hear. His leg doesn't lift. "Do it yourself," she cries. Across the field, steps crunch the gravel of the parking lot. She stumbles to her feet and bounds through the trees toward the deepest darkness, her heart as loud in her ears as the crash of her running—too loud for her to know if some burly, outraged emissary of justice is running after her.

She runs the straightest line she can manage, simply *away*, till the trees thin and the wind is strong. She has arrived at the bluff to the south of where they meet, closer to the beach. Scrub trees, dark sky over water. Her lungs burn, and so do the bottoms of her feet. She has her jeans on but no shirt or shoes. Her hair is matted with twigs and leaves like a wild boy's.

She puts her arms around a narrow tree trunk, the last entity this side of the void. The bark moves in and out against her chest as if it too is breathing. Once upon a time there might have been people she hugged like this, but she can't remember whom. Her Texas grandpa, who died when she was eight? He's not even a smell anymore. Her eyes closed, she is breathing into the bark, deciding how long to stay here, when from the woods behind her comes a crack of branches too clumsy for an animal. A murmur: "Diana. Goddess of the moon."

It's Garth. He sings "Diana" into her ear. Yes, he is young and she is old—she feels eons older than he is. His voice soars into falsetto, still as sweet as an angel's: *"Oh please, stay by me . . ."* She turns around and steps back, crossing her arms over her chest. "You total shit."

He jabs an imaginary knife into his breast, staggers, drops to the ground, and writhes at her feet, which would have been funny at one time.

"You're out of your mind," she says. He grabs her foot. She shakes him off. "How could you? How could you sic Dad on me!"

He flaps his empty arms on the grass. "You don't exactly run like an Indian scout."

He hasn't cut his hair this summer. It's a wild mass all around his head. She wonders, irrelevantly, if their father asked him to cut it and he refused. "Garth, listen to me. I have my own life. Please don't ruin it." Moonlit, his face is pale and bony as death, but he is more beautiful than ever. His body is shuddering; she kneels down and touches his shoulder. "I have my life and you have your life. Did you hear me?"

He lies on his back, sprawled and still.

Stop that! she wants to shriek. But she speaks softly, keeping her arms modestly folded. This is her brother, whom she used to baby-sit, whom she taught to read, whose lunches she made when their mother was drunk. "Garth, don't you see, this desire thing? It's hormones, the juice your glands secrete." She fixes on the hand covering his eyes. "It's just a state of mind. Which you can get control over." She scoots closer, pleased, moved, strengthened by her lucidity. "The bad stuff too! When Dad calls me a slut, I have a choice! I can take it in and feel like shit. Or I can barricade my mind against him. I don't even have to convince him, I just say to myself: If a slut is someone who has lots of sex, then I'm a slut, so what? The good or bad is just society's opinion, and who's society but you and me? We have our own opinions: Sex is good, therefore a person who has a lot of sex does the world some good. *Is* good! So I'm good, I'm great! What's the matter? Is this something you already know?"

His arm lifts, then falls across his eyes. His mouth is a tight seam. She tugs at his hand. "Take incest. What a creepy word. 'We committed *incest.*'" She makes her voice thin and horror-struck. "But we don't have to think of it as *incest,* quote-unquote. The Bible says no to incest because you get weird kids, but that was before birth control. On the level of *real* there's nothing wrong with what we did. No one was hurt by it." She's not sure what she's saying is true, but she wants it to be true. It *ought* to be true. "We can walk away with our heads up!"

She prays for him to move, and he does after a while. "Who's *we?*" he says.

"What?" she says, smiling encouragement.

"Who says what *we* want? Suppose I don't want to walk away? Even down in Florida, all I thought about was you." He sits up. His adolescent voice rings like an old bell. "I don't think of it as *incest,* quote-unquote; I don't think of it as anything. I want to hold you. I want to be inside you again. That's all."

He takes her hands and presses them to his cheeks. His face is wet and salty. Tears spring to her own eyes. "Teddy," she says, the name she used to call him when he was three years old, as warm and soft as a stuffed animal. She kisses his head as she did then, like a mother, with simple affection, until she feels his tongue at the junction of her lips where Saint's had been. And there's that feeling again, spreading from her groin into her legs and chest, a mélange of pleasure and pain that's part heaven and part a torture out of the Middle Ages, her limbs tied to horses all raring to go in four different directions. She puts her hands on his chest, though she can't make herself push him away. "Please. I'm not into that."

"You *were,* Vera."

She swallows. Pushes a little. He doesn't move.

"You were," he repeats. "What happened?"

She stands and steps back, inserting salutary space between them. She wrings her hands, the good and the bad one. *I love you, Teddy.* She wills the words into her brother's mind, a protective shield for him out in the world. "It shouldn't have happened, Garth."

"What do you mean? Don't you want me anymore?"

The answer to his question is so complicated her mind stalls out. His body twists from side to side with a pain she understands but must not assuage. "You've got to get out of here. Away from me. For both of us. Garth, I'm begging you!"

He is shaking as if with fever, in uncontrollable pulses. His eyes and mouth are open wide, pulling her in. She doesn't move, willing him up, willing him free from their precious and hideous tenderness. Their eyes are locked on each other. Then a sound comes from his lips, lost, forsaken, as desolate as an abandoned house. Dragging his gaze from her face like some poisonous tentacle, he pulls himself to his feet and plunges back into the woods.

23

Saint

———

Saint feels around in the dark wet grass for his clothes and dresses quickly, but he can't arouse in himself a sense of urgency. He feels languid, like a sultan so fully satisfied that the aftermath can be only sleep. He puts a sock on, can't find the other. Should he be frightened? All around him the world seems suffused with love; inside him and out there is love. If a wild beast approached, teeth bared, dripping saliva, he would soothe, welcome it to the happy human world. As for the Pledge—he doesn't take it seriously, nor does he believe that Vera does. Vera is happy. "Vee," he says into an imaginary mouthpiece, "where the fuck is my sock? Over and out."

He puts on his sneaker without the sock, is about to tie it, his thoughts and his fingers moving very slowly, when he sees two figures near the playground. The beam of a flashlight flits over the ground, illuminating a table, a trash can. This is not, he thinks, a good thing, and he steps back into the trees. He drags the blanket back a couple of feet, along with his book and backpack. But it remains hard for him to locate the spot in himself where fear abides. He picks up Vera's shirt, so small though it's big on her, puts it to his face, carefully folds it into his backpack. He rolls up her small pack and squeezes it inside of his. Did she take her shoes? The key to the scooter is in the ignition: He could put it in neutral and try to follow her path, but they made no plan about where to meet. He looks over the ground for more of what belongs to her, unwilling to leave this spot to which she might return. He can't imagine anything happening to her out in the sparse woods; they are completely familiar to her. His concern is losing her, having to ride home without her, and tomorrow having to face her hurt and anger.

Now the second figure is gone, but the flashlight seems to be crossing the field. The light bobs; the patches of ground it illuminates swell and shrink. But although the flashes seem random, their movement seems to be in his direction, as if the light is a missile and his heat what it's seeking. A beam strikes a tree behind him, brushes past the scooter, then seems to linger. Hairs rise on the back of his neck. There are trees between him and the light and the man who wields it, but he feels *seen*.

In danger mode now, he rights the scooter, wheels it to the far side of the blanket, and leans it against a tree. He unlocks the carry-all, removes Vera's brother's gun, and loads the one bullet. What a joke, this little gun, next to what they had on the West Side, though all he ever shot at were stop signs and SLOW CHILDREN CROSSING signs to impress the Badger Boys. With a self-conscious flourish he stuffs the gun into his pants under his T-shirt and feels a little safer. Stronger. Calmer. He has done nothing wrong, or at least nothing that will get him arrested. Kids hang out in the summer woods after park hours. At worst they're told to get their horny asses on home. He smooths out the blanket, sits down, crosses his legs, and tries to count his breaths. Then it's like the goo has just washed out of his eyes because he can see now between the tree trunks. Vera was right. Walking toward him, in uniform, holster and all, is her father.

Nam myoho renge kyo.

In his two years at Lourdes Senior High, Saint hasn't had what his priest had called an *episode,* but he has had to be watchful. When Cathy Kirk pretended not to see him, or giggled with her girlfriend as he passed in the hall, he'd wanted to grab her by her ponytail and slap her snotty face. He'd have preferred to put her in her place with a few choice words, but even afterward nothing came to mind, which may have been the problem. He was three, his mother said, before he regularly put words together; complete sentences came slowly to him. And when he tried to speak and wasn't understood, he'd fly at the person, growling like a dog, or beat the floor with his hands and feet until quelled by the predictable violence of a spanking.

Starting school, though, he was obedient and good-natured. He was intrigued by the mysterious order of the painted circle on the floor, of children his age raising their hands to answer questions, listening to stories and craning to see the pictures in the teacher's book, singing in a group. He obeyed any rules that were made clear to him. He couldn't bear doing less than very well, and his occasional outbursts were lost in the daily small violences of the city classroom. In fifth grade he fell in love with Sister Mary Perpetua and labored for her *Excellent* in red at the top of his paper. Then a test came back with three red X's and *You can do better, St. John,* and he rammed his chair against the desk behind him. Then, in the lunch line, a boy named Charles asked to see his quarter, put it in his own pocket, and wouldn't return it though St. John had explained that it belonged to him. There seemed to be no choice. He head-butted Charles to the tiled floor and kept on punching, even after the boy stopped struggling and blood dripped from his nose and mouth.

In the principal's office the next morning, St. John learned that he had broken Charles's jaw. "I was shocked," said the sister to St. John's mother. "He's usually one of the good ones." In the large wooden chair beside his mother, who wouldn't look at him, St. John felt himself growing dimmer and more mysterious to himself. He remembered hitting Charles but not the feeling in his stomach and throat that made him hit. If he was no longer among the good ones, where did that place him?

"He's turning into his father," his mother said despairingly.

St. John was eleven years old then and rarely saw his father. When his father called, St. John refused to talk to him, and his mother didn't make him. "Too little, too late," she said into the phone. Sometimes St. John said it to himself: *Too little, too late.*

That's what he said to himself while the principal, who had pale wet eyes and seemed thousands of years old, lectured him about self-control—if everyone did just what they wanted to do, the world would be chaos, as in the time before the birth of government. But he hadn't *wanted* to hit Charles. He had wanted, above all, to curl into a ball and roll away. On top of Charles, with the boy's blood running out of his nose, he felt small and weak and easily hurt. Even while he was punching. Even as they pulled him away.

It was Father Barnett at Most Holy Redeemer who gave him a handhold. His mother had brought him there on her day off. "He has a rotten temper," she told the priest, a very young man with pimples on his face. "What'll it be when he's bigger, that's what I worry about."

"Life is long," said Father Barnett.

St. John was startled by the pimples, and by the fact that the priest looked about as old as a high school kid. "Are you truly sorry?" said Father Barnett, his bright blue eyes shining, radiantly resigned to the world's sins and maybe to his own complexion.

"Yes!" said St. John, to stop further talk on the subject, but he couldn't stop the priest from clasping his and his mother's hands and asking God to forgive them all the sin of anger. On the wall over the priest's desk a wooden crucified Christ looked resigned and radiant like Father Barnett.

Thereafter, when someone pushed into the tender space around him where words refused to assemble, St. John would conjure a resigned, radiant crucifixion. He kept a journal, in which he wrote: *I think of Jesus hanging from those nails. One day I will be empty and free.* And after they moved to Lourdes, despite the setback with Cathy Kirk, he found that rage came less often. The Buddha replaced Jesus but proffered equal tranquillity. He had friends who wanted to hear what he had to say. And the lake bordering the town spread in all directions, vast enough to absorb almost anything.

. . .

Saint is seated in meditation, the thumb and middle finger of each hand completing the circle that links his mind to the mind of the universe, when Officer DeVito arrives. The bright police-issue flashlight plays over the Tao Te Ching on the blanket, over Saint's crossed legs and up past the slight bulge of the gun, which feels unduly warm on Saint's skin. "Hey you," says the policeman, loud in the quiet woods. "Friar Tuck!"

Meditating or not, Saint would like to lay the man out. The urge is distinct and unalloyed. He knows Vera's stories. He could head-butt the officer, knee his nuts, and have his own gun out before the asshole unsnapped his holster. He'd make him crawl to his car, dazed and humiliated. But all his life Saint has been training for this moment of self-governance. He knows how to keep revenge in his pocket like a joint in a baggie or a gun he'll never use. *The Tao that can be told is not the eternal Tao. The name that can be named is not the eternal name.* The little gun doesn't hurt his side when he sits erect. He allows his gaze to reach Vera's father's face and says amicably, "Hey, Mr. D, sir."

The flashlight shines on the book. "Nighttime reading?"

"What?" The light flashes at his eyes, but Saint will not flinch. "Oh. Yessir." He unlocks his legs deliberately and sees his dangling shoelace. The lapse irritates him.

"So what's happening, bud, a solo picnic? Me, myself, and I?"

"It's a good place to be quiet, sir." Should he say he was meditating? It being a hippie thing, he decides against it. He tries to tie his shoe, but his fingers are clumsy. He doubles one lace, winds the other slowly around it, while the light investigates his backpack.

"Anything in there?"

Just a little smack, he wants to say. *To sell to the school kids. Do you have a warrant?* "Personal stuff," he says quietly.

"How personal?"

The man steps deliberately onto the blanket. Saint gives up on the tying, puts the book into his backpack, and holding the pack against the gun in his pants he rises to his feet. "I've got to get going. Got work tomorrow." His voice is even. He tugs at the blanket lightly to pull it out from under Mr. D. "Excuse me, sir."

The man's flashlight is trained on Vera's small sandal, on its side at the base of a tree. He plants a heavy foot on the end of Saint's shoelace. Saint stumbles, lands on his knee. Shame and rage make him gasp, but he is mindful. *Who can wait quietly while the mud settles? Who can remain still until the moment of action? Observers of the Tao do not seek fulfillment. Not seeking fulfillment, they are not swayed.* He observes the man standing over him. "I haven't done anything, Officer DeVito. What do you want from me?"

Mr. DeVito isn't tall—Saint has four inches on him and weighs almost as much—but he seems to swell before Saint like a blow-up doll. He grabs the back of Saint's neck and squeezes, punctuating his speech with jerks of Saint's head. "You pathetic piece of dog crap. You tell my daughter to get her ass home if she expects to be able to sit on it anytime soon. Tell her that."

The hand tightens. Saint's jeans unsnap. He works his hand around the pack to catch the gun before it falls, imagines it tumbling out at DeVito's feet. He wants, horribly, to laugh. "I will, sir. If I run into her."

The policeman gives him another shake, then pushes him away as if overcome with disgust. "Get the fuck out of here. You can twang your twanger in your own outhouse. And from this moment on, if you so much as wish her good morning, if you say hi, you queer piece of shit, you won't have jack to jack off with!"

The man's gaze burns through Saint's retinas to the delicate meat of his brain. The Tao has fled from Saint, every soothing, puzzling line. What's left are the pale bags under Mr. D's eyes and his crooked bottom teeth and his nose too small for his nostrils, too small for him to take an honest breath through. The man deserves to die; that is clear to Saint. Less clear is whether or not to be his executioner. With a bullet in the gut Mr. D would be more respectful. Under cover of his backpack, Saint feels for the gun's trigger.

Then the policeman lowers his flashlight and suddenly his nose looks just like Vera's nose, small for his face, the kind of nose you have to fight to protect. The man is a dick but no threat, a middle-aged creep with sour breath. *The ancient masters were subtle, mysterious, profound, responsive. Watchful, like men crossing a winter stream. Courteous, like visiting guests. Yielding, like ice about to melt. Simple, like uncarved blocks of wood.* Saint sits back on his heels, still holding his pack, a posture that keeps the gun in place and looks natural. The width of the blanket separates them, a span Saint has no need to cross. "I hear what you're saying, sir."

Mr. D shakes his head as if he understands everything about Saint that he will ever need to, and he spits on the blanket. "I'm going for a beer. One quick beer. If she's not home when I get there, you're going to hear from me."

With the swagger of a man who has no idea how close he just came to death, he walks back across the field, calling out for Garth, high and furious. Saint can't move, even when a little later the headlights go on in the parking lot and the car drives off.

Even with everything silent again, Saint remains on the blanket, trying to understand what has just happened. He feels like a stone sinking in water of uncertain depth, waiting to touch bottom. *Other men are clear and bright, but I alone am dim and weak. Other men are sharp and clever, but I alone am dull and stupid. Everyone else is busy, but I alone am aimless and depressed.* He sets the gun down, refastens his pants, tucks his shirt in, while shame crawls up his spine. He had a gun and he let someone shit on him. He could have nailed the man. Made the world a better place. With all his self-governing he is fundamentally stupid.

The one thing he knows for sure is that he has to see Vera. He's trying to decide whether to search for her or wait here a little longer—he's about to get his watch out of the carryall and put the gun back—when he hears the crackle of underbrush. A tall, lanky boy enters the small clearing. It's Garth, Vera's brother. Saint is almost glad to see him. "Hey, bud," he says to Garth, smiling, "where's the big sister?"

The boy walks toward him, head down. He looks skinnier than usual, jeans low on his hips and held up by his belt. He has blond hair like Vera's, not as long as hers but way beyond school regulations. Saint has always liked him. Respects him, even, for a cockiness that seems unfeigned. As if he genuinely doesn't care what other people think. He says louder, "This might sound weird, Garth, but she took off when your dad showed up. You didn't run into her, did you?"

Garth punches him in the stomach.

"Hey!" The blow was clumsy and didn't hurt, but it annoys him. What to do when a younger, smaller kid starts a fight? You can't fight back, and you can't not fight back. It's a dilemma. "What's with you?"

Garth comes at him again, and his arms are long enough to reach him, but there is no force in his blows. Saint gives him an almost tender look and blocks a swipe at his face. "Cut it out. What's wrong with you?"

"Leave her alone," Garth says. His eyes send out serious hatred. "You keep your hands off her!"

"What? Who? Vera?"

Garth's chin trembles. "Have you done it with her? You better tell me!"

Saint feels his cheeks heat up. "It's none of your business!" He'd laugh, but he doesn't want to hurt Garth's feelings.

"Fuck you down to hell! I swear I'll kill you!"

Saint smiles, but Garth lunges for him. Saint holds him by the arms. Garth shrieks, "Tell me the truth, you bastard!"

Saint is tired of Garth, but earnest ferocity shines from the boy's face. "Look," he says lightly but also, he hopes, respectfully, "you don't want to be like your father." Garth flings more obscenities.

"What's it to you? Are you trying to guard your sister's honor or something? Vera and I love each other."

"And?"

"*And?*" He snorts at the absurdity. "Obviously, we . . ." His ears feel hot. This is not a topic for Vera's brother.

"Obviously what? Do you guys fuck or not?"

Saint smiles like an idiot, almost apologetically.

Garth stands up straight. The boy is tall but gaunt, like one of those starving kids in Africa that need your donation. For a moment Saint wants to put an arm around him, this earnest boy with his bizarre loyalty. Then Garth says, "Us too."

The tone hits Saint first, the ferocious pride. His knee twitches. "What do you mean?"

"What do you think I mean?"

"You love your sister," Saint says. "I know that."

Garth laughs shrilly. "Eat your heart out, man."

It takes some moments for Saint to fully grasp what was implied. Then he tells himself that Garth is a sick kid. "You shouldn't lie about a thing like that."

"No, you shouldn't." Garth has mastered himself. He is looking straight at him, eye to eye to eye to eye. Saint makes himself look back. "Ask *her*, if you have the guts."

Garth's voice is challenging and sulky, like the voice of a small boy who thinks he's finally got the pointless advantage. Their eyes are locked, Saint can't look away. All he can do is will the boy out of his life. He wants to go home, lie down, fall asleep, and wake up days later with his mind clear.

Then it seems to Saint that it is he who has been willed away. He feels like a spirit wafting up and away from this craziness. He looks out over the field. The moon is behind a cloud, but the stars are thick. Light gleams on Garth's belt buckle. As in a dream, Saint sees the belt unbuckling, the already loose jeans bagging down, the long, bony back and torso, the dirty fingers with their nervous bitten nails touching all the private places in the fragile body that he too has loved. Loves. With the howl of a crazy dog he drives his shoulder into the boy's gut.

If Garth is hurt he keeps it to himself. They circle, arms out. Saint is stronger and heavier, but Garth is lithe and slippery, lacking in substance for Saint to damage. Their feet move on and off the blanket. They vie for the advantage; no one can get in a blow. Then Saint's sneakered foot knocks against the gun, which he'd actually forgotten. He swoops down for it before the boy can get to it and holds it pointed at the ground, his other hand stretched out in a kind of plea. "Admit," he says, "you're a liar." The face of the boy across the blanket moves in and out of focus. Saint wants to instill fear in Garth, to reduce him to the size of a bug to be stomped underfoot, but Garth remains unfazed. It's as if he can't even see the gun. Saint releases the safety, not to shoot, just to make that distinct, authoritative click. There are no limits to a gun's authority, not just over people but over reality, it seems to Saint. The gun is the guardian of truth. "This is your moment," he says to Garth. "You can't go around telling lies about people."

The boy looks at him gravely. "You *wish* I lied." He makes no move, but it's as if he did. Saint steps back, raises the gun. His knees are shaking. "I told you the truth," Garth says, his face aglow. "The whole truth and nothing but the truth."

Saint takes aim, but the gun is so light it won't stay still. It's wobbling all over the place. "Shut your face," he says, sounding ridiculous to his own ears. "I mean it," he adds.

"We screwed," says Garth. "We made love to each other. She was completely into it. She panted and screamed. Like this." He reproduces the panting, which seems comical to Saint in some inaccessible part of his mind. But Garth's face is pale and solemn. "She loves *me*," says Garth, "better than you. More and deeper than you."

"Shut the fuck up! I'm warning you. Please!" Saint feels sickeningly weak. He's pointing the gun at Garth, but it's more like he's handing it over to the boy. Begging him to take it.

"Shoot. I dare you." Garth steps toward him with his arms out. "I'll give you a hand. Give me that gun."

Even now there is more than one thing that Saint can do. He can hurl the gun into the darkness behind them. He can put the safety back on, return the gun to his pants. In the prolonged fractional second in the adrenaline pump of a fight there's time for consideration. He straightens his back, trying to maintain possession of the gun along with some trappings of the dignity that Garth seems determined to shred. Once uttered or even hinted at, a threat cannot be retracted. Not if you want to walk the earth with your head up.

Across the blanket, Saint can see Garth's face, so much like Vera's that he can't bring himself even to hit the boy, let alone blow his brains out. But Garth is grabbing at the gun and Saint's finger is hooked around the trigger, and what can be done? Even before the blast Saint feels it coming, but the hand is slower than the mind. Which, even before Garth falls to the ground, perceives the future as pure, empty space. Like an old TV screen, contracting to a line, then a tiny point, then, after a moment, winking out.

Part III

24

Flight

We drove south toward Chicago. The plan was to find a motel near Interstate 80, a crappy place where no one would question us. In the morning we'd head west toward San Francisco. It was CJ's plan. I had no plan.

After an hour or so, in which CJ monologued and I sat in dead-feeling silence, he pulled into a rest area. Toilets, drinking fountain, Plexiglassed-in map (YOU ARE HERE). Got to powder my nose, he said, and tap-tapped into the small building, steady in his high heels like he was born wearing them.

I couldn't smile. I stayed in my seat praying for something to change. *4EVER* was indelibly inscribed across my calf, but where it had been in my mind was a gaping hole. People said don't put all your eggs in one basket, but I had only one basket, the best imaginable basket. Without which I was (ha-ha!) a basket case?

He returned with two cups of coffee, one for me, along with a packet containing two saccharin tabs. He smelled of air freshener. "Ladies' is nicer than Men's," he said. "I had a feeling about that." He was carrying long gloves and he put them on, pulled them toward the twin small swells of his biceps. He smoothed his skirt. "We have met the enemy and he is us. Now, let's drown our sorrows." He sipped from his cup and put a gloved arm around me. "Have you ever wanted to make it with a girlfriend? I hear it's nifty. So much surface area."

I was running on shock. I didn't even try to keep up with him. "Did you get high in there?"

"I'm high on you, dear. On the freedom of the night."

I let him hold my hand. But his lips were bright red, and his female face made me woozy. My tactic for quashing despair (besides eating) was sharing pain with another person—two grieving hearts better than one—but he was jabbering away as if nothing had happened. I said, "I don't understand you at all."

"You're in the majority, Kay. Along with me, myself, and I."

He smiled. I felt even more tired. "Doesn't anything ever get to you? Is everything a joke?"

"There are good jokes and bad jokes."

"I hate when you do this."

"Do what?" he said.

I put my mouth to my coffee but didn't tilt the cup. In some ways it was like when my mother died. Bleakness to infinity. "I don't know about this."

"You mean this trip? Should we go back home?"

I closed my eyes. For a moment I hated all four of us, the glitter of our self-conscious pain. Our pride, as if pain was heroic. I sat in my seat, stiff with self-revulsion. "It's like you're always onstage, CJ. Always acting."

"Is that a good thing or a bad thing?"

I'd meant to insult him. His neutral question opened a little space in my mind. Maybe it was fine to be theatrical. He was never at a loss, never seemed to flounder as I did. "Do you ever"—I paused— "examine yourself?"

"There madness lies."

"What do you mean?" He started the car. He didn't seem to want to explain. "Don't you get depressed?"

He gave a twisted smile. "When it threatens, I do the first thing that comes to mind no matter what. Any crazy act, however humiliating, is better than nothing."

I examined his made-up face. I touched his gloved arm. He pulled back involuntarily, then exaggerated the recoil, batting his eyes at an imaginary third party. "She's coming on to me. I've waited so long."

"Be quiet."

"You mean, 'Shut the fuck up, asshole.'"

"I said what I mean, asshole."

He cocked an ironic eyebrow and smiled so painfully wide that I put a hand to my own jaw. His narrow shoulders looked like my mother's at the end. "Shall we stop in Chicago and play with the hippies? Or spy on them from afar?"

"Just go."

Back on the highway, I couldn't drink my coffee. I lowered my seatback and tried to doze to the dual hums of the engine and tires on asphalt. Signs flashed by: WALHALLA 23. Every three or four minutes we passed something or something passed us. SPEED LIMIT 65, TRUCKS 60. I thought about hippies, kids with long hair driving Volkswagens, starting communes, having communal sex. Hippies were fine. WALHALLA 12. I knew Walhalla from Norse mythology, heaven for brave men who died in battle. Greeks had the Elysian Fields. I pictured rolling hills full of poppies, lupines, grasses soft on the soles of your feet. Both seemed more credible as well as aesthetically preferable to Christian heaven, the fluffy clouds and horn-blowing angels.

I closed my eyes, tried to feel love for CJ; I willed it. Vera had Saint, so I had CJ; I could do the math, $4 - 2 = 2$. The group was supposed to be 4EVER, but things had changed—all my life I was training to roll with punches. Saint loved Vera, Vera loved Saint, two pairs of hands holding each other with no need for anyone else's blessing or permission. "CJ, you know," I said, "you're really a good person."

"Wrong again. I'm a shithead."

"But you're a good-hearted shithead."

"Don't overdo it."

"I always overdo it. I like to overdo it."

I lowered the window and let my hair blow in the wind. I took off my shoes, stuck a foot out the window, and wiggled my toes in the rushing air. Just beyond the shoulder of the highway, trees seemed to slap at the car, one, two, three, four. CJ sang "Light My Fire" along with the Doors on the radio and directed me to his purse in the back with its joint-rolling materials. Would I do the honors?

I wasn't always good on pot. Sometimes it made me giddy and talkative, but sometimes it turned me inward so far I'd get claustrophobic and panicky. But now I dragged hard on the joint, toking several times before handing it over. Sky's the limit, I said to myself. I wanted to see what would happen, to burst out of my miserable skin. I looked out the window. WALHALLA, NEXT RIGHT. I'd wanted to die in battle for honor's sake. For the dark thrill that would curl around my heart. I turned the radio up loud. "Could you drive a little faster, CJ?" He hit the gas and the engine roared, the music roared, the wind roared in my ears. And we were inside a wind tunnel, little hydrogen atoms, once considered the smallest particle of matter to exist as its whole self, atomic weight one, till they were blasted into electrons and photons and then quarks, and probably one day there would be something even smaller, I could easily imagine that—our quest for the essence of things. I stuck my head out the window, face to the wind, to be blasted into my own essence. There were no other cars on the road, no lights but ours. "Step on it, buster! Faster!" Then, as our speed increased and the rush of sound thickened around us, I felt myself growing larger. Not fat; simply massive and accruing ever more mass, agglomerating the onrushing O_2 and N_2. I was everything around me. For the first time in my life, size equaled power equaled freedom from pain and fear. And the faster CJ drove, the more mass I accrued, till thought stopped and infinity loomed like God, like matter nearing the speed of fucking light.

An hour or two from Chicago, CJ turned off the highway. He needed a rest. We drove down a series of asphalt roads without center lines named with letters, then narrower nameless roads, unmarked intersections that materialized in the headlights, then, poof!—gone. The radio played static; I turned it off. Depression was back. "Let's do one more joint, CJ?"

He didn't respond, but I rolled one and toked, trying on futures. With CJ in San Francisco in an airy apartment with a view of water. We'd host dinners for our many friends who enjoyed his mind and understood his vulnerabilities, and mine too. I imagined myself without him, in a dorm room at the School of the Art Institute of Chicago, with a roommate who didn't wish she had been paired with someone else. How about an upscale mental hospital for the troubled children of the well-to-do? Pale gray walls, a window giving onto a soothing landscape? I took another hit. "Where are we? My God, where are we going?"

I was sinking. The blackness inside the car was relieved only by the little dashboard lights, the blackness outside only by the twin beams of the headlights, and there was fog on the country road turning darkness into light as opaque as the darkness. I couldn't help moaning.

"Are you nauseous, Kay?"

"Maybe a little."

The car braked sharply and turned. Gravel clacked under us. We went a short ways down a leafy tunnel, jounced then stopped. Lights off, engine off. Darkness and silence, like the cut of a sword.

He opened his door. The world stayed black but in poured a stream of insect-hum, an occasional small cry or rustle. He went around and opened my door. "Here's a good place to puke. Blend with nature."

I tried but produced nothing.

He lit another joint, offered it to me.

"Not now."

He led me through brush toward thinner darkness, talking for my sake. If you don't sweat, you won't attract mosquitoes. If you wear a scarf over your mouth, you can live months without water. We reached a cornfield and open sky and he pointed out constellations, though he might have been making them up. Two weeks ago we'd have seen swarms of shooting stars, the Perseids, named for Perseus, who saved Andromeda from the sea monster. I gazed obediently upward. The stars stayed put and had nothing to do with me. I was panicky, a feeling that might not even lift when the joint wore off; the thought made it worse. I felt myself falling under the weight of the Pledge and my family and my superfluous flesh, compounded with the weight of my helplessness in the face of despair. *Man, woman, birth, death, infinity.* Infinity was the quintessence of pointless. And death? It might not even bring an end to the sensation of falling.

I was staring at nothing when CJ put his arm around me. He was humming to himself, and I thought how different we were. When he was depressed, he got silly or nasty; me, I ate. But there was nothing in the car to eat, no food for miles and miles. Then it occurred to me: What was there to lose? Giddily, recklessly, I said to him in a husky voice that came from God knows where, "Let's go back to the car and have sex, okay?" His theatrical shriek cut the night, but I took his hand; I tugged him back along the lane. "I've never made it with a girlfriend, and you're my girlfriend, right, CJ?"

He opened the door but didn't get in. He was nervous but worked to sound amused. "Let me call the men in the white coats. I'll visit you on weekends."

"Am I too fat for you?" I spoke not plaintively but as a challenge. "Come on, boy, in the dark we all look alike. Pretend I'm Marilyn Monroe. Brigitte Bardot."

"You're being weird, Kay."

"I know that!"

In the dark I felt the heat from his face. He was embarrassed, frightened. But I was too, and when I rethought the idea of having sex with him, I reached the same conclusion. My virginity was a door to be opened. It was useless to me except as an offering to the god of self-transcendence. "Come on, man. As a favor. As my best friend on earth?"

He didn't say yes, he didn't say no, but he got in the car. We tried the radio again: static. The clock said 1:15, gleaming along with other familiar lighted dials, the 1 2 D N R P of the gearshift. The clock said 1:16, with 13,287 miles on the odometer and God knows how many more to go.

He lowered his seat to match mine and we lit another joint. Thoughts passed without stopping to deposit their loads. Past and future lifted off like helium balloons. There was no space but the space of the car, no time but now, nothing required but breathing, which ensued without effort or will. We took off everything but our underpants, separately, like children. We kissed with dry lips, like children.

Then I was shaking. I was Katherine Elizabeth Campion, who believed in God and had gone with Mom and sometimes Dad to St. Mark's Episcopal Church, though once when Mom was out of the house, I picked up the upstairs phone to call my friend Cynthia and heard my father say to someone who probably wasn't Mom, "I want to be inside you," violin-sweet and smooth, and I hung up before I heard who it was. And once, longer ago, on my mother's nightstand I found a paperback with a pretty red-haired woman on the cover, her eyes closed, lipsticked mouth half-open, and thumbing through, lackadaisically seeking what I know now was my mother's spirit or soul, I came upon: "She held up her breasts for him to kiss." Sick, I thought, whatever drove the woman to make this sort of offering. The image penetrated to my nine-year-old marrow, and here it was again, warping the image of my own maturing breasts, open to the air now, and large enough to be held in my hands.

"Kay, methinks thou art having second thoughts?"

Was I? My thoughts were coming crazy fast, one after the other. Before we went through with this there was a story I had to tell him.

He and our other friends knew my suspicions about Arlyn and my father, but I recapped the seamy details for him. She had been Dad's accountant, and sometimes she came to our house to bring him work or pick it up. One night, from my bedroom window, I saw him walking her to her car. He opened the door for her, like a gentleman, and I watched, waiting for her to drive away so I could get back into bed. Then he leaned into the car and kissed her mouth— I could see it in the overhead light. It was winter, snow on the ground. He wasn't wearing a coat.

"Hmm," said CJ, "that is kind of a turn-on."

I winced, but I had more to say. Lowering my voice, though there was no one for miles around: "I *told* her, CJ. I told my mom what they did. So she could stop it. Make them stop. And she . . . you know."

He shuddered, and I almost loved him then. He pushed his hair off his forehead, and I liked his face that way, framed but not intruded upon. He said, "Did you think it was your fault?"

A deep groan formed in my stomach, but it came out of my mouth high and thin. "Why would it be my fault?"

He shook his head back and forth. "Kay, it *wasn't* your fault!"

It was strange. Now all of a sudden I wanted to kiss him, this boy who was trying to be nice. Who *was* nice. And maybe he felt the same, because our mouths came together. Our bare chests came together. Our tongues slid across each other. We kissed and touched for a few minutes, softly, almost apologetically. *Is this nice? Do you like this?* Then he stopped.

"Kay, I should tell you about this, a crush that I have . . . that I used to have. . . ."

I hid my breasts against his chest, my hot face on his shoulder. "You don't have to tell me unless you want to."

"The thing is," he said, "I keep obsessing about . . ."

He didn't say the name but I knew who he meant. "Me too," I said. "All the time. Useless."

He looked so relieved I started to laugh. Tenderly I took hold of his face, fragile and beautiful. Under his mother's perfume I inhaled the metallic smell of boy. "To be continued?" I said.

"Yes, for sure," he said.

We put our clothes back on, and he told me what had happened between him and Saint, and I felt good with him, comfortable, like he was my brother. He was crying. Tears sprang to my eyes as well, and I looked for a tissue, found nothing except a pair of socks on the floor. I held one sock in my hand. "We can make a puppet out of it. We used to do that, sew on little buttons for the eyes." I sounded demented. I put the sock on my hand and bobbed the puppet head up and down. In a high puppet voice I said, "I seem to be demented!" Then, in my own voice: "Why do we both love him so much? He's just some guy."

He put the other sock on his own hand. We touched sock-puppet heads. "If I had any power over anything, I'd give you what you deserve, which is everything you want in the world."

"Enough. *Please.*"

He shook his head no, then took my hands and held them to his face. "That's the great thing about you."

I stared. His face was still wet. It's hard to do irony well while you're crying.

"You don't have the faintest idea how great you are."

"Shut up!"

"I mean it."

"Please," I said, aware of my many deficits, any one of which would blight a person's interest in me.

"Kay, dig. I'm a faggot. If I weren't you'd be first on my list."

I wanted to laugh. How to adjust to this new, open-hearted CJ? "Okay, you're a . . . well, got it. Now what?"

If I sounded brusque he didn't seem to mind. We kissed again, awkwardly, then we were back on the road. When reception returned we found a lively deejay, heard "Blowin' in the Wind," then news:

"It's fairly quiet tonight at the Amphitheatre but things may be livelier elsewhere in Chicago. So far over sixty people have been treated at local hospitals for bruises and concussions, and the numbers are rising. In Lincoln Park, Black Panther party chairman Bobby Seale urged the crowd to defend themselves from the police by any means necessary. Mayor Daley's widely reported remark seems to capture the general mood: 'The

police aren't here to create disorder, they're here to preserve disorder.' This is Ralph Donleavy reporting live from Grant Park, where the sweet voices of Peter, Paul and Mary are calming things down. Go, Mary."

They segued into the middle of "The Cruel War" and we sang along. Happiness seemed, if not ours, at least imaginable. The plan now was to stop in Chicago, where CJ might find his fellow queers and we could get a taste of tear gas. "Hippies are our people," he said. "Wouldn't you like to join a larger group?"

"I was fine with four," I said. I sang it out the window. I bellowed it out into the night.

25

The Cruel War

Vera sits on the sparse sandy grass by the bluff, tending to her feet, which are sore from her run. Moonlight trembles on the lake's dark surface, a band of shifting broken bits. Should she worry about Garth? One day, he will pull free of her; he will be happy without her. The thought brings a certain kind of relief, like setting down a heavy pack she has carried so long she forgot she had it.

She stretches and turns and looks back where she came from. The woods are thick overhead, the ground choked with brush; a few feet in, there is darkness, a clotted web between where she is and where she wants to be. She thinks of the Pledge, as she has been doing lately—this door she has shut and locked on her future, and that of her friends as well. The image of a heavy iron door, to a jail or a dungeon, wavers under her scrutiny. Could it be opened? The thought frightens her, but she can't shoo it away.

Then into the weave of her thinking and of the many small, repeated night sounds comes something sharp, like a gunshot. Some creep offing a squirrel, she thinks. Still, her heartbeat has quickened. She stumbles up, wipes sand off her legs, shakes out a foot that has gone to sleep, tries to figure the time that has passed. She must get back to Saint.

The breeze has stiffened; she enters the woods, shivering, wanting her T-shirt. The moon is down or behind a cloud, or it might be the air, thick like water, that keeps her from moving fast enough to get warm. But her body knows where to go. She imagines Saint on the blanket where she left him, the soon-warmth of his arms around her. In thirty hours or so the Pledge will come due; should she ask to rescind it? Would they despise her?

Not far from her destination, another concern squeezes her chest: that Saint got sick of waiting and left. Tomorrow he'll be pissed, remote. Or he won't show up. She increases her speed. A bead of sweat rolls into a corner of her eye. Something might have happened between Saint and her father, who can do some crazy things, and Saint too. She thinks of the gunshot, then blots it out, scanning the slithery darkness. "Saint?" Her voice quavers as if she has become younger suddenly or decades older. Her father is perfectly capable of starting a fight with Saint, then carting him off to jail feeling righteous about it. She pushes into the small clear space where their blanket was, and her breathing is loud in the silence. "St. John?"

It's lighter here at the edge of the woods. She can see her feet on the ground and the trunks of trees. But the blanket is gone, if it ever was here—the plaid wool on which, hours or years ago, she and Saint fell to their knees and, even before it settled, sprang at each other. Her gaze moves over the pebbly grass, the mat of old leaves, and finds his scooter close to where they left it, though now it's propped against a tree and the carryall is open. Into the blank dark of earth and bark and branches, the indifferent shushing of leaves, she calls out, "Saint!" then snaps her mouth shut on whatever else she might conjure up.

A dozen steps away but hidden by night and close-growing trees, Saint sits with the empty gun in his hand. Every so often he puts it to his temple, pulls the trigger, unflinching at the hollow click. Bugs bite the backs of his hands. At each new injection of hot, numbing insect poison, he thinks, *Go for it! I'm all yours!* If a wild animal went for his throat he would stay put. He'd offer himself to it.

Then the sound of his name sweeps into the enclosure and falls upon him, light and sticky as spider silk. He begins trembling. It comes again louder. He drops the gun, or rather he has forgotten that he was holding it. Rising, with the mindless will of someone approaching his execution, he moves toward the sound.

Miraculously, it seems, Saint is standing before her. With an involuntary cry she opens her arms. His body warms her skin. Shaking with joyful relief she kisses his shoulder, his hands. "I was scared, can you believe it!" She presses his hand to her cheek. "I ran into my brother. No, actually, he found me. And I told him to stop creeping around. He was . . . oh, I don't know. Forget it." She looks up at his face but has trouble seeing it. "Say something, Saintly! Was Dad his normal turd self? I was afraid he'd start something and take you in. Seriously." She shimmies against him, loving how safe he makes her feel. Like he could carry her in his hand. She looks around for her shirt. Her teeth are chattering, but she feels unaccountably happy. She wants—she admits it now—release from the Pledge, which seems to belong to a distant epoch, when she was young and arrogant enough to believe herself in charge of her life. "You know, Saint, maybe tomorrow when we see Kay and CJ, we should talk about the Pledge. Reconsider? What do you think? I hope they're not too mad at us. What time is it now?"

He remains still for a moment, straight and tall and unengaged as a tree. Then he takes her hand and leads her a few steps into deeper woods. Here she finds their packs, her shirt, and her sandals neatly side by side. She laughs, dresses. "Thank you, my responsible friend." When her eyes adjust to the new darkness she sees her blanket rolled around what looks like a wide, flat log. Her mouth opens slightly while the image expands to fill her mind. With a mental jeté she thrusts herself toward the next thought, the next picture, but nothing comes; her mind is filled with log. She looks up at Saint, who seems to have grown inches taller.

She is considered brave, she knows that. And she takes pride in the part of herself that can look square into the face of things. "Vera" means truth. She can handle truth. She can suffer disappointment, even shame, anything but this thrashing in the muck of uncertainty. Forcibly she directs her gaze to the blanket, which it's clear to her now encases not a log (no log is so flat and lumpy) but a human body.

It's her father.

The thought arrives, solitary, lucid, unsullied by feeling. Then there's a shudder, the recognition of an emotional gap in herself. What might have been grief is just the residue of a loss she mourned a long time ago and made adjustments for and set aside as well as she could. She presses her fingers to her temples. *Father. Our Father. Who art in heaven. Yeah, right,* comes quickly to mind. She turns to Saint, who has been standing before her with his head down. "Saint, talk to me!" He shakes his head. Terrible laughter bubbles in her throat. "Shit. All right. Listen to me?" She tries to get him to look at her. He won't give her his hand; she takes hold of his arm. "This is terrible, of course. But there are worse things. I mean it. You didn't know him." He stares. Her eyes burn; she blinks rapidly. "I shouldn't say this, but in some ways—I don't know—it's an improvement in the world?" She shakes him, as if trying to wake him up. "We'll get through this. I can imagine what happened. I'm not angry, I can easily imagine." Tears come to her eyes. Her throat hurts. "I know I sound like a cold bitch. One day I might start to miss him, parts of him. But he was a shit to me. To Mom and everyone." In the dark of the woods she tries to see Saint's face. She feels the first squeeze of a fear without boundaries. "Saint, what? Do you hate me? Am I a cold bitch?"

He stares at her, blank, empty.

"God, I'm sorry. I'm not thinking right. Saint, don't worry, you won't have to go to jail or anything." She tries to gaze back into his eyes. "Or not for long, I'm sure, because I'll tell the truth about him. He hated you. Hated you with me. Please, don't look like that!"

A sound comes from Saint, but it's not his voice or any human voice; she thinks of an old chair giving under someone's weight. Then he bends over the blanket and pulls back a corner.

It's hard to see in the dark, and at first she seems to be looking at herself on the blanket, her own face, wide lower lip, narrow pixie chin, pale hair. She must shake herself awake from what logic would deem a nightmare. Then her hands rise to cover her face. She falls to her knees, but it isn't low enough.

Gently, lovingly, she touches her brother's cheek. It's how she woke him on Saturdays in second and third grade. Up, Garthie. Soccer time. "Hey, buddy," she whispers as she whispered then. "Garth," she says, a magician's command. *Open sesame.* His lips are slightly parted, as if he wants to speak. He is achingly, preposterously beautiful. But his eyes stay closed. In his wool cocoon he is motionless.

She looks at Saint, but his face explains nothing. Garth's head seems loose on his neck. There's no way not to see that her brother is dead, but it's a state of affairs she cannot accept. She wants to shake him awake, or restore him with a kiss like the Prince with Sleeping Beauty. She takes hold of his hand. It's cold, but so is her own hand. In a small voice, reasonably, she says to Saint, "He isn't a fighter. He has a big mouth, he can shit-talk you, but he's a softie. He wouldn't hurt anyone." She takes in air but not enough for additional words. On his knees beside her, Saint gazes out through his robot eye holes. Looking at nothing. Nothing at nothing.

Then a wave of red passes through her brain. She backs away from Saint, whom she hates with every cell in her body. She growls, a sound that hurts her ears. Her hands curl into fists. Then she runs at him and hammers at his back, his head, his face—she has boundless energy to destroy. He sits motionless, making no move to protect himself, and she pounds at his blankness, daring him to hurt her, cut her—just whip out his Swiss Army knife. Or the gun! What's the matter, asshole? She pounds his face till blood runs from his nose. "Come on! Kill me too! Do *something,* you piece of cowardly shit!" Eyes half-closed, he sits like a monk, worlds away from earthly fray. "Fuck that *blank* business! You're *nothing,* St. John, nothing and nobody!"

She's on fire, her lungs are burning; she could spew dragon breath. But her words clink like stones into an empty pail. She steps back, then hurls a kick at him, all her nuclear heat compressed into the warhead of her foot. She feels no pain, just heat in the side of her foot, and she kicks again. He sits like a rock. She continues to kick but with decreasing force, as if she were kicking underwater, as if there were no bones in her legs.

Only when she stops does she realize that something is wrong with her foot, but it's far back in her consciousness. She lies down beside her brother and wraps her arms around him in the blanket that contains him. "Garth, baby. Sweet, sweet Garth." With her cheek to his, she dreams their lives together exactly as he described them to her, the two of them joined against their parents and the world, laughing, conspiring. He always closes his eyes when he laughs and she loves his eyelashes, darker and thicker than hers. She loves the smell of his breath, clean and sweet unlike the breath of older boys. A pulse in her foot vies for her attention, but it's mere sensation. She lies with Garth on the blanket on the sandy leaves in the shallow woods, waiting for things to change back to how they were.

Gradually, she becomes aware of Saint watching her, his nose dripping blood. "I can tell you what happened," he says in his strained, blank voice.

The fact of Garth's death assaults her again, and she sits up, her back to Saint and his bleak, ruined presence. She shudders, trapped between flesh into which she can't breathe life and living flesh that she loves and abhors.

Saint is still trying to speak, to lay it out before her as he ought to and as she deserves. She puts her hands over her ears. Nothing will change anything. They sit in the dark in the little clearing while she waits for the universe to respond to the catastrophe. The earth could open at their feet, for example. When nothing transpires, she stands abruptly, knowing at least what to do next. "Let's get moving. We can't just leave him here."

. . .

Garth's death, the just-before and the moment of it, is a balloon in Saint's skull, pressing his brain flat. The little mental space in working order is busy trying his case, not that he grants himself a case. An observer might see Garth's death as an accident, but the word "accident" seems shameful to Saint, a plea for forgiveness he doesn't deserve. That the gun went off as a result of the interplay of both their hands doesn't weigh in his favor. Without a gun he'd have strangled Garth or broken his neck; his hands burned to do it. That Saint isn't a hundred percent sure he wishes Garth back alive is the final damning piece of evidence. Case closed. He's glad Vera doesn't want to know the story. Whatever he'd say would sound like he was excusing himself.

So, mindless, a humble servant, Saint follows Vera's directions and lifts Garth's body in its shroud of a blanket onto his shoulder. They are a funeral procession heading to the lake, Vera in front. It's slow-moving. After a few steps the blanket loosens and flaps in his face. Already his shoulder hurts, though it might be from the beating that Vera inflicted. "It doesn't hurt enough," he whispers.

"What?" she says shrilly.

"Nothing, thanks. I'm sorry." An odd spate of courtesy. Though he's not sure he spoke loudly enough to be heard. It's hard to separate inside from outside. His load is getting heavier by the minute, but it might just be the burden of his thinking, over which he has no power. *Nam myoho renge kyo* passes through his mind, words he's unworthy of, but they come again. Foot after lumbering foot he treads the hard-packed sand of the path to the lake.

Then the sand is dry and gives under his weight. He hears waves, smells water. They are near the low point in the bluff where the stairway of railroad ties slants down to the beach. He wants to shift the bundle to his other shoulder, but he's scared he'll drop it. He tries to rotate his sore shoulder.

"Is there a problem?"

"No."

He firms his grip, toeing for the top stair. It's too dark to gauge the spaces between things. He kicks his shoes off, toes off his socks, trusting his feet more than his decrepit brain. After several steps the back of his load snags a branch. He moves forward, then back; the blanket is caught. He's streaming sweat but gives a last determined tug and the branch snaps. Time to rest. But there's no resting for him. He steadies the body on his shoulder, his arm tight around Garth's legs, then sees Vera beside him holding her brother's hand. *Her lover's hand?* Below, waves crash on the rocks but not loud enough to stop his mind. Turning ninety degrees on the narrow path, he drags Vera into the brush until she lets go. In full, solitary charge of his burden, he plunges down the tilting steps.

By the time Vera arrives on the beach, he has settled—say it!—the body of the boy he killed onto the damp sand. He has quashed his excuses for what he hopes is the last time, his absurd and shameful need to self-justify. He takes off his belt and buckles it over the blanket around Garth's waist and one arm. The other won't fit inside. Vera makes a frustrated, annoyed motion. He wants to tell her he plans to pay for what he did, but even in his mind the words sound phony. Garth's sneaker must have fallen off; she restores it to her brother's foot, ties a double knot. "I'm very close to being crazy," he says, not exactly to her. The words just come out, but they generate more words. "That's not an excuse, just a fact." She's so close he smells her sweat. His flesh creeps and he longs for her, an ambivalence that's nearly insupportable.

She says, "Should I feel sorry for you?"

He closes his eyes till her heartfelt words echo and die away. "When we're done with this I'm going to the police. I'm turning myself in."

"Don't be stupid."

He looks at her. There must be something left in him of self or ego, because her words increase his anguish. Her hand moves toward him in a gesture that could be conciliatory. He steps back, stomach heaving. Her pale hair glows in the moonlight, ghostly but still, achingly, pretty. His hands wring each other. He doesn't know what he'll do if she touches him. He must do no more harm.

"Tomorrow we have to meet Kay and CJ," she says. "We owe them."

He remembers loving Vera, but he doesn't remember why he ever did what she said. The plan in his mind is to give himself over to community justice. He has read *Crime and Punishment*. Not that he can repay this sort of debt. But he has to give himself over to something more substantial than Vera. Lay his head on the block if need be. Lay his head down somewhere.

"We have to let them out of the Pledge," she says. "They aren't part of this."

She drops her pack on the sand, takes off her sandals, tucks Garth's feet inside the blanket, and picks up the end. "Come on. Help me." She's walking backward toward the lake, pulling Garth by the blanket. "Take your end!" she cries. "Hurry."

"I'm not sure we should do this. The police won't like—" he starts to say; she shakes her head in disgust.

"There are three cops in this town, and one is my father. He's not going to read you your rights and let you call your mom. Do you understand that?" Her voice breaks, but her face is stony. She peels off her clothes, throws them onto the sand, and drags the blanket and its burden toward the small waves at the shore. "Will you give me a hand?"

He kicks off his shoes and scrambles to do her bidding, realizing too late that he too should have undressed all the way; he'll freeze in wet clothes. Can he never learn anything?

But half-wading, half-swimming, she's already got the bundle that is Garth into the water, and Saint is up to his knees, trying to keep a grip on the head and shoulders. The water is icy cold; his feet and legs are going numb. When the cold reaches his waist, he thinks of Socrates on his deathbed, drinking the hemlock as if it were wine. The poison hit Socrates's veins like ice water, Saint has read, paralysis starting with his feet and moving upward inch by inch. Not that Saint dares to liken himself to Socrates. But in the Socrates execution story, there's a line Saint keeps repeating as he maneuvers his burden through the water: *Soon he couldn't feel his legs anymore.* Words that pull Saint ever deeper into the lake till his lungs fill up and his mind freezes like his feet.

Garth is dead, Vera knows. But as the floor of the lake slopes down past the sandbar, she can't stand the thought of her brother's head under the water. Waves swell and subside. She, Saint, and Garth in the blanket go up and down. "Trade ends with me," she says to Saint.

"What? Why? This end is heavier."

"Do it!"

With the water holding the body up, they accomplish the switch. A giant swell lifts them off their feet, but Vera kicks, keeping Garth's head above the waves, *sweet Garth, sweet baby Garth, whom she taught to swim,* till she swallows water and, choking, swims for the surface. She treads water, bobbing in the troughs and crests, scanning the frothy horizon. She swims farther out. Now the swells come in flocks. For a moment atop a surge she sees a dark shape against the sky. Then a wave breaks over her, and when she surfaces there is only undifferentiated dark all around, not even a line where lake meets sky.

Back onshore, dressing, she notices for the first time that her foot hurts. But the pain is hard to distinguish from what emanates from other parts of her body, including the tattooed spot between her breasts. She prays for Garth's soul as if there is such a thing as the soul. She prays to God as if she believes in God. *Protect him. Shelter him.* She hopes she has done right. Hindus, she has heard, put their dead in the holy water of the Ganges, the midpoint of flesh and spirit. Vikings put their dead on boats or rafts burning in the night. Overhead the sky is cloudless, nearly pure black, and the Milky Way shines the pathway to heaven. She prays for Garth's soul to be received through Christ our Lord in heaven, as if heaven could exist without the other place. *My words fly up, my thoughts remain below.* And where does that come from?

She is rotating her ankle to see if it's sprained, when she glimpses Saint crossing the sand toward the terraced stairs. "Wait!" She lurches after him, foot and all. "Where are you going? Didn't you hear me back there?"

He is climbing the bluff, fully clothed and dripping onto the sand behind him. Her sandals are down on the beach, but she doesn't retrieve them. Despite her foot, and her rage—because there is nothing her brother could have done to Saint to merit his death—she follows with one goal in mind: He cannot go to the police. At the top she finds him shivering and trying to wring out his T-shirt. She holds the other end of the shirt and they wring together, turning the cloth at the same time in opposite directions as if they are still a pair. She hangs it on a branch to dry.

There's a log by the trail. They sit. Her ankle is a bit swollen but doesn't hurt if she keeps still. It's the middle of a night that feels endless, although she knows better, knows that dawn will come soon enough, but for once she waits; she doesn't try to make something happen or try to prevent it from happening, despite her near-overwhelming urge to control her life. And then Saint starts to talk. In the tunnel of overarching trees, where she can't see her hand in front of her, where she thought she had it all figured out—that Saint's rage toward her father had exploded at the innocent son—a new scene unfurls in her mind. Saint's words come slowly, with long pauses between them, but the events ring with their truth, she can hear Garth's voice telling Saint what he came to tell him. What Saint couldn't at first believe and tried not to believe, that cannot exist alongside his fragile, mistaken love for her. "Was he lying, Vee?" Saint's voice is thin and hopeless. "I'm not even sure I want to know."

Instead of answering she flexes her ankle. She can't suppress a moan.

"What?" he says.

The pain blooms and shrivels, but there's no release. "You're right," she says. "It was my fault."

"That's not my way of thinking."

"*Je suis merde,*" she whispers. She was older. The responsible one. She could have said no. "I'm a piece of shit."

"I didn't say that."

"No, *I* did."

He takes a small sip of air, as if that's all he's allowed; she could cry for him. She says, "Isn't it obvious? I should have done it when I planned it. No delay. Alone." He shakes his head no but without force. "Saint, be straight with me. There's nothing left to protect me from." Saint knows everything about her that there is to know. That ought to create some ground for her to stand on. "You hate me, don't you?"

"Way less," he says, "than I hate myself."

She nods. That's how she feels but in reverse. So they are still confederates. She looks at his face, trying to decide whether it's ugly or beautiful, as if it will give her an idea of her own face. "Should we run away? To the real Haight? There's an underground scene. Or L.A. I have cousins there."

"We could stay with them till they turn us in."

She isn't used to sarcasm from him, but she's glad for talk of any sort. She babbles on, half-aware that she's reprising Garth's crazy scenario. "In California we could do mushrooms together. Or peyote? To make us forget?"

"We'll go berserk and kill innocent people."

"In L.A. there are no innocent people."

"Not anywhere," he says.

She nods fervently, though she doesn't think he means it. She wants to take his hand but forbids herself, as if Garth were watching. She looks out into the darkness for a sign. "If we lived in Japan," she says, "we'd commit hara-kiri. It's what you do in the face of unresolvable conflict."

"They don't do hara-kiri in Japan anymore. They throw themselves in front of commuter trains."

"That would create a lot of civic inconvenience."

"It does, actually. That's what I read."

They smile into the dark with the complicity of bank robbers.

"But before we do anything, we have to meet Kay and CJ." Vera feels the world starting to reorder itself, at least on the periphery. There are plans to be made. "Kay's out of jail. But they might feel weird about us. We should call to make sure they show."

"Why would they feel weird?"

She shrugs. "I don't know. They both have phones in their rooms. What time is it?" She stands up, starts walking.

"You're still in charge, aren't you? You think I'll do what you want."

"But don't we want the same thing?"

They walk while bickering, he protesting her authority, she asserting, insisting. It's surreal and funny and horrible and ordinary. Her foot hurts, but the pain is tolerable, and she conceals her limp till they arrive at the pay phone near the restrooms. "What time is it?" she asks again, without expecting an answer. It's definitely past midnight, too late to call where a parent might pick up the phone, but CJ has his own number.

She tries CJ but no one answers. She dials Kay. Arlyn picks up. "Hello? Who is it? Who is this? Please answer me!"

Vera drops the phone, then hangs up quickly. "It's the stepmother. She sounds kind of frantic. Should I call her back?"

They ride the scooter to CJ's, but his room is dark, the windows shut. Vera has a few dollars left over from babysitting. Saint has a paycheck he can cash. But even if they had enough money they can't chance a motel.

The answer occurs to them almost simultaneously—Vera's hideaway, the little stone room in the rocks along the lake. If their friends don't show for the morning meeting, they'll try calling again.

26

We Enter History

These days "hippie" means tree hugger. Privileged pot smokers from "back in the day," who had anxiety-free sex and didn't bother their idealistic little heads about employment. But to many of us in 1968, hippies meant a new hierarchy, an inversion of values, a fairer distribution, among other things, of popularity. What was down, meaning young people and black people and weird people, was up, and vice versa. And on the eve of the Democratic National Convention in Chicago, there would be people our age, or just a little older, who might love us for exactly what thwarted us in Lourdes. So on Pledge Day minus one, in the middle of that night of terror and hopefulness, CJ and I looked for a place to park in downtown Chicago.

We found a legal spot on Lower Wacker, a belowground run of streets lit by creepy green light, then made our way to the surface. Not a soul was in sight. Our green shadows would vanish only to reappear in front of us, stretched to infinity. On the open street, the night remained surreal, sidewalks empty, the sky the same purple-red that had hung over Wells Street when there were four of us. We didn't talk about that, though. CJ walked barefoot, carrying his high-heeled shoes. It was three A.M. CJ had a dim sense of where things were from a Fourth of July weekend his family had spent at the downtown Hilton. His father had opened the drapes of their hotel room and shown them the bejeweled nighttime city as if he'd invented it himself, a glittering web spreading north and south, cut off to the east by Grant Park and then the darkness of Lake Michigan.

When we hit Michigan Avenue, CJ put his shoes back on. The surrounding streets had been still and silent, but in the early hours of Wednesday, August 28, 1968, Grant Park was rocking. People lay in sleeping bags, under tarps, clustered for protection at the base of trees, while others slept out in the open like the world was their bedroom. It was warm enough. Most were awake, in groups large and small, talking, arguing, singing, or listening to people playing musical instruments. Their clothes weren't that different from ours in Lourdes, jeans more rumpled, shirts more flamboyant, hair a little longer, a few beards. But in his mother's dress and shoes, CJ looked like no one else. It was an experiment. *Real* hippies wouldn't see the clothes, just the person underneath. Surprisingly steady on his feet, he crossed the street.

Less sure of a welcome, I followed watchfully. Who were these people, so pleased with themselves and one another? They seemed to have important business that they conducted merrily and whimsically, and what did we have to offer them? More to the point, what did *I* have to offer (I asked myself), feeling the kind of ugly not even a hippie could tolerate. Not only was I fat, I was deluded, having thought Saint might return my love. So much was wrong with me.

CJ had run ahead of me across the street, and now he was back, loping toward me over the grass, carrying his shoes again. "I thought you got lost, girlie." I was so glad to be found that he looked good to me. Not male or female, just good in his beaded black dress, his skin shiny with sweat and the damp air. All through the park was a buzz and hum, as if from insects or small animals. We moved within it slowly, trying not to step on anyone, toward what we didn't know, perhaps the heart or head of this body of people, its energy source. We felt something we had no word for but "energy," impersonal and benign. Barely older than we were, these kids clustered in groups, but they weren't protective of themselves like a high school clique. The clusters were part of something larger that was in its essence benign. Four friends were too few, I thought. Here was teeming humanity, none of whom, so far, had rolled their eyes at either one of us.

Eventually we arrived at the band shell, where CJ and his family had heard "The 1812 Overture" and authentic-sounding cannon fire. On the grass in front, people were listening to a pair of musicians, a guy playing a guitar and a young woman playing a mandolin; under her gauzy shirt you could see she wasn't wearing a bra. Nearby, a man in a red bandanna toasted marshmallows over a camping grill. CJ and I sat down behind him, famished but not wanting to beg.

I was swallowing my saliva and trying not to look at the food when the man turned around. "Cool duds," he said to CJ.

In my fly-on-the-wall shorts and T-shirt, I was embarrassed, but CJ didn't bat a false eyelash. He fluffed his skirt with a fussy little theatrical gesture. "This? It was the first thing that came to hand in my closet this morning." The man laughed, then blew out his flaming marshmallows, stuck them with a chocolate bar between two graham crackers, and offered them to CJ. "Land of plenty," he said, and made one for me.

CJ took the treat a bit warily, but I was babbling. "This is so nice of you. We've been driving all night. Are you from around here?" Beside him, a girl with round glasses and Pippi Longstocking braids, who was probably older than she looked, was crocheting something with multicolored yarn. They went to the University of Chicago, had seen Godard's *Weekend* tonight instead of getting tear-gassed, then felt like elitist shits and drove up from Hyde Park. She was making a hat for her new nephew in Maryland. Her name was Amy; his, Joel. We told them where we were from and we all made Lourdes jokes. A man my dad's age lurched over, the kind of guy people in Lourdes would have pretended not to see or told to get a job, and he too got a s'more. He sat down with us, reeking of booze. "You're a bunch of good kids, I don't care what they say."

After a while, our hosts put out their grill and lay down together,

and we found a spot near a flagpole that offered the illusion of protection. "They're so *nice*," I whispered to CJ.

"Brigadoon," he said.

But the next day, even more people were roving about in the already hot sun with the American flag flapping overhead. Joel handed
us cups of coffee as if we were family. Every once in a while a group of
uniformed police would pass through like soldiers, blank-faced inside
their riot helmets, but talk in our group continued. How to behave
when arrested: fight, play dead, and make them carry you away, or go
along, hoping not to be injured? "We have to resist, that's why we
came," Amy said. Joel snorted. "What? You're going to stab them
with your crochet hook?" He wasn't a martyr, had no interest in getting clubbed. "I need my brains to finish school." People laughed,
some uneasily. "The question is," he said, "what is worth dying for?"

Talk was loud now. Someone handed Joel a motorcycle helmet;
he gave it to Amy. I saw a few other people in helmets or hard hats.
My skull felt exposed and vulnerable, but I actually liked feeling
vulnerable. I was aroused at the thought of new choices, of onrushing extraordinary, momentous events when CJ and I and all of these
people might have to put our lives on the line. What *was* worth
dying for? The question linked Chicago and Lourdes, the throbbing
heart of their quest and ours too. In my mind I was trying out
variations on this idea to express to the group around me (braving
possible ridicule), when two policemen halted in front of us. "I'm
going to have to ask you for that," one of them said to Joel. He
meant Joel's little camp stove, which sat on the ground under the
percolator. New coffee was burbling.

I smiled at the policeman, confident suddenly in this place where
no one knew my limitations. Besides, I wanted to impress Joel.
"We're just making coffee," I said, upturning my round face, whose
youth and innocence would surely shame him. Amy said, "Would
you like a cup?"

He had no interest in us. "No grilling on city property except in
designated areas."

"It's not a grill," Joel said quietly. "No briquettes, Officer, just propane. It's not dangerous." He set the percolator on the grass and shut off the gas.

"I won't ask you twice," said the cop.

"It's off. No heat." Joel waved his hand over the burner. "I won't use it again." He unscrewed the burner from the small blue tank. He was holding one harmless item in each hand when the cop went for his stick.

I had been preparing for martyrdom with my new, coffeed-up energy. But before I could throw my body in front of Joel's, cop number two grabbed the first one's arm. "Cool it, Frank." At which Officer Frank grabbed the tank and the two marched off. "Motherfuckers," Amy said, but not loud enough for them to hear. Joel tossed the useless burner into the air and caught it. "Brave new world," he said.

"In the shadow of the American flag," CJ offered.

"He was nice enough to leave us the pot," I said goofily on purpose, and held out my cup for more. Joel laughed and poured and I drank. I loved the bitter taste of coffee, how it made me a part of it all.

CJ and I had planned to start our westward journey today, head out for the territories, but the scene wouldn't let us go. It was getting hot; CJ unzipped his dress. More and more people kept arriving, some with signs:

END THE WAR IN CHICAGO. SEND THE COPS
HOME.
CLEAN FOR GENE!
BLACK IS BEAUTIFUL

A boy was walking around with a parrot on his shoulder. Helium balloons sporting peace signs bobbed in the wind. This was our place, these were our people. The enemy wore a uniform, so you knew whom to hate, which left everyone else to be loved, if you were so moved. Stories circulated about power abuses, a Yippie leader arrested eating breakfast in a diner because he had FUCK written across his forehead. Arrested and jailed. For a *word*, for Christ's sake!

For a while we drifted through the crowd, pausing on the outskirts of discussions. In one group, a pretty woman with yin yang circles on her cheeks declared that she hated Gene McCarthy as much as President Johnson. More, because McCarthy had gotten people's hopes up then dashed them! Someone spoke in support of McCarthy, and the yin yang woman got upset. "The Soviets marched on Prague. No big deal for McCarthy! *Not a major world crisis*—he really said that! Then he quit, did you see the *Trib*? He said Humphrey had it all sewn up!" I couldn't follow her argument, but I believed her sincerity. I could love this woman.

There were speakers now on the band shell. A man with thick black glasses stood at the lectern, his face wholly encircled by black curly hair. People sat down on the grass and quit talking. Something big was happening. Holding hands in order not to lose each other, we edged that way. The man said he would read some poems. There were whistles and cheers. *"America you don't really want to go to war. America it's them bad Russians."*

I knew Emily Dickinson, Robert Frost, Sylvia Plath, but not yet Allen Ginsberg. He read as if he was making fun of things I didn't know could be mocked. He made me nervous, and I didn't want to be nervous; I wanted to be impressed, aroused, illuminated. "CJ, do you know this guy?"

CJ just listened. *"America I'm putting my queer shoulder to the wheel."*

His bare back was getting sunburned, and he had draped a glove across each shoulder. It made him sit straight. "That was a great poem," I said, not quite fraudulently. I felt on the edge of appreciation, that one day those words would stir me. CJ nodded without looking at me. He couldn't take his eyes off the stage.

Speakers followed whose purposes were easier to fathom. A guy with brown hair down his back described himself and friends going to face the New York City police with bags full of blood that they had garnered from local slaughterhouses. When a cop raised his billy club, they broke the bags over their own heads. "All this blood pours out," the guy said, "and they totally freak!" Then someone else took the mic and made an announcement: The peace plank had been voted down.

CJ and I felt the gravity of that event through its effect on the people around us. They booed; they cursed the Democrats. A few were crying. Someone yelled, "Bomb the Pentagon!" The clamor swelled. *Fuck the whole stupid country.* Waves of fury looking for direction. Across the grass a skinny boy, very young, was climbing the flagpole toward the American flag that had presided over our sleep. Onstage someone was chanting, "Om." Then the boy was gone from the pole and so was the flag, and another flag was going up, a piece of white cloth that looked like it had been dipped in blood. Things were happening now too fast for understanding. A troop of police wearing gas masks and holding rifles topped with bayonets were pushing toward the flagpole, to chants of *"Sieg Heil!"* Someone yelled, "Stick those guns up your ass!" A guy near us said, "See how mad they get when you fuck with their flag!" People threw things—eggs and water balloons filled with what we hoped was food coloring. We heard coughing and choking. And then we were coughing.

Tear gas hurts. My burning eyes wouldn't open. CJ and I stood up, but we couldn't move in the packed crowd. We held on to each other, trying not to fall, while around us was the world gone crazy. From the stage someone was urging battle in the streets. A cop yelled, "Get the nigger!" and cops converged on someone I couldn't see. "Keep your head down!" someone said near my ear. Chanting rose and fell: "The whole world is watching, the whole world is watching." Occasionally a bullhorn pierced the din, but the commands differed:

"We're marching on the Amphitheatre."

"Everybody sit down!"

"It's time to leave the park. Exit in small groups."

Our eyes and noses streaming, half-blind, we kept our heads down and held tight to each other's hands and tried to reach what we hoped was the edge of all this.

"Be cool! Await instruction."

With the bullhorn to orient us, we threaded our way through the churning crowd. "Stay together. Hold the line," cried a black man in a suit. Then he went down. On hands and knees he tried to crawl away, but cops surrounded him. One cop kicked at him, another used his club. Blood streaked the back of his neck. *Somebody, do something,* I kept mouthing silently, like a crazy person.

I hadn't forgotten my quest for martyrdom, but I was confused. I had lost hold of CJ. There were people all around me, but I seemed to be the only one aware of the man's plight. And if no one else saw it, could it really be happening? *CJ, where are you?* The man was crawling toward the sidewalk. A fence barred access, but it was a snow fence, half-down already. Was that blood running from his ear?

Then, in the noise and the pressure and odor of bodies around me, someone stumbled against me. I grabbed the nearest handhold, which happened to be the blue sleeve of a policeman. He shook me off, but now I was moving. I'd lost sight of the man on the ground, but in front of me was a cop with a club in his hand, and while he leaned forward I jumped onto his back the way I would jump onto my father's for a piggyback ride. I didn't know if this was the evil cop, the one who had actually used his club. I knew some cops meant well and some did not. I don't know if I thought I couldn't be harmed, or if I just didn't care, or if I thought I was Joan of Arc. I remember my arms around his neck and my legs around his waist, laughing. I was riding *piggyback*—riding the back of a *pig*! I held him by the helmet, yelling what my mother would say when I misbehaved, "I'm a*shamed* of you!" squeezing the strap against his neck to make him drop his club, which may or may not have happened. At some point he bucked me off. Then CJ was pulling me through the broken fence.

Out on the street the mayhem was less fraught, with an element of humor. Kids were trying to overturn a police car while someone danced on the hood screaming, "I am the universe." There was no sign of the beaten man. CJ took off his shoes and we ran, past the Palmer House, where a middle-aged woman was being handcuffed while she tried to hold on to a boy who was probably her grandson. Past a man who yelled in our direction, "You pitiful fag!" Some blocks away was a Woolworth's, where we ate bacon and eggs, drank coffee, waited for our hearts to slow down. There were two more days for the convention to run, two more days of the political theater that was Chicago. Safe now, we were high on it. We had been embraced as equals by older kids, all of us morally superior to the adults misrunning the world. My arm was bruised and my side hurt when I breathed, but I didn't mind. I was glad for what CJ called my war wounds. And there was more for us to do here, and so much more to learn.

Scheduled for the afternoon was the protest march to the Amphitheatre, where the presidential nominee would be chosen. We planned to join it, but there was one thing we had to do first. The war in Chicago transcended personal matters, including P-Day, it seemed to us. It was crucial—essential—that Saint and Vera know about it. If we were lucky, they could ride down on Saint's scooter and join us here.

We found a phone by the door and put our change together. We had to avoid Vera's father, so Saint was obviously the one to call. We flipped a coin. I won, but together we worked out what to say. This thing was bigger than 4EVER. It could change our lives.

Saint's mother answered the phone. At the sound of my voice she gave a shriek. "Thank God! Thank God!" She was laughing and crying. "Kay, where are you!"

I put my hand over the mouthpiece and whispered to CJ, "She knows we're gone!"

He took the phone. "How are you, Mrs. Scully?"

She seemed equally glad to be talking to him, and she kept thanking God. Then she asked for Saint; she had to talk to Saint. "Please, just for a minute. I have to know he's all right."

"He isn't here," CJ said. "We're looking for him too." Her groan was audible. "I'm sorry," he said.

The news was frightening. It wasn't just Saint who hadn't come home last night; neither had Vera or her brother, Garth. Mrs. Scully was crying. CJ apologized again and again. Then, not knowing what else to do, he hung up in the middle of whatever she was saying. We looked at each other, but we didn't have to discuss it. We went for the car.

27

Playing House

———

Saint and Vera ride the crest of the dune until the path ends, then abandoning the bike they slide down the slope. Her foot is seriously swollen now but she makes no sound and will not ask for help as they clamber over rocks in the dark. A point comes when she has to sit. Her ankle is actually hot to the touch. But relatively speaking it's nothing. Flesh. In a minute or so she'll get it together.

They're still a ways from their goal. Saint picks her up like she's a doll; she's almost glad now for her incapacity. She puts her arms around his neck—she has to, in order not to fall—remembering a late-night family outing, being carried from the car to her room and tucked into bed without having to brush her teeth or wash her face or take her daytime clothes off, then drifting off to sleep with the faint pressure of someone's lips on her forehead. At the mouth of their haven Saint sets her down on a flat rock. The sky is pale over the darkness of the lake. She rests her head and feels herself relaxing, pain and all. She is where she is, and there is nothing she can do about anything. The sensation is completely unfamiliar, with an edge of euphoria.

Now tears are running down her cheeks, with no choking or sobbing. In the course of her life she has rarely cried, and never like this, without trying to make it stop. Saint lifts her down to the sandy floor of the bunker where she used to play as a child, alone and safe, and she feels warmth from his body through his damp clothes. She leans closer, her face directly in front of his, and touches his face, neck, shoulder, his warm, alive skin, and what has no other name but love pulses from her to him.

They lie, exhausted and empty, side by side but separate in their rock shelter. In her dream they are dancing, she in the white dress of a bride. Then they are driving somewhere in a large, comfortable car, and the backseat is full of children, laughing with pleasure in one another, which she shares, she floats on it, till their screams of delight edge toward wildness and she turns in her seat to quiet them. They all look like Garth.

They sleep late and wake up starving. Vera's ankle is yellow and double in size. Saint hoists her out of the hole so she can pee. Soon, though, they will need food.

He makes a noontime foray through the woods back to the picnic area, trying to blot out everything except simple, attainable goals, and manages to steal a thermos, a package of hot dogs, and a jar of mustard from a family organizing their children's baseball game. There are eight hot dogs in the package. Even cold they taste good, especially with the mustard. They eat them all. The thermos contains lemonade, which they sip chastely, leaving as much as possible for the other person.

All afternoon they sit or lie inside the bunker, still separate, with occasional remarks on their immediate situation, the pleasure of not being hungry, the state of Vera's ankle, the likelihood of being discovered, the chances their friends will show up. Do they want their friends with them? It's hard to understand the notion of "want." A gull peers down through the opening over their heads, then takes off with an indifferent cry. A beetle crosses the sandy floor. Saint doesn't ask Vera what she's thinking; truly, there is nothing he wants to know. Sometimes she seems to want to touch him—her hand seems to linger on his arm when he helps her to stand. But for the most part she's oddly passive. She doesn't complain or criticize, which proffers some relief. His one conscious wish is for time to pass, which will happen without effort on his part. Tomorrow will come, when they have pledged to jump. *Nam myoho renge kyo*. But Zen doesn't seem to work in cases like this, or else he's a lousy practitioner. His mind is locked into images more vivid than anything around him, what she did, what he did. When he thinks of what he did, he still wants to give himself up to an authority, but not to someone like Vera's father. He wants a master who is pitiless but fair, who views evil like a Zen master and will mete out the kind of justice that restores balance to the world.

Then he thinks of what *she* did.

After dark has fallen and the park has supposedly closed, Saint returns to the picnic area. Hunger is back, his stomach is cramping. There are no cars in the lot, but he's cautious now: Around this time yesterday Vera's father showed up.

Working quickly, he rinses the thermos at the fountain and fills it with water. On the far side of the fountain he finds a decrepit wheelchair with a note taped to the seat: *Hail Mary Mother of God*. The writing is large and painstaking, like third-grade cursive. *Shit*, he says to himself. He drags a garbage can over to the light by the restrooms. It offers up only a picked-at bunch of grapes and a bag of Fritos, but in the next can there's a half-full tub of Kentucky Fried Chicken, including an apparently untouched thigh and an almost full container of red beans and rice. His stomach growls. Plasticware is easy to find. He's washing the forks in the men's room sink when a car drives into the parking lot. He peeks out of the restroom door. Two women emerge, one of them seemingly dressed for a party. They look disheveled, maybe drunk, and offer no threat. This is his first thought. Then, as if in a dream, he sees—although it can't be!—Kay and crazy CJ, in the dress Saint remembers him wearing—when? last night? It seems like years ago.

Our midnight encounter occurred long ago, but in memory it's crystal clear: Saint in his dirty, smelly T-shirt, CJ half-zipped into sequins, and me in my Bermuda shorts looking almost respectable. The light over the pay phone shone on our three-way embrace and on Saint's beautiful dirty face, his hurt-looking eyes. We were back in Lourdes, Chicago distant and out of mind. Saint was alive, and I was shaking with relief and love for him. CJ too, it seemed.

We wept, laughed, tried to speak. There was so much to say and find out. I held one of Saint's hands, CJ the other. CJ spoke first. "You look like a bum, man."

"And you look like a hooker," I said to CJ with a scowl, then to Saint, "We were afraid you guys left town. I thought we'd never see you again!" He could hardly look at us, as if we were a source of too-bright light. I couldn't let go of him. I went on about our worries for him and Vera, waiting for information.

"It occurred to us," CJ said, a bit stiffly, "that you might have done the deed on your own. Without us."

"I kind of thought you eloped, but that's just me!" I said. "Hey, is Vera okay? And Garth, where's Garth? We talked to your mom on the phone. She's really upset."

Saint kept hugging us but answered no questions. When, after some minutes, we let go and stepped back, I saw that his face was blank, as it often was, but his jaw was trembling.

28

Last Supper

When night falls on Lourdes, Michigan, and someone's teenager is not where he said he'd be, after Hamburger Heaven, which closes at eleven P.M., the first place to check is the busy Burger Boy. Two grease-stained locals are cleaning up when Officer DeVito walks in, out of uniform but known and formidable. Cops up here are not called pigs. The employee with the mop knows Garth from Cub Scouts. He knows Vera too. (DeVito scans for sexual innuendo, finds none.) "Not either one of them came by here," says the mop boy, shaking the mop and his head at the same time. "Hey, good luck, sir, Officer, sir. Mr. D."

There are a couple of bars with two A.M. licenses, Granma's and the Dew Drop Inn, but the high school kids hate Granma (a middle-aged man named Lenny, who wears a ponytail), and the husband and wife who own the Dew Drop have children in junior high and won't let minors in the door. They and he concur as to the sleaze-bags some of these kids are (for example, the fifteen-year-old moron who made his case for lowering the drinking age by pissing on the floor). So his best guess means more stumbling through the woods. And Deedra's waiting, and she gets mouthy when he cancels, and anyway, how long can it take for him to satisfy her?

But of course it takes longer than he figured, and when he finally gets back to the park, the goddamn scooter's gone, and why search, with the kids probably home by now? He calls the house; the phone rings on. Which signifies nothing. Their phone answering is erratic, and by now Yvette is well beyond picking up.

The question, then, is whether to call for backup, but the thought of what his partner, Brod, may light upon (a teen porno flick starring his daughter?) makes him reluctant to do anything till he's sure of the need. He races home like a maniac. Then *Fuck-shit,* he says to himself, running down to the basement, then up to the second floor, throwing open doors onto not one but two empty bedrooms. Passing Yvette's door he spits in disgust. Her kids could be in the hospital and Sleeping Ugly's snoring away.

But he doesn't really think they're in the hospital; he thinks they're out disrespecting him. At some pot party, when they know what he's paid to do. Enraged, he calls Brodkey but gets no answer. He calls Jane in the upstairs room of the firehouse that serves as the local police station, and howdy doody, she's there. Good Jane. But Brod doesn't answer her either. He can see the fucker parked on the dark side of some residential street too dead asleep to hear the beeper, and sleep is what he needs too if he's going to do any kind of job tomorrow. No big deal, he says to Jane, who is a fine lady. Thanks, babe.

Before turning in, though, he walks downstairs. Detective work begins at home. In Garth's desk drawer he finds, not surprisingly, a matchbox filled with marijuana (a quarter ounce) and a vial marked TETRACYCLINE 250 MG containing seven fat black capsules that look like horse pills but aren't.

Feeling a twinge of annoyance at his son's nonchalant selection of a hiding place (does he want to get caught?), he climbs the stairs to Vera's room. If Garth's illicit possessions could earn him a felony indictment, only God knows what his wild daughter might have. He rifles through underwear, shirts, sweaters. He pulls sheets from the bed. He ransacks. Between her box spring and mattress is a book of Victorian pornography, but it isn't that steamy.

Shit, there's no way he can sleep now. With a muscle twinge of long-thwarted rage, and needing a helpmeet, as the Bible says, he enters his wife's bedroom for the first time in six months and shakes her awake.

But even if Officer DeVito had found the Pledge folded inside the pocket of Vera's winter coat and followed its lead directly to the park, he wouldn't have known about her little stone refuge. And even with many more hours than the twenty-four that ensued, he wouldn't have known the bar that was hosting the four compadres' reunion. Sixteen miles north of Lourdes, so new it wasn't even in the phone book, on the corner of a Vincentian seminary that had become a prep school and then the Academy of Cosmetology, was the one place local underage insomniacs could buy alcohol and be left alone. As far as Mr. D knew, like most of the adult residents of Lourdes, you went there to learn how to cut and set women's hair or get a discount dye job from an advanced student, but in August of 1968 it was two years since the last hair dryer had been carted away. As for its ecclesiastical past, all that remained besides the Friday fish special was the name, Seminary, in white on the green awning. That and a photograph over the cash register, a yellowing aerial view of the Regional Seminary of St. Vincent de Paul bedotted by robed seminarians now dead, frozen in midstroll. In its current incarnation (by two brothers from Detroit), the Seminary Tavern and Grill offered greasy fried fish and an inexpensive, locally brewed Jackalope Light at any hour of the day or night to whoever had money to pay.

Now it's after midnight, a Thursday, dawn will come in five hours and the Seminary cook has gone home. Besides booze, the fare is reduced to the simmering bottoms of two tubs—Manhattan chowder or "Diehard" blow-your-brains-out chili—so the bartender informs the newly arrived party of four and points to a chalkboard behind the bar. The kids stumble, totter, and lurch to the restrooms, then emerge, all but one of them, and seat themselves at the booth on the end, farthest from the handful of other patrons. "Lookin' good," the bartender says under his breath. He just got out of high school. This is a decent job. He can take it till he gets drafted.

It's CJ who has stayed in the men's room, and he's taking the time he needs. After thirty hours in his mother's dress, some of the sequins are dangling, but he's zipped at least, hands and feet washed, makeup freshened. He plans to be cool in the face of what he'll hear from his friends (ex-friends?), because he thinks he knows what's coming: The happy boy and girl are running off to Disneyland or Florida or Buenos Aires (fuck the Pledge!). Predictable, if sad. Boring. And maybe Vera's—alas—in the family way? Steady in his high heels, he swings out into the rank-smelling barroom. Why the fuck did they come back?

Involuntarily (he can't help it), he scans himself in the bar mirror, noting the extra inches the shoes add to his height. He bats his eyes at the stud bartender (can't help that, either) while the compadres watch from their booth. The bartender makes a remark that's probably about him, probably defamatory in the crass local style. A listener snorts, meaning *I see your point.* Two women on adjacent stools regard him with smiles like he's a good Halloween show. He blows them kisses like a beauty pageant contestant might, adjusts with a black-gloved hand the scoop of his neckline, feels, without looking, his sequins glitter. He's Miss America (albeit moist and malodorous). Adrenaline has flushed from his brain the dregs of rumination. Oh the boy needs his Librium.

His pals call to him, Kay clucking and shaking her head. Is he sick or something? Time's a-passing. But he isn't ready for time to pass. He sits down beside dear Kay and across from Saint and Vera and says the first thing that comes into his head. He wants to write a book about Adolf Hitler. A novel, actually. He wants their advice.

The level of attention isn't stellar, but he presses on. It will be a historical novel like *Napoleon and Josephine,* and since Hitler was queer, his book will be called *Adolf and Ernst.* Ernst Roehm and Adolf Hitler not only started the Nazis, Hitler let Ernst call him

Adolf, not Mein Führer, and gave him the storm troopers to lord it over. "And right after the party took power, guess what?" he asks. "Hitler arrested him and had him shot. For treason. But I ask you, ladies and gentlemen of the jury, could there have been another reason?"

"CJ," says Vera, "what is your problem?"

"CJ," says Kay, "please try to calm down!"

"We have to tell them," says Vera to Saint, who shrugs.

But CJ is boiling over with Hitler lore. "There's a dispute here," he continues. "Some folks think Hitler's buddy Hermann Goering convinced him his lover was a traitor, but elsewhere you'll find that Ernst was threatening to tell the world Adolf was queer. He called Adolf *du*, the only guy allowed to get so personal. In my humble opinion, though, Adolf killed him out of jealousy. There was Rudolf Hess in their club, another queer Nazi. Isn't it amazing how many Nazis went that way?" CJ raises an eyebrow at Saint's blank face, then he's on to Rudolf Hess, who had called Hitler a "profoundly sexually attractive animal." And Goering was supposed to be a transvestite! God, his mind is going gangbusters. He eyes the other three, silent in their chairs. "Oh dear. Am I talking too much?"

Before anyone can reply, the bartender passes by the booth, a guy who went to Lourdes, whose name is right on the tip of CJ's tongue. Jock-type head, wider at the jaw than the forehead, short blond jock hair. Cartoon good-looking. One of those Aryan assholes who, in the Nazi days, would have dared his Deutsch schoolmates to kick the Jew-boy. (Otto? Helmut?) CJ waves. What he really wants—it comes to him now—is to be lusted after by other people, male and female alike. As much as his fucked sexual preference, he hates the inequity in personal gifting that grants one human being charisma while others receive only the infinite capacity for longing. On the table in front of him, the red candle lamp is out, out, out, brief candle. He looks through his beaded bag for matches, finds none. Feels over his shoulder someone's eyes on him, but when he turns, everyone's minding their business, including Helmut, who is ignoring him, or is that more paranoia? How he would like to stop talking. Be the strong, silent type.

He shuts his mouth—he can do that—and tries to attend to his friends' concern, whatever it might be. If an abortion is needed, he can help with money, he thinks, picturing skinny Vera with child, like a snake that swallowed a basketball. But she declared once that if she was stupid enough to get pregnant she would have the kid, and Saint would concur. CJ suspects the forthcoming talk to center (alas) on rescinding the Pledge and taking (egad) responsibility for your screwups. The one extra puzzle piece is Garth's disappearance. But Garth has vanished before.

Then abracadabra, voilà, straight from *der* Hitler *jugend,* here's young Helmut standing before them, so clean-cut his cheeks shine. "What can I get you folks?"

In theatrical slow motion, CJ peels a glove down the length of his arm and picks up the unlit candle lamp. "*Mein herr,* old chap, would you mind terribly?"

His friends are obviously embarrassed, but so? Helmut's blond fingers snap a match. CJ nods approval. "And could you wipe down the table? It's a mite, you know, *schmutzig.*"

Out comes the Handi Wipe. The table gets a rudimentary rub.

"Now, how about four brews, my man. Brewskies, as vee say in Varsaw!" CJ taps his high heels against the floor as Helmut heads for the bar, then says louder than he has to, "Never trust a pretty face. Not even yours, Mr. Saint."

Saint suddenly—surprisingly—looks at him. Those blue eyes, long pale lashes. Aryan lashes, not that Nazis liked Catholics much more than Jews. CJ remembers with a surge of grief what he thought was the dawn of love for him and Saint, dawn in the dawn, of forever love in the Eden behind his house—he believed and dreamed for a day or two—a dream, he understands now, that Saint didn't share and never would. To Saint he says, "You look like a Greek fucking god, but you haven't a clue." Then, as the beers approach, "Now, if maybe you focused on internal beauty? Like our Kay here?" Kay seems less than pleased with her representation; he elaborates. "That's why we all love her." He pulls a ten-dollar bill from his bag and hands it to the bartender. "Keep it, babe."

The door opens up front. Enter a man his father's age in a pink and green palm tree tourist shirt: his father minus fifty IQ points. He has a kid in tow, age three or four, maybe, and the kid's got one of those wooden paddles with the ball attached by a rubber string. It's a cheap toy and hard for most people to get the hang of, and the kid basically is chewing on it. And here is what wrings his heart. Dad, good Dad, just takes it out of his mouth, lifts him onto a stool, and hands it back. No scolding, no look of annoyance. The boy twirls on his stool, then stops, facing the row of booths, and points the paddle at CJ.

"Daddy, is that a girl?"

A laugh spurts among the four or five people who overhear. One of the women, both of whom have stiff, curled, beauty parlor hair, sends CJ a look of sympathy. He feels his ears flush. Then out of nowhere it comes to him, the bartender's name: Isaac Johansson. Swim team. Isaac's younger brother was Jake, for Jacob probably, another O.T. name. On the precipice of laughter, CJ refuses to fall. Neither looks Jewish. "Hey there, Isaac," he calls out, "are you named for the Old Testament Isaac? The kid whose father would have done him in? Or are you Isaac as in Ike Eisenhower?"

"That's *Dwight* Eisenhower."

The bartender's hand has curled into a fist. In a minute he's going to punch CJ. Who is nodding vigorously. "You're absolutely right, Isaac. I was wrong and you were right. How does it feel to be extremely intelligent?"

"Shut up, CJ," says Vera.

"Don't make trouble," says Kay.

Even Saint looks like he might say something. CJ curves his mouth in a goofball smile. *"Liebchen,"* he whispers, "don't walk away."

Isaac retreats without hitting him. CJ doesn't know whether to feel triumphant or bad. He doesn't feel triumphant. His feet hurt in his mother's shoes. "Is anybody hungry?" he says to the booth in general. "Have I done something wrong?"

When the bartender returns, CJ orders four bowls of chili. Kay apologizes—our friend is high, he's kind of nutsy, we're really sorry. Vera and Saint concur. The bartender plants himself next to CJ's ear.

"I don't care if you come in like a queer Barbie doll, but one more shit-eating word and I'll kick your fag ass down the block. Is that clear enough?" He lingers half a second while the words implant, then turns on his heel.

4EVER was done for, it seemed, a shooting star that had streaked across the sky of our lives. CJ was locked into his avoidance game, with Vera and Saint trying and failing to get a word in. If nothing else, CJ's performance had welded them more tightly together. They had walked into the bar hip to hip, arm in arm, and now it looked like they had gone beyond being lovers, like they were married to each other; I wondered if this was the news they wanted to impart. Our being here with them seemed almost shameful to me, trying to save these people who didn't need saving—who sat in a sexual synchronicity I could feel without ever having experienced it. I wanted to run out of the place or else, wickedly, force them to honor the pact they seemed to have outgrown. When Saint shifted in his chair no matter how slightly, Vera did too. And I'd thought the story of our Chicago adventure would illuminate the world for them. I'd wanted to offer it to them like fire to the Neanderthals, when here they were together, warm as toast. When I could imagine myself no lower in anyone's estimation, I put my hand over CJ's mouth.

"I'm sorry, guys, but I can't wait another second. Are you going to tell us your news? Or are we supposed to guess?"

CJ went silent then. Vera glanced at Saint, who went still. Country music played on the radio. Then news. *"On the first ballot Senator*

Hubert Humphrey of Minnesota has received the Democratic nomina-tion for president of the United States. Outside the convention hall the rioting goes on." Then Vera began, in a whisper. We bent over the table to hear.

Food came, four bowls of chili, ultra-dense and burned-smelling. Vera picked up her spoon, set it down, and with a crazy squeak in her voice said the name Garth. Garth and Saint. Garth, Saint, a gun, and a secret, a terrible secret that gave rise to an act that only made sense in light of the secret, and maybe not even then. Saint stared into his bowl. We leaned in over the sticky table in the beery dark of the restaurant and the story went on, grotesque, absurd. Vera spared no unimaginable detail. When she stopped, we floated in dead si-lence. CJ bit down on his spoon and it flew up and hit him in the forehead, but he seemed not to notice. "It's not true," I said auto-matically, but I didn't doubt it was true. How could I ever have cried for myself when there was *this*? I ached for Vera, her strong mouth and fierce pixie chin. And for Saint, gazing past us with his con-demned eyes. "Don't look like that," I said to him, then, "Sorry, that's typical of me," looking into his eyes of a man who had just refused the blindfold. Blank-faced, Saint asked me the time, his first words since we'd met in the park. I showed him my Mickey Mouse watch: two A.M. "Four hours," he said.

"But it's different now. It's not for the Pledge," Vera said. "You guys don't have to join us. It's our mess." She looked for a better word. "Our evil. Sin. Crime. It's just what we have to do."

"It's what *I* have to do. Not you," said Saint to Vera. Then to us: "Or any of you."

I understood then they weren't united. I shivered up from the soles of my feet. "We all know you didn't mean to hurt anyone," I said to Saint. "You were angry. It's *understandable*, how betrayed you must have felt!"

My words were lame, but I was feeling a glimmer of hope. Their guilt wouldn't just disappear, but expiation was possible. Sins could be atoned for. I hadn't known I believed, and even now I wasn't sure, but there is a lot to be said for confession and absolution, a system that lets you make mistakes. I started brainstorming, and the more I talked, the clearer it seemed. We had to get Saint a lawyer. "Arlyn's first husband was a lawyer, she knows *tons* of them. And CJ's dad has connections." Saint was gazing at me with tenderness; it spurred me on. "You're a minor, Saint. You don't have a criminal record. I mean, it's horrible, tragic, but it was an accident. You and Vera are *good*. It will turn out for you!"

I looked from Saint to Vera and suddenly remembered. It wasn't only P-Day, it was also her birthday. She sat with a stiff back and a blank white face. I grabbed both of her arms. I shook her a little. "Happy birthday!" I almost shouted, and then, absurdly, "And many more!!"

I started to laugh, perhaps hysterically. I couldn't stop, and after a bit the others joined in, even Vera. When we had calmed down, I went on with more confidence. "I confess, I was blaming you, a little bit," I said to Vera. "I was mad at you, but that was just envy. I'm sorry. Love is so strong and illogical." Woozy with self-renunciation, I labored to accept Saint and Vera together in some happy future—I had to, to convince them. "This is the worst thing that can happen, ever. It happened, and you lived through it. It's natural for you to blame yourself, and who wouldn't? But now you can work to make up for it! So you *have* to stay alive!"

My argument was logical and seemed incontrovertible. I went on fervently for as long as they let me, spinning straw into gold, though after one statement concluded, I had no idea what to say next. I was merely, resolutely, throwing out strings of words to hang on to while the great ship of our lives sank beneath us in the storm. Then Vera touched my arm. "Garth was my twin. Sometimes I think he's my soul, if I have one." She gave a wobbly laugh, looked at Saint, then back at me. "You and CJ—you're, well . . . free. You're beyond this. Saint is too, though he won't accept it."

I was arguing with myself about whether I was in any way free when CJ burst in passionately, "I don't want to be free. I don't *feel* free."

"Cut it out, CJ. Whose side are you on?" I looked from face to face. Vera's was paper-white; Saint's large features jutted as if from a mask. CJ blushed red.

"I signed the Pledge," he said, and raised his mug and drained it. The other two followed suit.

A shudder rose from my groin to my chest. It was happening again. Bigger than life, Saint and Vera sat before me like Jesus and Mary Magdalene, with CJ like Peter, who denied the Lord but turned into a rock strong enough to hold up the Church. All three glowed like separate suns, and me, a poor little moon with my borrowed light in my eternal subordinate place in our galaxy. I tilted my mug and gulped bitter fizz. New arguments came to mind. How would Saint's mother feel, and his brothers and sister? I recalled what we had felt down in Chicago, CJ and I, the warmth of that glorious, selfless, disaffected community. But my heart was going so fast there were no separate beats, just a thin buzz.

Then Vera took one of my hands, Saint the other. CJ extended his smooth, narrow palm. Our eight hands grasped one another, as they had two weeks earlier. "Us four forever."

I'm not sure who said that, but it might have come from me as well. We started gorging. The chili was cold but peppery-hot in my mouth, and I savored the burned taste. I was glad for our table, not the perfect square of a bridge table but a rectangle narrow enough for us to see everything in the faces on the other side. "So this is our Last Supper."

"Good one." CJ compounded our mythos with a tale of Jewish martyrdom. In A.D. 70, in a fortress at Masada, the last Jewish citizens of Israel took their own lives rather than surrender to the Romans.

Saint said, "Remember the Alamo."

"Fuck remembering," said Vera. "I want to forget."

We toasted Masada, the Alamo, and martyrs Jewish and Christian. We toasted one another. We toasted remembering and forgetting. We sat, ate, breathed together, in the fortress of our conjoined myths. Then CJ pulled some napkins from the table dispenser, took my pen, and wrote in small, cramped, neat capital letters:

ON AUGUST 29, 1968, CJ WALKER TOOK HIS OWN
LIFE. TO ANYONE SO SHORT-SIGHTED AS TO MOURN
HIM, HE OFFERS CONDOLENCES, WISHING TO
REASSURE SAID PERSONS THAT RESPONSIBILITY FOR
HIS DECISION LIES WITH THE STATE OF HIS PSYCHE
AND CHARACTER AND THE UNIVERSE AT LARGE, AND
NOT WITH THOSE WHO BROUGHT HIM INTO THIS
HARROWING WORLD; THEY KNEW NOT WHAT THEY
DID.
    TO DANIEL M. WALKER HE BEQUEATHS HIS BOOKS
AND MAGAZINES, SPECIFICALLY WHAT IS TO BE
FOUND ON THE LEFT-HAND SIDE OF HIS BED
BETWEEN THE MATTRESS AND BOX SPRING. ENJOY,
DANNY BOY. GO TO ICELAND OR IRELAND OR ISRAEL.
GET HIGH. FUCK YOUR BRAINS OUT. DON'T THINK
OF ME, OR IF YOU MUST, THINK BADLY OF ME. IF
THERE IS A GOD, I'LL GET WHAT I DESERVE. IF NOT,
THERE'S NO NEED TO WORRY ABOUT ME OR
ANYTHING. YOU ARE STRONG.

The writing covered the front and back of two small napkins. He signed it *Love*, and I wanted to cry. He was a good soul. Then Vera took the pen; her writing was so light you had to squint:

To whom it may concern: Once upon a time a princess was born without a nose. People fell in love with her but for only as long as she held a hankie or a fan to her face. One day she gave a grand ball that began with a contest. She would marry the first man who could ballroom-dance with her without losing his lunch. Those who tried and failed would, as was deserved, lose their shallow, too fastidious heads, the executioner to be the princess herself.

As it happened, the best dancer of course was her brother the prince. They waltzed all night around the ballroom quite gracefully, her hands in his hands, her face mere inches from his, but in the morning he too was beheaded. Why? Historians have debated. In one version, dizzy from all that circling, the princess mishandled the ax. Others blamed her father the king. Perhaps the truth will never be known. (Fin.)

I read with a shudder and took Vera's hand. CJ kissed her on both cheeks. Saint, though, seemed unaware of her missive lying on the table in front of him. He hadn't read CJ's either; he took the pen and wrote, keeping his eyes on his napkin, and he wouldn't let any of us read it.

I wrote:

Here lies one
departed but not dearly
who left this life early
but not early enough.
If she died before she grew fat
and guilty for being fat,
for taking more than her share
of light and air,
if she died before the angels fell
down to hell
then she'd have died
at peace.

I turned the napkin over and continued on the back, not that people would necessarily keep reading:

But peace is not
what I had thought.
Love is more
worth living for
or dying for

if that's in store.
And so I'll die
without complaint
if I can lie
with Vera and CJ
and Saint.

CJ asked my permission to read it aloud. After he gave a thumbs-up, Saint squeezed my hand, and even Vera nodded unsmiling approval. I bowed in my seat; I was rather proud of it. Then we all turned to Saint. "Last but not least!"

On his napkin were two short lines. CJ started to read it to us, but after a few words his voice trailed off: *Dear Mom, Megan, Sean, and Percy, please forget about me. Every single thing I ever did was wrong including this. SJS.*

We argued with Saint, tried to make him elaborate, leave his mother and the world a more detailed legacy, or at least one with love in it. But he was done, he said. It was all he had to say.

29

4EVER

———

On the bluff side of the fence, with nothing but loose rocks and sandy scrub grass and blackness beyond, my heart is knocking around in my chest. Vera sits on one side of me and Saint on the other; in front of us CJ belts out songs from *South Pacific* into the void over Lake Michigan. Under cover of CJ's reverberating voice and the crash of waves two hundred feet down, I'm trying to prepare myself. I push my toes into the pebbly sand, press back against the chain-link. Leaning one way I touch Vera's knee, the other way and Saint's thigh is under my hand. I float in the pocket of warmth between them. "I love blackness," I whisper. "It's soft."

"Like sleep," says Saint.

"Like forever." I laugh like crying. "Like it always was and always will be."

"The birds are starting up."

That's Vera—high, clear, peremptory, not just acknowledging the approaching day but summoning it. At the end of the row she remains central somehow. I lean toward Saint's more diffuse energy. Time stretches before me like Lake Michigan, whose western shore I imagined as a young child imagines the span of her life. "Listen," says Vera. But I have been listening, under CJ's sweet tenor voice, to the hushed repeating sounds of the endless middle of the night. There's a flicker in the sky that might be a falling star. My teeth want to chatter; I clamp my jaw. Vera says, "Who knows the time?"

It's too dark to read my watch. Saint's is locked in his scooter. All our other personal effects—wallets, jewelry, our napkin-testaments—are in our backpacks aligned on the park side of the fence. Vera repeats her question. "Does it matter?" says Saint. "Like we could miss sunrise?"

"But how will we know exactly when?"

"Well," I say, trying to be agreeable, "how about when light first hits the water out there?"

"It could cloud up. Oh dear, oh dear, oh! A stay of execution!" CJ giggles and sings, *"When the sky is a bright canary yellow / I forget ev'ry cloud I've ever seen. . . ."* so charged that sparks seem to fly from his lips. Saint and Vera don't look at each other, still at odds, it seems, but it no longer excites me. In the black in front of me hangs a feather of light. The term "heat lightning" comes to mind, though I read somewhere that the phenomenon is simply ordinary lightning so far away that the sound of the thunder never arrives. I move closer to Saint and he puts a heavy arm around me. I would speak if my tongue weren't stuck to my teeth, if I weren't so freezing cold.

Vera rises abruptly and limps the five steps to where the ledge narrows. I can see she has hurt her foot, but she ignores it. She wants to jump right now out of the clingy wrap of her skin. She wants the wet pulsing heart of hers to explode into the wet of the air, wants to merge her heat with the heat of the universe like the first part of a grand jeté, a lift with no ankle-jamming drop. Behind her Saint and I are murmuring together, but she has no mind for me. She loves Saint's face, his long straight nose of a Roman emperor, his wild hair. Her eyes rove the darkness for the invisible line between air and water. CJ is on "Bali Ha'i" now, and his stagy baritone calls out to her. She squats behind him. "Excuse me. Is this seat taken?"

"I was saving it for you, gorgeous."

She sits down on a portion of the satiny material he's on, his mother's dress turned inside out. "My God! Are you wearing *any-thing*?" She pats his hip, feels the silk of his boxers. "I guess you don't want to meet your Maker in drag?"

CJ starts a new song, in sweet falsetto, *"I'm gonna wash that man right outta my hair. . . ."* She pats his head. The moon is down, it's dark over the lake. When he quits singing she mock-punches his flat midriff. She has always liked his frank, amiable spitefulness. That he doesn't pretend to be nicer than he is. "I might miss you, boy."

"No need. We're going to the same place."

"Are we talking hell, CJ? The everlasting flames? When was your last confession?"

"Jews have hell too. With a different name. But I meant our gore, mingled on the stones of the beach."

"Are you testing me?"

He snorts. "Why not? Here's a joke, Vee. What does the optimist say as he jumps out the window?"

"Tell me, asshole."

"So far so good!"

She laughs, a ripple of genuine, unreflecting mirth, then runs her two hands, the perfect and the imperfect one, down his hard, narrow chest. "It's been you all along, darling." She places his hand on her breast. "Pay attention. I'll turn you on yet." He pulls back. She says, taunting, "Do you think I'm disgusting? Come on, relate to me. Time is running out." He shakes his head as if to wake himself up. As if his mind is elsewhere. Maybe she does put him off. "Just give me your demented opinion, CJ. Is it a sin, you know, what I . . . what we . . ." She can't say Garth's name, but he must know what she means. "What do the rabbis say?"

"I didn't know 'sin' was in your vocabulary."

She presses her hands together. "Beam me up, CJ. There are vicious aliens on this planet."

"You'll handle them. I have full confidence." He's staring out into the blackness. "Sex . . . desire, whatever you call it—it's just fucked up. Nobody gets it."

She nods energetically. "Is there such a thing as a normal sex drive?"

"I didn't know 'normal' was in your vocabulary either."

"I was being wry. Ironic. I didn't think it would be so hard for you to get."

"I'm aging, the faculties are clouding." CJ turns away and takes hold of Saint's hand. "My turn," he says to Saint. "Got to have my fix."

He sounds snide as usual, but the earth is turning, dawn is coming. He looks at Saint fearfully, shyly, as at the face of God. It occurs to me how vulnerable men are, with their parts all dangling out, much more so than women. No wonder they need guns. Vera, though, vies for CJ's attention. She leans toward him and murmurs, "Saint despises me. I can't stand that."

"He hates you. It's every bit as strong as love."

"I prefer love."

"They're a package."

"Maybe you're right. I hate him too."

She speaks loud enough for Saint to hear, but he says nothing. She badly wants to touch someone, Saint most of all. But CJ's lips are pressed to Saint's palm, and Saint hasn't pulled away. With me on Saint's other side, there's no place for her. She takes two cigarettes out of her pack and offers one to CJ; he waves it away. She puts one in her own mouth. "How about a light? Do you have matches? Thanks, CJ."

It hurts CJ to let go of Saint's hand when there's so little time left to hold it, but he can do this small task for Vera (there's no need to die a complete asshole). In his mother's purse is a silver lighter from her smoking days. He lights Vera's cigarette and then his own. Then it occurs to him: Not only does he not want to die in drag, he doesn't want to die with any suspicion of it, doesn't want that notion of himself on anyone's lips or in anyone's mind. He wraps his mother's sequined gown around her gloves, bag, and shoes, moves to one side of the ledge, and touches the lighter flame to an edge of the fabric. When it ignites, he'll throw the whole flaming bundle over the bluff. But the fabric burns poorly. There's a rising, knotting thread of sour smoke, then nada, a stink. "Shit," he says. He could throw it all over unburned, but that would leave female finery scattered about the beach for people to have opinions about. He tries lighting the cloth again.

"What the fuck are you doing, man?"

It's Saint's first spontaneous remark. CJ holds the flame up to Saint's face. Saint the beautiful. "If I had a few more years, I'd study sculpture," says CJ. "There's a Norse god you remind me of. Do you know Baldur the Beautiful? The god of purity and light? Everyone loved Baldur. Well, everyone but Loki. But why bring up Loki?" He lights the fabric a third time, in several places. It smells like burning wire.

"You're sending out smoke signals," says Saint. "Do we want a party here?"

"Lordy, how sensible we are. But the world is sleeping." Bundle in hand, he scrambles up and over the fence.

We watch in silence as he gathers twigs and scraps of litter and starts a small campfire in the grassy dirt that quickly exhausts its fuel. He goes over to the picnic area and finds a big trash can. He throws in the clothing, mixing it up with whatever's in the can. Behind our fence we see it smolder, then a flame rockets up. While the sparks fly he runs to his car in the parking lot, then to the bathroom, and returns to us clean-faced in anonymous boy clothes—jeans, T-shirt, hiking boots. "Dressed for success," he says. When the flames fade into a plume of rotten-smelling smoke, his female persona will be a pool of synthetic glop in the bottom of the can, and he will be dressed for his yearbook picture, dressed like a figment of his father's imagination, dressed to make the man proud. "It can now be said," he says, "that I died with my boots on."

He's blustery, but he seems genuinely relieved. He crawls down the row of us, kissing cheeks. "It's an honor to share this eternal moment with you good people. I look forward to continued love-play and good conversation in the Elysian fields, or on the shores of Valhalla." He giggles. "Did you know that's the name of an actual town? It's not that far. Instead of offing ourselves, why don't we just move there? Ha. Just kidding!" He has brought back a lighted joint and he puffs, holds it out. "First one's free!"

When Saint accepts the joint, CJ starts crowing. "Aren't you *glad* we're doing this? Seriously, think of the shit we're escaping! World War Three, for one thing! Terminal pollution! Lung cancer!"

Vera scoots over to join in the riff. "We'll escape wrinkles and gray hair."

"Senile dementia," Saint offers. We lean in his direction, warmed by his verbal return to us. "Old-age homes."

"Where you get raped by the orderlies," says CJ, then after a beat: "Or is that a plus?" With no response from us he tries something else. "I won't have to worry about getting rejected from Harvard."

"Or me from Lansing Community College."

That's my contribution. CJ laughs; I love him for it. "Everyone gets into Lansing," he says. "It's open admissions."

"There's always a first," I say.

"That's the spirit, Kay!"

I know the words to maintain the group of us; I know the tone. But I'm only mimicking my old part in our revelry while, with an increasing sense of futility, I look for a way to derail this train. The riffing proceeds, other evils we'll escape by dying early: soul-crushing jobs, abusive mates, evil children. What about trying to get a prom date? Or getting one! Going to the prom! CJ is king of the hill, albeit a hill about to bulldoze itself. But he loves the hilarity he has stirred, he wants to stir it further. He offers me a hit.

"No thanks."

"What's up, dear? We won't get busted. Your political future is safe." He blows smoke in my face; I wave it away. "All right," he says, "I can take *no*. It's a sign of my new maturity." I make a laughlike sound. "Uh-oh! What's happening, baby?"

What's happening? God knows. Almost since we sat down here, I've been in a muddle. CJ is looking at me.

"Oh dear. Tell me if I'm wrong, girl. But are we perhaps in the process of maybe changing our little minds?"

I shake my head, fast, back and forth in the dark. I haven't changed my mind. "I'll abide by the group decision."

"Hmmm. I detect a *but*, my love."

"No!" I'm choking; I cough it out. "I want to do what's right. What we agreed. It's just so . . . *final*."

"Ah, but that's the point! Remember how weary, stale, flat, and unprofitable are all the uses of this world?"

"I know. *Hamlet*. To be or not to be."

"And the answer to that riddle? Not!" he proclaims, pointing to emphasize, smoothing back his hair. " 'Final' is the wrong word. Think of the end of *Alice in Wonderland*. They're about to chop off the girl's head and she says, 'You're nothing but a pack of cards.' That's us, Kay. We jump and it's just down the rabbit hole." He looks out at the water we can't see, then up at the sky, where the stars seemed to have vanished. "No, wait. This is better. We jump, and the camera pans up to a row of four bright stars. We've been translated into a constellation like the Seven Sisters. An astronomer observes us. Historians call us by his name, *Quadrus Rosenburgus*, but forever after little kids will point us out to one another. See that line of stars? Those four bright ones? That's the Four Friends! Isn't that touching?"

"Oh, Christopher Joseph."

"Kay, you rebel you."

I'm shaking my head. I don't know what's right. My feelings keep changing.

"Don't cry, dear. That's *my* scam."

I choke out a tight-jawed laugh. "But really. It's like I'm hypnotized. I keep trying to shake myself out of it."

"Beats our prior state, wouldn't you say?"

Does it? I'm stiff with fear. He takes my hand, puts it to his cheek.

"You know, I sometimes think that if I'd been born to different parents, I could have been a remarkable person." His earnestness embarrasses him; he says more lightly: "No need to support me on that."

"But I know what you mean."

"You usually do."

My teeth are chattering. I'm holding him by the shoulders. Under my hands is the fresh cotton of his shirt, in which he thinks he'll be proud to be caught dead, and one thing is clear to me: I don't want him to die. "CJ, you know, you're already kind of remarkable."

"Isn't it pretty to think so?"

I thought I'd quit hoping for a miracle, but I'm off and running. "No, seriously. You don't even know what your limits are."

"Oh, oh, oh, oh, oh! Get thee behind me, Satan."

He's joking, but I've made him nervous, I know. Starting down that old familiar road. "You know, CJ, we still haven't told them about Chicago," I start to say, but he has turned to Saint.

"Buddy, she's having second thoughts. All thoughts are lethal, but second thoughts are the worst. Can you give me a hand here?"

"I never wanted anyone else to do this," Saint says. "I'm the only one who's fucked completely."

I say piteously, "You *aren't*!"

"If you only knew," says CJ. Saint shakes his head almost imperceptibly, but it's a dismissal. At which CJ starts twitching, head and shoulders, a caricature idiot. "Shee-it. 'Course, my shit ain't nothin' by yours, Mr. Saint." At the same time he's leaning toward Saint, taking him in, his smell, the dried blood on his shirt.

"Saint doesn't know his own goodness. And neither do you, CJ!" I'm shaking his arm. "There's this innocent, kind, sweet part of yourself, don't you see that?"

"On the rocks down there, I'll be even sweeter. CJ on the rocks. A new beverage. A cocktail!"

I groan.

"Shit, Kay. Don't you know that my unaccustomed good nature

derives from my awareness of having slightly less than an hour left on the earthly plane? I hear the waves, and the blood beating in my veins, and if I thrill to it, it's because I'm about to lose it. Take away the dawn leap and I'm the same old asshole."

I put my hands over my ears.

"Listen," he says. "If it was just me jumping into the void, it wouldn't mean anything. Another teen suicide. One more failure for psychiatry. The kid just couldn't hack it. With two jumpers, it's still mental illness. Folie à deux. Dismissable. But with us four it's a *manifesto*."

Saint is listening; CJ seeks even stronger words. "It's our fourfold middle finger at everyone who ever fucked with us! Our 'Hell no, we won't go.' It's our barbershop quartet, our band's latest hit, it's 'Vera in the Sky with Diamonds.'" He starts up with the Animals song—*"We've gotta get out of this place, if it's the last thing we ever do"*—and afterward the lyrics ring in our ears. "Best of all," he says, "we're leaving an *idea*. About the meaning of friendship. The love of members of a group for one another. It's more important than life."

Vera: "I know where you're coming from."

Saint nods agreement.

"I do too," I cry. "Believe me!"

CJ kisses my lips like he means it. I'm squeezing his arms so hard it's got to hurt. Then he takes Saint's big face in his hands and kisses him all over.

Saint tolerates CJ's affection as he would that of an exuberant dog. He doesn't move, even after CJ lets go. CJ flings himself onto his back, kicks his feet over the edge, chortling, but Saint is tired unto death, and he wants it all to be over. In most ways, he thinks it's already over. Whatever's left of him resides in Vera sitting in the shadows at the end of the row, but there's nothing she can do for him. Nothing he wants her to do.

And yet? But still? When the red tip of her joint moves in his direction and she's squeezing down next to him, he can't help but thrill to her proximity with all the hairs growing out of the pores of his skin. For the past weeks he has either breathed her in or talked to her image in his mind. He has devised detailed mental scenarios in which he tells her everything about himself down to the most abject, pathetic weakness, and still he wins her love. He shuts his eyes tight, against this train of thought and every other, because he knows exactly where they lead. A little effort and he can stay cool till it's truly over. Half an hour, by the color of the sky.

Vera says into his ear, "Please don't be a dick to me."

He sighs, swallowing it back like a yawn. There's no point to more talk. He regards her out of the tunnel of his hard-won calm.

Her lips come closer. "You did what you did. That can't be taken back either."

He nods. He agrees. Nothing can be taken back.

"I don't want to die with you hating me," she says.

"I don't hate you. I mean it."

"So why are you acting like that?"

She is as near him as she can be without touching. Against his eardrums pound the waves of her voice, upon his retinas the glow of her hair in the dark, upon the nerves of his skin the heat of her body. But he can sit still, he can stay centered, and they are mere phenomena. All his life, it seems, people have wanted to know why he did something or other. As if he had intentions. In a minute he won't remember what she said. He has already forgotten.

"You're such a phony, Saint. You did . . . what you did and I still love you. I do. Maybe I'm insane."

Om. Om. He does what he always does, sits like a rock while the world storms around him.

"Please," she says, "do you want me to beg you?"

Om namah shivaya. "No. Please don't."

"I will if I want to! I'll get down on my knees!" she says with an uncharacteristic quaver. "Listen. I hate myself, isn't that enough?"

He wants to put a hand to his head, which aches, but he won't. He resists. He will be still.

"Don't you blank out on me!"

She takes his arm, then quickly lets go. She seems sad, even fragile, but he remains straight and stiff, his limbs under control. He won't try to defend himself, though he'd like to scream into the tender hole of her ear, *Never in your life have you done anything you didn't want to do!* He promised her once not to be possessive. He said she could screw whomever, and it was fine with him. But it was not fine. And he must shut out her glow and her fierce breath and the heat of her skin, because if he opens himself he'll have to admit another image, clear in his mind's eye all the way to death. And why, minutes from death, should he invite more pain? *Do you still love him?* At the thought a groan rises to his throat. But he will not ask and start an argument he can't win and doesn't want to win.

Then her face is against his shoulder. He feels her hands on his back. Her fingers touch his face like a blind person's, tracing his features, his large nose, wide mouth, everything out there on the surface asking for trouble. And into the darkness stretching in front of him like a pair of maternal arms, he feels himself emptying. His rage balloons up and out, taking his breath—private anger that he has carried nearly all his life like an unregistered gun. And he howls. He howls like a dog to the moon no one can see, till he's empty and as weak as a child, with no energy to want to be otherwise. It isn't satori, perfect and instantaneous enlightenment. But he can rest for a bit.

Vera, though, is still touching him. He feels her lips on the side of his neck. "You're so gentle," he says.

"That's me," she says, and he doesn't care whether or not she's being ironic.

Overhead, very near, comes the squawk of a waking bird, impatient and gruff like a throat being cleared. I am kissing CJ, the first boy

I've ever kissed, and he is kissing me, and if we are thinking of Saint we don't mention it. Then he pulls back, and my forlorn mouth moves involuntarily in his direction. I love kissing him. I seem to love this new pastime, kissing. He runs a friendly hand over the top of my head. I tremble like a puppy.

The bird squawks again, then another bird farther away. The night's hold has cracked like an egg. There is a sense of general waking, as in preschool after the midmorning nap. The sky is indigo. The lake has a wrinkly surface. "Soon," Vera says.

Words charge through my brain, trying to signify. *Saint darling, you won't go to jail, or not for long, and when you get out you can marry Vera. Vera, just quit being stubborn, okay? CJ, you're so nice when you aren't trying not to be.* I look from one friend to another, again struck by their perfection. "You are the only people who ever loved me— the seeing, knowing kind of love," I say, and they nod. They know what I mean. They knew before I said it. "Are we sure," I whisper, "that this is what we want?"

CJ cocks his head, ready for something new to laugh at. Vera gazes into the middle distance, not quite smiling. Saint's hand is on her knee. They have reconciled—I see that. "I just don't want us to make a mistake," I say.

Their smiles, it seems, become more radiant. Over the lake a chain of purple-blue clouds has appeared. At the horizon line the water is salmon pink. I squeeze my eyes shut, but they won't stay shut. "The world is full of light. Don't you want to keep on seeing it?"

My friends gaze warmly at me as if they fully agree, but maybe they're thinking of something else. I point out an orange cloud in the dark blue. "Isn't that weird, with the sun on the total other side of the world? Wouldn't it be sad not to hear birds anymore, won't you miss birds? God, do I usually talk this much?"

"I've heard birds," Vera says.

CJ giggles. "Heard one bird, heard 'em all."

"No, we haven't! The world is big. There's so much to do. We can make up for everything." I think of the kids in Grant Park, their humor and gravity. I think of the space between here and Chicago, between Chicago and San Francisco and Vietnam. And the moon. Room to be lost and found and lost and found a million times.

"What time is it?" Vera says.

I take off my watch, throw it over the bluff, wait for the splash.

"Kay," says Saint, "why did you do that?"

"That reminds me of a joke," CJ says. "Why did the moron throw the clock out the window?" He laughs, then whispers, "He wanted to make time fly! No offense. You know, I've always wondered why people say 'no offense' just before they give offense. To rub it in?"

"Kay," Vera says, "you shouldn't do this if you don't completely want to."

She sounds solemn, like a judge or a teacher. Cold shame congeals in my backbone. Without looking at anyone I feel their attention. My mouth is shut tight.

Vera says, "Kay, tell the truth. Do you want to get out of this?"

I shake my head no.

"If you don't want to do it . . ." Vera says. "Listen, honey, if you want to get out of it, it's all right. Truly."

"Yes," Saint says. "No blame."

"Oh no, oh no," CJ says. "You signed. You have a contractual obligation."

"Ignore him," Vera says.

A very small part of me tries to smile, but my face hurts. Their gazes remain affectionate, but I feel them retreating. Shrinking back, moving ever so slightly, not away from me but nearer to one another. Nothing has happened, but I feel like one against three. Excluded. Outcast. *Please love me.* Silently I beg them to love me enough to stay alive with me, despite misery past and to come. Is that asking too much?

"When we pledged, we were babies. We didn't know any better. This is for real." These words come from Saint, who seems unearthly calm, older than any of us. "Kay," he goes on, "there are right and wrong reasons to do things. If life is calling you, if it means something to you . . ."

He eyes me, but at the same time he's drifting away. "Life." Out of his mouth the word sounded tawdry. They're all drifting away, watching me with the indifferent, terrifying love of angels. And I'm tumbling through the hole of my terror, faster and harder than I'd fall from the bluff. *How can it not mean something to you,* I want to say, *no matter what you did?* I was crying silently, but now I'm gusting with sobs. "Life doesn't call me. Nothing calls me but you! I believe in the pact! Don't leave me alone!"

"Are you sure?" Vera speaks like a good teacher, strict but fair. "Really, think about it. Are you absolutely free of doubt?"

I look out at the lake, from which the gleam of pink is already gone. The sky is white. Birds squawk like nasty girls in the lavatory telling lies about someone they've decided not to like. "Life or death, compadres! Count on me. Either way I'm with you."

"To die, even?"

"The group rules."

"Kay," says CJ, "there is no one like you."

"That's what they say about God," I say, and they laugh as if it's funny. I feel their relief, which wouldn't be so intense if they didn't love me. Vera and Saint guide me into the warmth between them. Vera strokes my hand. Saint kisses the side of my face. CJ's eyes are fixed on me, as if I'm about to say something important.

Vera stands up to check the horizon then returns to her place. I sit with my eyes closed, as if I can somehow make the sun stand still.

Then one of the sounds floating in the back of my mind swirls up as a siren. I cover my ears, but it gets louder. The ground starts to shake. My friends stand up while I'm squeezing my knees to my chest against whatever it is—a real live earthquake in our pseudo California? The thundering hooves of the Four Horsemen, the end of everything for everyone? I tuck my head between my knees as we were taught in grade school in the event of a nuclear bomb.

"What the fucking shit?" says Vera.

I look, eventually. Dim across the field, a pair of faint lights might be headlights. There's the pulsing red of police. A siren wails in measured beats.

Vera eyes CJ. "Good work," she says.

"What? I didn't do that!"

"Yes, you did. Your damn smoke signals."

CJ hits his head with the flat of his hand. "Fuck me!" He's almost crying. "But it died down almost immediately. Oh God!" He looks doubtfully down the row of us. "They can't see us. We could run," he says.

"Why? Nothing's changed. Except time of death." Vera wipes her hair out of her eyes. Her voice is firm and cool. She stands up, then one at a time we rise and stand beside her on the edge of the bluff, lined up like good schoolchildren. We join hands. *Red Rover, Red Rover, let Jesus come over.*

I have my chosen place beside Saint, but I'm absurdly irritable and everything makes it worse. The birds sound squabbly, mean-spirited. The siren subsides with a dying wail, but the engine roar is as loud as our discussion of whether to link arms or hold hands. I hate it all.

A police car emerges out of the fog, then men with red fire extinguishers. We watch through the fence as they attack the trash can. We entwine our arms, ending in held hands. If we can hold on we'll fall right next to one another. Below, the rocky beach is in shadow, but the field of light on the water is spreading fast.

"One, two, three!" Vera blurts it, a goof. Her teeth are chattering.

CJ giggles.

"Ready?" she says, and gives my hand a friendly shake. A kiss moves along the row, CJ to Saint to me to Vera, like Pass the Orange.

"It's like a little kid's birthday party."

"We're being silly."

"It's time," says Vera.

I love that my arms are squeezed between Saint's arm and his side and Vera's arm and her side. I am more than included. There's nothing, no one, to whom I am not connected—this lake, that tree— because we are four together, 4EVER, heads raised to the intensifying light with death snapping at our feet. "Let's count to three," says Vera, "then I'll say 'go.'"

"As usual," CJ hoots. "Little Napoleon!"

A second car enters the lot.

"Fuck-shit," says Vera.

Behind us, red canisters train the last of their contents on the smoldering trash can. There's a continuing hiss, a tower of smoke. But louder in my ears are the intake and expulsion of our breathing. On either side of me, Saint and Vera bend their knees like divers. Saint says, "Holy Mary mother of God, pray for us sinners now and at the hour of our death."

"Now! Go!"

I feel the thrum of the force of their intention, its manic holiness. Then through my closed eyelids comes the red hotness of sun. My four-strong body starts to expire head by head, till there's only mine dripping sweat. I know what happens to an eye when its mate is blinded, and to a Siamese twin when its sibling dies. I also know the sound of a tennis ball when it hits the exact middle of the racket, its firm, sweet sound. Like Lot's disobedient wife I turn around. Alone on a tennis court, Gary Landry is practicing his serve. And while I'm not, even for a moment, a pillar of salt, my legs won't move. In the face of the thought of being forever alone, stranded on the island of myself, I let go of my friends' hands.

They leap and there's the rush of wind. For a moment I seem to be falling with them. Then a low-voiced moan rises to my ears. CJ, curled in a fetal ball on the ledge at my feet: "I know, I know, I know, I know! My innate cowardice." One of his feet hangs over the edge as if he's still daring himself. His hand is balled into a fist under his cheek, such a sad, helpless hand. "He let go. I would have done it, but he let me go! I'll never, *never* forgive him." He heaves another moan. "Was there a crash? A splash? I didn't hear anything." I sit down beside him, taking fast, hard, sharp breaths that seem to clang against the back of my throat. In my ears, over and over, sounds the scream that didn't come from our friends. For now, it's all I can hear.

Then "Hey," says a man. "There's somebody over there!" Heavy steps tread the grass. "Couple of kids!"

"Wouldn't you know." That's Vera's father, uncharacteristically nervous-sounding. "Motherfuckers."

"Vera?" That's Vera's mother, wailing as if she already knows. "My sweet, beautiful girl?"

But I am not Vera, I'm Kay Campion, scratching as if for a hand-hold in the dry, stony earth of the ledge. To hang on to the moment for as long as it will allow, I lie down beside CJ and put my lips to his springy curls. His arms enclose my waist. Beautiful, appalling, the shades of Saint and Vera hover in the warming air.

Afterward, after the confusion and the crying and the search for whom or what to blame, after school started and I wouldn't leave my room, and Elise went off to college, and CJ got into his car and just drove away, without a note or a word, my family moved to San Diego. Where they could play golf the year round and I could get "distance" on the calamity—they assumed or at least hoped. San Diego was on the far side of the moon from Lourdes, a gentle, barely perceptible slope to the beach. The white sand was as soft as sugar, the ocean warm and salty. Its water held me up better than the lake's; I could swim out until I couldn't see shore. I lost weight; so what? Arlyn and Dad urged counseling—gently, respectfully, I'll give them credit. But I had no interest in "moving on"; I hated the very words. Toward what or where should I be moving? I didn't *want* to change or weaken what I felt for my lost friends. I didn't even want to forget that I couldn't save them.

But they were already gone, Elise said in one of her letters. *I don't mean to put them in any kind of box, but I think they were fated, you know? Like Romeo and Juliet? It would have taken a miracle!*

But that was it. I'd wanted to work a miracle. We were in Lourdes, after all.

Our first few months in San Diego, Arlyn and Dad walked on tiptoe around me, as if I were terminally ill. Then postcards from CJ started coming to our house, from Zurich, Jerusalem, Bombay, Kyoto. He was questing—on a track that might lead him somewhere. That spring, without anyone's urging, though the parental units were pleased and relieved, I applied to a community college, and got in without a single credit for my senior year of high school. A miracle of sorts, someone might have said. The following year, at Berkeley, I took a course in Eastern religion, and we were assigned a book Saint had read, *In Search of the Miraculous.* Disappointingly, it was a little dry, and I didn't see why, for the Miraculous, you had to go East, but I loved the title, which described my own quest. In my dorm room I wanted Mary, mother of God, to appear haloed before me with the living bodies of my friends in her holy arms. I wanted my mother to come for Parents' Weekend and say she was proud of me, and lie about how beautiful I was, and smart, etc., or just hold me hard and tight in her formerly big arms. I wanted, and I still want, to live in a world where miracles can happen, not constantly but every once in a while. I want to watch someone with hideous facial boils drink from the fountain at the entrance to our Haight and jog away, clear-skinned. I want the world's parents to understand their children, or at least try to understand, or at least not harm them while they try to understand themselves. I want to change our story.

Yes, my Saintly, I have many wants. I'm stuck on the wheel of birth and rebirth.

And every once in a while I think maybe *that's* the miracle—that days pass in their dailiness, years go by, and I'm still on the wheel. I remember August 1968 in Lourdes, Michigan, with a clarity that refuses to fade. Sometimes I'll even wake in the dark with a burning sensation on my leg where the tattoo abides, and I weep for what's lost, which, in bad times, I'm on the brink of returning to. But I can't, or I don't, since on the edge of the bluff that summer dawn, I chose not to die. And so I was born.

ACKNOWLEDGMENTS

I want to thank, first, my agent, Lauren MacLeod, who said yes to this manuscript that I'd been working on for twenty years, and then—so quickly!—found a place for it in a house where they lovingly and painstakingly edit the books they publish. In this regard, I want to thank my editors Cindy Spiegel and Annie Chagnot, who went over not only every line but every character interaction, and made it a better, deeper book. Thanks also to my assiduous copy editor/fact checker Jennifer Prior, who noticed discrepancies and inaccuracies almost too small for the human eye. And to Beth Pearson, who managed the copyediting and proofreading—with all its demands and complexities—with a graceful and easy expertise.

Special thanks to the brilliant and warmhearted women in my writing group—Rosellen Brown, Janet Burroway, Garnett Kilberg-Cohen, Tsivia Cohen, Maggie Kast, Peggy Shinner, and S. L. Wisenberg—who penned their comments on multiple drafts without saying, "I thought this was finished?" or "I'm sorry but my eyes are starting to glaze over." Then there is Joyce Winer, who is no longer in the group but has commented on my work and encouraged me over many years with her usual wry acuity. And, of course, Barry Silesky, my beloved husband, whose faith in me runs wide and deep.

Thank you, Purdue University, and especially the English department, and within that the creative writing program—original members Patricia Henley and Marianne Boruch—which hired me to teach fiction with the first, now much rewritten, chapter of *Once*. Thanks also to members of Purdue's Center for Artistic Endeavors, headed by my colleague Don Platt, who granted me a fellowship and thus a free semester to work on this book.

And thanks from the bottom of my heart to my parents, Myron and Ruth Solwitz, ninety-eight and ninety-three, respectively, who have never flagged in their encouragement of their at times wayward daughter, and have been good enough to stay alive for some well-earned *naches*.

ABOUT THE AUTHOR

SHARON SOLWITZ is the author of a novel, *Bloody Mary*, and a collection of stories, *Blood and Milk*, which won the Carl Sandburg Literary Award from Friends of the Chicago Public Library and the prize for adult fiction from the Society of Midland Authors, and was a finalist for the National Jewish Book Award. Several of her stories have been featured in Pushcart Prize anthologies and *The Best American Short Stories*. Other honors for her individual stories, which have appeared in such magazines as *TriQuarterly, Mademoiselle,* and *Ploughshares,* include the Katherine Anne Porter Prize, the Nelson Algren Literary Award, and grants and fellowships from the Illinois Arts Council. Solwitz teaches fiction writing at Purdue University and lives in Chicago with her husband, the poet Barry Silesky.

sharonsolwitz.com
Facebook.com/sharon.solwitz